A Different Slant of Light

THE SEQUEL TO
INCOMPLETE

J.D. LEVIN

A DIFFERENT SLANT OF LIGHT

A NOVEL

J.D. LEVIN

NOT-SO-SILENT LIBRARIAN BOOKS

Not-So-Silent Librarian Books
Ventura, CA 93003
www.notsosilentlibrarian.com

Library of Congress *Cataloging-in-Publication* Data
Levin, J.D. (Joel David)
A Different Slant of Light: A Novel / J.D. Levin
LCCN 2021920832
ISBN 978-1-7377569-0-3 (hardcover)
ISBN 978-1-7377569-2-7 (paperback)
ISBN 978-1-7377569-1-0 (ebook)
1. Adolescence — Fiction. 2. Popular Music — Fiction. 3. Rock groups — Fiction. 4. Composers — Fiction. 5. High school students — Fiction.
813'.54 — DC23

Book design and layout by J.D. Levin

Printed in the United States of America
DOC 10 9 8 7 6 5 4 3 2 1 (Counting is fun!)

Once again, this is for my daughters,
Alexandra and Charlotte.
You're more important to me than rock and roll.
Thank you for making my life complete.

INTRO RIFF

PROLOGUE
"Sail Away"

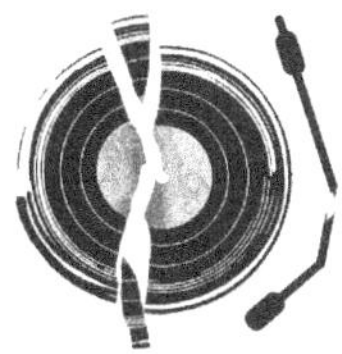

Winning the war is only the first half of the story.

Growing up, we encounter countless books and songs and films that culminate in the hero's long-awaited moment of glory. We salivate over these stories, ascribing mythical qualities to the fictionalized fantasies that we devour like movie theater popcorn.

If you're anything like me, you probably geek out over the sublimely static story arc: the mild-mannered zero transforms into a superhuman hero, overcomes the overwhelming odds, and rides off into the sunset with true love in tow. Perhaps you invest a few hours of your life into the intricately woven threads of a hero's journey, tracing lines of lineage across the fabric of the narrative. Along the way, you witness the protagonist ascending to the apex of the mountain and basking in the radiant glow of the humble heavens overhead – or, in my case, ending up with a major label recording contract and a hit song. You would think that such an ending would wrap up the disparate strands in a tidy bow: the protagonist lives happily ever after with his beautiful wife and his everlasting rock and roll glory, ensuring that his legacy will be cherished for eternity.

But that's not the way life works.

One might assume that a lifetime of fame rests upon the weary wings of the victor, the humble hero who braves the tempest-tossed seas and cleverly escapes claustrophobic islands – but still survives to tell the tale. Perhaps, you anticipate that the golden shores of home allow him to bask in the beaming rays of his unfettered accomplishments. You know, the standard Hollywood feel-good ending: roll the credits, cue the lights, and chomp down those last few bites of popcorn before you leave the theater and head home.

I'm here to tell you that it's never as simple as a movie-script ending. There's no gentle fade to darkness, no inspirational song blaring from the speakers as the credits scroll indefinitely down the screen in a black-and-white epilogue. Our lives linger on, like incomplete novels with an infinite number of chapters that stretch on for eternity.

Until, of course, they don't.

Sure, some of those real-life stories fit snugly into the Hero's Journey archetype. Even in the romanticized realm of rock and roll, you've got a few figures who have ventured to hell and back, barely surviving to tell the tale: Johnny Cash, Tina Turner, Ray Charles, Elton John… and my namesake, Brian Wilson. Everything works out for them in the end, and they live out the remainder of their days in peaceful tranquility. Kind of.

Some artists are capable of catapulting themselves to a musical Mt. Olympus in the heavens, where they spend eternity with the Gods of Rock and Roll. But that's not everyone's story. Some become producers. Some invest in real estate. Some open restaurant franchises.

As for me, I became a high school English teacher.

Call me Brian. Or Mr. Smith. Or even "Brick." I know it's not as catchy as Ishmael, but it'll have to do. After all, when your freshman football coach thinks you look more like a white whale than a peg-legged captain, your nickname is bound to be a little bizarre. Obviously, if you've read this book's predecessor, you've heard all about my life story – and you know that the stormy seas of adolescence can be cruel.

It's a miracle that I survived.

Of course, as you'll see soon enough, I almost didn't make it.

This is the story of how I flew too close to the sun.

As a stubborn high school kid, I daydreamed of a lifelong career in the music industry. With my bass guitar in one hand and a songwriter's notepad in the other, I enveloped myself in wings made of wax, pledging to fly away from my labyrinthine home in the scorching Ojai Valley to the cool, comforting shoreline of Los Angeles. Heck, I even got accepted to UCLA and met my future wife in the dorms. For a while, it seemed like the future was full of boundless potential, rife with radiant possibility. I stretched my arms to the firmament and coasted on the cool winds of victory, sailing high above the tumultuous oceans below. I figured that even if things didn't work out – even if I crash-landed in the waters beneath me – I would simply sail back to shore, my arms coolly caressed by the brisk baptismal waves.

But things didn't work out that way. After all, the ocean is a terrain of terrible uncertainty. It will suffocate you just as quickly as embrace you.

And, when I was twenty-one years old, I almost drowned.

Of course, I wasn't the first voyager in my family. When my great-great-great-grandparents sailed the tempestuous tides from Russia to the United States in the early 1900s, they couldn't have foreseen the complicated world that their aching ancestors would inherit. Those Smith forefathers renounced their homeland of *pogroms* and protests and persecution for the promise of a new home: America. Though they might not have faced sirens and cyclopes along the way, they inevitably endured heartache and hopelessness when they left their old world behind. My forebears were long-suffering sailors, searching for salvation across the stubborn seas. They were *proto-surfers*, if you will. But these ancestors were Cossacks dressed in cassocks and caftans, instead of Californians clothed in swim trunks and Huarache sandals. *Surfin' U.S.A.*, looked a lot different in the early decades of the twentieth century.

Fast-forward a hundred years, and my ancestors' great-great-great-grandson was making waves in the music industry. When I was twenty, I felt like a rock and roll Hercules, ready to tackle any lion or hydra or three-headed hellhound that came my way. But, in reality, I was much more like Icarus: a headstrong child who failed to recognize that his waxen wings would melt in the heat of the sun. And, when I tumbled from the sky, it nearly destroyed me.

But this isn't some gory Greek gameshow. If you want blood, guts, and glory, go read *The Iliad*. As for me, I'll stick to *The Odyssey*. Sure, my band, Call Field, raged into battle during the late-1990s rock and roll renaissance, like a Trojan horse of pop-punk – but we didn't even last long enough to put out a *Greatest Hits* album. Instead, like Odysseus's crew on the island of Thrinacia, a few band members mutinied.

It didn't end well for Odysseus's men.

And it didn't end well for Call Field.

After the Trojan War, when Odysseus set sail for his homeland, he had no idea just how complicated the ensuing years would become. He didn't realize that a ten-year military campaign would transform into *twenty* years away from home. Odysseus's tragic flaw was his *hubris* – his excessive pride – and the Greek gods punished him for his arrogance. Even as he sailed towards Ithaca, desperately wishing to be reunited with his wife and son, he got lost along the way.

Although it didn't take me an entire decade, I got lost on my way home, too. Odysseus paid the price for his pride. And so did I.

This is where things get dark and ugly.

There's a reason I tried to forget my adolescence, to shroud those years in the blackout curtains of repressed memories. And, for two decades, I was able to hide in the humble anonymity of my middling middle-class existence. It was a welcome respite from the smothering silhouettes of my teenage years. Until, of course, one of my favorite students uncovered my deep, dark, depressing secret…

I used to be a rock star. Kind of.

I thought all those turbulent waters were behind me, like liquid shadows trapped and trailing in my wake. I thought the catalyzing crescendoes of those crashing waves were relegated to my yearning yesteryears. But I was wrong.

After I confessed the cruel calamities of my youth, I was forced to confront the conflagration that had consumed my adolescence. Thanks to that precocious star student of mine, I had to revisit a painful era of my life when I was set adrift at sea.

As I discovered, though, the interminable odyssey returning to your home isn't always resolved by sailing across vast oceans. Sometimes, the journey home is in your head. And in your heart.

Like it or not, I need to look backward to gaze forward – to embrace the eye of the hurricane before I can slap those waxen wings back on my shoulders and reclaim my rightful place in the immortal nighttime sky.

It's time, dear reader.

It's time to confront the specters of my youth.

It's time to sail back into the past.

SECOND VERSE

"Pet Sounds" was playing in my Mustang
On the night we shared our first kiss.
Suddenly, I didn't feel so lonely:
I found salvation when I touched your lips.

CHAPTER ONE
"The Times They Are a-Changin'"

*R*ight foot. Left foot.
Right foot. Left foot.
Repeat for an hour.

It was an early afternoon in late October, a sinfully sunny Sunday of the casual California variety. While my wife and daughter were gardening in the backyard, embracing the festive fall glow of simmering sunshine, I was stomping away in the cavernous corners of my garage, racking up mile after mile on my trusty treadmill.

In many ways, it was just a typical weekend: I was at home with my beautiful wife and our adorable daughter, squeezing in an hourlong workout before I returned to the laborious task of grading essays. It's the Sisyphean fate of every Advanced Placement English teacher. My wife, Mel – technically *Noelani Mele'kauwela Aukake'ho'opae-Smith*, but I've lovingly called her "Mel" since we were in college – was looking casually gorgeous in denim shorts and a tank top, letting her golden skin soak up the sunshine as she tended to our makeshift garden in the backyard. Our daughter, Samantha, was huddled on the ground next to Mel, her diminutive fingers digging deeply into the soil that nourished our homegrown pumpkins and tomatoes. I, on the other hand, was forcing myself to repeat endless footfalls on the treadmill. As with many other aspects of my life, I was constantly moving, but going nowhere.

To the outside world, the scene probably looked like a benign barometer of our static suburban lives.

But this particular Sunday was different.

The day before had been emotionally exhausting: one of my star students, a precocious seventeen-year-old kid named Veronica Jones, had irritatingly insisted that I sit down for an interview and recount the complex chronicles of my youth. After stumbling across a music video of my old band on YouTube, Veronica had confronted me about my former rock-and-roll life, nagging me endlessly about my path to the fringe territories of stardom. And, since she's my daughter's favorite babysitter, I begrudgingly agreed to lay my cards on the table and tell her all about my complicated childhood.

Reluctantly, I related my experiences growing up in the 1980s and 1990s. I told her about my childhood as an obese wallflower with an undiagnosed social anxiety disorder. I told her about my tortured high school romance, the claustrophobic love triangle between my teenage crush and the lead singer of my band. I told her about my prodigal path making music – that salve of salvation that had transformed me from a pushover preteen to a confident young man with prodigious potential. And I told her about how all of those disparate elements of my life led me to write Call Field's one hit song, "Incomplete (Just Like Your Smile)."

It was ugly. It was uncomfortable. It was undermining the stability of my static suburban life. But it also had some unintended side effects.

Though my adolescence wasn't painless or carefree – not by *any* means – it did have some remarkable moments. Those hazy summer days of playing rock and roll in my garage provided some pretty potent memories, and it was hard to extricate the accomplishments of my youth from the person I had become in the ensuing years.

Maybe – just *maybe* – I might have missed making music.

And writing songs.

And playing shows.

And glancing into the audience to see random strangers singing back the words I had written and humming the melodies that I had composed.

But what could the forty-year-old Brian Richard "Brick" Smith do to recapture those transient memories of lost youth? It's not like I had a record label anymore. Or an album. Or even a band, for that matter.

Oh, to be an artist without his art…

So, there I was, less than twenty-four hours later, stewing on the situation as I clocked a few more miles on my NordicTrack treadmill. The epic conversation with Veronica had kick-started something in my heart, something I hadn't wanted to revisit – or even think about – for a long, long time. For so many years, I felt like Orpheus in the underworld, desperately avoiding the desire to look back behind me. Now, however, as my neck craned at awkward angles to focus on forgotten fields of vision, I was forced to stare into the abyss of my adolescence.

And it hadn't been as cataclysmic as I anticipated.

I thought about Veronica, that star student who embodied the picture-perfect, all-American kid: earnest, overachieving, thoughtful, and kind. And curious. In theory, Veronica should have been more concerned with church and grades and boys and prom dresses and social media and her future career plans as a dentist. Instead, she was singularly focused on my short-lived career in the music industry.

For some bizarre, baffling reason, Veronica thought I was *cool*. God knows why, but this high school kid wanted to research my life – as if I was Alexander Hamilton or Jerry Garcia or Kobe Bryant. Little did she know, I'm just a mild-mannered English teacher who had a brief brush with fame. Sure, being in a major-label rock band *sounds* romantic and dreamlike. The reality of the experience, however, was fierce and fleeting.

But try telling that to Veronica Jones.

I've never been cool. I've been on the *periphery* of cool, but that's not the same thing. For God's sakes, I'm a *high school English teacher*. There's nothing cool about that.

Veronica Jones, however, disagrees.

And that, dear reader, left me in a bit of a pickle.

Right foot. Left foot.
Right foot. Left foot.

Repeat.

My life has become a comfortable routine in the time since Call Field's short-lived encounter with fame. I wake up, shower, head to work, spend the evening with my family, grade papers, plan lessons, go to sleep, and repeat the whole process, day in and day out. Maybe I squeeze in some exercise on alternating afternoons, like this particular sunny Sunday. But it's always soothingly predictable, with very little variation.

The wheels keep spinning the same way, over and over.

The motor keeps humming.

The rollers keep rotating.

And my legs keep moving.

Right foot. Left foot.
Right foot. Left foot.
Repeat.

When something comes along to break the routine, it's a bit jarring at first. Your body has been conditioned to wake up every morning at 5:00 AM, your internal clock begs you to climb into bed at 9:45 PM, and you can't help but feel the never-ending cloud of anxiety and stress looming over your shoulder. When a weeklong vacation (like my school's October break) interrupts your daily rituals, you have a hard time adjusting. But then, after a few days, it clicks in.

It's hard to accurately articulate the beauty of a weeklong vacation to those friends and family members who don't work in the field of education. A lot of people labor for forty hours a week: they clock in, sweat through an eight-hour shift, clock out, and forget about their work responsibilities in the evening hours.

With teachers, that's never the case. There's always another paper to grade, another lesson to plan, another parent to call. So, when that routine is snapped, that spell is broken, it feels absolutely liberating.

Instantly, you're free. You aren't shackled and chained to the overwhelming obligation of caring for an unreasonably large number of students. Instead, you can care for your family…

And you can care for yourself.

And you can focus on all of the aspects of your life that you've put on hold. Your hobbies, that laundry list of books you've wanted to read, your overflowing Netflix queue, those exotic restaurants across town… The world is suddenly full of limitless equations for happiness and health and home.

And you have time to think – *really think* – about the twists and turns that your life has taken over the years, the seemingly disconnected series of events that ultimately led you to where you are today. Maybe you'll just talk about it.

Or maybe you'll begin to write it down.

As long as you keep moving, keep working, you'll be okay. Stay the course and remain on that treadmill.

Right foot. Left foot.
Right foot. Left foot.
Repeat.

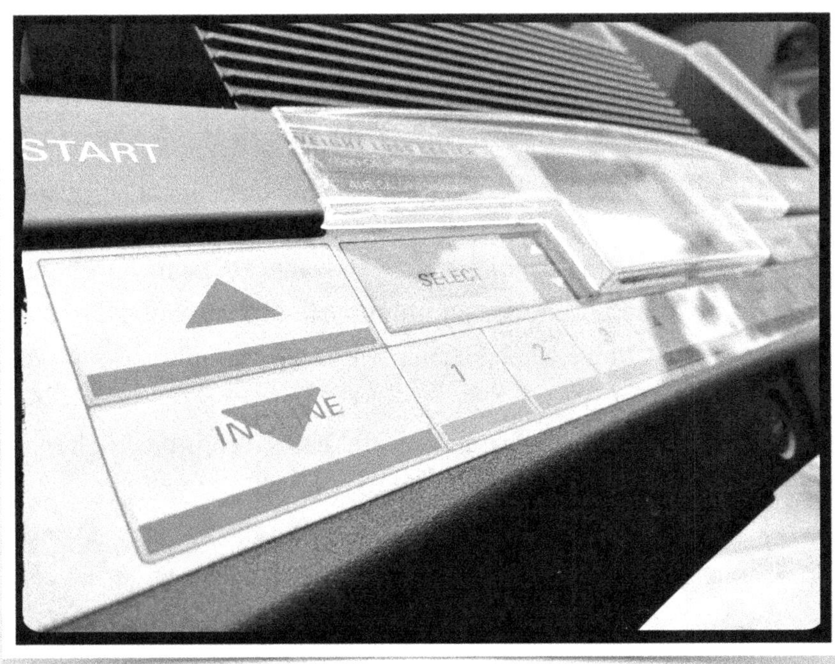

CHAPTER TWO
"Do You Remember?"

Twenty-ish hours earlier, when I finally returned home after my hours-long interview with Veronica, I was decidedly *not* in the mood to jump on the treadmill. All that recoiling recollection left me more exhausted than any number of miles I could have spent jogging.

By the time that I walked through the front door, Mel had finished her dinner preparation, and the smell of broiled chicken permeated the house. With the oafish motions of a graceless adult, I closed the front door behind me, kicked off my shoes, and unbuttoned my plaid shirt. And I had just enough time to breathe before I was tackled by my favorite tiny tyke.

"Daddy's home!" Sam yelled, dropping her watercolor brushes on the table and rushing up to meet me in the entryway. She wrapped her willowy arms around my waist and looked up at me with beaming hazel eyes.

I tugged on Sam's right hand to free myself from her grasp and stretched out my arm, pulling a pectoral muscle in the process. Ignorant to my suffering, Sam did a little ballerina twirl and gave me a goofy, toothy grin.

"How was your big interview?" Mel called from the kitchen. "Did Veronica get everything out of you that she needed?"

"Not *exactly*," I sighed as I led Sam down the hallway towards the kitchen. Though it was cold and drizzling outside, I was struck by the waves of warmth emanating from the oven. "That smells good. Trying out a new recipe?"

"Nope," Mel nonchalantly replied. "Just good old-fashioned barbecue chicken in the broiler." She leaned over Sam's elfish figure and gave me a brief kiss.

"Hi, beautiful," I whispered as her lips pulled away from mine.

"Hi, handsome," Mel answered.

Sam tugged gently on the sleeve of my shirt. I twirled my daughter around one last time and patted her on the cheek.

"Are you all done with your artwork?" I asked, pointing at the muddy watercolor paints and scattered brushes that lay anarchically askew on the tabletop.

"Nope," Sam answered. "I'm still working on a mermaid for Mama."

"In that case, sweetie, you better wrap it up before Mama finishes dinner."

Sam did an about-face and marched back to the dining room table. I yawned and stretched out my arms, feeling a bit more exhausted than I would have anticipated on a Saturday evening in late October.

"So, tell me about your conversation," Mel casually commanded. "What did you and Veronica talk about?"

"*Ugh*," I moaned. "I felt like I was giving her the play-by-play breakdown of my entire inconsequential life."

Mel rolled her eyes and frowned at me in the artistically sardonic way that only wives can pull off. "Seriously," she ordered, "just give it to me straight. Without all the melodramatic flourishes."

I took off my glasses, set them on the kitchen counter, and rubbed the bridge of my nose. "Fine, fine," I relented. "I told Veronica about my childhood and learning to play music and high school romantic drama and Call Field and UCLA and writing 'Incomplete.'"

"So, it wasn't *that* bad, right?" Mel asked, eyebrows raised.

"Well…" I grumbled, "I stopped before I got to all the heavy stuff, so I didn't completely unburden myself. But I could still feel the weight of everything that I *didn't* tell her."

Mel tiptoed forward and curled her right arm around my hips. She looked up at me with a concerned expression and delicately traced the line of my cheekbone with a finger. "How's your anxiety?" she asked, her eyes never wavering away from mine.

I took a deep breath and wrapped my hand around her finger, caressing her bare knuckles. "It's okay," I told her, shrugging my shoulders. "Better than I thought it would be."

It dawned on me then that my marathon interview session with Veronica hadn't produced anything even remotely resembling a panic attack. Normally, when the subject of Call Field came up, I could feel myself tensing up like a latex balloon overfilled with helium, expanding and expanding until there was no room for air in my lungs.

The *absence* of that anxiety was alarming.

"Good," Mel whispered, noticeably relieved. "So even all that stuff with Serena and Steve… that didn't get to you?"

"Surprisingly, no," I answered.

You'd think that the arrogant lead singer of your band stealing your almost-kind-of-girlfriend would be an incendiary action that could cripple you for a lifetime… but the torturous love triangle of my youth felt more like the numbed ridges of a scar than the raw cliffs of an open wound. Twenty years later, that Grand Canyon of pain seemed more like a mildly irritating microcosm than an insurmountable chasm. It's amazing how much you can change in a few decades.

Still, though, I couldn't help but feel haunted by those menacing memories of my youth. Even if I wasn't self-flagellating my soul with the regrets of yesteryear, I couldn't shake the sensation of uncertainty that clouded my vision. It felt a bit like staring out at sheets of fog as your boat humbly drifts away from the shore.

I didn't like it. At all.

As I let the silent air between us hang dormant and dull, I turned my head to look at Sam. From my vantage point, I could just see her with my peripheral vision: she was diligently painting her canvas with watery blue paint. She seemed so calm, so at peace. I envied her zen innocence.

"Maybe you're outgrowing some of that old baggage," Mel suggested. "And maybe those periodic panic attacks will start to subside. Your psychiatrist *did* mention that the last time you saw him, right?" She looked at me with a conservative concern in her face, her twinkling eyes betraying her cautious optimism that things would get better.

That *I* would get better.

"People don't change, Mel," I said with a pessimistic frown.

"Except when they do," she countered back, her right hand placed firmly on her hip. "*You've* changed. And I've witnessed that firsthand during the last twenty-one years."

She had me there.

"Here's the funny thing," I said, bunching my lips up into a tight ball. "I almost…"

My words trailed off, dissipating in the dim distance between us.

"You almost… *what?*" Mel asked.

I took another deep breath. "I almost *missed* it," I admitted. The entire notion was disconcerting, to say the least, but I couldn't ignore the gentle pull of those wayward tides. "There were times when I was telling Veronica about the excitement of being onstage and the thrill of writing songs… I almost felt weightless."

Mel didn't say anything at first. She quietly turned away to the silverware drawer and took out a triplicate set of spoons, forks, and knives. I reached into a cabinet, grabbed a trio of placemats, and trailed my wife to the dining room.

As Mel and I walked to the dinner table, Sam was still studiously painting her undersea scene, adding colorful flourishes to the mermaid figure on her canvas. Mel and I weaved around her, setting the table and talking over her head (literally and figuratively).

"I think there's something there," Mel said.

"What do you mean?"

Without looking up at me, Mel scrunched up the right side of her face. "Well, if talking about all these memories didn't provoke anything negative in you, didn't trigger any physical or mental earthquakes, then perhaps you've turned a corner."

I was of two minds. Part of me wanted to scoff bitterly at the suggestion… but another part of me recognized that Mel might not have been too far off the mark.

"Maybe you're right," I sheepishly admitted. "And maybe there's a part of me that actually *misses* making music. And writing songs. And playing shows."

Even as the words left my mouth, I realized the intense contradiction of my thoughts. How could I possibly go from having panic attacks to whimsically thinking about the not-so-good old days? It was cognitive dissonance at its finest.

"Maybe your life is incomplete," Mel suggested, eyes glued to the table in front of her as she meticulously rearranged the crooked placemats I had haphazardly set out. "Not 'Incomplete,' like my song," she clarified, "but *incomplete*... as in unfinished. Like something's missing."

I walked around the table, leaned my forehead against Mel's, and draped my arms over her shoulders. "With you and Sam, my life could never be incomplete," I reassured her. "It's just nostalgia."

Mel instinctively batted her eyelashes and crinkled her eyes. "Nostalgia is beautiful," she said.

"Nostalgia is a *beautiful liar*," I clarified.

"That might be true," Mel countered, "but maybe you're lying to yourself in other ways."

That stung. Mel was right. As usual, my wife was right.

Adding insult to injury, Sam chimed in. "You know, Daddy…" she sighed with a weary expression far beyond her eight years. "Lying is bad. Maybe you shouldn't do it."

Mel and I looked at each other and broke out in voracious, all-consuming laughter. At the same time, my eyes unexpectedly welled up.

"Maybe your daughter is giving you some good advice," Mel giggled, stifling more laughs as she dabbed the corners of her eyes with a napkin.

"I feel like there are a lot of *maybes* in this conversation," I said between chuckles.

"*Maybe* you're right," Mel said with a wink.

That's one thing about having a wife and daughter: you're outnumbered and outvoted on every issue – even the ones that seem caged inside the confines of your soul.

CHAPTER THREE
"Be Here in the Morning"

Something funny happened the next evening, after I finished my five-mile run and showered off the gritty grime of sweat that coated every inch of my skin. We were seated at the dining room table behind steaming bowls of ramen, delectable fumes billowing towards the ceiling. As usual, our conversation danced between the dying art of newsprint and online journalism and students and finances and vacations and even *Star Wars* (Sam's newest obsession). We were all excited about the impending release of *The Rise of Skywalker*, so we regularly found ourselves discussing the credits and deficits of each movie in the trio of trilogies.

"*A New Hope* will always be the best film in the series," I argued.

Sam, frequently eager to play devil's advocate, was trying to argue the merits of the prequel trilogy. "But, Daddy," she explained, "it doesn't have Princess Amidala, and she's the best character. What's so great about the original movie?"

"Well, Sam, *Episode IV* introduces all the characters and the concept of the Force and sets up all these story arcs for the rest of the *Star Wars* films."

"But the other movies have more adventure," Sam asserted. "And aliens. And different-colored lightsabers. And Ewoks."

"That's true," I reluctantly agreed. "But sequels are never as good as the original in a series."

"How so?" Mel asked, effortlessly balancing a pair of chopsticks in her left hand.

"Sequels never live up to the expectations of the audience," I explained. "It's just too hard to recapture the magic that comes with the first movie. Or book. Or whatever."

Just as I was about to plunge into a diatribe about why I passionately disliked *The Phantom Menace*, something interrupted me: I felt a sharp, unexpected crack in the lower right corner of my mouth and I let out a truncated yelp.

"Are you okay?" Mel asked, dropping her chopsticks on the table.

I mumbled something vaguely obscene, my jaw throbbing in intense pain. After a few moments of this unexpected spasm, something like a pebble seemed to mysteriously appear in the middle of my mouth. I reached in, grabbed the rock-hard object, and pulled it out.

And there it was: a small stone, roughly the size of a pea, oddly shaped with rounded edges on one side and a jagged crack on the other.

It was a tooth.

Or *half* a tooth, technically.

Panicking, I ran my tongue along the back of my jawline and felt a gaping hole where my farthest molar should have been. Instead of the smooth, rigid surface I was accustomed to, there was a serrated edge at the fault line and a vacuum where that tooth used to be.

"What's wrong, Daddy?" Sam asked, her eyebrows knitted together in earnest concern.

I stared at the small nugget of an object in the palm of my hand.

"I broke a tooth," I said aloud, almost incredulous. "I can't believe it. I broke a tooth eating *ramen*."

"Oh, god," Mel muttered with an involuntary flinch. "Does it hurt?"

Reflexively, I put my right hand against my cheek. The pulsing pain continued unabated, the stinging repeating with every heartbeat like a sadistic metronome.

"Yes," I answered. "It hurts. A *lot*, in fact."

Mel grimaced in sympathy. "You should call the dentist, Brian. Right now."

Normally, I would have tried to tough it out – perhaps I would've even recycled one of my father's old, staid phrases about delaying the inevitable. This time, however, I acquiesced immediately.

"You're right," I agreed, just before I was hit with another intense bout of throbbing pain. Even the simple gust of air that filtered through my mouth felt like a tornado of suffering. I immediately reached for my phone, flipped through the address book until I found my dentist's number, and hit dial. I paced back and forth in the kitchen, the phone ringing a few times before a mechanical click echoed through the speaker.

The answering machine began prattling off the usual prerecorded greeting, reminding me that "the office staff is only available during normal working hours." *Blah, blah, blah.* You know the kind of message I'm talking about. However, the next part made me panic: "Our offices will be closed until October 31st for construction and remodeling. If this is a medical emergency, please call our help line and an on-call professional will get back to you shortly. Thank you!"

"Oh, God," I muttered, absolutely terrified. "Their office is closed for the next *week*."

I'm not sure which was worse: the thought of writhing in pain for seven days while I waited for my dentist's office to open, or the idea of some stranger sticking his oversized, over-sanitized paws into my poor mouth. Neither option sounded very appealing to me.

I ended the call and sullenly placed my phone on the kitchen counter.

"They're closed until Halloween," I whimpered. "What am I going to do?"

Mel tapped her foot nervously as I rubbed my cheek, hoping the staccato stinging would magically subside.

It didn't.

"Wait," Mel said, her eyes widening with inspiration. "What about Veronica's dad? I'm assuming his office will be open."

"Do you think they'll take me?" I asked, hope cautiously welling within my chest.

"I'll call him," Mel assured me, grabbing her phone. "Give me a minute."

She flipped through her contacts, dialed the phone number that Veronica had given us months ago when she started babysitting Sam, and waited for someone to pick up on the other end. Mel gave a brief anticipatory gasp when the ringing stopped.

"Hi, Veronica!" Mel spoke into the phone. "I'm sorry to bother you at dinnertime, but is your dad around?" My wife nodded her head slowly towards the invisible figure on the other end of the call, then spoke again. "Thank you, Veronica." As she waited, Mel covered the receiver with her hand and whispered to me. "She's going to get her dad right now."

I gave Mel a wary thumbs-up, trying to ignore the aching agony in my jaw.

"Hello, Dr. Jones!" Mel greeted Veronica's father on the phone. "I realize that this is a big request, but… well, Brian broke one of his molars at dinner tonight, and he's in a lot of pain. Is there any possible way that you might be able to see him in the next few days? I know it's kind of last minute, but maybe if there's some small window to squeeze him in…?"

I couldn't hear the response on the other end of the line, but I could tell from Mel's relieved facial expressions that the Jones family was coming to the rescue.

"Thank you so much, Dr. Jones!" Mel finally said. "You're a saint!"

I tried to breathe a sigh of relief… but it hurt too much when the air entered the cavity where my tooth used to be.

Meanwhile, Mel pressed the *End Call* button on her phone and set it down on the counter. "Well, Mr. Messed-Up Molar," my wife announced, "you're in luck. Dr. Jones will see you tomorrow afternoon at 2:00."

"That's perfect!" I said, relief flooding through my body.

"And it's your lucky day. He said he's bringing Veronica as his dental assistant."

My initial flood of relief immediately transformed into a dried-up desert of dismay.

Great, I thought to myself. *Another Veronica interrogation on the horizon.*

This time, however, I would have a very valid excuse to avoid talking.

Twenty miserable hours later, at 2:00 sharp, I entered the lush office of Dr. Thomas Jones, DDS, MAGD. I didn't know what to expect, though I had a sneaking suspicion that the interior of the dental practice would look identical to every other dentist's office that I had ever seen.

I was wrong.

Instead of sterile white walls, Dr. Jones's office was decorated with beautiful murals and paintings showcasing variations on familiar ocean landscapes. One dark blue painting depicted the Oxnard Harbor at twilight; another orange image captured the sunset over the Port Hueneme Pier. This was no ordinary office: it was something special, unique, replete with a welcoming spirit of adventure. It was like the Disneyland of dentistry. I had the sudden urge to go sailing on the open waters or ride a cresting wave on a surfboard. Miraculously, the extreme anxiety I had felt for the last twenty hours fizzled into a subdued nervousness.

Moments after I walked through the jingling glass door at the front of the building, I was greeted by a familiar voice.

"Mr. Smith!" Veronica called out to me. "Long time, no see!"

Situated behind the receptionist's desk (and looking rather casual for such a reputable facility), Veronica was dressed simply in blue jeans and her favorite BYU sweatshirt. The young Miss Jones had a clipboard with legal forms that she promptly handed me, along with an oversized pen that was emblazoned with the logo of some fancy pharmaceutical firm.

"We've got to stop meeting like this," I joked with her – just before an intense pain shot up through my jawline and forced my whole body into an abrupt convulsion.

"Are you okay?" she asked, her eyebrows furrowed together.

"I'm fine," I reassured her. "Just dealing with some fresh wounds."

When Veronica's father walked in, I almost didn't recognize him: prior to this, I had only seen him in jeans, polo shirts, and flip-flops. In sharp contrast, the illuminated figure in front of me was garbed in a spotless white lab coat, like an immaculate angel of medicine. It felt a bit like seeing a theatrical *deus ex machina* descend from the rafters… except, you know, **dentist** *ex machina*. Or something like that.

"Thank you so much for seeing me on such short notice," I said, reaching out to shake his hand. "I know you've got a busy practice going on here, so I appreciate you making time for me."

"It's no worry," Dr. Jones reassured me. "After all, it's the least I can do, considering how much you've helped Veronica with her college applications and whatnot."

Veronica made her way from behind the receptionist's desk and cut in between the two of us, grinning puckishly. "So, when do we get to slice him open, Dad?" she asked.

"There's no time like the present," Dr. Jones said with a roguish smile.

Between the weekend's emotional excavation and the impending medical procedure before me, I was ready to be liberated from the pain that had derailed my pleasantly monotonous life.

"I guess it's time," I sighed in defeat as the two Joneses led me from the reception desk back to a gleaming white room.

"Before we start to slice and dice," Veronica interrupted, "do you mind if I put on some music?"

"Be my guest, Ronnie," Dr. Jones said as he placed a surgical mask over his chin. "Just make sure it's something soothing." He pulled the elastic straps over his ears and added one more caveat: "But nothing too sleepy, either."

"I've got just the thing," Veronica said mischievously.

From my vantage point, I could see her fiddling with a computer workstation, scrolling through Spotify or iTunes or some other streaming platform as she searched for her selection.

"Found it!" she squealed.

Once again, the familiar sound of distorted power chords and a distinctive guitar riff filled the air. Shortly thereafter, an unforgettable voice rode in on the wave of crunchy guitars.

"California can be cruel in the summer…"

I scowled at Veronica from where I sat. She either didn't notice or didn't care, but I could just imagine her smirking and laughing maniacally to herself as she punished me in this makeshift torture chamber.

"Good choice!" Dr. Jones called out to his daughter. "This *really* takes me back!"

As I sat there trapped in my seat, forced to listen to the ghosts of my youth, I felt nauseous and angry and sad and bitter. And yet, I also felt a slight, unmistakable twinge of something else: nostalgia.

"This really takes *me* back, too," I mumbled sarcastically, just loud enough for Veronica to hear me from where she sat across the room.

She simply smiled, seemingly enjoying my solitary suffering.

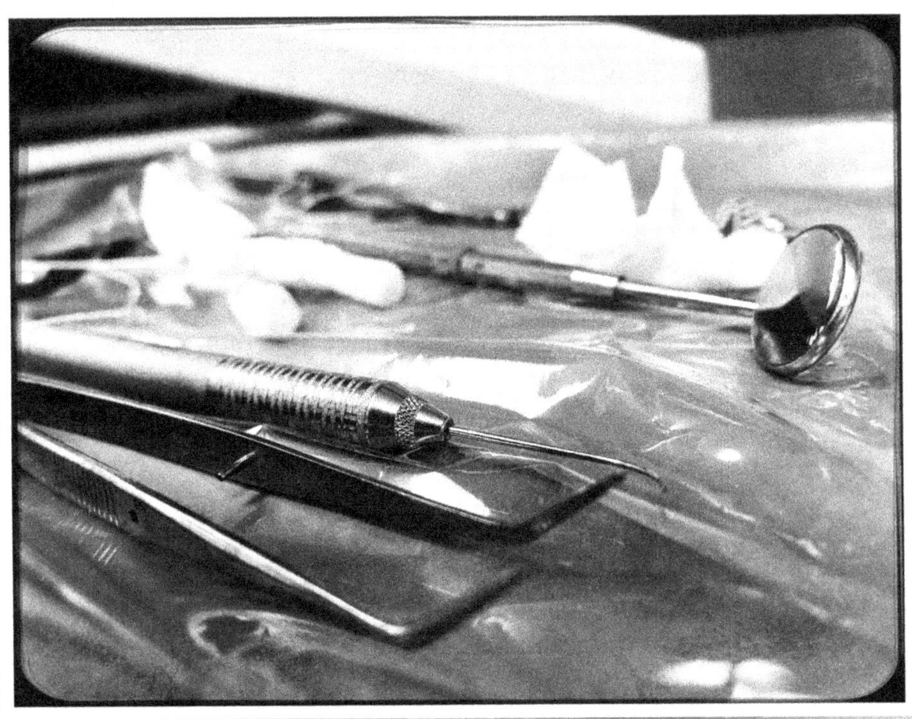

Within a matter of minutes, I found myself politely propped up, prostrate and anxious. Though I completely understand the need for regular dental checkups, this was something more unnerving, more invasive. I guess an innate fear of medical professionals is one more thing I inherited from my father.

Thanks, Dad, I thought to myself bitterly.

Looking for a diversion – from both the dentist and Veronica's selected soundtrack for the appointment – I cast my eyes around the immaculate room. Of course, there was the usual treatment chair, the tray of shining sterilized metallic instruments, and the pristinely polished sink. Nothing too out of the ordinary. Something on the walls, however, caught my eye: framed vintage posters from the 1996 summer Olympics in Atlanta, Georgia. Fidgeting with my fingers, I turned to Dr. Jones, who was stretching out a pair of latex gloves to fit onto his hands.

"Judging from the posters, I assume that you're a swimming fan?" I asked him, trying to make some uninspired small talk to quiet my nerves.

"You could say that," he chuckled, his hands gracefully adjusting the surgical mask that covered his mustachioed mouth.

Veronica laughed loudly, with an indelicate snorting sound that echoed off the walls.

"What's so funny?" I asked, feeling like I was on the outside of an inside joke.

"My dad *competed* in the Olympics," she beamed proudly. "Those posters are from the year that his relay team won a gold medal."

"Wow," I muttered, half to myself. "That's incredible."

It was kind of jarring to think that this real, live human being in front of me had once been a famous Olympic athlete – and a medal winner, nonetheless. Growing up, I spent countless hours watching superhuman athletes perform all kinds of heroic feats on television; knowing that one of those retired superheroes was casually investigating my teeth in a nondescript office on a quiet Monday afternoon seemed absolutely surreal.

"Open your mouth, please," Dr. Jones directed, using his fingers to deftly pry open my jaw.

I did as he commanded, widening my mouth until I could feel the tendons in my face stretching to an unnatural tension, and I blinked hard as the light fixture above my head nearly blinded me with its luminescence. Dr. Jones seemed to sense my discomfort; he eased up with his hands and casually started some conversation.

"It was a long time ago," he reassured me. "In fact, sometimes it almost feels like someone else's life entirely."

"That sounds familiar, doesn't it?" Veronica chimed in, giving a pointed look in my direction as she placed a surgical mask over her own face.

I scowled at her from my awkward position in the treatment chair, though I was quickly distracted by her father, who was examining my gum line with his latex-gloved hands. Like a spelunking explorer, Dr. Jones was venturing into the natural architecture of my mouth, feeling his way around with the help of a glowing bulb affixed to his forehead.

"Now, let's see what we have here," he said, his gentle voice punctuating each word with a staccato rhythm. He went straight to the point of impact, tracing his pointer finger along the crater where my tooth used to be. He gestured to Veronica and waved her over.

I felt a little like a curiosity – like the featured attraction of a dental freak show, on display for all to study.

Come, one and all, to the horrendously hazardous mouth of Brian Smith! There will be thrills! And chills! And dental floss!

Dr. Jones grabbed a sharp-looking probe instrument (which vaguely resembled a crescent sickle) and a tiny mirror attached to an elongated metal cylinder. In my head, I envisioned a miniature Grim Reaper grasping these tools and plunging into my mouth looking for nerve-endings to harvest.

"What do you recognize here, Veronica?" he asked his daughter, as he delicately poked around with the pick.

Veronica squinted harshly, as if she was studying a calculus textbook rather than her AP English teacher's teeth.

"It looks like a deep cuspal fracture on *number thirty-one* with an exposed nerve," she hypothesized.

"You nailed it," Dr. Jones said proudly. "There's also advanced decay here, too."

Veronica leaned in a little bit more, so close that I could smell the lingering traces of baby shampoo in her hair – a saccharine, childlike scent that clashed with the sterile cleanliness of the room.

"Dang it!" she scolded herself. "I can't believe I missed that!"

Veronica might be a sharp kid, I realized. *But she's still just a kid.*

"And what are the next steps we need to take, Ronnie?" Dr. Jones asked his daughter.

"It looks like a root canal to me," she responded confidently. "So, we need to clean it and make a temporary crown to tide him over until he gets the invasive stuff done. It'll definitely need a permanent crown in the end, though."

"*Exaaaactly…*" Dr. Jones confirmed, drawing out the sound of the three syllables as he withdrew his instruments from my mouth.

A root canal? A crown?

This verdict did not sound appealing to me. At all.

"So, what caused this?" I asked Dr. Jones as I rubbed my cheek. "What happened?"

He pulled the latex gloves off of his hands, snapping them loudly as he did so.

"I can tell from the coloring and texture of your teeth that you brush and floss regularly, so I know you're not neglecting your dental hygiene…"

"Then what do you think it is?" I asked.

"To put it in simple terms," he explained, "some people just have brittle teeth – which, combined with high acidic levels in a patient's saliva, can lead to significant decay. Even if you're not doing anything unhealthy, recurrent clenching and grinding can wear down your teeth. It's funny, because tooth enamel is actually the hardest substance in the human body. But, no matter how strong it might be, a tooth sometimes simply breaks."

So that was it: the hard, seemingly indestructible enamel of my tooth just cracked. The foundations of my jawline and my smile that I had taken for granted for so many years – those bricks of the human mouth – were actually much more fragile than I imagined.

"And a root canal is the only option?" I asked, afraid to hear the answer.

"That's correct," Dr. Jones stated matter-of-factly. "A specialist will have to clean out the infected tissue of the pulp, and create a fresh, clean space for the post and core. Once the diseased tissue is removed, the endodontist will do a core build-up. After that, they'll send you back to your dentist to put in a permanent filling and crown that will hopefully last you for the rest of your life."

I could feel the blood rushing out of my face, and I must have blanched ghostly white at that point. The thought of scraping out tissue from my mouth seemed particularly unsettling.

"What would happen if I just let it stay as it currently is?" I asked, desperately hoping for an alternative option. "Wouldn't it just heal on its own over time?"

Veronica snorted loudly at my ignorance. Even Dr. Jones chuckled to himself.

"Actually," Dr. Jones informed me, "it would only get worse. You know the aphorism that *time heals all wounds*...? It doesn't work that way in the world of dentistry."

"How so?" I asked.

"It isn't a matter of *time healing wounds*," he explained. "On the contrary, that cavity where your tooth used to be will fester and rot, and the infection can actually spread to the rest of your jaw. Apart from spending the rest of your life with an exposed nerve ending that would painfully interfere with eating and drinking, the resulting infection could have severe – even *deadly* – repercussions. In this circumstance, you need to face your problem and directly address the matter at hand. You can't hide from it."

So, there it was: take care of this festering wound or it would destroy me.

While Dr. Jones wasn't able to perform the full root canal right there on the spot, he did promise me that he would put in a temporary filling and crown to help ease the suffering I had been feeling for the last twenty hours. Despite the fact that it wasn't a full-fledged procedure, I remember spending an uncomfortable amount of time horizontally immobile, my mouth pried open with some strange metallic contraption, while Dr. Jones used a vibrating instrument that sounded like a miniature chainsaw.

From my limited vantage point, I could see little clouds of dust flying into the air like early morning mist. It was kind of amusing… until I realized that I was watching the microscopic fragments of a tooth – *my* tooth – sawed away into oblivion.

The procedure took about an hour, during which time I was laid flat in a rigid chair, listening to Veronica's father share stories about his life. I won't pretend that I'm an expert in dentistry; after all, my entire background is in the analysis and creation of literature, not in dental science. I do remember, though, some small sensory details – the funny feeling of anesthetic numbing half of my face, the nutmeg-scented medical-grade clove oil that tasted like a Christmas campfire in my mouth, the blaring white light that shone above me from the fixtures overhead, the whirring saw that eroded the seemingly indestructible structure of my molar. And, of course, Call Field's album playing in the background the whole time.

Over the course of the hour I sat confined in that padded pleather chair, Veronica was intently reading a copy of *Pride & Prejudice* – barely glancing up from her book as she handed her dad various intimidating metal instruments. Occasionally, when the good doctor took a breath and removed his hands from my mouth, I was able to sneak in a question or two.

"Do you *mitthhh* it?" I asked him at one point, my tongue numb from the anesthetic and unable to produce the sibilant sounds of standard speech.

"Miss what?"

"The Olympic *ttthhh-tuff.* The *crowd-ttthhh* and the *ttthhh-potlight.*"

Dr. Jones snickered to himself. "The thing about the Olympics," he explained, "is that it's a brief blast of intense, high-pressure athletics. You spend your whole life training to be a part of something special, and then the Olympics come and go within a matter of weeks."

I silently nodded my head in understanding, while Dr. Jones used the wrist of his latex-covered hand to rub an itch on the bridge of his nose.

"It didn't feel like *ttthhh-ome* kind of pinnacle or *ttthhh-omething...?*"

He gazed off into the distance, his eyes piercing through the impeccably clean walls towards some invisible horizon. There was a hint of wistful longing in his expression, a momentary distraction from the medical procedure at hand.

"It's a simultaneously gratifying and humbling experience," he said, reflexively twitching his nose behind the surgical mask. "In some ways, you *do* feel like you're on top of the world. But then you remember that you weren't fast enough to place in the individual races, and you only got a gold medal because you were a member of a *relay team.* Even though you spend your whole life training for that one moment, you're only able to achieve your goal because you were one part of a four-man team."

"But a *gold medal,*" I blubbered through my inconveniently invaded mouth, "*that-ttthhh ab-ttthhh-olutely* incredible."

"True, true," the doctor agreed, his face turning away from the imaginary horizon and back towards the patient in his treatment chair. "But as an athlete, especially one on a relay team, you're just one small piece in a much larger machine. After all, there's the fact that you're only there for your *one* group event. Meanwhile, there's a seemingly endless number of sports happening all around you. And, unless you're Mark Spitz or Michael Phelps, you're just another face in the crowd."

I had never thought about it that way. Like every average American citizen, I just assumed that such a victorious achievement would be the absolute pinnacle of someone's life.

But what happens after that kind of spotlight fades? I wondered.

"*Ttthhh-o, doe-ttthhh* everything *afterward-ttthhh ju-ttthhh-t* feel anticlimactic?" I asked, my mouth awkwardly askew. "After you're done and you go home with your medal?"

Dr. Jones chuckled to himself. "It *is* rather surreal," he admitted, his vision focused intently on my jawline. "But, believe it or not, the best moments of my life actually happened *after* all the gold-medal craziness. That summer at the Olympics wasn't the climax of my life. It was just the beginning."

"How *ttthhh-o…?*" I asked.

"Well, for starters, I got married, finished school, had children, and started my own dental practice."

"The most important part," Veronica interjected impishly, casually looking up from her book, "obviously being the birth of *me.*"

The good doctor good-naturedly scoffed at Veronica's comment. "Yes, one of the highlights was definitely the birth of my *humble* daughter," Dr. Jones said, placing extra emphasis on his ironic adjective. "In many ways, I would venture to say that the Olympics was only an antecedent of things to come. Everything since then has been much more rewarding and enjoyable."

Only an antecedent of things to come, I internally repeated to myself. My eyes darted from the fading poster on the wall back to the middle-aged man who towered over me in his medical coat.

"Do you *mi-ttthhh ttthhh-wimming* competitively?" I asked through the distracting discomfort of my medically induced lisp.

"Ironically," he said, without breaking his concentration on whatever mystery task he was doing in my mouth, "swimming now is actually a lot more fun."

"How *ttthhh-o?*" I asked, slurring my words with the sea of saliva in my mouth.

"When I go swimming now," he explained, "I do it for *me.* There's something kind of pure and liberating about that." As he spoke, Dr. Jones used a suction tool to siphon my spittle. "It reminds me of being a kid again," he continued, "swimming for the sheer joy of it all and not worrying about medals or personal records or the next big race."

"*Ttthhh-o* now you do it *ju-ttthhh-t becau-ttthhh* you *enjoy* it?"

"I do it because I *love* it," he said. "I love it with every fiber of my being." He paused, lifting the drill from the back of my mouth, and returned the focus of his attention to my eyes.

"*Becau-ttthhh* you love it," I echoed back.

"Surely," Dr. Jones said, "you have something like that in your life."

Instinctively, I grimaced.

After a solid hour of dental work, I was numbed and exhausted – physically and emotionally. Before leaving the office, I filled out the requisite paperwork and handed over my insurance cards to Veronica, who dutifully played the role of front-office assistant.

"I owe you big time," I said with a fat, numbed lower lip, shaking the hand of Dr. Jones and then repeating the cordial gesture with Veronica.

"Yes, you do," Veronica smirked. "And, just like Rumpelstiltskin, expect me to collect on that obligation in the future."

"Oh, hush," Dr. Jones said to his daughter with a loving tap on her shoulder. "You're such a ham, Veronica."

"That doesn't make the debt any less real," she countered mischievously.

"Just remember," Dr. Jones reminded me, "this anesthesia and filling are only *temporary*. They won't solve your problems in the long-term. Make sure that you schedule a follow-up appointment for your root canal soon. That will provide you with a final solution to this chronic problem."

The numbness will wear off, I thought to myself, *and then the pain will be back in full-force…*

Unless I do something to finally address the long-term problem.

In a slight daze, I walked out of the office into the overcast afternoon air. I dragged my numbed tongue over my back molars, but I was unable to feel anything with the anesthesia coursing through my jaw. So, I reached my right pointer finger into the back of my mouth, feeling for the spot where my lost tooth had been replaced.

The zinc phosphate certainly *felt* like my old tooth, though I knew that it was only a temporary composite filling the void. Something newer and stronger would have to take its place eventually.

Sometimes, we take for granted the permanence of the things and people in our lives. It is only when we touch the craters left behind in their absence that we notice their importance.

It's true for molars.

And for human beings.

CHAPTER FOUR
"Santa Claus Is Comin' to Town"

What was it that William Faulkner wrote?

"The past is never dead. It's not even past."

Though good ol' Faulkner composed that line more than half a century ago, it still rings true – especially for those of us living in an era of email and texts and social media and digital footprints and instant messaging.

Not even death can stop the past from coming back to haunt you.

After an emotionally torturous interview at Veronica's house – followed almost immediately by an equally torturous (but more excruciatingly painful) dental procedure at her father's office – I was feeling the weight of the past on my humble, haunted shoulders. Veronica, for all of her wonderful traits and talents, had become something of a psychological necromancer, resurrecting the corpses of my youth. And, as I dusted off the mental cobwebs and soil from the coffin of my consciousness, I naively hoped that Veronica would let the ghosts of my past dissolve back into the ether.

Sure, under different circumstances, it might have been fun to revisit those old haunting grounds of my punk rock past – to play a tourist in the backdrop of my rock and roll memories – but I had absolutely no desire to move back home into a haunted house.

A week later, Veronica hadn't made a peep about our interview – or about the aforementioned "debt" that I accrued from my emergency dental appointment. Periodically, though, I would glance across the room in the middle of a lesson and catch her looking up from her pile of essays with a strange expression on her face. You remember that old game *Mousetrap*, wherein you build these elaborate Rube Goldberg-esque contraptions? There was something about Veronica's demeanor that told me she was developing an intricate strategy in that brilliant mind of hers.

It only took a week and a half before Veronica pounced with her plan. We were back at school after our weeklong October break, and I had just finished a Friday morning lesson on *The Narrative of the Life of Frederick Douglass.* As my eleventh-grade AP students boisterously filed out the doorway with promises of weekend freedoms, Veronica confidently walked up to me at the front of the class, her Honors Physiology textbook clutched tightly to her chest.

"I would like to preface this conversation by reminding you that you owe me," she said matter-of-factly, like a lawyer making an opening statement. "So, before you shoot me down, remember that the only reason you can comfortably eat food right now is because my daddy saved you from dental misery."

She had me there. I took a deep breath and thought about my options. I could gracelessly shoo her away. I could dramatically fake an illness. I could frantically run out the door. Or, I could patiently listen to what she had to say.

I opted for the last – albeit most intimidating – choice.

"Okay, Veronica," I conceded. "Tell me what's on your mind."

Her eyes instantly brightened like luminous headlights being switched on, and she started intently tapping her left flip-flop-adorned foot on the tile floor of the classroom.

"Next month is the school talent show," Veronica started to explain.

"That *Winter Spectacular* thing?" I asked. Though I had been teaching at Oxnard Shores High School for more than a decade and a half, I hadn't actually been to one of the annual holiday-themed talent shows on our campus. Alas, it's just too hard to come out for a weeknight event in the last few days before winter vacation.

"That's the one!" Veronica squealed. Her flip-flop was tapping even louder and more rapidly than before. She reminded me of the little rabbit Thumper in *Bambi*, unable to stay still for more than a few moments at a time. "I've been wanting to sing a Christmas song at the Winter Spectacular since I was a freshman, and this is my last chance before I graduate."

"Sounds pretty exciting," I said, almost afraid to ask what her demands might be. "But how does this involve me?"

"Well, being the musical snob that I am, I *hate* karaoke…" Her voice trailed off into the static of the classroom's air conditioning.

"And…?" I asked anxiously, waiting for the other shoe to drop. Or flip-flop, as it were.

Veronica took a deep breath, mustering her courage. "And I can't sing and strum a guitar at the same time so I need a guitarist to play with me up onstage and I don't know any guitar players," she blurted out, "so I want *you* to be my accompaniment."

This girl had no shame.

My knee-jerk reaction was to say *"no."* In fact, I believe that I was on the verge of spouting a frantic *"hell, no"* to the little seventeen-year-old student in front of me.

Veronica clearly sensed my hesitation. "Before you say '*no*,'" she interjected, "I want you to simply *think about it*. During our interview a few weeks ago, you told me how pivotal music was to your childhood. Don't you want to revisit that part of your life? Don't you want to get up onstage and make notes come alive from your fingers on those guitar strings? Just like when you were an inspired teenager?"

I sighed nervously. "I don't know, Veronica…"

"I think you *do* know," she interrupted. "I think there's a part of you – deep, deep down inside you – that *misses* playing music. And if I'm wrong, then I'll critique a million AP essays without complaint."

She had me there. I was left mentally scrambling for excuses, but I couldn't think of a single valid justification for why I shouldn't agree to her request.

"Plus," Veronica added slyly, "you owe me. My dad squeezed you into his *very* busy schedule and fixed your busted tooth for you on super-short notice. And the only reason you know my dad is because of me. Basically, without me, you'd still be reeling in pain from your broken molar."

I scowled at her. In a joking sort of fashion, of course. Or half-joking, at least.

"Like I said," she continued on, undeterred, "just think about it over the weekend. Promise me that you'll think about it."

"I'll think about it," I told her, squinting hard. "I promise you."

Veronica readjusted the backpack haphazardly slung across her sleek shoulders. She squinted at me puckishly, her cheeks crinkling into a devilishly dimpled smile.

"And remember," she added coolly, "I have some leverage. I know all about your former career as a rock star."

Veronica turned on her heels to go, and, with a twist of her long black hair, she marched out of my classroom.

I was almost beginning to resent that precocious kid.

CHAPTER FIVE

"Diamond Head"

I tend to overthink things. A lot. Obviously.

Frequently, I find myself trapped inside my own head. You know that line from "Incomplete" – *"I get lost sometimes in the melodies of my mind"* – that you've undoubtedly heard by now? Though I'm older, wiser, and exponentially balder than I was when I wrote those lyrics, the part of me that psychologically dwells on significant subjects hasn't changed much in the ensuing years.

Is it a sign of my mental illness? My burgeoning bipolar disorder? Or simply anxious artistry? I suppose you'll have to come to your own conclusions in the pages ahead.

It should come as no surprise that I spent the rest of that day distracted by Veronica's request. There were a few comical moments – spilling coffee on my favorite tie, photocopying the wrong set of worksheets after school, missing a turn on the drive home – but it didn't feel amusing at the time.

Like it or not, I was at a crossroads.

A high school talent show crossroads.

Sound familiar?

After taking an alternate route home from work (due to the aforementioned distracted misdirection), I made it through my front door close to dinnertime. As the heavy oak door creaked open in its frame, I could hear distant voices echoing in the tile hallway. I kicked off my dress shoes, loosened my newly coffee-stained tie, and glanced at the clock in our entranceway. The clock read *4:45*. Yikes.

In our household, 4:45 is in the middle of dinner-preparation time. If you show up closer to 5:00, there will be no one to greet you at the door or throw loving arms around you. During that hour, it's a culinary classroom at *La Casa de Smith*. Arriving home as late as I was that evening, the girls had started making dinner without me.

Yes, I know that it's a reinforcement of traditional gender roles and stereotypes that my wife does 99% of the cooking, but I'm absolutely useless in the kitchen. Mel, on the other hand, learned a bunch of tricks growing up around her family's restaurant. So, Mel cooks, and I clean. Thus far, it's been an egalitarian equation for our marriage.

Does that make us marital caricatures? Perhaps. But we're *well-fed* marital caricatures. With clean dishes.

Because my arrival had gone unnoticed, I was able to creep around the corner in my sweaty black socks, barely making a sound on the tiled floor. As I inched closer to the kitchen, I could see the backs of Mel and Sam, both of whom were facing away from me. Mel had a cutting board and a sharp knife on the kitchen counter in front of her; Sam, perched casually on a stepping stool and wearing a child-sized Darth Vader apron, stood next to her.

Their voices sliced through the still silence of the house, the sounds of their conversation punctuated by the rhythmic chopping of a kitchen knife. I could hear Sam's giggles wafting through the air, accompanied by the occasional laugh from Mel.

I stealthily slumped against the doorframe of the entranceway, unseen and observing them from a distance. In this culinary classroom, Mel was the teacher and Sam was the student – while I was simply a spectral spectator in the foyer.

"When can I have some pineapple, Mama?" Sam asked, her pint-size fingers tapping against the granite countertops like a nervous stenographer. She fidgeted with her apron, untying and retying the strings that kept it in place.

"Not yet, sweetheart," Mel reminded her. "We have to disassemble it first."

"What does 'dis-semble' mean?" Sam asked.

"'Disassemble' means to *take it apart*," Mel answered calmly, snapping off the Mohawk-like crown at the top of the pineapple. "You have to get rid of all the exterior – the *outside* of the pineapple – before you get to the fruit on the inside. The part that you can actually eat."

"Oh," Sam muttered.

Mel brushed her nose with the back of her forearm and turned towards Sam. "And what's the very first thing you have to do before you *disassemble* the pineapple?" Mel asked.

"Well, before you *dis-semble* it…" Sam began.

"Dis-*a*-ssemble," Mel corrected gently.

"Before you dis-*a*-ssemble it," Sam over-enunciated while rolling her eyes, "you have to flip it upside-down." Then, she paused and her eyebrows furrowed intensely. "But why do you have to flip it upside-down? I forgot."

"Good question, honey. You see, when a pineapple is hanging in the same position for a long, long time, the sweet juices all settle at the bottom." Mel demonstrated by picking up the fruit and dangling it between her hands. "When you flip it," – at this point she turned the prostrate pineapple on its head – "it shakes things up and the sweetness redistributes…"

"What does that mean?" Sam asked, interrupting the cooking lesson. "*Re-dis-tri-butes*?"

"It means that it spreads out evenly, instead of being stuck in the same little spot. You have to shake things up to bring back the sweetness to the rest of the fruit." Mel shook the pineapple like a giant maraca before placing it back on the cutting board.

"You're silly," Sam giggled.

Mel reached out and tapped Sam on the nose. "That's what mamas are for, right? Being silly?" She scrunched her eyes in a goofy smile and then reached for the shiny, oversized chef's knife. "And while the sweetness *redistributes* in the pineapple, we can start slicing off the sides."

Sam leaned forward, staring intently at the jagged surface of the fruit in front of her. "Why is it so prickly, Mama? It looks like hundreds of little hooks."

"It's actually an illusion, *keiki*," Mel said. "Look."

She took Sam's right hand and dragged it delicately across the skin of the pineapple. The seemingly intractable spikes swayed and bent under the slight pressure of her elfin fingers. Inquisitively, Sam pressed down on a sharply curved hook only to see it retreat like the petal of a wilted flower.

"What's really interesting about pineapples," Mel continued, "is that they only *look* scary. That's nature's way of keeping animals – and people – away. But if you're not too frightened, and you make your way past the intimidating outside, your prize is the sweet, sweet fruit on the inside."

Waving Sam's hands away, Mel used the chef's knife and deftly sliced the right edge off the pineapple. She rotated the fruit, continually cutting away at the exterior, until all that remained was a single cylindrical shape of yellow flesh. When Mel was done, she sliced a small triangle off the top and handed it to Sam. Without hesitation, Sam placed it squarely on her tongue and began to chew. Mel cut off another small piece and popped it into her own mouth.

"And *that*, Sammy-Sam," she said between bites, "is how you get to the sweet stuff."

For a brief, unsolicited moment, a distant memory flashed in the back of my brain: my father teaching me how to properly fasten a necktie back at our old house on Lago de Paz Court in Ojai. Despite my best efforts, my eyes teared up as I thought back to that tender time in my life. A couple of rogue drops streaked down my cheeks, and I took a deep breath as I wiped them away.

I swear, fatherhood has turned me into a big old softie.

When I sniffled, wiping away the tears from my eyelids, Mel turned around and spotted me standing in the hall.

"Hi, honey," she greeted me. She squinted and – even without her glasses – saw my red, runny eyes. "Are you okay?"

"I am now," I told her. I made my way through the kitchen and walked up to my two beautiful gals. I squeezed Mel tightly, and kissed Sam on the top of her head. "I am now."

That evening, I thought long and hard about Veronica's proposition. After Mel and I put Sam to bed and finished our nightly cleaning rituals, I found myself tossing and turning in bed, unable to find any comfortable position. With every twisting bedsheet I wrought, every valley my head formed in my pillow, sleep and solace kept slipping away.

Like I said, I tend to overthink things.

After the umpteenth time that I uneasily flipped sides like a fish on a sailboat's deck, Mel dragged her right arm across my frustrated frame.

"Are you okay?" she asked, her left hand cushioning her horizontal head. She looked cool and comfortable in her cotton pajamas, a Zen mystery draped in argyle patterns.

I sighed deeply, heaving the air out of my listless body. "I've got a lot on my mind," I told her. "And I'm having a hard time quieting my brain."

Mel began a delicate dance with her fingers, carefully caressing my clavicle. "Let's talk about it," she said gently, her voice softer than silk. My wife might not be perfect, but she knows how to coax the truth out of me.

"Veronica asked me to perform with her at the school talent show next month," I said. "She wants me to play guitar for her so that she can sing a Christmas song."

Without hesitation, Mel's eyes lit up like jewels. "That's great news!" she said, sitting up in bed and drawing back her fingers towards her cheerfully parted lips. Then she paused, studying my reaction (or lack thereof). "Wait… that *is* great news, right?"

I didn't say anything.

"So that's *not* great news?" she asked, raising a single eyebrow. "It seems like this could be a pretty fun opportunity for you."

"How so?"

"Well, having the different parts of your life brought together… It could be therapeutic."

"I don't know…" I began. I rolled over onto my side and gazed up at my wife.

"Don't know… *what?*" Mel pressed on, her petite body towering over me.

I sat up in bed, but kept my eyes fixed on the crumpled sheets between us. Slowly, I threaded the fingers of my right hand through hers. "I just don't know if I want to have my world turned on its head," I admitted.

"Don't be so *dramatic*," Mel answered, casually rolling her eyes. "It's not like you're performing in front of the Pope or serenading the President or anything. It's a *high school talent show*." She punctuated every word of the sentence with a tap on my shoulder. "I think this might be a really great opportunity for you. And you'll get to do something nice – a *mitzvah* – for Veronica. She's a good kid."

"I guess," I mumbled back at her.

"Plus," she added coolly, "it might be healthy for you to get your world flipped upside-down. You know, shake things up a bit."

"I am not a pineapple, Mel," I said with a half-hearted scowl.

"No," she smiled. "You're much sweeter."

CHAPTER SIX
"Child of Winter"

My dad once told me that he stopped playing guitar the day my sister was born – and he didn't pick it up again for a decade. As he explained it, between the ridiculous requirements of teaching and the hectic demands of parenting, there was no time to fiddle around (or strum, technically) with something so trivial.

"When there are diapers to change and essays to grade," he rationalized, *"there's no opportunity for an old man to waste time on his guitar."*

Very true, Pops. Very true.

As I sat in my office that weekend grading essays on *Narrative of the Life of Frederick Douglass*, I kept hearing that quote over and over in my head. In-between the blue pen marks that I was scrawling on the interminable pages in front of me, I would find my eyes drifting over to the silent and dusty Martin guitar that stood in the northwest corner of the room. Just as I would begin to lean back in my leather office chair and arch my body towards the instrument, I would catch myself and turn my attention back to the stack of essays on my desk.

Normally, I have some kind of instrumental soundtrack playing in the background while I work (improvisational Grateful Dead jams seem to be the most conducive for grading), but the room felt eerily silent that Saturday afternoon. I could just barely make out the soft crashing of waves against the distant shore. But, when I looked out my window, the sky was a dark, unforgiving shade of gray that shrouded the coastline in rolling curtains of fog.

The ocean waters, normally smooth and rapturous, seemed a bit more tentative and reserved in their gentle cresting. They kept moving, of course – in and out and in and out across the shore – but the waves seemed uncertain, distracted.

"Why do you keep Grandpa's guitar in your office, Daddy?" Sam asked from the doorframe, scaring the life out of me. Most of the time, kids are like petite elephants, stomping loudly across the floor; occasionally, though, they're like little stealth ninjas, slithering behind you undetected… until they strike and nearly give you a heart attack.

"Oh, jeez, Sam," I puffed, swiveling my chair to face her and capping the blue pen I held in my right hand. "I didn't see you there."

She smiled impishly at me. "That's because I was using my *ballet moves*," she explained, quietly prancing across my office floor and delivering a mini-arabesque.

I clapped stiffly, like a stuffy old Englishman from *Downton Abbey*, and gave my daughter a goofy grin. "Excellent, my dear," I spoke in a ridiculous caricature of a British accent. "That was bloody brilliant."

Sam curtsied and gave me an over-the-top bow. She's a complete ham – just like her dear old dad.

"You didn't answer my question," Sam said, returning to her upright stature. "Why do you have that guitar in your office?"

I rolled my chair over to where she stood on the cold, wooden floor. "Well," I began, wrapping my hands around hers, "who gave me this guitar?"

"Grandpa Smith," she answered matter-of-factly. "Right?"

"Right," I reaffirmed. "This guitar used to belong to my dad – your grandfather. Then, when I got old enough to play it, it became *my* guitar." I smiled at her, my eyes stinging a little. "And one day, Sam, this will be *your* guitar."

Samantha walked over to the Martin and hesitantly ran her hands along the headstock of the instrument. As she did so, the guitar shed a thin film of dust, sprinkling a grimy powder onto the hardwood floor.

"It's all dusty," Sam noted. "You haven't played it in a while."

"Not for a long time," I admitted solemnly.

"You should play the guitar more often, Daddy," she told me. Slowly, her eyes opened wide with hope, like a flower blossoming in a stop-motion video. "Will you play it for me?" she asked.

I could feel the tug of desire within me, the yearning for a chance to reconnect with that piece of my past. Ultimately, though, the flicker faded and I resolved myself to the silence.

"Not right now, sweetheart," I said firmly, turning away from the guitar and looking back at the pile of papers on my desk. "I've got too much work to do. There's just no opportunity for an old man to waste time on his guitar." As soon as I said it, I was hit with a slight pang in my chest.

There's just no opportunity for an old man to waste time on his guitar. The words echoed in my head, unraveling from the recesses of my memory like an unfolding origami sculpture.

The luminescence of Sam's eyes dimmed slightly and her previously hopeful expression faded into a despondent frown. It hurt me to see the disappointment spread across her face so quickly, as if my own distractions darkened my daughter's mood.

"You know what, Sam?" I said instinctively, as I rushed to counter the encroaching sadness. "Veronica asked me to play guitar for her at the school talent show next month."

Oh, God, I thought, as the words came tumbling forth. *What am I saying?*

Sam's indomitable joy slowly crept back into her dimpled chipmunk cheeks. I couldn't help but feel a flood of relief as her smile was resurrected from the ashes of disappointment.

"So… maybe Veronica and I can play some music for you very soon," I offered. "Will that be okay?"

"My favorite babysitter and my favorite Daddy!" she sang out gleefully. "I can't wait!"

"For right now, though, sweetheart," I told her, "your daddy needs to go back to his homework. Do you mind if I do a little more grading before dinner?"

"That sounds *boring*," Sam intoned dramatically. "Playing guitar would be much more fun." She casually glanced around the confines of the office before turning back to the door. "I'm gonna' go play in my room. Bye, Daddy!" And with that, she joyfully bounded out of the room.

I watched her exit through the doorframe, and I stared out into the darkness of the hallway for a few lingering seconds after she was gone. At that moment, I knew that my fate had been decided. Good ol' Brian Richard "Brick" Smith was begrudgingly coming out of musical retirement for a high school talent show. And a *Christmas* talent show, at that.

Bah, humbug.

Before I could dwell on it any longer, though, I turned back to the stack of essays and uncapped my blue pen. Mechanically, I found the spot in the middle of the paragraph where I had left off. Yet again, I returned to grading papers from my AP English class.

Back to business.

CHAPTER SEVEN
"Santa's Beard"

To say that Veronica was excited would be a dramatic understatement.

"YES! YES! YES!" she screeched inelegantly in my classroom, as she jumped up and down like a pogo stick with a backpack. "You won't regret this! I promise you!"

I had just given her the news that I would, indeed, be accompanying her on guitar for the Oxnard Shores "Winter Spectacular" talent show. Based on her over-the-top reaction, however, you would have thought that I had just handed her a puppy.

"But don't get too excited," I warned her. "I'm *really* rusty. I haven't played guitar in a long time. A *long* time."

She looked up at me with a curious expression. "So…?"

"Like a *really* long time," I emphasized. "You know those old, broken-down tractors you see collecting rust in the strawberry fields around town? The ones that haven't moved an inch in years?"

Veronica shot me a quizzical look. "What are you *talking about*…?" she asked with furrowed brows.

I adjusted my horn-rimmed glasses on the bridge of my nose. "Well," I explained, "at this point, I'm sure that those immobile machines work better than I do. I'm an old, busted contraption, Veronica. I can't guarantee that this –" I gestured wildly with my hands. "– our musical collaboration – will be a smashing success."

"Do you always have to talk in metaphors?" She frowned at me. "I know you're an English teacher and everything, but it can be kind of frustrating."

"Frustrating metaphors or not, Veronica, you're kind of stuck with me."

"You're right, Mr. Smith," she nodded. "And, to use your overly complicated metaphor, I have complete faith that you'll brush off those mental cobwebs and get that musical engine running again."

At least that made one of us.

So, Veronica had strong-armed me into serving as her musical accompaniment for the Winter Spectacular. As the next few weeks sauntered by in the November nuances that lead up to Thanksgiving, Veronica and I carved out a few minutes here and there for lunchtime and after-school practices in my classroom. Each time, Veronica would bring one of the multitudinous friends in her social circle to keep her company and serve as a mini-audience for our rehearsal.

"Mr. Smith!" the friends would inevitably announce with shock when they saw me cradling my dad's old Martin in my hands. "You play guitar…?"

"You have *no idea*," Veronica would smirk at them cryptically.

It was pretty rough at first. Picking up the guitar again after so long of an absence felt like putting on a pair of tight-fitting blue jeans fresh from the dryer. Alas, the many intervening years since I departed from Call Field had not been kind to my musical muscle memory. The fancy fingerpicking techniques that my father had taught me during those late-night jam sessions in our garage had atrophied – faded and floated away into the ether.

But slowly – *very* slowly – it all started to come back to me. My fingers, at first clumsy and insubordinate, began to move in familiar rhythms. It felt like reciting a forgotten prayer from childhood. Strumming those steel strings unlocked parts of my heart that had lain dormant, like hibernating beasts during a long winter. I never made it back to the skillful ease of my late-1990s heyday, mind you, but at least it was an improvement over the stilted motions that plagued me at first.

The old *Brick Smith* was back. Kind of.

For the Winter Spectacular, Veronica had selected "Santa Baby" as the tune she wanted to sing. It wouldn't have been my first choice, mind you, but she clearly felt a connection to the old Eartha Kitt holiday tune.

"Don't you think that 'Santa Baby' is a bit too provocative for a high school audience?" I asked her, secretly hoping that she'd pick a different selection.

"Not at all," Veronica answered.

"But the lyrics sound like a greedy laundry list from a lusty lover," I told her, concern etched on every corner of my face. "Not very Christmasy, if you ask me."

Veronica rolled her eyes at me. "Okay, Boomer. It's a song addressed to *Santa Claus*, not Hugh Hefner. Get your mind out of the gutter, old man." With a narrowing of her eyes, Veronica's dismissive distaste swiftly transformed into self-righteous anger. "Why do Baby Boomers always try to ruin the playful innocence of old songs?"

"For the record," I shot back defensively, "my mind is *not* in the gutter, kid." I gave her a bitter scowl. "And I'm not even *close* to a Baby Boomer. I'm Gen X. Or Gen Y. Or Gen Z. Or something."

"Whatever," she answered with a scoff. "You're still old."

That Veronica. What a kidder.

For a seventeen-year-old, Veronica possessed a surprisingly sophisticated voice. She sang with an earnest, unassuming tone – a vintage style that reminded me at times of Norah Jones or Zooey Deschanel or even Amy Winehouse. I'm not sure how a sweet, straightedge, suburban kid managed to sound like such an old soul, but when Veronica sang, I felt like I was being transported to a bygone era.

It was jarring. But, I have to admit, it sounded impressive. *Really* impressive.

"It's because I grew up listening to a lot of music from the 50s and 60s," she hurriedly explained to me after practice one day.

Her friend, Rita, who had been sketching something while we rehearsed, was tapping a watch impatiently, giving Veronica the cue that it was time to leave.

While Veronica could have undoubtedly rhapsodized for days about her favorite artists, she was in a rush to leave my classroom that afternoon. "I love Aretha Franklin and Etta James and Janis Joplin and all kinds of other singers from the decades before I was born," she quickly explained. "There's so much passion in their voices. The closest thing to that now is someone like Adele. There's not much else in today's musical landscape that speaks to me in the same way."

"That's unusual for someone your age," I noted. "I don't know many high school kids who listen to that kind of music. Of course, I don't know any other teenagers who want to be dentists, either."

"And *I* don't know any other teachers," Veronica shot back, "who used to be rock stars."

"What was that?" Rita shouted from the doorjamb.

"*Nothing!*" Veronica and I answered simultaneously.

I turned back to face my superstar-student-turned-musical-collaborator. "*Touché*, Veronica," I said with a scowl. "*Touché*."

Finally, the big day (or night, as it were) arrived. When I was at home getting dressed for the event, my hands were shaking uncontrollably. I remember staring hard at my reflection in the mirror as I fumbled with my necktie over and over again: I had to knot, unknot, and re-knot it until my unsteady hands could do the job correctly. Maybe it was because my interview with Veronica had dug up so many old memories of my adolescence, but I couldn't help but think back to that long-ago afternoon when my dad had first taught me how to flip up my collar and forge a Windsor knot with silk folds of fabric.

"The wave washes over the beach once," he had explained, *"then washes over it again, and then the wave creeps back into the ocean."*

This time, though, my father wasn't standing next to me. I was all by myself.

As my uncertain fingers fumbled with the silk fabric, I tried to quiet my brain with a calming image: each time I filled my lungs with air, I imagined a wave cresting and then receding on the shore.

I breathed in. I breathed out.

Cresting and receding. Cresting and receding.

I breathed in. I breathed out.

Cresting and receding. Cresting and receding.

I can do this, I told myself. *I can do this.*

After all, it was just a high school talent show. For a middle-aged man who had played dozens and dozens (perhaps even *hundreds*) of venues over the years, why should the dilapidated floorboards of a high school stage seem so intimidating?

Despite the tightening in my chest and the quaking of my hands, I knew that this talent show was no overwhelming opponent. It was just a small, amateurish event at the place where I worked.

I can do this, I told myself yet again.

I slid the big end of the necktie through the folds of silk, pulled the knot, and tightened it above my clavicle.

I can do this.

Lugging my guitar from my car to the auditorium took significantly longer than I had anticipated. The average guitar weighs a little over four pounds, and a hard-shell case weighs about nine pounds; yet, the instrument in my hands felt infinitely heavier, like I was shouldering the full burden of a musical casket. I looked down at the smooth, solid-black, four-foot case swinging down from my right hand, and I almost stopped in my tracks. It felt like an insurmountable gravitational force – like an anchor dropping – as if I was a submerged ship, stalled on the course to meet my destiny.

For a brief second, I entertained the idea of running back to my car, ditching the show, and leaving town for Canada or Mexico or some other destination hundreds of miles away. As I paused in my tracks, the echo of my footfalls temporarily silenced in the hallways of Oxnard Shores High

School, I realized that such an escape plan would merely be delaying the inevitable.

You can't cheat death, and you sure as hell can't outrun your destiny. Or out-sail your destiny, for that matter.

With that in mind, I took a deep breath, put one foot in front of the other, and continued on to the theater down the hall.

Right foot. Left foot.
Right foot. Left foot.
Repeat until showtime.

The drama teacher at Oxnard Shores, Jonathon "Jack" Franklin, was a stocky, bespectacled teacher of medium height who vaguely reminded me of a good-natured bulldog. He was a former high school and college wrestler, and the depth of that history lingered like an intimidating shroud over his persona. Despite his physically daunting stature, the man was absolutely hilarious, reducing his casts and crews and classes to nonstop laughter in his presence. And yet, for all of his comedic qualities, the man ran a tight ship: his drama productions were always professional-quality shows, and his students knew to take him seriously – lest that old competitive wrestler reemerge from the remote recesses of his personality and start barking orders at the mischievous parties involved.

Fortunately, Mr. Franklin seemed to like me. He was a transplant from the Pacific Northwest with a deep passion for 1990s grunge music, so we bonded over our shared love of Pearl Jam, Soundgarden, Alice in Chains, and Nirvana. Though he was a few years older than me, Jack considered me an egalitarian equal and treated me with reverential respect. The man obviously understood how to communicate with kids, as the multiple "teacher of the year" awards adorning his classroom walls illustrated, but he also knew how to commune with his colleagues.

As I sat anxiously in my uncomfortable, dilapidated, duct-taped theater seat in the green room, Jack sauntered over casually and plopped down next to me in a similarly shabby, ramshackle seat.

"You ready for tonight, bud?" he asked.

I nodded my head deliberately, more to assuage my own anxiety than to answer his question. "As ready as I'll ever be," I told him.

He gave me a crooked sidewise grin and cracked his knuckles like a mafia enforcer. "You never mentioned that you played guitar," he said. "We should get a band together and do a number at next year's show. Maybe a Neil Young song or something?" He instantly launched into a Robin Williams-esque rendition of "Rockin' in the Free World" – much to the amusement of the students huddled nearby.

"That could be fun," I answered noncommittally. "If I can survive tonight, obviously."

"Are you nervous?" he asked.

"Yeah," I mumbled. "It's just been a long time since I've been onstage. I'm not sure I'm ready for all that attention."

"You'll be fine," he assured me. "Besides, everyone's going to be watching Veronica, anyway. The lead singers always get all the attention."

"*You're telling me*," I knowingly snickered. "Isn't that how it always is?"

"Yup. But that's what teachers do. We lay the groundwork for kids like Veronica to shine." He leaned forward and examined some loose cotton stuffing emerging haphazardly from the upright cushion of the seat in front of us. Squinting at the torn vinyl surface of the seat, he diligently poked and prodded, forcing the cotton batting back into its cracked container. It was a Sisyphean task: all he managed to do was temporarily stuff it back in place before it seeped out like an angry cloud.

"You're right," I agreed. "In fact, I don't think I'd even be doing this show if I hadn't been coerced by Veronica."

"You know that she's like your biggest fan, right? And that's a high honor. She's basically the president of the *Mr. Smith Fan Club*." He kept poking at the cotton stuffing, doing his best to repair the imperfections adorning his less-than-perfect seats.

"Who?" I asked.

"Veronica," he answered casually, still focused intently on the cotton emerging from the cracked cushion in front of us. "She talks about you all the time, spouting off all the things she's learned from you. She says you're like a second father to her. And if you can make that kind of an impact on a kid's life, you know you're doing a great job. I mean, we could all use another good father figure in our lives, right?"

His words were sinking in slowly, but I couldn't take my mind off the decrepit state of the green room's seats. The whole time we had been talking, Jack had been fighting a losing battle against the cushion of a chair – not exactly a glamorous occupation for an adult with several post-graduate degrees.

"So, what's up with the seats?" I asked finally.

Mr. Franklin let out an angry grunt. "I've been begging the district to repair these for *years* now," he explained, "but I always get the same answer. '*We don't have enough money,*' they tell me. '*There just isn't sufficient funding set aside for the arts programs.*'" He aggressively increased his attack on the seat, but his anger had little effect on the cotton batting that he battled.

"Have you thought about fundraising?" I asked him.

He whipped his head around and scowled at me. "Sometimes, I feel like that's *all* we do. But this theater is so old," he said with a dramatic gesture of his hands, "it's just a money pit. When we get any influx of cash, it's hard to decide where to start."

Following his gesticulations, I casually looked around me at the modest facilities. Oxnard Shores High School was half a century old, and the decades of wear and tear showed in every crooked corner and damaged doorjamb.

"What kinds of expenses are you looking at?" I asked gently, afraid to broach what was clearly a sore subject for my colleague.

Jack grunted and shifted his position so that his back was arching forward like a broken balance beam. "Well, I just used a huge portion of our ASB account to buy a new dimmer pack for the auditorium, and we still need to pay for all the restoration of our main stage."

"That sounds like quite a Herculean task," I told him. "And there's no one who can help you out?"

"There's just never enough money for arts programs," he said, circling back to his original point. "We make do with what we have, but we'll never be able to live up to our full potential without a better facility."

"That's a tragedy," I mumbled, head bowed.

Mr. Franklin nodded in agreement. "Sometimes," he explained, "I feel like Cinderella showing up for the royal ball in ripped-up rags. Sure, I can train our kids to do magic onstage, but it's impossible for Oxnard Shores to compete with professional theaters unless we make a *ton* of improvements to our facilities."

"How much do you think it would cost to redo the theater?" I asked.

Jack let out an epic breath of air. "Oh, man," he said, "I'd venture to say about $20,000. We need a new backdrop curtain, some new borders, a new proscenium, a new drive motor for the main curtain…"

"That's a lot," I said dully, unable to conjure a more eloquent response to console my colleague.

"And, of course," he said, thumping indelicately on an adjacent chair, "dozens and dozens of reupholstered seats."

Even as empathetic educators, it's easy to forget the struggles and challenges of those around us. I guess I'm guilty of staying hyper-focused on my own problems – on the challenges of my classroom and household – and completely forgetting that my colleagues on campus are facing their own overwhelming obstacles.

"That's where we stand," he sighed. "And that's where we'll stay."

I stared at my folded hands as they perched atop the metal rim of the chair in front of me. "If there's anything I can do to help…" I offered in a subdued voice.

"If you have any suggestions," he muttered, more a rhetorical statement than an actual plea, "let me know."

It was at this point that our conversation was interrupted by a frantic student calling from the backstage area.

"Mr. Franklin!" she shrieked, her thin voice echoing through the green room. "One of the microphones is malfunctioning!"

He looked over at me and shook his head. "A teacher's duty is never done."

As he got up to leave, I reached my arm out to shake his hand. "Thanks for the pep talk and the conversation, Jack," I told him. "I needed that."

"Go out and knock 'em dead," he called back to me, striding off towards the darkness of the stage.

The minutes cruelly ticked by as I anxiously awaited my turn to face the spotlights. In the green room, I was surrounded by a gabby gang of gangly high school students, all of whom seemed to be caught in little microcosms of joy and terror and camaraderie. It never ceases to amaze me how these young human beings, constantly posturing for adulthood with preternaturally sophisticated clothing and language and makeup and hobbies, are really just overgrown kids at heart. Waiting there in the backstage holding area, I thought of Serena Rios, my teenage crush, tottering in heels at her *quinceañera.* Despite our best attempts to appear like we were all grown up, we were nothing more than children playing dress up. I guess things haven't changed much in the quarter-century since *I* was a high school student.

Looking out across the green room at the small crowds of kids dressed in ball gowns and cowboy hats and sparkling uniforms, I couldn't help but wonder what the future might have in store for them. How many would achieve remarkable things in their lives? How many would fall short of their ambitions and expectations? How many of them would live in the aftermath of Friday night lights or Olympic medals or rock star dreams? And how many of them would tragically pass away before their time, leaving grieving lovers and spouses and children and families and friends?

High school is a way station for life, a purgatory-like waiting zone in which so many of the important activities – the things that *really* matter – get put on hold for the sake of diagramming sentences and balancing equations and filling beakers and running endless miles around an infinity-shaped track. As a teacher, I'm sometimes guilty of playing into those predictable tropes of meaningless academic treadmills, contributing to that overwhelming malaise of factory-like education. But I also know that public high schools can foster powerful experiences for our students. Nights like this one – when brave, dedicated kids with cultivated talent can flourish under the beaming spotlights of an amateur stage – these nights mean something.

I would wager that Veronica will remember that talent show performance for the rest of her life. She'll remember giggling backstage with her friends. She'll remember wearing a floor-length sparkling red gown. She'll remember standing center-stage with the incandescent lights beaming down on her. She'll remember what it felt like to have hundreds and hundreds of people in the audience applauding and cheering and screaming.

And she'll also remember the nerdy, balding, bespectacled English teacher who strummed his guitar in the background while her voice sailed through the rafters like an unchained eagle in a limitless sky.

Despite my fears and trepidation, I knew that I didn't *really* have any choice in the matter. I was going to break my decades-long absence from the stage in service of someone else. Someone I believed in. Someone who apparently thought of me as a second father in her life.

And we all know how valuable and irreplaceable a father can be.

After hours of waiting in the green room – where kids applied and reapplied make-up, warmed up their voices, stretched their muscles, and rehearsed their magic tricks – it was finally our time.

"*Veronica Jones*," the stage manager calmly called out into the room. "You're up next."

Eagerly, Veronica walked up the aisle to the back of the room where I was sitting uncomfortably. She beamed a smile at me. The normally cool, levelheaded Veronica was amped with excitement, wearing an expression of sheer joy that rivaled Samantha at her giddiest.

"Are you ready, Mr. Smith?" she asked.

I stepped out from my seat, unlatched my guitar case, and pulled out my father's old Martin guitar. Steadily, smoothly, I looped the leather strap around my neck and gripped it tightly in my arms.

"Ready as I'll ever be," I told her.

"Then let's go make some magic," she said, her eyes twinkling like Christmas lights.

We walked up the aisle together, Veronica anxiously leading us through the crowded backstage area as her sparkling red dress reflected every inch of iridescence in the darkened halls. We stopped in the wings, stage-right, as a student with a telecom headset silently motioned for us to wait for our cue. Stoically holding out her arm, the student directed us to halt in our tracks; however, as applause for the preceding act bounced off the walls of the auditorium, the student waved us forward to a pair of stools on the blue-lit main stage. The teaser and tormentor curtains were drawn tightly, hiding us from the view of the audience. An eerie halo of light surrounded us as we hustled forward from the wings, glowing neon tape providing a subdued illumination in the darkened space that surrounded us.

Reflexively, I reached out my right hand to touch the hem of a curtain. A small layer of felt seemed to melt off onto my fingers before crumbling into dust and gliding to the floor. I immediately rubbed my hands together to wipe the revolting remnants free.

With each creaking step forward across the stage, the floorboards moaned and croaked obnoxiously. Not even a ninja (or Samantha at her quietest, for that matter) could make it across *this* stage discreetly. I was mortified that the theater at *my* school could be in such a state of disrepair.

"Man, you weren't kidding, Veronica," I whispered as quietly as I could. Not that it mattered, of course, considering how loud the wooden boards beneath us squeaked with our steps. "This stage is in bad shape. Like *really* bad shape."

"Pretty sad, huh?"

"It's not just sad. It's embarrassing. This whole theater is shoddy and falling apart. It's like an OSHA violation just waiting to happen."

"And look at these curtains," Veronica pointed out. "Gross, right?"

"I'm pretty sure I still have some remnants stuck to my sweaty hands," I said, choking back my disgust.

I had an epiphany right then – a grandiose idea that I probably should have just kept to myself.

"You know, Veronica," I brainstormed aloud, "you should consider doing some kind of fundraiser to get this place back in decent condition."

"Like what?" she asked.

"Maybe like a benefit concert or something?" I suggested, my eyes straying from the proscenium to the fly gallery to the dim corners behind the stage.

"A benefit concert...?" Veronica asked, echoing my words back to me.

"Yeah, you know," I clarified quickly, "a benefit concert. Remember how I told you about the first time that I saw Brian Wilson? It was at one of Neil Young's Bridge School Benefit Concerts in Northern California."

"Right. So...?"

"Well," I continued, "over the years, Neil raised *hundreds of thousands of dollars* for students with severe speech and physical impairments. I'm sure that you could probably figure out something for Oxnard Shores High School."

"A *benefit concert...*" Veronica repeated again, as if she were tasting the words for the first time.

"If you can get the right performers in here, I'm sure you could raise a few thousand dollars towards the renovation of this Performing Arts Center. It's just a matter of pooling your resources."

Veronica's eyes suddenly widened, doubling in size as an idea struck her – a revelation, it seemed. In quick succession, a mischievous grin coiled up her face and her eyelids slithered into slits.

"You are a genius, Mr. Smith," she said. "That's *exactly* what I'm going to do."

I didn't realize it then, as I waited in the shadows of that decrepit auditorium, but I had just planted an incredibly potent idea in Veronica's head...

An idea I would come to regret in a short time.

A *very* short time.

"*And next up,*" a booming voice announced to the crowd, the monolithic sound reverberating forcefully through the venue, "we have senior superstar Veronica Jones. Veronica will be singing a special holiday tune, accompanied by our very own Mr. Smith on guitar. Please welcome them to the stage with a round of applause!"

The crowd hooted and hollered in anticipation as the scraping curtains screeched in retreat, unveiling us to the audience below.

I couldn't see anything beyond the blinding lights that broadcast the brightness of the sun into our blinking eyes. My first instinct was to recoil in pain, throw my arms up, and block out the spotlights…

Instead, I started playing my guitar.

Dum-SNAP-dum-dum-SNAP-dum-dum-SNAP-dum-dum-dum-dum-dum-dum.

Despite my quivering breath, my hands fell into an old familiar rhythm, muscle memory taking over my fingers and operating my body like an airplane on autopilot. As my right thumb kept time on the bass strings of the guitar, I found myself unconsciously tapping out the tempo with my left foot. Each stomp of my Doc Martens boot echoed across the stage, adding a touch of percussion to our quiet little duo.

"Go, Mr. Smith!" someone in the middle of the auditorium yelled out, piercing the stillness of the air. Immediately after the cry, a small chorus of whoops and cheers swelled from below. Despite my teetering anxiety level, the crowd's response gave me the confidence to keep going, to keep moving my hands across the guitar strings.

And then Veronica began to sing.

"Santa baby..." she crooned into the microphone.

Mr. Franklin was right: all eyes were on Veronica as she glittered like a red disco ball, dazzling every person in the audience. She was a quiet revelation that evening, a star emerging from the darkness. I'd known the kid for almost a year and a half at that point – I'd even seen her perform as the lead in Rodgers and Hammerstein's *Cinderella*, for goodness' sakes – but she was something altogether different onstage that night. Her voice had a singular quality to it, a breathy brilliance that belied her age. As she confidently contoured each note, adding just the right amount of old-fashioned drama to the lyrics, she had the crowd enchanted, captivated. You could hear a pin drop in that theater, each unconscious cough and clutter from the crowd audible in the obvious stillness of the room.

Veronica skillfully maneuvered through the first verse of the song, singing about chimneys and fur coats and 1950s convertibles, keeping the audience spellbound the entire time. On the middle eight section, my shaky voice began softly harmonizing behind her. I might have been the rock and roll veteran in our little duo, but in that moment I was merely a grunt guitarist trailing my musical lieutenant on the microphone.

As I followed Veronica's lead vocal, strumming behind her and matching her melody with my own harmony, I could feel a soothing sensation emanating from behind my heart and flooding through my limbs like the balm of a welcoming bath. The hairs on my arms stood at attention, and a warm wind whipped through my veins. You know that feeling of déjà vu, when something triggers a long-buried memory in the synapses of your brain? There was something about being onstage again, about supporting a truly talented and singular singer, that took me back twenty years.

For a split-second, I wasn't thinking about Oxnard Shores on a brisk December evening; I was transported back to my own alma mater, Sespe Creek High School, in the dim atmosphere of an all-too-familiar auditorium, wavering in the heat of a spring talent show. I thought of my lead-singing sister, captivating the audience as a proto-incarnation of Call Field (then known as *Marina and the Bookhouse Boys*) rocked a Weezer song onstage. Eventually, my mind wandered to Call Field's lead singer, Steve – that remarkable showman whose thrilling voice and dashing looks pulled everyone in with a gravitational force of attraction.

Veronica was like a combination of these two lead singers from my past: she had Marina's compassion and composure, but she also had Steve's daring and showmanship.

And yet, she was also something entirely different. Though I'd only known her for three short semesters at that point, Veronica felt less like an academic acquaintance and more like an adopted member of my family – a recently reunited niece or a long-lost second cousin. And, like any invested teacher, I felt a swelling sense of pride flowering in my chest as I softly strummed behind this precocious teenager.

When I squinted under the twinkling brilliance of the spotlights, I almost felt like I was watching a grown-up version of Samantha onstage, a wide-eyed little girl with endless possibilities and the entire world in front of her. During the time that we had spent together, Veronica had become something of a surrogate daughter to me, and watching her perform in front of hundreds of people in that auditorium made me feel like a proud parent. And, though this wasn't a *real* father-daughter duet, I still found myself tearing up a little bit.

Like I said before: fatherhood has turned me into a total softie. That goes for my biological child, Samantha – *and* for the precocious pupil who had become something like a surrogate daughter to me.

Veronica and I waltzed through the rest of the song gracefully, an occasional chirp of adoration wafting through the auditorium from the peers and parents who filled the seats. My star-student-turned-singer was a starlet of holiday spirit, cheering up every single grump and Grinch in the venue.

And, I have to admit, it felt *really* good to be strumming a guitar onstage again.

As the subtle sounds of our final notes evaporated into the auditorium, I could feel a momentary sense of relief flood my limbs, the pressure of performing gently emptying out from my body like a deflating balloon. And, just as quickly, the audience thundered their applause, cracking open the stillness of the moment without reservation.

Veronica melodramatically blew a kiss to the audience while I waived from the safety of my wooden seat. The curtains cinched closed with the friction of creaking runners, the MC dashed onto the stage, and we were left in virtual darkness.

And it was done.

Before we could bask in our glory, the student stage manager impatiently ushered us offstage with a manic flailing of her arms, wildly gesturing for us to head to the green room. Veronica awkwardly scurried through the darkened halls in her sparkly getup while I serenely strolled behind her, distracted by the fleeting feeling of victory after finally appearing onstage again. I was no longer shaking, no longer twitching involuntarily; rather, I felt calm and collected, like a radar wave drawn ineffably to my destination.

The scene backstage could only be described as a casually chaotic celebration. While a few students had abandoned their posts in the green room and inevitably filtered out into the cool air of the twilight hallways, the area was still swamped with kids in costumes, flanked intermittently by bored-looking chaperones.

I took a deep breath and marched to the back of the room, where my guitar case sat undisturbed on a wobbly poker table. Methodically, I flicked the clasps and opened up the top of the case. Once again, my father's guitar would be tucked away into hibernation. This time, I didn't know how long it would stay there.

"*Mister* Smith," a child's voice giggled from behind me, laughing at a joke that only she could understand. "Surprise!"

I turned around just in time for Samantha to plow into me like a miniature linebacker. Slowly making her way up the aisle behind Sam was Mel, whose chic leather jacket, black jeans, and kitten heels made her stand out from the throngs of high school kids in their overwrought costumes and oversized t-shirts.

"Nice work, hubby," Mel grinned, reaching up to peck me on the cheek.

"You made it!" I beamed.

"We did!" Sam chimed in. "And you did great, Daddy!"

Mel reached down and tussled Sam's hair. "*This one*," she gestured down to our daughter, "wanted to beat the crowd backstage and visit with Veronica before we hit the road. And see you, too, of course."

"Of course," I echoed back. "It's hard to compete with the lead singer, right?"

"Veronica!" Sam shouted, running off and throwing her arms around her favorite babysitter's sparkly waist. "You were *amazing!* You should be a *movie star!*"

"Awww…" Veronica sighed, curving down to return Sam's hug. "I'm so glad that you could come tonight!"

With the two girls momentarily locked in a candid embrace, I reached behind Mel and wrapped my arm around her back.

"Thank you for coming," I whispered in her ear.

"I wouldn't miss it for the world," she said, crinkling her eyes as she smiled up at me.

I stood there with my arm around Mel, watching the room buzz with the chitter and chatter of excited high school students. Though it was nearly a lifetime ago, it was strange to think that *I* was once one of those children, thrilled to play my first talent show with Marina. Back then, I was oblivious to the convoluted course my life would take as the waters of my destiny ran from the dry hills of Ojai to the flowing coastline of Oxnard Shores.

If I could go back in time, I would tell the fourteen-year-old incarnation of me that everything was going to work out. The loneliness would subside, the anger would fade, and my life would feel nearly complete – even without some of the key elements that defined who I was during that adolescent era.

Three of the most important people in my life – Mel, Sam, and Veronica – were all sharing the same room at this critical juncture of my story. I felt grateful for all three: for the wife who pulled me out of darkness and desperation, for the daughter who brought new meaning to my life, and for the precocious student who served as a catalyst in my musical resurrection.

It was a bit of a challenge to pry Samantha away from Veronica, but we finally coerced our daughter with a bribe of strawberry ice cream. I took Sam's little hands into my own and curled my arms around her.

As I did so, Veronica brushed past me and walked up to Mel. "Can you give us a second?" she asked me, gesturing to my wife with a quick twitch of her thumbs.

"Uh, sure…" I answered bemusedly. I kneeled down to Samantha's eye level and placed my index finger under her chin. "Do you want to go see some of the other performers, Sam?"

Her eyes lit up feverishly and she dashed down the aisle, dragging me behind her with our fingers intertwined.

Sam and I made our way through the throngs of audience members, pausing to shake hands with the students and staff we recognized. I stopped by to chat for a minutes with Jack Franklin and a small coterie of students who had gathered around him; all the while, Sam's eyes traced lines across the room, slowly taking in the stupefying sequins and flabbergasting fashions that floated around us. Periodically, I would glance back at Mel and Veronica, who seemed to be engaged in a rather intense discussion.

"Daddy..." Sam eventually interrupted. "Can we go now? I'm bored."

I looked up at Jack's satisfied smile and shook his hand one last time. "I guess that's my cue, Mr. Franklin," I told him. "Have a great weekend, and congrats on a great show!"

"You, too, bud," he said with a slight upward jerk of his chin.

Sam and I dodged bodies like conjoined automobiles driving into oncoming traffic, gradually creeping back to Mel and Veronica. From our vantage point a few yards away, I could just make out the faint hum of their conversation.

"...Do you think he'd want to do it?" Veronica asked, her eyebrows furrowed together.

"No," Mel answered with a snicker. "But I think he *needs* to do it."

As Sam and I finally approached, I interjected myself into the conversation. "What are you two gossiping about?" I asked.

Veronica jolted backwards, as if she'd been caught stealing cookies from a cookie jar. "Oh, just the usual girly stuff," she quickly replied.

"You know," Mel clarified with a conspiratorial glance over at Veronica, "like overthrowing the patriarchy and taking over the world. Frivolous female conversation."

I shot the two of them a quizzical look, but Mel just ignored me.

"Alright, Sammy-Sam," Mel announced, "it's time for us to head home."

"And I can still get my strawberry ice cream?" Sam asked eagerly.

"Yes, sweetie," I reassured her, tussling her hair. "A sweet treat for my little sweetheart."

I arched my back and leaned in to give Mel a kiss on the cheek.

"I'll see you at home?" I asked, my voice suddenly sounding more depleted than playful.

"Take your time," Mel reassured me with a wink. "I've got some work to do." She gave me a quick wave and then turned away with Sam trailing behind her.

As Mel shuffled Sam off to the car, I walked back to Veronica to say goodbye.

"You were so great up there, kiddo!" I told her. I raised up my hand to give her a high-five, and she slapped my palm so hard that the sound echoed through the entire room.

"And so were you!" Veronica called back, her giddiness barely contained beneath her giggling voice. "I couldn't have done that without you, Mr. Smith!"

"I was just the backdrop," I told her. "No one was paying attention to me during the performance. You totally stole the show."

Veronica dismissively waved her hand in the air, ignoring my comment. "I can't thank you enough, Mr. Smith. This really, *really* meant a lot to me." Her smile was simply irrepressible, incandescent in the muted lights of the green room.

"It was nothing, Veronica," I reassured her.

"You don't understand, though," she continued on, "I've been wanting to do this show since I was a little girl – like since I was Samantha's age. I remember watching my older brothers perform at the Winter Spectacular, and I just sat in the audience all wide-eyed and gushing."

"Kind of like Sam was doing tonight, fawning over you," I reminded her.

"You're right," Veronica continued. "That was me ten years ago. And you gave me the opportunity to make that dream come true. I know it's silly to place such importance on something so trivial…"

"It's not silly at all," I reassured her. "When I was in high school, it was a big deal for me, too. A *really* big deal. I remember the thrill of that first performance all too well."

I could feel my vision getting blurry, the saline stinging my eyes as they filled at the edges. My lacrimal glands were betraying me.

"Don't get all soft on me, old man," Veronica said as she punched me in the arm. "If you start crying, I'll start crying. And I really don't want to wipe off my mascara in front of all these people."

I chuckled to myself, half-laughing and half-stifling tears. "I'm sorry," I said. "It's an occupational hazard of getting old." I dabbed at the corners of my eyes with my wrists.

"What I'm trying to say," Veronica continued, "is *thank you*. Thank you for helping me do something that I had only dreamed about until tonight."

I nodded my head in agreement, taking a deep breath to staunch the potential tears that threatened to pour forth from my eyes.

Right about that time, Veronica got a little bleary-eyed herself. "Darn it, Mr. Smith!" she pouted. "You're going to make me cry, you jerk!" She scoffed at herself, unwilling to accept that she – the one and only Veronica Jones – might be susceptible to something as undignified as crying in public.

"In that case," I said, taking another deep breath, "I'm going to head out of here. Thanks again for coercing me into playing this show."

"It was my honor, *Captain, My Captain*," Veronica said with a ridiculous little salute. As she started to walk away, she offered one last parting shot. "I still want to hear the rest of your story, you know. You're not getting off that easy."

I chuckled.

"We'll see about that, Veronica. We'll see."

By the time that I got home, Sam was already fast asleep. I gently crept through the shadowy house, careful not to make any noise that might wake my sleeping daughter. From upstairs, I could hear the white noise of a TV set seeping through the door to our bedroom, cascading in volume with the canned applause of a television audience. Probably *Golden Girls*, I thought to myself. Mel likes to fall asleep with the TV on, and though it wasn't *too* late, I had a feeling that she was already passed out.

Quietly, I tiptoed up the flight of stairs, precipitously balancing my guitar case as I made my way up the stairwell. The creaking hinges of the handle seemed inexplicably loud in the stillness of the house, as if the instrument was desperately calling out for attention. Still, I did my best to mutely maneuver myself upstairs to the second floor of our house.

With the precise movements of a father trying not to wake a sleeping child, I gently pushed open the door to my office. Since it shares a wall with Sam's room, I had to be extra careful not to run into anything – which, if you know how clumsy I am, can be quite a challenge. With each step, my feet swept the hardwood floor, my black socks picking up specks of gray dust from the ground.

As I gently set my guitar case on the floor, I looked up at the framed Stuttering Surfers record on my wall. It hung there immobile, resolutely refusing to move or change or shift. It was one of the first things I mounted on the walls after we bought our house so many years ago, and it served as a constant reminder of the fragility of the past. After a few seconds, I turned away and reached down to my prostrate guitar case.

Tenderly, I flicked the locks and opened the lid. My dad's old Martin guitar didn't look any different than it had a few hours earlier, but there was something about it that now begged me to pay attention. I took the instrument out of its case, ran my fingers horizontally across the steel strings, and formed a chord on the fretboard. I wanted to strum and sing and celebrate my triumphant return to the stage. But I knew better.

There's no time for that, I thought to myself. *Everyone else in the house is asleep.*

I begrudgingly placed the guitar on its makeshift throne, leaving it to hibernate for a little bit longer. The Martin sat there, mute and motionless, as I backed away.

Unceremoniously, I turned off the lights and shut the door.

CHAPTER EIGHT

"Can't Wait Too Long"

Although *real* rock stars get to stay out past curfew and sleep in late and bask in the glow of a post-show high, normal human beings don't have time for such self-indulgent revelry. Despite my best wishing and praying and pleading, Samantha tends to get up bright and early every single morning… even on weekends, when Mom and Dad would rather be sleeping in. The day after the Winter Spectacular was no exception.

"Good morning, Mommy! Good morning, Daddy!" Sam chimed, a plush bunny rabbit doll cradled in her pajama-ed arms.

As I opened my exhausted eyes from the deep comfort of snoozing, my eight-year-old daughter stood a foot away from my face, beaming with an unusually wide grin.

"Good morning, sweetheart," I grumbled quietly. I rubbed my eyes with the palm of my right hand, wiping away the crusty crumbs of leftover slumber stuck in my eyelashes. I glanced over at the clock on my nightstand, the face of which read *6:05 AM*. "Sam, you know you can sleep in on the weekends, right? It's barely even six o'clock."

"What's the point of sleeping in?" she asked, still beaming. "We have the whole day ahead of us!"

I let my left arm drape limply over the side of the bed, blood slowly flowing back into the numb regions of my elbow and hand. I clenched my fist, feeling the poorly circulated blood sluggishly returning to the extremities of my fingers.

"We can still have the whole day ahead of us if we sleep in another hour, Sam," Mel groaned, groggily stretching on her side of the bed.

I could tell from Sam's expression, though, that she disagreed.

"Cinnabun and I are ready for breakfast," she intoned dramatically, holding out her plush rabbit for us to see. In her little arms, Samantha clutched her favorite stuffed animal, a little beige bunny that smelled faintly of cinnamon and nutmeg. Originally, Sam christened the doll *Cinnamon Bunny* – but the name was later truncated to *Cinnabunny* and ultimately shortened to *Cinnabun*.

As you can tell, we're big on nicknames in my family. I'm *Brian* and *Brick* and *Mr. Smith*. My wife is *Mel* and *Lani* and *Noelani*. Our daughter is *Sam* and *Samantha* and *Sammy-Sam*. And then there's the aforementioned plush rabbit. I guess "Brick," "Mel," "Sam," and "Cinnabun" are all birds of a feather. Or bunnies, as it were.

"Alright," Mel yawned, "you win. We'll go make breakfast for you."

"And Cinnabun," Sam added.

"Yes, Sam," Mel said sleepily. "And Cinnabun."

A few minutes later, I was setting the dining room table with placemats, napkins, and silverware, while the bittersweet smell of coffee exhaled forth from the gurgling Keurig machine in the kitchen.

"Do you want pancakes or waffles this morning, Sam?" Mel asked.

"*Well…*" Sam answered. "I want pancakes. But Cinnabun wants waffles."

"In that case," Mel said, "Daddy gets the tie-breaking decision."

"I vote for pancakes," I called from the dining room. "Blueberry, please."

"Blueberry pancakes, it is!" Mel announced. "Tell Cinnabun that I'm sorry she won't get her desired menu option this morning."

Sam squinted her eyes, deep in thought. "Cinnabun is disappointed," she informed us.

Mel sighed. "What if I add some cinnamon to her pancakes?"

Sam's face lit up. "In that case, I think she'll be okay."

My daughter is such a ham.

After breakfast, I threw on an old set of raggedy clothes: oversized jeans with widening holes, a sweat-stained shirt with a fraying collar, and graying tennis shoes marked with the irregular green blemishes that appear after countless hours maneuvering through shredded grass clippings.

As I looked outside, through the transparent (albeit finger-smudged) glass partition of our sliding door, I could see clouds shifting and churning like rat-gray cotton candy in the sky. Even though California frequently finds itself in longstanding drought conditions, we *do* actually get periodic rainfall that cleanses the earth and nurtures the soil. Of course, it inevitably interferes with the best-laid plans of English teachers and gardeners.

It looked like it was going to be a race against time with Mother Nature.

Would I finish the lawn before the heavens parted and rain started hurtling towards the ground? Would I accomplish everything I needed to do, or would I find my time prematurely cut short?

The foreboding firmament taunted me with its encroaching darkness. It was time to get moving.

I pulled my battered UCLA hat tight against my scalp, put on a set of wireless Sony noise-cancelling headphones, queued up the Beach Boys' *Holland* on my iPhone, and exited the sliding glass door that led to our modest backyard. As Blondie Chaplin's voice surged with the opening lines of "Sail On, Sailor," I grabbed my electric weed whacker from the toolshed out back, plugged the extension cord into a power outlet on the side of the house, and started my work. The beautiful harmonies of the Beach Boys were muffled by the indignant hum of the weed whacker as I made my way around the backyard, meticulously edging the lawn and striking down any unwelcome weeds that had encroached upon our property.

Right foot. Left foot.
Right foot. Left foot.
Repeat until the task is done.

As I circled the verdant grass in our backyard, my thoughts kept returning to the night before and my brief time on stage with Veronica. Despite the violent thrumming of the weed whacker and the resplendent harmonies emanating from my headphones – sounds that I desperately hoped would suffocate the static in my brain – I kept repeating our performance over and over again in my head. The decrepit stage of Oxnard Shores High School wasn't the Ryman or the Fillmore or Madison Square Garden, but it was *something*. For a few brief moments onstage, I had felt temporarily transcendent, struck by an irrepressible magic that couldn't be contained within the confines of a four-minute pop song. I know how silly it sounds, to be filled with such a powerful emotion on the decomposing stage of a public high school, but that's how it felt to be performing again.

As I finished the edging and weeding, I swapped out the weed whacker for an electric leaf blower and started propelling the scraps of grass and weeds onto the main section of the lawn. The whole time, I found myself daydreaming about strumming my guitar behind Veronica's singularly sophisticated voice. In fact, I lost track of time, almost forgetting where I was and what I was doing as I circled the backyard over and over.

Right foot. Left foot.
Right foot. Left foot.
Repeat until the task is done.
And then, suddenly, I was brought back to reality.

I felt it first on the back of my neck. It was that familiar stinging sensation, like a child's finger flicking against bare skin, followed immediately by a shrill chill that coursed from my head to my arms. Little dark spots started to appear in anarchic patterns on the sidewalk as drops of rain made their descent from the heavens.

The rain was starting to fall.

I knew that I still had a few minutes before any blinding sheets of rain would come gushing down from the sky, but the race was on: Brian Richard Smith against Mother Nature. As I felt small pellets of water periodically shoot onto my bare arms and face, I wondered to myself…

Will I finish my work before I run out of time?

I dashed to the toolshed, tucking away the weed whacker and leaf blower onto rusty shelves, and wheeled out my old Toro lawnmower. Glancing up at the grim sky, which seemed more ominous than before, I was hit on the forehead by a few bitter droplets of water.

My time was running out.

I pulled the cord to start the lawnmower's engine and guided the machine across the perimeter of our backyard, mechanically making my way back and forth across the lawn. As Blondie Chaplin's yearning voice in "Leaving This Town" crept out from my headphones, I hunkered down, pushing the lawnmower faster and faster across the expanse of the yard.

Right foot. Left foot.

Right foot. Left foot.

Repeat until the task is done.

I was cutting it close. Or mowing it close, considering the circumstances. The rain was falling harder and harder, slowly soaking my clothes and shoes. I had so many ambitious plans for yard work that afternoon (mowing the lawn, pulling weeds, and trimming the overgrown skeletal branches of the trees in our backyard were all on the agenda), but I quickly realized that I couldn't complete all the tasks I had laid out for myself. I turned up the volume on my headphones and pushed the lawnmower more aggressively, crisscrossing the yard over and over until the bag of grass clippings sagged from the weight of its waste.

The battle in my brain kept raging: the roar of the mower, the luminescent harmonies of the Beach Boys, the memories of my performance with Veronica, the impending torrential downpour that threatened to derail my best-laid plans... My head was a hurricane of emotions, each aching thought angling for my attention.

All the while, I kept moving, snaking my way back and forth across the patches of green between our house and the weathered picket fence of our property line. My clothing was so permeated with water that I felt like I was wearing dish towels. Finally, after several rain-soaked minutes navigating the puddles that were quickly forming on the grass, I realized that I couldn't go any further without risking a bout of pneumonia. I killed the engine for the lawnmower, kneeled down, and removed the stained grass-catcher bag; as I did so, the confetti-like shreds clumped together, while little rogue cuttings breezed away onto the grass below. By the time that I dumped the lawn trimmings into our beige yard waste bin, the rain had nearly thickened into a squalling soup, coming down sharper and with more intensity.

For a second, I looked back at the branches of our apple tree, the one that I had planned on trimming before calling it quits. The long, skinny branches looked like bony hands cupping the interminable faucet of the clouds – like the emaciated fingers of a battered old man attempting to strangle the sky. I stood there in the yard, pummeled by rain, as a snippet of a song I had written so many years before popped into my head.

"My arms reached out like skeleton trees..." I sang softly to myself. I could hardly hear my own voice over the thumping precipitation, but the melody triggered something in the recesses of my memory. I had written that line in the throes of romantic heartache during my freshman year at UCLA; but, now, the fiction of my songs had become manifest before me. The skeleton tree in my yard, the one I had planned on thinning that day, would have to wait.

"I'm not done yet," I murmured to myself.

But I was out of time.

There was no extended revelry for me that day, no hungover remembrances of a carefree night celebrating my victorious return to the stage. In true suburban style, I spent the morning racing against the clock, performing a fool's errand as I tried to outrun the elements.

I wasn't basking in the sunlight and bathing in the afterglow. Rather, I was drowning in responsibilities – and soaked to the bone.

After two long hours of soggy yard work, I was sweaty and sore – doused in cold rain and ready for a hot shower. I took one last look back at my newly trimmed (and newly drenched) yard, and I entered the garage through a creaking side door, leaving the chilling precipitation behind me. Without much fanfare, I stripped down to my boxers and threw my messy, soiled clothes into the laundry hamper.

Quivering from the cold, I sprinted upstairs to the master bathroom and hopped into the shower. The hot water and steam coursed over my exhausted body, a welcome respite from the bitter cold I had faced only minutes before. I let the water flow over me, let it combat the accumulated chill of my body, while I used my hands to clear away the small shreds of debris and smudged dirt that still covered my arms. As I wiped away the grime, my mind traveled back once more to my performance at the Winter Spectacular the night before – and remembered what it felt like to be back onstage after so many years.

I have to admit, it felt good.

Really good.

In some ways, it almost felt like going home. Not to an address or a street sign, mind you, but to an inscrutable feeling – a faint, trembling wisp of nostalgia that reminded me of younger times, simpler days.

Not necessarily *happier* times, of course. But *different* times.

Nostalgia is, after all, a beautiful liar. It twists and turns and mocks with velvet tendrils, making you forget the harsh thorns that stabbed you in classrooms and on playgrounds. You don't recall the punctured skin or the gashes in your hands; you only remember the soft and gentle moments that made you feel young and alive and invincible and infinite.

Nostalgia is sweet and beautiful and seductive.

But it isn't true.

And that's easy to forget.

You have a lot of time to think when you're doing yard work.

You have a lot of time to think when you're in the shower.

You *don't* have a lot of time to think when you're grading papers.

I'm sure normal human beings with normal jobs spend their Saturday afternoons in movie theaters and malls, searching for small semblances of happiness that help ease the suffering of the working week. English teachers, however, are constantly weighed down by a perpetually insurmountable load of essays to grade. Even during the weekend, with its promise of relaxation and relief, English teachers are hunkering down in their bunkers, scratching endlessly on crumpled papers of unpolished (and frequently unfinished) student writing.

We're just trying to earn our haloes, one essay at a time.

Weekends are precious commodities in the Smith household, with limited windows for grading papers and planning lessons. Between my yard work and Sam's swim practices and Mel's gym workouts and whole-family grocery-shopping trips to the supermarket, those two precious days evaporate like a sprinkler's water stains on the summer sidewalk. Alas, a teacher's work is never done. Nor is a parent's, for that matter.

So, there I was, once again grading papers in my office on a sad, soaked Saturday afternoon when I would've preferred to spend time with my family and friends. Apparently, I wasn't the only one feeling that way: I could hear a rhythmic bouncing from down the hall, a monotonous thumping that was slowly making its way in my direction.

Bounce. Bounce. Bounce.

"Hi, Daddy," Sam's voice called from the doorway. "Want to play with me?"

I wheeled my chair around to face her, my posture crooked from a morning of tedious yard work and an afternoon hunched over a desk grading essays.

"I wish I could, honey," I told her with a sigh. "But I've got too much work to do."

"But I'm *lonely*," Sam whined, swinging her checkered soccer ball back and forth in her arms. "Mommy is at the gym and I can't play outside because it's raining and *someone* needs to keep me company."

"Sam," I intoned, "you are *eight years old*. You don't need someone to keep you company every single minute of every single day."

Undeterred, Samantha stubbornly soldiered on. "If you're not going to come *out* with me," she stated matter-of-factly, "then I'm going to stay *in here* with you."

I love my daughter with all my heart. She is sweet and smart and thoughtful and clever.

But she's also just a kid.

She's stubborn. She's challenging. And she makes mistakes.

Sam cradled her soccer ball in her lap and unceremoniously plopped down on the ground. Scooting backwards across the hardwood floor, she positioned herself against the south wall of the office, kitty-corner to the doorway. Then, she sat up straight, leaned against the eggshell-white wall, and crossed her arms.

It was clear to me that she was preparing for battle. You know the kind: when a strong-willed child refuses to budge or back down without a fight. These circumstances rarely end well for any of the parties involved.

I spun around to face the window, closed my eyes, hemmed and hawed to myself for a second, and then turned back to face my daughter. "Look, Samantha," I said. "I have a lot of work to do. I'm sorry that I can't play with you right now, but I have a ton of papers to grade."

I held up the stack of essays as evidence of my workload.

She did not seem impressed.

"What's more important, Daddy?" Sam asked, her eyes scrunched into scowling slits. "Your work or your family?"

Damn, that kid is smart, I thought to myself.

"That's not really fair, Sam," I argued.

"I don't care if it's not fair," she snarked. Samantha twirled her soccer ball around and around in her hands, looked up at the opposite wall, and looked back at me mischievously. Without taking her eyes off of me, she raised the ball in her right arm and launched it across the room.

With a loud *thud*, the ball hit the wall, shaking the frames that hung daintily in place. The ball bounced on the floor and then boomeranged back to Sam's place on the opposite wall.

I immediately went into stern parent mode.

"Samantha, we do not throw balls in the house," I told her, repeating that familiar age-old aphorism. "You know that."

My daughter simply ignored me, continuing to throw her soccer ball rhythmically against the opposing wall – only a few feet away from my precious office decorations. I could see my framed Bob Dylan poster shaking, my first "teacher of the year" plaque trembling, and my vintage Stuttering Surfers record quaking.

My Stuttering Surfers record: that one-of-a-kind antique artifact, carefully encapsulated in glass, and proudly mounted next to all my other meaningful memorabilia.

Samantha's soccer ball kept ricocheting against the wall –

Thud. Bounce. Thud. Bounce.

"Sam, please stop that," I calmly commanded.

Thud. Bounce. Thud. Bounce.

She didn't respond.

"*Sam*," I repeated, this time more forcefully, "please stop throwing your ball against the wall like that."

Thud. Bounce. Thud. Bounce.

"This is the third time I'm asking you, Sam," I said once more, barely keeping my cool composure. "You need to stop it. Right. Now."

Still, my daughter ignored me.

Thud. Bounce. Thud. Bounce.

"*SAMANTHA!*" I yelled – a bit more forcefully than I intended. "*STOP IT!*"

I could see Samantha's slim frame twitch as my voice scared her and broke her rhythm. Right at the moment of release, she jumped in her seat on the floor. With a jarring motion, her arm slipped and the soccer ball flew away from its intended target. The checkered black-and-white sphere soared higher and farther than anticipated, veering off to the left and missing its mark on the blank, unadorned section of the wall. Instead, it sailed off course, smacking right into a valuable artifact.

The Stuttering Surfers record.

For a split second, the framed vinyl shivered on its nail. Then, without any further pause, it slipped off the wall and dropped, gravely wrested down with the unstoppable force of gravity.

Though it was only a six-foot drop to the hardwood floor, the record hit hard. Really hard. Glass shattered everywhere. Little shards spat out from the mounting and recklessly cascaded onto the ground. After colliding with the hardwood floor, it landed face down, the vinyl obscured by the rim of the frame.

"Oh, my God," I whispered, shock seeping in like an uninvited flood. "*Oh. My. God.*"

I darted out of my seat, stepping on glass splinters that angrily bit into my feet. Without hesitation, I flipped the frame over in my trembling hands.

It was broken.

The vinyl record that I had treasured for so many years was cracked into thick, lifeless pieces. I could feel myself consumed by anger and heartbreak as I flipped around, steam practically fizzling out of my ears. I shook an accusatory finger at my daughter.

"*WHAT DID YOU DO, SAM?!?*" I screamed, less of a question than an accusation. "*WHAT – DID – YOU – DO?!?*"

Needless to say, it was not my proudest moment as a parent.

The shocked, scared look on Sam's face will haunt me for a long time. As I stood there fuming, glass digging into my bare feet, Samantha's expressions cycled through a flurry of emotions: from the frantic darting of her eyes around the room to the recoiling sense of fear that revealed itself in her collapsing posture to the guilt that soon came streaming down her face in thick, hot tears.

My anger swiftly subsided into despair. I crumpled to the floor, falling first to my knees and then on my side to the glass-covered floor.

"*This is all that's left,*" I whispered between weeping whimpers. I curled myself into an oval, pulling my knees up to my chest as I clenched splintered pieces of the record in my hands.

I sobbed.

I felt fractured, like the jagged pieces of vinyl scattered on the floor and grasped between my bleeding fingers.

I felt alone and abandoned and broken.

I felt incomplete.

For a few seconds, the only sound that penetrated the silence was the muted tap-dance of rainfall on the roof and windows. I lay there on the floor, choking on my sorrow, while scattered drops of rain hit our house, threatening to drown the architecture of my life. Waters slid silently down the window and tears coursed quietly down my cheeks, and I wasn't sure whether the house or I would suffocate first.

Suddenly, I could feel the almost imperceptible, feather-like weight of a small hand on my back. The fingers slid forward, towards my shuddering chest, and two small arms wrapped themselves around me.

"*I'm sorry, Daddy*," Sam sobbed. Her small frame heaved as tears flooded forth, my daughter bawling with every stilted breath.

We must have made quite a sight: a 200-pound grown man curled up in the fetal position, while his 80-pound daughter held him tightly, throwing her tiny arms around his much larger frame and awkwardly trying to console her father. It was a strange inversion of roles, a moment in which everything seemed emotionally upside-down.

Eventually, I mustered the strength to speak, turning to face her and enveloping her in my arms. "It's not your fault, honey," I assured her between sniffling sighs. "You didn't mean to do it." I wiped tears off her cheeks, though they were quickly replenished by fresh ones that mirrored my own.

"Will you still love me if things get broken?" she asked, her eyes dense with tears.

"I will love you no matter how many things get broken… or how broken things get," I told her. I squeezed her tightly in my arms, trying to keep my heart from breaking into so many irreparable shards like the vinyl that spilled across my floor.

"I love you, Daddy," Sam blubbered.

"I love you, too, Sam," I told her between my own sniffling. "More than you can ever know."

And then I broke down again.

We cried together for ten minutes – out of grief and sorrow and loss, out of fear and guilt and confusion. Sam didn't understand the weight of what had happened with that small moment of wrecking and reckoning.

But I did.

It was a reminder that some things are simply lost forever –

With no chance for return or resurrection.

CHAPTER NINE
"I Just Wasn't Made for These Times"

Glass can be swept away.

Broken frames can be discarded.

But shards of vinyl can never be repaired.

The fine, seamless grooves cannot be glued or stitched to make whole again.

The sounds and spirits captured on those seemingly infinite circles are simply lost for eternity.

No matter how much you wish they would return.

CHAPTER TEN
"Shelter"

For the rest of the evening, Samantha carried the weight of guilt and shame on her diminutive shoulders.

And, for completely different reasons, so did I.

Instead of her usual boisterous, bouncy self, Samantha was subdued and quiet. It was almost as if the gravity of her guilt – and, of course, my less-than-calm response – had cast a shroud of darkness around the entirety of her petite frame. At the dinner table, I tried to engage Sam in small talk, asking her questions about *Star Wars* and Disney films and her week at school. Despite my best efforts, though, she remained withdrawn.

Clearly, something was amiss.

Maybe it was a remnant of our painful experience with the broken vinyl record that afternoon. Maybe it was the loneliness that accompanies the solitary existence of an only child. Or maybe it was just something in the air, something intangible that slipped between our hearts and minds like the mid-December evening mist.

Even during our nightly reading of *Harry Potter* right before bedtime (I think we were on the fifth or sixth book in the series back then), Sam seemed pensive and reserved. She snuggled into my armpit as I awkwardly balanced the behemoth of a book in my hands – not an easy task with a small child covering half of my left arm.

"Daddy," Sam mumbled tentatively, gripping Cinnabunny tightly to her chest. "How does Harry feel with both of his parents dead?"

I slipped my tongue between my front teeth and the inside of my upper lip. When Sam asks a hard question like that, I tend to revert to "teacher mode," ricocheting the inquiry back to her without giving my own opinions. It's a little trick I use with my students: *never provide a solution when you can ask your student a question and get the same answer.*

It works beautifully with high school students – and, surprisingly, with your own children.

"Well," I started, sitting up straight against the stiff couch cushions, "how do *you* think he feels?"

Sam's eyes drifted up towards the ceiling as she studied the popcorn acoustics that protruded like tiny stalactites from a snow-white surface.

"I think he must feel sad," she answered. "Very sad. Like his heart is broken into a million pieces."

"I agree, Sammy. It's hard to move on after something like that. Even losing *one* parent can be devastating…" I didn't mean to, but my voice caught a little as I finished speaking.

Sam didn't say anything right away, but she squeezed me tightly. My left arm was still trapped between her little body and the couch cushions, but I used my right hand to wipe the corners of my eyes.

"Can we keep reading, Daddy?" she asked.

"Of course," I whispered, my eyelids stinging slightly. "Where were we…?"

There is something innate in all of us, a fear of being abandoned by our parents, that all children encounter during their first years of life. I wish that I could tell Sam that it gets easier, that your heart gets bolder and stronger as you age.

But it doesn't. The stakes only get higher, the older that you get.

Each goodbye, each parting, each closing salutation bears the knowledge that it might be the last time you see someone that you love…

Years later, it hurts just as much as it did in the beginning.

CHAPTER ELEVEN
"Tell Me Why"

Fate has a funny way of humbling me. Whenever I feel like I've reached some artistic apex, when I stand tall at the top of a massively monstrous mountain, basking in the sublime elevation… Fate kicks me from behind and laughs as I topple from those towering heights. It's kind of a cruel joke.

Whether I like it or not, my life is constantly balanced by highs and lows of weighted measure. During my twenties, just as I should have been basking in rock and roll glory with my successful punk band, everything fell apart. Two decades later, just as I was celebrating my semi-triumphant return to the stage, Sam accidentally shattered a pivotal piece of my past.

And, just as I was gearing up for a winter vacation free of stress and pressure, I got trapped in a classroom with a captive audience – and nowhere to hide from the truth.

The following Monday, when I arrived at school, I found a sealed square envelope waiting for me in my mailbox. The front simply read "Mr. Smith" in an unfamiliar cursive signature, and there was no return address or other demarcation of identity.

When I ripped it open, however, I discovered that the mystery letter from a mystery person was actually a greeting card from Veronica's parents. The front of the card featured a fancy embossed, metallic image of a Christmas tree – but it was the message between the folded paper that held the real holiday magic. In calligraphic cursive, Veronica's mother thanked me profusely for playing the Winter Spectacular and helping her daughter check off that glittering, tinsel-shaped box on her bucket list. I have to admit, the glowing gratitude Mrs. Jones expressed – coupled with the lavish superlatives she heaped on your humble narrator – made me tear up a little bit.

As much as Veronica Jones could be a pain in the posterior, it was clear that our partnership had evolved into something special: a familial bond that transcended the cardboard barriers between teacher and student. Veronica knew it. Her parents knew it, too. And I was slowly starting to realize that Veronica had become more like an adopted daughter than I ever could have anticipated. After wiping away at the creases in my eyelids, I slipped the envelope into my jacket pocket and made my way out of the office towards room 23.

The morning came and went with the usual tedium of classroom preparation: photocopying handouts, shuffling essays, entering grades, and the like. It was *supposed* to be an easy day. My eleventh-grade AP English Language classes had a presentation in the auditorium with their guidance counselors, so I had been gifted with a few glorious hours of teacher prep time. With my trusty blue pen in hand, I planned on grading papers for most of the morning and afternoon – and, during first period, I would have my trusty TA, the infamous Veronica Jones, to help scrawl insightful feedback on student essays. Based on past experiences, I figured that the two of us would crank through a few dozen essays and then go our separate ways for the day.

Boy, was I wrong.

As the bell for first period rang, I swore that I could hear some vague rumbling emanating from the distance. I didn't think anything of it at the time – and I didn't have time to investigate further, because Veronica casually sauntered into the room, her shoulders weighed down by the impressive load of AP textbooks in her backpack. I waved and greeted her.

"How's it going, Miss Singing Superstar?" I asked. "Did you have a thrilling weekend full of starstruck paparazzi hounding you with flashing lightbulbs?"

"You're *soooo funny*, Mr. Smith," she grumbled sarcastically, rolling her eyeballs farther back than I thought humanly possible. Unceremoniously, she dropped her hefty backpack onto a student desk and stretched her neck muscles. When she turned back to me, though, she was beaming with pride. "But how cool was it being in the spotlight? Wasn't that just the most amazing experience ever?"

"It *was* pretty remarkable," I admitted. "I spent a lot of the weekend thinking about how great it felt to be strumming a guitar onstage again. And please thank your parents for me. Their card was really sweet, and I…"

That incessant thrumming in the distance was growing louder, a deep fluttering sound that reminded me of a locomotive engine thrashing rapidly as its wheels mechanically spun around in blurry circles.

"What's that noise?" Veronica asked, her forehead scrunched up with equal parts confusion and irritation.

"I'm not sure," I said. As the seismic rumbling increased in volume, however, I recognized the whirling sound for what it was. "I think it's a…"

"Helicopter," Veronica chimed in, the realization hitting her at the same moment.

Suddenly, the air was pierced with a blizzard of buzzing bells. The sharp, painful halcyon shrieked a Morse code message that signaled for us to close our doors, shut the blinds, and crouch onto the dirty tile floor of our classrooms. Seconds later, the principal's voice broke through the shrill cacophony with a warning.

"*LOCKDOWN! WE ARE ON LOCKDOWN!*" She announced on the intercom, her voice barely audible over the screaming alarm.

"Oh, crap," Veronica muttered.

As the blaring bells continued belting out their monotonous noise, I twirled on my heels, ran for the door, put my key into the handle, and twisted the lock until it clicked. My heart pumped faster than a hummingbird's, the propulsive rhythm coursing through my veins.

To be fair, lockdowns are fairly common in public schools: any time there's a high-speed police chase or a suspicious entity in the vicinity of campus, schools follow a tight-knit safety plan for staff and students. Still, the minute those bells ring and the principal's voice blasts out from the intercom, my pulse quickens and my brain races with a myriad of morbid possibilities. After everything we've seen on the news the last few decades, it's impossible to *not* ruminate on the macabre things that could happen in a public high school. And it's not just staff members who go into "fight or flight" mode when the lockdown bells ring: it's students, too.

"What's going on?" Veronica asked, a trace of panic escaping from her otherwise composed voice.

"I won't know until I check my email," I told her. "Give me a second…"

I dashed over to my work computer, brought up my email, and scanned my inbox. Right at the top was a message from the principal with "LOCKDOWN" spelled out in capital letters in the subject line.

Speed-reading through the message, I gleaned the important information: there was an armed robbery a few streets over from the school, but the police had blockaded the surrounding area. We were – for all intents and purposes – *safe*.

I literally breathed out a sigh of relief. "We're going to be okay," I said aloud. "We're not in any imminent danger."

"What's happening?" Veronica asked again, somewhat more urgently this time.

"There's a robbery three blocks down on Harbor Boulevard," I explained, relaying the contents of the email. "They want us locked down, in the unlikely event that the culprits decide to run for it."

As Veronica's expression decompressed and worry evaporated from her furrowed face, I pulled my iPhone out of my pocket and started texting Mel.

Damn, I wrote, tapping away in tandem with my thumbs. ***We're on lockdown.***

Veronica followed suit, whipping out her phone and proceeding to tap away on her screen at a rapid-fire pace.

"I guess that's a relief," Veronica mumbled, her thumbs still flying across the touchscreen of her phone. She finished her text message and laid her iPhone flat on the desk in front of her. "Still kinda' spooky, though."

"Yup," I agreed with a heavy sigh. "And we're probably going to be stuck here for a few hours."

"It's a good thing I showered today," she joked.

I was grateful that Veronica hadn't lost her sense of humor.

For obvious reasons, it's a bit awkward for a male teacher to be trapped in a room alone with a teenage girl – even one as wholesome and trustworthy as Veronica Jones. With that uncomfortable thought in the recesses of my mind, I scooted back my rolling office chair behind my desk, trying my best to leave a little physical distance between us.

Undeterred, Veronica marched over to where I sat and plopped herself down in a beaten-up desk in the front row of the classroom.

"Here's a pile of essays," I said, passing over a stack of student work that was several inches thick. "Let's see how many we can get through while we're stuck here."

Veronica recoiled, as if I was handing her an overflowing box of venomous spiders rather than a heap of ink-stained papers. She dramatically thrust up her hands, refusing to take the papers from my outstretched arms. "I can't concentrate on reading essays at a time like this," she whined. "I need something to get my mind off the oppressive stress of this lockdown!"

"Well, then, Veronica," I said warily. "What do you propose?"

Her eyes coolly darted back and forth across the room, until they finally settled on me and met my gaze. She smirked back at me. "I can think of one thing that would be a very productive, academic use of our time," she answered, her eyes narrowing mischievously.

"What's that?" I asked. My chest tightened, afraid of her response.

"I believe you have a story to finish, Mr. Smith," she snickered, rubbing her hands together like a silent movie villain. "A story that I've been waiting to hear for a very long time…"

I couldn't help but think once more about William Faulkner's statement: "The past is never dead. It's not even past." I sometimes wonder what Faulkner would think of our modern world, in which every notable action is captured and curated in websites and text messages and email and social media. In this digital era, it's nearly impossible for the past to remain buried. Instead, every flickering image and sound and sentence excavates the past from its malleable mounds of slumbering soil.

So, there I was – unable to escape, captured by a captive audience that wanted me to exhume the earth of my personal history.

"Listen, Veronica…" I started to say.

And then my phone buzzed, lighting up with a new message.

"Saved by the bell," I said, looking down at my screen. "Or saved by the *buzz*, in this case." I held up my index finger, indicating that Veronica would have to wait. "Give me a minute to text my wife."

Veronica nodded her head with an impatient frown. She swiped her own phone from the desktop in front of her, and proceeded to tap away at the glass surface.

Meanwhile, I stared down at my iPhone's shimmering screen, reading Mel's text messages and typing away my responses.

Damn. We're on lockdown.

Oh my god! Are you okay?

Yeah, it's more of a safety measure than anything else. I think it's going to be a little while before they release us, though. 😫

Are you with your students?

Just one. Veronica. All the rest are at an assembly in the auditorium.

At least you've got good company with Veronica there. Should I pay her for babysitting you, too? 😉

You're sooooooo funny. 😑

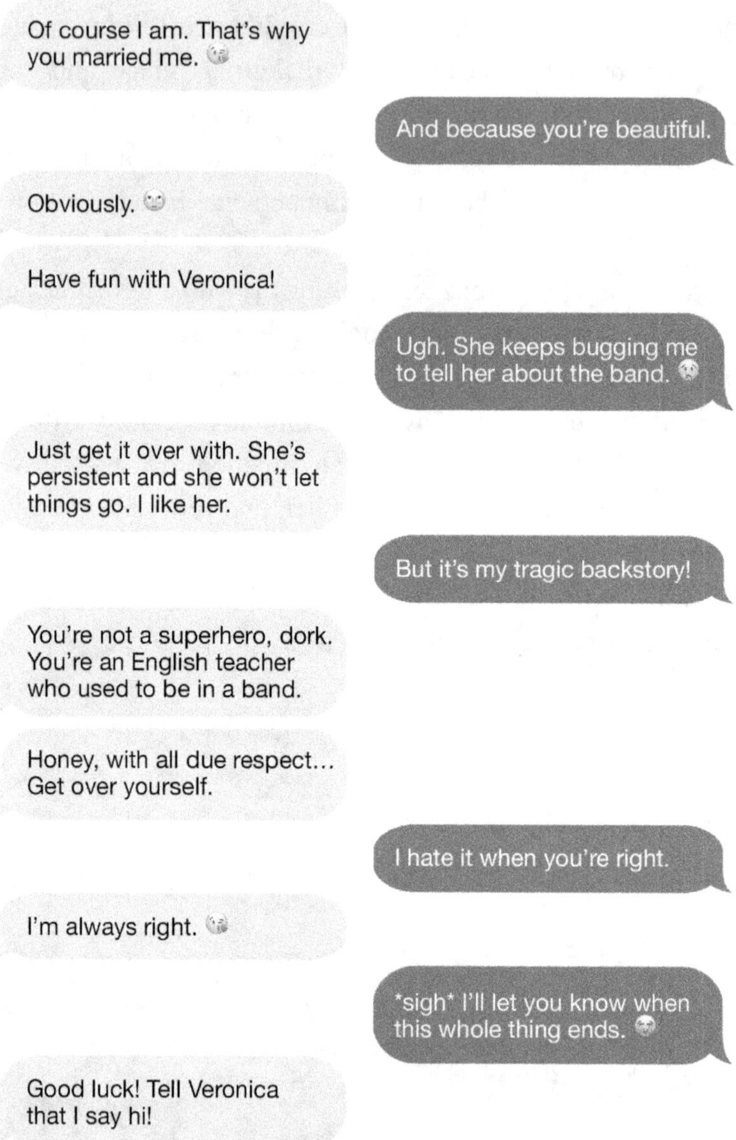

I placed my phone down on my cluttered desk and slid it away from me in defeat.

"So…?" Veronica asked.

"My wife sends her regards," I sighed. "And she said that I should tell you my sad story."

"YES!" Veronica yelled.

"*Sssshhhh!*" I hushed her. "We're still on lockdown!"

"But you said that we're not in any *'imminent danger,'* right?"

"Right," I admitted. "We're safe. For now."

"And we're going to be stuck here for a few hours?"

"Correct."

"And there's no one who can interrupt us or hear what secrets you confess?"

"Once again, you are correct," I begrudgingly agreed, scowling in frustration.

"Well, then," Veronica said, "in that case, I think this is a sign from God. He works in mysterious ways, right? And it can't be a coincidence that you and I got locked up together during this non-dangerous lockdown. It's like this is meant to be."

"I don't really believe in signs, *per se...*" I grumbled, rubbing my hands against the temples of my head. "But this is going to be hard for me, Veronica. I don't like talking about this stuff. With anyone. Ever."

Her face softened, the impish countenance fading to a more earnest expression. "I promise that I'll listen respectfully," she said, her voice reduced to a velvet whisper. "And I won't judge you or blame you or criticize you." Her forehead creased in concern, and then she added one final afterthought. "Your secrets are safe with me."

"But there's some ugly and embarrassing stuff in there, Veronica," I warned her. "Will you promise to keep this conversation private?"

Veronica scrunched up her mouth like a frustrated child and knitted her eyebrows sympathetically.

"You're like my second dad," she said reassuringly, "or my really ancient older brother."

"Way to make me feel old, kid," I laughed.

"You know what I mean," she said, slapping the top of her desk. She thought better of it immediately after, however, and gently pushed her palms across the wooden surface as if she were smoothing wrinkles out of a stubborn bedsheet. "I just wish I had some popcorn..." she joked, looking around the room for comic effect.

I closed my eyes and sighed, realizing that there was no way to avoid this confrontation any further. It was time to reach my hands into the soil and dig up the corpse of my past.

"So, where were we?" I asked.

"You had just written 'Incomplete'," she answered with eyes ablaze. "And Call Field got signed to a major label."

"Right," I said, exhaling deeply. "And that's when everything started to fall apart…"

SECOND CHORUS

I get lost sometimes in the melodies of my mind,
where I've tried to find what I need.
But the crashing tide has swept me off my feet,
and left me incomplete for a while…
And it's just like your smile.

CHAPTER TWELVE
"Celebrate the News"

So, there we were: four college kids with a major label contract.

It seemed incredible, implausible, improbable – if not entirely impossible. We weren't gods or saints or geniuses. We were just young, preternaturally experienced musicians with the right sound and the right look at the right time.

Though it was mid-November when we got the news from Lowercase Records that they wanted to sign us and put out our first full-length album, they wasted no time in getting us into a studio. The label had a laundry list of suggested producers – everyone from Mark Trombino to Jerry Finn to Michael Beinhorn to Ric Ocasek. At first, it seemed like they wanted to steer us in the perfect direction: Lowercase entertained the idea of molding us into the next Weezer or blink-182, which was a dream come true. We had visions of headlining tours, gold records, and annual invitations to the Warped Tour – where we could chum it up with the very same punk-rock acts that we had worshipped in our high school years.

Ultimately, though, Lowercase Records settled on an in-house producer with an epic résumé stretching back to the 1960s: Jimmy Storforsen. If you haven't heard the name before, double-check the liner notes to some of your favorite records. Jimmy had a hand in producing, recording, and/or engineering some of the greatest albums of the twentieth century. Highlights of his storied career include records from Social Distortion, Neil Young, Bruce Springsteen, and the Ramones (to name just a few). The clincher for me, though, was a record Jimmy had helped engineer in 1966, the greatest album ever made: The Beach Boys' *Pet Sounds*.

It was, it seemed, a match made in heaven.

As Jimmy explained to us in the months that followed, he had been a teenager when he started working in recording studios, initially sweeping storage rooms, making coffee runs, and performing a litany of other tedious tasks. Eventually, he finagled his way into the control room – "where the magicians wave their wands," as he put it. But he wasn't just some talentless gear-head: Jimmy had been a piano prodigy in his preteen years, playing Rachmaninoff better than precocious students twice his age. Somewhere along the way, though, he developed an affinity for rock and roll, and he kissed his classical roots goodbye.

"It was Leon Russell," he told us. "That guy played on all the great songs of the 1960s. And he just had this soulful way of rollin' his notes and hittin' his chords. Once I got Leon in my head, there wadn't no looking back, ya' know?"

Storforsen (or "Storf," as we later nicknamed him) was a badass. An aging badass, yes, but a badass nonetheless. And he would play an integral role in my life for the next few months.

When we first met Jimmy, we wrote him off as another pencil-pusher. It was shortly after we finished signing our contracts with Lowercase, and I just remember a flurry of paperwork: lots of highlighted sections that required signatures, forms that indemnified the label in case of lawsuits, and other miscellaneous legal documents that seemed indecipherable to a bunch of naïve college kids. They were the first contracts we signed, but they weren't the most dangerous. That would come later. By comparison, this paperwork all seemed innocently innocuous – not like the death warrant I would soon stupidly sign.

But I'm getting ahead of myself.

The afternoon that we met Jimmy, we were all stationed around a fancy-looking conference table that probably cost more than my entire year's teaching salary. In the depths of the commercial building that was the headquarters for Lowercase Records, the air conditioning was set at a frigid 65 degrees, keeping us uncomfortably chilled like fresh vegetables in the refrigerator. It was almost like Lowercase was trying to preserve our youth, our image, and our sound – before we ripened too far past our expiration date.

When Jimmy walked into the room, we mistook him for an accountant: his slight frame, exceptionally tall height, thinning salt-and-pepper hair, and boxy glasses made him look like an aging spelling-bee champion, an archetypically awkward square with meticulously refined edges – not a guy who had worked on some of the most important gold and platinum rock records of the last few decades. At that point, Jimmy was hovering around his fiftieth birthday, and his age was beginning to show: he bore heavy creases on his forehead and long, sagging lines at the corners of his eyes. There was nothing remotely rock and roll about his appearance.

But, as we know, appearances can be deceiving.

"Ya' must be the band," Jimmy whined in his distinctive Bronx accent. "It's nice ta' meet ya', boys." He nodded at each of us and shook hands with everyone at the table.

"And who are you?" Steve asked skeptically.

"I'm the guy who's gonna' make ya' rich," he said with a big grin.

Storf wasn't kidding around. Though we had always prided ourselves on a certain level of tight musicianship, aiming to be one cohesive unit instead of four disparate limbs, we quickly learned that our respectable level of professionalism wasn't nearly as professional as we had assumed. From the get-go, Jimmy picked apart our playing, dissecting the musical body of Call Field with surgical precision – and offering an unvarnished estimation of our abilities.

"Ya' kids are good," he told us, "but not good enough. Yet."

We discovered pretty quickly that Storf had no filter. Maybe it was his age. Maybe it was his ample experience in the business. Or maybe it was just the simple fact that he valued cold, hard truth above all else. Whatever the reason, Storf told us exactly what he was thinking – egos, be damned.

"We're gonna' have to change some things when we start recordin' the album," he warned us after one early rehearsal. "Whatcha' been doin' onstage works fine… *onstage*. But ya' gotta' step up yer game if ya' wanna' put out a major label record."

"Just tell us what to do, and we'll do it," I reassured him. The rest of the guys in the band seemed a little more hesitant, but their reluctance was overshadowed by my desperate desire to create a punk-rock masterpiece of an album.

"Good," Storf said, scratching at the faded skeleton tattoos on his left forearm. "First off, yer singer can't play guitar for crap. Secondly, we're gonna' need to beef up yer sound. Either ya' need another member or two in the band, or we overdub like hell on this record. Either way, even if we do plenny a' overdubs in the studio, once ya' get out on the road ya' won't be able to replicate the sounds live. Finally, ya' gonna' need to practice a helluva' lot more. These songs need to be tighter than a cheerleader's prom dress or else it'll take us *years* to get this album done. And I ain't got years, kids."

The air drained from the room as we took in Storf's criticism. I was still quietly processing his critiques, but I could tell that Chunk and Ethan were shocked by his blunt feedback.

And Steve… well, Steve was less than thrilled.

"What do you mean I '*can't play guitar for crap…?*'" our fearless leader fired back, anger seeping through his voice like battery acid through cracks in a terminal's casing.

"I *mean*," Storf responded matter-of-factly, "ya' ain't good enough yet. Ya' keep falling off time. Ya' rhythm is inconsistent. And ya' struggle to shift chord positions. Unless the Devil makes ya' the same deal that he made with Robert Johnson, there ain't no way that ya' gonna' be ready in time to record. So, someone else is gonna' have to track all yer parts for ya' on this album."

Without thinking, I immediately chimed in. "I can do it," I sputtered. "I wrote the songs on guitar, anyway, so it won't be a problem for me to record Steve's parts."

Perhaps I volunteered a *little* too quickly. When I glanced over at Steve, his face had turned a violent shade of crimson. For a split second, I had visions of Steve storming off after I beat him out for a singing slot at our high school graduation. That same frustration and anger – and, as I would soon find out, *distaste for me* – rushed to the surface with more force than Noah's fabled flood.

"Good," Storf said to us with his nonchalant New York drawl, "now that *that's* settled, let's talk about the recordin' process…"

The weeks that followed were incredibly humbling for us. Storf's collected criticism served as a blow to our egos – especially Steve, whose guitar playing was deemed too amateurish from the very first chord. Still, though, we gritted our teeth and let ourselves be molded into a pristine pop-rock band. It didn't come easily, of course: I remember playing for hours and hours on end, repeating fragments of songs and transitions between choruses until my calloused fingers ached.

It was kind of like rock musician boot camp. Except we sure as hell weren't singing "Kumbaya" by the campfire.

Eventually, after weeks and weeks of dictatorial rehearsals in the studio, our little band of college kids started to shine with a new musical lacquer. Our songs – the same ones that I had written in dorms and bedrooms and garages – sounded tighter, smoother than ever before. As we followed Jimmy's guidance, we saw some of our rawer edges and our punk influences smoothed down to a mercurial fluidity. Ethan's buzzsaw guitars became less distorted, Chunk's drums less violent, my bass less punchy. Even Steve, our gravel-throated god in Levi's jeans, found a new silky luster in his verses and a new emotional capacity in his choruses.

Though I was on the ground floor of this rebirth, willingly molded by Storf's mentorship, it was still a sight to behold: these young California punkers were being transformed into something smoother, something calmer, something shinier.

Something more palatable.

Something more marketable.

We were being sculpted from the clay of amateur art into a coveted commodity for mass consumption. Remember that show *Queer Eye for the Straight Guy*, in which fashionable guides transform hopeless men into stunning, star-like studs? It was almost like we were living in *Pop Eye for the Punk Guys*, in which an established producer turns regular SoCal punk kids into young, attractive, viable pop stars. So much so, in fact, that the record label found us a team of stylists who decked us out in scrupulously selected clothing for photoshoots and interviews. There were trips to swanky Beverly Hills boutiques to improve our fashion sense, visits to Guitar Center to upgrade our instruments, and stops at salons to tame our wild hair. It was simultaneously beautiful and bizarre.

This was, Jimmy reassured us, just part of the star-making process. "Do ya' think Bon Jovi or Bruce Springsteen kept the same faded flannel after hitting the big time? Hell, no! Those fellas traded in their old rags at the first opp-uh-tunity!" He cracked his knuckles so loudly that the noise ricocheted through the studio. "If ya' wanna' *be* rock stars, ya' gotta' *look* like rock stars first."

It seemed to be sage advice, but it didn't sit well with me. As thrilling as the transformation might have been, I never lost that nagging feeling that I was somehow losing myself, like I was shedding pieces of my well-worn identity. As my old, faded, torn blue jeans were swapped out for designer denim – as I was *looking* different – I noticed myself acting differently, thinking differently. And I didn't like it.

Steve, on the other hand, *loved* the wardrobe assistance from the label. His jeans got tighter and his haircut more pristinely coifed. He even died his hair black for more of a James Dean/Johnny Depp look. Whereas I just felt like an imposter in expensive clothing, our lead singer felt more at home than ever before, as if he'd been roughing it with plebeians his whole life but was now ready to ascend to his throne. I swear, that guy was born to be a star: not only did he have the flawless physical appearance that begged for an audience's admiration, but his confidence and swagger made you *believe* in his rock and roll sovereignty.

I never felt that way.

The other guys in the band had mixed reactions. Ethan welcomed this new promise of wealth and slid right into the limelight as smoothly as his fingers slid across the frets on his guitar. But Chunk seemed to struggle just as much as I did.

I should note here that Chunk was going through his own personal transformation. He'd been frequenting the gym on a daily basis and his wide frame was quickly slimming down to a remarkably smaller size. Whereas Chunk and I had always been the "big guys" in the band (especially compared to Ethan's svelte frame and Steve's athletic build), I suddenly found myself outnumbered by skinny boys. Along with his changing body, Chunk's personality started to change as well: he became more withdrawn, more independent, pulling away from his old friends and spending less time with all of us. He was more short-tempered, too, snapping back at Steve and Ethan for any number of transgressions. I always seemed to remain in my cousin's good graces, but I still felt him slipping away like refined sand through my callused fingers.

Chunk had always been more of a brother to me than a cousin or a bandmate. Now, however, I felt a dark shadow of defiance creeping between our solitary silhouettes. He was withdrawing – from me, Ethan, and Steve. Especially Steve. As solid and consistent as Chunk was on his drum set, keeping meticulous time and setting the musical meter for the rest of the band, something profound was happening to my cousin. He was changing.

Chunk wasn't Chunk anymore. He was someone else.

But I was too distracted and self-involved – too busy with Lani and music and school – to even notice.

It wasn't just the individual members of the band who were evolving, though – Call Field was being reshaped by outside forces. The label was giving us all musical makeovers, working hard to manipulate us into a commodity they thought would sell to the masses.

Upon Storf's recommendation, we started incorporating new arrangements and sonic textures into Call Field's songs. Jimmy's first suggestion was to work keyboards into the band. "Ya' gonna' need to pad the recordings with some synth or organ to flesh out the sound," he stated matter-of-factly. "Any of ya' fellas play piano?"

I reticently raised my right hand. No one else in our quartet had experience tickling the ivories, so (by default) I was the only one who could pull it off.

"Great," Storf said. "So, you'll be playing bass, guitar, and keys on this album. And you wrote the songs, too, right?"

I nodded quickly, grinning with pride. As I glanced over at the rest of the guys, though, I noticed that my enthusiasm and cheer were not shared by everyone else. Chunk seemed preoccupied, but Steve and Ethan wore expressions more akin to contempt than complicity.

"*Kiss-ass teacher's pet…*" Steve muttered under his breath.

My cheeks flushed crimson. As soon as Steve made his snide comment, I felt like I was in high school all over again – balancing my own insecurities with prominent peer pressure from the "cool" kids. But I was a different person now: as opposed to my days at Sespe Creek High School, when I would have sunk in my seat and cowered, I bolted upright and turned towards our singer.

"Screw off, Steve," I shot back. "We wouldn't need a *'teacher's pet'* if you could actually play your own instrument."

A chorus of "oohs" filled the room, as Chunk and Ethan – and even Storf – giddily covered their mouths and laughed. Loudly, I might add. And, as bitter and defensive as I was, I couldn't help but snicker along with the others.

Steve was not thrilled. His crystal blue eyes shimmered with anger as lines formed above his temples.

Whether I meant to or not, I was challenging Steve's authority.

And he did not like it one bit.

I think Steve had always considered me a sidekick, someone whose chief duty was to supplement the lead singer and make him look good. Years before, Steve had no problem muscling his way into my life, taking over my band and swooping in on my adolescent crush, Serena Rios. Somehow, though, I had flipped the script in the intervening years, miraculously gaining an upper hand over my old almost-nemesis. I was no longer a hanger-on in the Hollywood fantasy story in which he starred; instead, I was turning into an antagonist, threatening everything that he held dear.

I was becoming a villain in his eyes.

In the ensuing months, I found myself thriving in the studio. I played better than I had my entire life, and I found myself inventing little riffs and fills to flesh out the recordings. Heck, I even got to layer my vocals in stacks of tracks, Brian Wilson-style. Of course, while Steve's voice remained front and center, it was *my* instrumentation and *my* harmonies that surrounded him like a protective force field and permeated every corner of those Call Field recordings.

It's hard to explain to someone who hasn't spent endless hours in a studio, but recording an album almost feels like assembling a three-dimensional jigsaw puzzle – except the shapes keep shifting and the pieces don't always connect in the way that you anticipate. Sure, you can put together a simple flowchart (preproduction with a metronome and scratch tracks, followed by individual players recording their instruments in isolation, with subsequent digital editing to clean up imperfections), but the time we spent recording our one-and-only major-label release felt more like constructing a Lego structure the size of an eighteen-wheel semi-truck. For every prominent vocal track, guitar riff, snare snap, and bass thump, there was an eye-opening amount of subtle, hidden layering: stacked harmony vocals, oblique organ padding, glimmering glockenspiel notes, doubled guitar parts, and countless other assorted accoutrements.

Rather than feel threatened or burdened by my ubiquitous presence, Storf seemed to honestly enjoy having me there. For a few months, I was like his musical sous chef – running errands, repositioning microphones, testing volume levels – basically doing whatever he needed. If he was bothered by my incessant questions about recording studio minutiae, he didn't show it at all. Instead, he tended to perk up in his cushioned leather seat, his eyes sparkling with excitement as he discussed some of his favorite recording tips and tricks.

For months, I spent every available moment in the studio. I tracked bass, piano, organ, acoustic guitars, electric guitars, glockenspiel, ukulele, tambourine, congas – basically, any instrument that I could get my hands on. Despite my best intentions, I found myself foregoing my weekend trips home, choosing instead to live and breathe the existence of a studio rat. How I managed to see Lani *and* attend classes at UCLA *and* get my homework done *and* record a major-label album during those intense months completely escapes me. It was probably sheer sleep deprivation that provided me with the hours needed to achieve those Herculean feats.

I *do* know, however, that I was eating way too much.

And I relied almost exclusively on fast food.

And I started smoking.

And I drank gallons of coffee and soda.

And I completely stopped exercising.

It caught up with me pretty quickly. I started gaining a few pounds a week, my clothes getting tighter and my belt buckle more constricting. By the time that we were zeroing in on the album's finish line, I had put on close to thirty pounds. Yup. Thirty pounds.

And that was only the start.

At some point, between Lani and UCLA and hamburgers and a variety of bad habits, I had the million-dollar idea that my dad should drive down to Los Angeles and record some guitars for the album. Of course, the tracks would be buried in the mix, but I figured that my music-obsessed father would be thrilled to have his name in the liner notes of a major-label album. We were nearing the end of the recording process, and we were on a tight timeline, but I figured my dad would do anything in his powers to participate. When I called to invite him, though, it didn't exactly go as planned.

"Wow," my dad intoned feebly over the telephone line. "That sounds like an amazing offer..." Despite the earnest appreciation in his words, there was a hesitation in his voice.

"But...?" I asked.

He coughed loudly through the phone receiver, the viscous phlegm lodged in his throat echoing over the line. "I just don't think I'm up for it right now. I'm sorry, Junior."

I was a bit crestfallen by his reply. It didn't make any sense to me: why would my dad, the definitive rock 'n' roll super-fan, not want to seize this once-in-a-lifetime opportunity? It just didn't add up. When I asked my mom about it, she wearily tried to fill in the blanks for me.

"Your dad hasn't been feeling well," she explained on the phone. "He's been fighting off this flu bug for a few weeks now, but he just can't seem to shake it."

"He should *really* go to the doctor, Mom," I told her. "If he's been sick for more than a week, it could be something serious."

My mom sighed. "You know how your father is. He *hates* hospitals. He keeps bragging that he hasn't been to the doctor in sixteen years. And he says that he's not going to break his streak now." She grumbled something inaudible into the telephone. "At this point, it's like he's more afraid of wounded pride than death," she added.

"Okay," I relented. "Just give him a hug for me and tell him that I love him."

"Will do, honey," she said.

I'd like to say that recording our one-and-only full-length album was a majestically magical, stress-free experience… but that wasn't the case. Though it's a far cry from flipping burgers or waiting tables (or even teaching a class full of high school kids), recording is still *work*. Yes, the process facilitates artistry and creativity and beauty – but it's also clocking endless hours to make a final product for mass consumption. There were rules to follow and timelines to adhere to, all of which made the recording process a bit more time-sensitive and taxing. Every hour that we spent in the studio cost the record label money, and we were accumulating a sizable bill in very short time.

Each recording session was an eight- to twelve-hour workday (hence my over-reliance on fast food and caffeine). As could be expected, after several five-day work weeks, recording begins to feel like a full-time job. Fortunately for me, the Lowercase Records studio on Ocean Way was only a short drive from UCLA, so I was able to dart back and forth between overcrowded classes and the spacious studio without too much travel time. Nevertheless, I felt like I was working two full-time jobs at that point: as a full-time university student *and* as a full-time recording artist. It was, for lack of a better term, *bonkers*.

As we stacked each brick in our wall of recording, Storf and I could see the architecture of Call Field's songs gradually becoming cleaner and clearer. Ethan, Chunk, and Steve had much less interest in the recording process: after they tracked their parts, they tended to vacate the premises and never look back. I, on the other hand, made it a point to be there for as much of the recording as was humanly possible. In fact, I may or may not have slept on the couches of the control room at various points in the month that we were there. Like I said, it was bonkers.

I lived and breathed Call Field's music for the entire month of February that year, and I felt like I was thriving. Other folks in my life, however, didn't necessarily agree with me.

"I feel like I never see you anymore," Lani griped at me after one particularly grueling late-night session. We had planned on grabbing sushi at a venue close to the studio, but I ended up having to cancel because I couldn't quite nail a piano riff. "And you haven't seen your parents since New Year's," she added.

"I'm sorry, Lani," I said, my eyes barely open after what seemed like a never-ending marathon of recording. "I swear that I'll make it up to you when this is all finished."

"You promise?" she entreated, her eyes pleading.

"I promise you."

"Good. Because I deserve your full attention, mister."

For a brief spell, I thought that it might never end.

Finally, though, after four jam-packed weeks of tracking, the album was finished. To celebrate, Storf offered to take all of us (and our significant others) to dinner at a hip, fancy *pho* restaurant in Beverly Hills. The four members of Call Field, most of us flanked by our girlfriends, sat at an elongated wooden table, speaking excitedly over steaming bowls of noodles. I was situated next to Jimmy, directly across the table from Steve. Poor Lani found herself in the awkward position of facing Serena, and the two of them paddled through contrived conversation while the boys in the band talked shop.

"Now that ya' kids are done with the album," Storf said between slurps of noodles, "I suppose that ya' have a tour planned?"

Steve leaned forward on the oak countertop, trying to position himself intimately close to Jimmy. "We've got it all mapped out," Steve explained. "The album drops in the middle of June, so the label is going to release our first single sometime in May. We're going to start our tour on June 21st, playing the Fillmore in San Francisco. Can you believe that? The *Fillmore!*"

"On my twenty-first birthday, nonetheless," I added, raising my chopsticks for emphasis.

Steve kept talking, completely ignoring my comment. "After San Francisco, we're going to snake on up through Arcata, Portland, and Seattle. Then, we're going to make our way across the flyover states. Eventually, we'll end up in New York City at the Bowery, and then we'll swoop down the East Coast and work our way through the South."

"Sounds pretty demanding," Storf commented, raising an eyebrow. "Ya' think that ya' kids are up for it?"

"Why wouldn't we be?" Steve asked. He leaned back and crossed his arms over his sinewy chest.

"It's a big commitment," Storf explained. "Ya' gonna' be away from ya' family and friends for a *long* time. Pro'lly all summer, I assume." He leaned forward, resting his wiry arms on the tabletop. "Are ya' sure ya' ready for that?"

From the corner of my eye, I could see all of the color suddenly draining from Serena's face. Her copper complexion had never seemed so pitifully pale.

"I don't care about anyone else," Steve suddenly shot back, oblivious to his girlfriend's reaction. "I'm ready to make this happen. I'm going to hit the road and never look back. I want to get out there and play as many shows as possible, and it doesn't matter who else is onstage with me."

There was an awkward silence. Chunk, Ethan, and I all looked up at Steve, studying his virulent expression. Didn't he realize that he needed us? That we were a *band?* We weren't just his hired guns. We were his peers, his friends. Or, at least, we *had* been.

Storf sensed our discomfort and quickly changed the subject. "Speakin' a' which," he interrupted, "did ya' get your live line-up figgered out?"

Steve fiddled with the straw sticking up from his drink, his forehead creasing into a concerted frown. Ethan and Chunk looked towards him earnestly, anticipating a response from our lead singer.

Instead of waiting for Steve, however, I chimed in. "I've got some ideas," I announced.

From my vantage point, I could see Steve's glaring eyes slowly work their way up from the table to my face. It was not a welcoming sight that I beheld.

"Oh, *really…?*" he muttered, cocking an eyebrow.

Undeterred, I explained further. "Since we've discovered how pivotal it is to have a keyboard padding the songs, I thought I'd move over to keys for our live shows."

Perhaps I should have brought up my idea with the boys first, before springing it on everyone in front of our producer. I could tell from the expressions on their faces that none of my bandmates were particularly enthusiastic about the idea.

"If you take over keys, who's gonna' play bass?" Steve asked skeptically. His doubtful look was mirrored by both Chunk and Ethan. Even Lani and Serena perked up, leaning forward to listen in on our conversation.

"What about Victor?" I suggested.

"Who's Victor…?" Steve questioned.

"Your old roommate?" Chunk asked, head cocked to the side.

"Wait…" Steve commanded. "The Asian dude?"

"Why not?" I answered, lifting my arms in supplication. "He's a better bass player than I am, and he's got tons of experience playing our style of music. And I was literally sharing a room with the guy when I wrote most of the songs on the album."

No one said anything. Ethan and Chunk looked down at their chittering chopsticks, while Steve skeptically contemplated my proposal.

"Victor's a good guy," Lani offered hesitantly, breaking the awkward silence. "He's reliable and trustworthy. And he's told me a bunch of times how much he enjoys your music." Lani's eyes looked searchingly across the table to everyone else, finally settling on Serena, who sat immediately across from her.

Everyone seemed to be waiting for a response from Steve, for him to offer his stamp of approval on the suggestion. Finally, he leaned back in his chair, stretched his arms out in front of him, and stuck his tongue between his teeth and his upper lip.

"Why not?" he acquiesced. He turned his icy gaze in my direction and added an afterthought. "Especially if he's better than you are."

CHAPTER THIRTEEN
"Let the Wind Blow"

The bond between Call Field's lead singer and its multi-instrumentalist songwriter continued to strain under the weight of our new dynamic. It seemed that every rock and roll rehearsal, every boring band meeting, every casual conversation became more and more confrontational. I suppose that I could have backed down at some point, that I should have stopped fighting our fearless leader for control of the band and simply followed him in lockstep like a good foot soldier.

Alas, I had developed too much pride at that point to simply give in and follow someone else's lead. As I saw it through my arrogant eyes, Call Field felt like *my* band playing *my* songs with *my* arrangements. And, since I had spent so many hours by Storf's side in the studio, I also felt like it was *my* album that we were recording. After all, *I* was the one clocking all the hours in the studio overseeing the recordings – not Steve or Ethan or even Chunk. That sense of pride, that sense of undue ownership helped set the stage for a punk-rock Greek tragedy.

You can see where this is headed, right?

I was Icarus, flying too close to the sun.

I was Odysseus, taunting the gods on my return home from war.

I was Achilles, roaring into battle with a false sense of invincibility, ignoring the fatal flaw that lay exposed at my heel.

I was headed for a fall.

CHAPTER FOURTEEN
"California Saga"

In the annals of rock history, there have been a few unique, one-off concerts when – because of circumstances beyond the control of the band – the group has to make some last-minute changes to the lineup. At a 1995 Pearl Jam show in San Francisco, Neil Young stepped in as the lead singer for the band because Eddie Vedder was too sick to go onstage; for the World AIDS Day concert in 2014, Bruce Springsteen and Chris Martin filled in for U2's lead singer, Bono, who was incapacitated and recovering from a serious bike accident; and, back in August of 1996, when Oasis taped its *MTV Unplugged* performance, the guitarist/ songwriter for the band, Noel Gallagher, handled the lead vocals because his brother, lead singer Liam Gallagher, supposedly had a "sore throat" (though there's some speculation that the Brothers Gallagher were simply feuding… yet again).

Though not as legendary, Call Field had a similar experience in the spring of 2000, just a few months before our album was released.

This is that story.

A little background: before Lowercase Records released our debut record, the label sent us out on the road to build some buzz for the band. These intermittent tour dates also provided us with a chance to break in Victor, the newest member of Call Field, who would be taking over the bass guitar duties from yours truly. As I had predicted, Victor was (from the get-go) a better bass player than I ever was: his nimble fingers fluidly maneuvered the bass's frets underneath the crunchy distortion of our power chords, and he seamlessly found his spot in our new live lineup.

Perhaps I should have felt a twinge of insecurity that I had been so easily replaced on the instrument. As it was, though, I was having so much fun experimenting with keyboard textures and riffs to worry about it too much. Historically, punk rock has not been very kind to piano players, so I saw this as a challenge: I would find a way to weave keyboards into our songs without sacrificing the grit or the integrity of the music. It was new and thrilling and completely outside my comfort zone. And I loved it.

So, under the label's advisement, we ended up taking weekend trips to San Diego and San Luis Obispo and Long Beach and Las Vegas – basically, anywhere within driving distance that we could play. One such excursion landed us in Berkeley, California, at the site of the legendary punk venue 924 Gilman Street. As the story goes, *Gilman* (as it's known by the cool kids) was one of the first venues to host Green Day, Rancid, Operation Ivy, Tiger Army, and a plethora of other punk-adjacent geniuses – and, as acolytes of Green Day's pop-punk sound, we jumped at the chance to play at the fabled venue.

When I think back to the career trajectory of Call Field, I see the Gilman show as a major milestone for us, a fork in the road that would eventually lead to the band's inevitable implosion. At the time, we just assumed the trip would be a fun romp up in the Bay Area, an opportunity for us to lay our claim as successors of Green Day's legacy. We were young and foolish, with seemingly endless horizons in front of us – like Jay Gatsby's emerald illumination mixed with our favorite band's musical legacy: *The Great Gatsby's Green Day Light*. And we all know how things ended up for Gatsby. Or at least my AP English students do.

The first sign that something was amiss was the drive up north. Usually, we were pretty good about sharing responsibilities: we would alternate driving shifts, letting the others goof around or sleep, and we would each take turns selecting CDs during the long haul. This mobile musical math equation worked incredibly well for a long time – until our fated journey up to Gilman.

For whatever reason, Steve decided that he was going to commandeer the driver's seat for the entirety of the trip. "I'll steer this ship," he told us, his eyes glued to the asphalt beyond the van's windshield. "The rest of you can just play passengers."

Chunk, Ethan, and Victor shrugged off his comment, turning back to the game of blackjack that they had set up on an overturned cooler stationed on the floor between them. I, on the other hand, wasn't able to shake it off so easily.

I couldn't help but wonder... Was this a thinly veiled threat? Was Steve trying to exert control over the band, trying to convert us from a democracy into a demagoguery? Or was I simply reading too deeply into his offhand comments?

As you know by now, I'm the king of overthinking things. Alas, I wasn't much different two decades ago in my nascent incarnation as the prince of pondering.

This time, however, I had tapped into some subconscious understanding of the band's changing dynamic. Somehow, a part of me knew that things weren't going to end well. But even *I* couldn't have predicted how this particular trip would turn out.

Uncle Jeff's passenger van, which we had borrowed for our weekend mini-tours, was a sturdy beast of a vehicle. Somehow, we managed to cram a drum set, amps, guitars, and my new Alesis keyboard into the back section of the van. Steve sat by himself in the front, a map spread out on the passenger seat alongside half-empty bags of Cheetos and Ritz crackers. Ethan, Chunk, and Victor squeezed themselves into the next row, the three amigos of the band bonding over a tattered deck of cards and plastic poker chips.

I, on the other hand, sat completely isolated and alone in the third row of seats, smashed against a wall of luggage and musical equipment, bracing the towering piles of items with my cumbersome form. The whole drive up north, I could feel the weight of it all pushing against me, trapping me between the van's door and the overwhelming mounds of musical instruments.

The others, preoccupied with their own distractions, paid no attention to my burden. It struck me as odd that not one of my bandmates turned back to face me, but I didn't place too much stock in the observation. It was just a road trip, right?

About an hour into our voyage, somewhere past scenic Santa Barbara and into the vaulted valleys of Goleta, Steve's musical selection (blink-182's *Enema of the State*) wound down with its fist-pumping closer, "Anthem." Assuming that we would continue our tradition of trading off album selections, I chimed in.

"So, who has the next choice for music?" I called out, raising my voice from the back of the van.

The three poker players sitting in front of me turned to one another and searched each other's faces. From my vantage point, I could see Chunk shrug and straighten his back. He dug around in his backpack, leaned forward with uncharacteristically stiff posture, and held out a copy of Weezer's *Pinkerton* in his right hand.

"How about…" he began to say.

"As long as I'm driving," Steve interrupted, "we're going to listen to *my* music."

Chunk immediately recoiled. He withdrew his arm, and leaned back into his seat wearing a look of consternation on his face.

I decided to speak up. "But I thought…"

Steve whipped his head around and scowled, his attention completely shifted from the road ahead and directed back towards us. "That's the way it's going to be from now on," he said. "And if you don't like it, you can jump ship."

Like it or not, things were changing. Our egalitarianism was eroding into a dystopian dictatorship.

For the next five and a half uncomfortable hours, Steve maintained his spot in the driver's seat, navigating the various freeways and off-ramps all by himself. As he had abruptly informed us, he was now the sole proprietor of the radio; meanwhile, the rest of us tried to ignore the various pop punk paeans that blasted too loudly from the speakers. Ethan and

Victor seemed to be unfazed by this, but I could tell that Chunk was distracted.

"What crawled up Steve's ass?" I whispered to Chunk at one point.

He scrunched up his eyes into thin creases and half-turned his head in my direction. "He's obviously pissed about something," Chunk agreed, murmuring conspiratorially. "It looks like our *fearless leader* is a bit more *fearful* about his leadership than we thought…"

"This doesn't sit right with me," I confided.

"Me, neither," Chunk admitted.

Steve's eyes darted up to the rearview mirror. Though the rest of his face was hidden from the thin rectangular reflection of the mirror, I could see his eyelids scowling harshly enough to light the van on fire.

"What are you two chicks gossiping about back there?" he yelled.

"We're talking about you!" I shouted to the front, cackling to myself.

Steve was not amused. If eyes can shoot daggers, I'm pretty sure Steve's irises were launching every last sword, knife, cannonball, and axe in his artillery.

I expected the other guys to laugh along with me, but only Chunk was chuckling. Ethan and Victor gave us piteous glances, shaking their heads with disapproval.

Whether we knew it or not, we were drawing lines in the sand.

As we wove our way through the Golden State, casually coasting by the various communities and coastlines, I stared out the window at the rolling hills of central California. I had made this trip a few times over the years (usually when we visited Marina at UC Berkeley), but something about this particular drive stood out to me. Though I had always admired the beautiful scenery and the majestic countryside, I hadn't really noticed the dilapidated buildings that littered the highways like discarded fast food wrappers. As we sped by, the world warped in a 65 MPH glimpse of other lives, I could see exposed beams and crooked floorboards, broken hinges and smashed doors. Those abandoned or half-completed shells of houses stood like sad monuments, intermittently reminding passersby that nothing can survive the damning hands of time.

I shuddered.

We soldiered on, Steve at the wheel, venturing past Santa Maria and San Luis Obispo and Salinas, veering away from San Francisco towards the East Bay, where our destination lay. As we took the 880 North to Oakland, the landscape dotted with the dinosaur skeletons of rhythmically rocking oil rigs, our little feud seemed to be fading into an overwhelming sense of excitement. We were headed straight towards ground zero of the pop-punk explosion, the home turf of Green Day. *Green Day*. For a band that got its start playing Green Day covers, this felt like an immeasurable milestone.

After six and a half hours on the road, exit signs for Berkeley dreamily swam past the windows: Ashby… University Avenue… and then, finally, Gilman.

Steve flicked on the turn signal, angling us off the freeway and onto the winding gray asphalt of Gilman Street. The venue was surprisingly nondescript, no billboard signs advertising that punk rock legends had once frequented this turf. Random tourists would have no clue about the rock and roll history that had transpired between these industrial walls. Call Field, on the other hand, recognized the gravitas of the scene, and we approached the front door as if we were on a sacred pilgrimage to Mecca.

As we pulled up to the venue, we were warmly greeted by the management: a tattooed elder statesman with thick salt-and-pepper hair, Buddy Holly glasses, and a multitude of silver-studded piercings. We shook hands with Mr. Buddy Holly Glasses, got a tour of the venue, and studied the walls for any artifacts of Billy Joe Armstrong's crew. The boys and I were abuzz with wide-eyed wonder, giggling with each other like kids on Christmas morning. When it came time for load-in, we were joking back and forth like the good old days, laughing with each other as we shouldered the heavy loads of our equipment. I thought for sure that this show would be a clean slate, a reset button – a chance for us to recapture the equilibrium that had somehow been disrupted over the last few months of recording and practicing and gearing up for our major-label album release.

I was wrong.

While I had assumed that this good-natured pre-show buzz was permeating every corner of Call Field, Steve had other ideas. Clearly, our interactions had left him feeling wounded and distant. He might have been our leader, but he was no longer fearless.

"I'm taking off to explore," he informed us coolly, throwing a leather jacket over his standard white t-shirt. "I'll see you guys at soundcheck."

So, while the rest of us unloaded our gear and set up our equipment onstage, Steve went sightseeing.

Now, this should have been a telltale sign for the rest of us – the lead singer of the band felt like the lackluster labor of a roadie was beneath him, so the other members had to pick up his slack – but we were either too intimidated or too non-confrontational to speak up. Instead, we just grumbled amongst ourselves and let him leave to survey the scenery.

Mind you, this wasn't the first time (or the last time) that Steve would pull this kind of trick. It was the same nonsense that we had witnessed two years before at the Ventura Theater, when we opened for blink-182 and the wheels of fate began their gradual grind towards our major-label record deal. We might have resented Steve for it, but we weren't going to rock the boat. We recognized the wealth of talent that he brought to the band, and we assumed we were nothing without our charismatic captain. Because of this, we begrudgingly assumed that the Gilman show would follow the same pattern: our too-good-to-roadie lead singer would go schmooze with the crowd while the boys in the band would do all the grunt work that was obviously beneath him.

This show, however, would end with a *very* different outcome.

As any gigging musician will tell you, there's an awkward downtime between load-in, soundcheck, and the actual show itself. There are different philosophies about how to deal with this temporal purgatory: many go sightseeing, others go shopping, some take naps… Yet, no matter how one chooses to utilize that bland buffer zone, there always seems to be a nervous energy that permeates the afternoon. At Gilman, I strolled around the venue for a long time, walking side-by-side with Victor, Chunk, and Ethan. I remember touching the walls, my hands caressing age-old graffiti and countless peeling stickers from the many artists who had passed through these halls. In some small way, we felt like we were staking our claim to rock and roll history, adding Call Field's name to the long list of bands that had graced Gilman's stage. And yet, despite the fact that the four of us were basking in this pre-show glow, it felt odd that Steve was strangely absent from the whole experience.

We're supposed to be a team, I remember thinking to myself. *What kind of a punk rock beast are we with our head cut off?*

I don't know what sparked it, but I found myself thinking back to Homer's *Odyssey*. Yes, I recognize how *incredibly* nerdy that sounds – to be thinking of Greek mythology backstage at a punk rock club – but I guess the breadcrumbs that steered me to my future occupation as an English teacher had already left a discernible trail in my heart. Just bear with me.

As I was saying, the synapses firing in my brain flashed through the multitude of mythical creatures that appeared during Odysseus's epic voyage back to Ithaca. And then I thought of the great hero Hercules (or "Herakles," if you want to be historically accurate) and his battle with the many-headed Hydra.

A quick refresher course: the Hydra was a serpentine monster from Greek mythology that had something like nine or ten different heads. However, as Hercules discovered, every time that one head got cut off, *another* head grew in its place.

Though we were about seven thousand miles away from Athens, I couldn't help but imagine Steve, Victor, Ethan, Chunk, and myself as a strange musical monster. In some weird way, I imagined, Call Field was like a five-headed rock and roll Hydra. The band was bigger than all of us – and it could live beyond the tenure of any single member. If one of our heads got cut off, the rest of the beast could soldier on and continue a reign of rock and roll terror.

I know. I'm a nerd.

As the afternoon wore on and the bright heat of the daylight began to fade into a dim twilight, we still hadn't seen Steve. At first, we weren't worried; after all, we had *hours* to kill before show time. However, as the hands of the clock spun around and around, lapping the numbers and tick marks on its face, we became increasingly concerned. After all, it's one thing to go on without an extra guitarist or a keyboardist… but to play a show without your lead singer? How would that even work?

Though we had arrived at Gilman hours ahead of schedule – with *plenty* of time before our set – we found ourselves facing this very real dilemma as we waited and waited for our lead singer to reappear. We paced up and down the backstage quarters that served as a dressing room, anxiously glancing up at the clock every couple of minutes as if that might magically transport Steve back to the venue.

Still, no word from our golden-throated leader.

As we inched closer to our set time, the management didn't exactly seem thrilled, either. "I don't think we need to remind you that cancelling the show means you forfeit your guarantee," Mr. Buddy Holly Glasses told us, rubbing his fingers together to indicate the money that would be lost if we failed to perform at the gig.

Needless to say, we panicked a bit.

Finally, after an interminable wait, we heard arrhythmic footfalls echo in the hallway outside the dressing room. There was a pregnant pause, and then a weak knock – more a sloppy thudding than anything else. The boys and I immediately bolted for the door.

What we saw before us was nothing less than a nightmare. There was Steve, his white t-shirt stained with vomit or some other unappetizing substance, propped up on the arms of two unseemly looking characters – and if you look unseemly in the presence of a punk-rock band at a punk-rock venue, that's quite an accomplishment.

"He's your problem now," Unseemly #1 said, pushing him in our direction. Unseemly #2 gave Steve one last pitiable look and then walked away in the direction of the exit, muttering something under his breath.

The Unseemly Duo cackled as they threw open the door that lead to the street.

Steve, meanwhile, was a complete mess. He stood with his feet spread apart in a ridiculous stance, swaying unsteadily and nearly losing his balance with every passing second. He tried to walk at one point, but he stumbled and collapsed into a ripped leather chair that clung to the wall of the dressing room.

When he looked up at us, Steve was glassy-eyed, his expression vacant and infantile. He absently fumbled with his hands, replicating the same lazy motions with his long, white fingers. His feet, previously tottering in the doorway, seemed loosely planted to the ground, as if his whole being was untethered from the gravity of the earth.

"I need to sit down," he repeated over and over mechanically. "I need to sit down. I need to sit down…" His words slurred sluggishly, like he was mumbling through a mouthful of marbles.

"You *are* sitting," Ethan said softly, kneeling in front of Steve. Ethan reached out his hands to steady Steve's off-kilter posture, holding our lead singer firmly in place.

Steve, undeterred, kept twisting his fingers with clumsy, imbalanced precision.

A loud stomping of Dr. Martens boots ricocheted through the industrial hallway. Seconds later, Mr. Buddy Holly Glasses poked his head into the room. "You guys are on in ten minutes," he told us, gesturing towards the stage with a nod of his head. "Better get out there, tune up, and take your places." Without waiting for a response, Mr. BHG made his way back through the hall, the echo of his boots subsiding with each step.

Victor was the first one to break the silence.

"What the hell are we going to do?" he asked, running his russet fingers through his spiky black hair. His eyebrows creased in on themselves, the wrinkled lines on his forehead betraying his nervousness.

None of us could muster up an answer. Ethan was chomping away at the nail on his middle finger, spitting out brittle fragments and biting deep enough to draw blood. Chunk anxiously twirled a drumstick in his right hand, rotating the wooden splint with increasing intensity while thumping his left foot on the concrete floor.

I just felt defeated, staring ahead at the ragtag collection of graffiti emblazoned on the eggshell walls of the dressing room.

My mind was racing. My heart was thudding louder than a kick drum. And I could feel a monolithic swelling in my chest. I didn't want to walk away from this golden opportunity – nor did I want to forfeit the venue's guarantee for our performance. But how does a band play if the lead singer can't even walk to the stage?

Desperate times call for desperate measures.

And we were desperate.

"Screw it," I muttered angrily, exhaling with equal measures frustration and inspiration. "I'll do it."

"Do what?" Ethan asked, simultaneously picking at his jagged fingernails and wiping away the blood that was refusing to clot on the quick of his middle finger. He kept his arms pressed securely against his chest, as if he could hold the world together by simply clutching his own body tightly enough.

I looked from Ethan to Chunk to Victor, feeling more determined and confident than I had in ages.

"I'll sing," I told them.

A wave of emotions flooded over the guys. Victor cocked his head in confusion, looking like a porcupine-haired rooster; Ethan uncrossed his arms and let them slide down to his waist, his chest deflating with a wave of relief. And Chunk… well, Chunk just smiled at me.

"Let's do it," Chunk said. "Brick wrote these songs. He knows them better than anyone else. Why not let him sing for the night?"

"What are we going to do about Steve's guitar?" Victor chimed in. "Ethan can't play rhythm and lead at the same time…"

"Actually," Ethan interrupted, "I can. It won't sound as good, obviously, but I can pull it off. I've listened to enough Jimmy Page to do the one-gun guitar thing."

"You won't need to," I said, gesturing into the middle of our semicircle with my shaking hands. "I'll play rhythm. I wrote most of the songs on guitar, anyway. And I just finished recording all the guitar parts on the album. It's all fresh in my memory."

"What about the keyboards?" Victor asked.

"We'll just skip the keyboards tonight," I answered. "I mean, does a punk band *really* need piano…?"

Ethan glanced over at Steve, then looked back at our little semicircle. "This is crazy," he said, "like absolutely ridiculous." He paused, let out a barely audible grunt, and then continued. "But we don't have much of a choice, do we?"

In the absence of Steve's increasingly dictatorial presence, I felt empowered – ennobled even. Once again, Call Field felt like *my* band. For this one show, I wouldn't serve as the supporting actor for some arrogant lead singer. I threw my arms over Chunk's and Victor's shoulders, and moved my head forward into a conspiratorial huddle. "Play it like you mean it," I told them, conjuring old half-forgotten advice that my father had once given me. "Play the hell out of it. Play like this is the last time anyone will ever hear us."

We looked back at Steve, who still lay motionless on the tattered leather chair that supported his limp frame. Our lead singer, unable to form a coherent sentence or even simply stand on his own, seemed a pitiable presence then. He was dead weight. But the rest of us would press on into the fray without him.

As much as I tried to look cool, I was nervous as hell. I don't think that I've ever felt so anxious in my entire life, though the nerves were counterweighted with an irrepressible sense of excitement. As I plugged Steve's Stratocaster into his Marshall amplifier, the lifeless instrument suddenly crackled to life. My hands were shaking so fiercely, though, that I could barely get the quarter-inch cable into its jack on the base of the guitar.

Chunk reached over from his kit, arching carefully over his snare and hi-hat, and tapped me gently with a drumstick. "Are you sure that you're up for this?" he asked.

"No, I'm not," I admitted, my head shaking feebly. "But it's not like we have any other choice, right?"

He nodded cautiously, then readjusted himself on his drum throne. "Then you better fake it, Brick. Harness that anger and put it to good use, you know?"

I nodded back at Chunk, then shifted my posture to face Victor and Ethan. "Let's play loud and fast tonight," I commanded. "We overcompensate with speed and volume for whatever we're lacking in stage presence."

"Sounds like a plan, Brick," Ethan said. He gave me a thumbs up, his chewed-up fingernails peeking through a balled-up fist.

Victor briefly made eye contact with me before shaking his head and looking askance, diverting his attention to the velvety, crimson curtains that framed the stage.

I knew that it was *do or die*. Or maybe *do or you won't get paid*. In that moment, however, it felt like a life-or-death matter.

The evening's MC, some elder punk with a bald pate of scalp and more piercings than a cactus, strolled onstage and grabbed the mic stand that stood in the center spotlight.

"This is Call Field from Los Angeles," he announced into the mic. "Please give 'em warm Gilman greetings and show some love to our out-of-towners."

A small smattering of applause trickled forth from the audience.

Wow, I thought. *Tough crowd.*

As I stepped up to the microphone and stared out at the skeptical sea of faces, I knew that I was facing a potentially humiliating scenario: a horrible half-hour of embarrassment in front of an impossibly cool group of onlookers. I couldn't help but think back to Serena's *quinceañera* and my one brief moment fronting the band. That evening hadn't ended well for me. At all. I wondered if this show would be any different.

"We're… uh… Call Field," I mumbled into the microphone.

I swear that you could hear crickets chirping inside that cozy industrial venue. A middle-aged bearded fellow who stood fifty feet back from stage left coughed loudly into his fist. No one else said anything.

Yeah, I definitely wasn't ready for the frontman gig.

I turned back to face Chunk and cued him with a jerk of my chin. It was time. Chunk nodded at me and counted out four beats. Right on cue, I flipped around and slammed a power chord on Steve's guitar as I pressed my lips to the chain-link surface of the mic.

"*I wanna' be your time bomb...*" I howled into the microphone. The voice that shot forth from the speakers surprised me, echoing out fiercer and more confident than I expected.

Is that really me singing? I wondered to myself. The grit and depth of the vocals were beyond anything I had been able to conjure before.

But, yes, it *was* me.

As I glanced over at Ethan and Victor for a split second, their faces mirrored my disbelief, and I could just barely see a grin spreading across Ethan's lips. Without hesitation, the band rushed in behind me, Chunk's drums thumping faster than usual while Ethan and Victor thundered along with him.

"*I wanna' detonate in your arms...*" I shrieked, plunging forward into the abyss and giving myself up to the music. I closed my eyes and surrendered to the fierce, frenetic sounds of the band.

When you're performing, it's easy to just go through the motions, mechanically strumming a guitar or reciting lyrics from memory. On special occasions, though, you might feel something primordial and spiritual surging through you like a tsunami's current – washing over you like a baptismal wave as you channel an ethereal force into your loose limbs and your tightened vocal cords. You become a conduit for a graceful, galvanizing power, and you know that you are the physical host of something bigger, more majestic than your flesh. It's familiar, instinctive – like it's been inside you forever and is only now rushing to the surface of your skin and outward into the heavens.

It's almost like punk-rock *tai chi*. And I felt it that night with every cell in my sweaty body.

By the time that we got through the first chorus of "Time Bomb," we had already started to win over the crowd. I could see heads subtly bobbing on otherwise stoic masculine faces, teenage girls in the audience swaying their hips side-to-side, even an occasional spike-studded fist pumping into the air. The audience – while clearly cooler than I would *ever* be – appreciated what we were doing on that small stage. They recognized a quality in us that we might have doubted in ourselves: *talent*.

That night, we played harder, faster, rawer than ever before. Our songs – *my* songs – transformed into a whirlwind force of nature in that historic music venue. Our Gilman show was very much a litmus test for the band: did our minor-league team have the chops and the talent and the songs to make it in the big leagues?

The answer was clear. We *did*.

I stared out past the stage and started counting heads: there were dozens of people there. It wasn't the smallest crowd we had ever played, though it definitely paled in comparison to our handful of Warped Tour gigs. But the limited quantity of audience members didn't dampen the power of our performance. We were intensely focused, unwilling to back down from this potentially cataclysmic crucible – and we were winning over the skeptical crowd, one-by-one.

While we weren't our usual fierce fireball force without Steve at the helm, we were still incendiary, lighting the room aflame with our sheer will. We were screaming for the rafters and thumping on the floorboards, and we would not let fate or circumstance cage us.

After thirty turbocharged minutes of fearless, frenetic playing, we glistened with sweat under the luminescence of the halogen bulbs above us. The crowd seemed equally lubricated, their initial skepticism replaced with unrepentant enthusiasm.

"Thank you for listening, Gilman Street," I spoke into the mic. "We are Call Field from Ojai, California. And we'll be seeing you again."

I couldn't help myself: I grinned like an idiot, basking in the glistening glow of that glorious moment.

However, as I unplugged the Stratocaster's guitar cables and started wrapping them up into loose concentric circles, I glanced over to the side of the stage and saw Steve. His shaking figure rocked in place – haggard and pale, glaring from the wings.

He was not amused.

Chunk grunted as he lifted his kick drum from the floorboards, hoisting it into his arms and briskly walking offstage. "Nice of you to make it," Chunk scoffed as he passed Steve's quaking form. My cousin's face revealed a mixture of anger and absolution, like a bruised child watching a belligerent parent fall face-first into the cold, hard ground.

Ethan just shook his head as he hurried past Steve, his stiff electric guitar case and Marshall amplifier alternately swaying as he marched offstage. Victor followed in quick succession, shrugging as he carried his Fender Precision bass and MESA/Boogie amp head through the darkened wings.

Unable to hide my sense of vindication, I grinned like a Cheshire cat as I made my way across the stage. Steve didn't flinch as I walked past him.

"You better watch out," I murmured to him. "I'm gunning for your job."

I was only half-joking.

As we loaded all of our gear into the van, Mr. Buddy Holly Glasses sauntered out with a thick wad of cash in his hand. He walked straight up to us and passed me the folded-up dollar bills, pressing the money firmly into my hand.

"You sounded different than your demo," Mr. BHG told us, his eyebrows knitted together beneath the barrier of his horn-rimmed frames.

"How so?" Chunk asked, grinning and shooting me a sideways glance.

"Not bad, mind you," he clarified. "Just different. A bit more raw and organic than I expected from a polished major-label band." He put his hand up to his beard, scratching his graying facial hair thoughtfully. "You sound like the dude from Smashing Pumpkins singing with the Ramones. I dig it."

Though Steve stood outside the compact circle, his muscular frame shrinking smaller and smaller, he seemed to smolder in the cool air of the Berkeley night. His hands thrust deeply into the pockets of his leather jacket, he swayed almost imperceptibly, his resolve shaken like his feverish limbs.

Watching us onstage, Steve had sobered up quickly – literally *and* figuratively. For a brief second, he glimpsed an alternate reality, one in which Call Field existed without him. For that one anomalous evening, I had been singing the lyrics that *I* had written, strumming distorted guitar chords for the melodies that *I* had composed. For once, *I* held the helm of our band, steering our unsinkable ship as I captivated the audience underneath the burning glow of the centerstage spotlight.

Steve had been forcibly shaken from his comfortable complacency, unceremoniously unseated from his rock & roll throne. And now he had to consume a hefty serving of humble pie while his bandmates celebrated without him.

Undeterred by Steve's moping, we shot the breeze with Mr. Buddy Holly Glasses for a while, listening to him recount stories of his own tenure in a 1980s post-hardcore band.

"It was a pretty unforgettable experience," he told us, his eyes squinting nostalgically beneath his horn-rimmed glasses. "It's been years now, but I still remember how great it felt to be onstage on one of the good nights. The crowds, the beer, the women, the camaraderie…" He trailed off slowly, gazing off into the distance as he vainly tried to conjure memories of his youth. "There's absolutely nothing like it."

"So, what happened?" I asked him, shifting my weight on the pavement and looking up from my Converse-clad feet.

"Just like most bands out there," he explained, "it came down to egos. The singer couldn't stand the keyboardist. The lead guitarist was jealous of the singer. The bass player wasn't as invested as everyone else. And the drummer got most of the action. It was a recipe for self-destruction."

"Which one were you?" Victor asked, his hands embedded in the back pockets of his jeans.

He gave us an impish grin. "The drummer, obviously…"

We talked with Mr. Buddy Holly Glasses for at least an hour that night before we finally made the call to drive home. We briefly entertained the idea of renting a cheap, haggard hotel room in Berkeley or Oakland, but our night's paycheck (though not really the point of the show, mind you) didn't leave us with enough profit to afford that luxury. So, with our wallets slightly more padded than hours before, we gassed up Uncle Jeff's van and prepared to hit the road. Just as I was replacing the gas nozzle into its station, however, Steve approached me and stuck out his hand.

"Give me the car keys," he demanded.

I was caught off-guard, and I stuttered for a second before I could force myself to speak. "Look, Steve… You're in no condition to drive."

His eyes narrowed viciously. "I'm fine now," he said brusquely.

"Steve," I snarled, "a few hours ago, you were so loaded that you couldn't even stand up. I'm not going to let you get behind the wheel so that you can steer us into a ditch."

He started picking at the calluses on the palm of his right hand, jagged fingernail edges scratching away dead skin. "I'm the captain of this ship," he said. "I'm the one who belongs in the driver's seat. Always."

I started to panic. After so many years of this tense rivalry between us, I thought Steve and I might finally come to blows – right there, under the flickering fluorescent lights of an Oakland gas station.

Luckily for us, Chunk chimed in and prevented a nuclear showdown from obliterating Call Field in a fiery fate of mutually assured destruction.

"For God's sake, Steve," Chunk called from the front passenger seat. "Grow up!" He slapped the side of the door's exterior and continued on with his diatribe. "Brick is driving. And you just need to deal with it. Shut your trap and get your ass in the van."

"Yeah," Victor called out from the dark recesses of the backseat. "I'm tired. It doesn't matter who drives, as long as we get home in one piece."

Steve was practically boiling under the wavering lights of the gas station. He looked like he was about to unleash a stream of profanities, but Ethan's voice suddenly echoed out of the van.

"Damn it, Steve! Just let Brick drive!" he yelled. "I want to go home!"

"There you have it," I whispered with a self-righteous smirk. "Four against one. I guess the decision has been made for you."

Steve sizzled with anger, but I could see him deflating as he realized he was unequivocally outnumbered. Our fearless leader was no longer the unchallenged dictator of our little group. As I twirled the car keys in my right hand, I watched him turn his back to me and flip his collar up against the brisk night air.

"I'm still the captain of this ship," Steve reminded me as he climbed into the backseat. "And don't you forget it."

I saw his body shrink into the darkness of the van and noticed – maybe for the first time – just how small he was. Though he always seemed so intimidating with his flawless, muscular physique, he was almost a foot shorter than I was. I was taller, broader, and denser than Steve – maybe even stronger, beneath the extra layers of flesh that hung off my sagging frame. Ever since that first show at Serena's *quinceañera*, Steve had always been Call Field's undisputed leader. But I was starting to see cracks in his armor.

True, I was only in the driver's seat temporarily, and Steve was still the captain of our ship…

But maybe it was time for a mutiny.

As I drove us home that night, our headlights piercing through the thick fog of California's central coast, the other members of the band all slept in the upholstered seats of Uncle Jeff's van. With only the mysterious mist beyond the windshield to keep me company, I thought back to our final conversation with Mr. Buddy Holly Glasses at the end of the night.

For some inexplicable reason, I felt like our talk with Gilman's tattooed, bespectacled club manager had provided me with a brief glimpse into our future. Would one of us in Call Field end up running a punk venue in some distant city, hundreds of miles from home? Would we recount tales of our glory days to some up-and-coming hellions on the verge of success? Would our dark hair wither and turn gray? Would our vision betray us, forcing us to don ironic eyeglasses?

I glanced into the rearview mirror, briefly glimpsing the sleeping faces of my bandmates. Victor's head was angled against the chilled glass of the window, Ethan had buried himself into a couple of blanched pillows, and Chunk was snoring in the front passenger seat. Even Steve was out cold – no doubt recovering from whatever fever-inducing substance he had consumed the afternoon before. In sharp contrast, I was gripping the steering wheel tightly, unwilling to let the tantalizing comfort of sleep distract me from the ceaseless road ahead. I nursed an oversized gas station jug of Dr. Pepper, cranking the car stereo with Paul Westerberg and the Replacements to keep me awake during the long drive home. As I steered us safely into the unknown darkness of the night, I felt a shudder of understanding: I might have been the one driving the van, but the rest of the boys were united in their slumber. I, on the other hand, was a solitary figure, sleepless and focused on the dim asphalt ahead of us.

Even in my hour of triumph, I was very much alone.

The miles ticked by on the odometer, the numbers creeping steadily higher as the gas gauge lazily sunk lower. We made it through San Jose into the long stretch of central California farmland that bridges northern and southern California, fields stretching out to the horizon or hugged by curved mountains that slumbered unmoving in the night. It was repetitive and dull, seemingly unchanging as I wove the van through indistinct roads and plowed forward into the blanket of night.

Five hours and countless cities later, I pulled the van off the freeway somewhere in San Luis Obispo, the vehicle lurching like a wounded animal. I was compelled to stay in the slow lane the whole duration of the 101, our poor borrowed automobile struggling to simply hover around 65 miles per hour. We were weighed down by all the baggage that we carried.

When the van curled onto the freeway off-ramp like a kitten stretching after a nap, the sun started to breach the mountains that obscured the horizon. As dark as the night had been, with all its endless miles of loneliness and isolation, the irrepressible luminescence of the sunrise ascended into the heavens. Shafts of light pierced the firmament, battling against the interminable darkness that had seemed inescapable only hours before.

A new day was dawning. Literally.

The change in velocity (and the inevitable inertia that followed) jerked the boys out of their slumbering states. Beside me, Chunk rubbed his hands across his face like a fevered soldier. In the rearview mirror, I could see Steve yawning, his mouth arching open as if to devour the entire world. Next to him, Victor gazed up with unfocused eyes, returning to the dry reality of the unsleeping. Only Ethan remained dozing, his arms curled under him like thin, unstuffed pillows.

"Why are we getting off the freeway?" Steve asked, wiping his eyes with the palms of his hands.

"We're just stopping for gas," I murmured back to him. "It'll only take a moment."

I drove the van to the first gas station off the Monterey Street exit of San Luis Obispo. As I twisted the key counterclockwise, letting the engine exhale and sigh, I arched my back and straightened my cramping legs.

"I gotta' take a piss," Steve informed us, sliding open the van's door and jettisoning himself from the vehicle.

Ethan and Victor followed him out, both of them stumbling on the loose gravel that littered the ground. Chunk, on the other hand, threw open the passenger seat door, walked around to the back of the van, and perched himself on the thick lip of the bumper. He listlessly kicked his legs in front of him and stretched his stiff shoulders.

As I reached for the gas pump and pulled the nozzle off its throne, I glanced up at the mountains that sprawled out westward, those large barricades that kept us estranged from the vibrant, unpredictable ocean. Swiping my credit card in the station's reader, I felt drawn back to the mountains and the luminous fingers of daylight that strained upwards into the sky.

The morning was cold, and every breath that I surrendered floated in a smoky specter in front of me. Something about the brisk morning and the encroaching light (coupled with the bizarre experience of the previous night's show) resonated deeply within my chest. I could feel myself changing, like the gears of a clock twisting and propelling its hands forward.

"Hey, Chunk," I called out.

"Yeah," he mumbled back, his quiet voice barely audible above the burbling gas pump. "What?"

I pointed off in the direction of the hilled horizon, just above the crest of the green mountains that towered over us.

"You see that?" I asked him.

"See what?" he murmured sleepily.

"That slant of light," I said, my finger arched towards the incorporeal incandescence that extended nimbly heavenwards.

"What about it?" Chunk mumbled.

A thought sprung from my subconscious, fully formed like Athena emerging from the head of Zeus. From deep within the recesses of my memory, I recalled a long-ago afternoon in my dad's AP English classroom – an image of my father flanking the blackboard with a battered collection of Emily Dickinson's poetry in his hand. It had only been a few years, mind you, but I had almost forgotten about that lesson – the one in which we analyzed the Bard of Amherst's poem, "There's a certain Slant of light." The synapses firing in my brain brought me back to that moment in time and my father standing tall in front of his captivated students.

"Do you remember that one Emily Dickinson poem we read in my dad's English class?" I asked him. "The one about the *'slant of light'*...?"

Chunk paused for a minute, squinting as he tried to recall that long-forgotten lesson. "Vaguely," he answered, his voice uncertain.

"The light..." I began to say, before my voice trailed off. Dickinson's poem was about a darkness of the soul, an overwhelming weight that even a simple strand of light can catalyze in the mind of those burdened by the *"seal Despair."* I had been there so many times before, it was like Dickinson was speaking directly to me, her words gliding from the graveyard across countless decades into the future.

But this moment felt different. For as long as I could remember, I had always focused on the second half of the phrase *"Heavenly hurt,"* dwelling in the piercing sting of depression that had plagued me for so many years. My adolescence might have had patches of heaven, but too much of it felt like purgatory to me.

This particular morning, though, didn't feel like an *"imperial affliction."* It felt like something else, like a rebel victory against the dark forces of the soul. It was different – an inversion of Dickinson's despair.

"It's a different slant of light," I muttered.

I was so caught up in the moment that I almost didn't hear the crunching gravel of footsteps that echoed behind us.

"What's that?" Steve asked, his gruff voice indelicately cutting into the conversation.

I glanced back at him nonchalantly, my eyes flicking first to him, then trailing over to Ethan and Victor. All three of them looked groggy, bundled up against the chilly spring morning, their hands wrapped around steaming styrofoam cups of coffee.

"That's what we're going to name the album," I told them. "We're going to call it *A Different Slant of Light.*"

Chunk cocked his head to the side and ran his tongue along his top teeth, as if tasting the words for himself. "I like it," he said, his eyes and smile widening broadly.

"I don't remember us voting on that," Steve groused from behind me.

"We don't need to vote on it," I laughed. "I wrote the songs, so I can name the album." I kept my gaze fixed on the distance and watched the sun breach the mountains, reliving the throes of its daily birth.

I didn't bother turning around, but I can venture a guess that Steve's face probably reflected the anger and dismay that I heard in his venomous voice. But I didn't care.

I had found a different slant of light.

There's an important epilogue to this story, something I need to share with you before I can move on with my tale. It seemed like a trivial matter at the time – something extraneous and inconsequential – but it ended up becoming a Rubicon for Call Field in just a few short months: the band constitution.

When we got back home from our Gilman show, the dynamics in Call Field had shifted dramatically. I'd spent years living in Steve's shadow, losing the girl and the band and even my sense of self-worth to our seemingly fearless lead singer. During that time, I had (with few exceptions) felt like I was perpetually deferring to the untouchable Steve Öken. He had become the voice of Call Field, the face of the band – the center of the universe with an inescapable gravitational pull. But, all the while, a centrifugal force had been building between us.

I no longer felt tethered to Steve – and, as the Gilman show proved to us, the success of the band no longer rested solely on his showman's shoulders. If, in some strange cosmic accident, Steve spontaneously combusted or was abducted by aliens, Call Field could soldier on without him. We were a band of five now – me, Steve, Chunk, Ethan, and Victor – and if one of us left, the rest could continue writing songs, recording albums, and playing shows.

No one was safe. Not even our lead singer.

Nor, as I came to realize soon enough, was the band's songwriter.

Steve showed up at the next practice with a sheepish apology and a proposition. When he arrived that day, his whole frame seemed to slouch inward, as if his body were folding in on itself. Once again, he thrust his hands deeply into the pockets of his leather jacket, his eyes focused abashedly on his scuffed-up Chuck Taylors.

"I messed up," he announced very earnestly, carefully drawing a sharp breath as he spoke to us. "I was stupid and irresponsible and I don't have an excuse for my behavior."

"You're damn right, it was stupid," Chunk interrupted. "Do you realize how badly things could have gone at that show? Without a *lead singer*? At *Gilman*, of all places?" Chunk was seething, his teeth bared as he belittled Steve. "You're just lucky that Brick stepped up to the plate. Without Brick, we would have been screwed."

As one might expect, I felt pretty smug. Perhaps I should have felt some sympathy, a little tenderness for a friend who had slipped up. Alas, in my hubris, I enjoyed every single moment of this disparagement. I gave the group a smug grin, knowing that I – the underestimated underdog – had finally had my day.

It. Felt. So. Good.

Steve just listened quietly as Chunk hurled vitriolic words in his direction. Our lead singer nodded mutely, taking the blows like a human punching bag, never rising up to challenge us. It was out of character for him to act so modestly, but I attributed it to the healthy serving of humble pie he'd been forced to eat.

Victor didn't say anything. I could only assume that, as the newcomer in the band, he was hesitant to assert himself as aggressively as the rest of us.

When Ethan finally chimed in, his words were carefully measured and premeditated. His statement was a simple one, straight and to the point. "It was a dumb move," he mumbled. "And it can't happen again." His eyes never lifted from the stained carpet below his feet.

Steve let the smallest semblance of a smile slip from his chapped lips. "I'm glad you're bringing that up, Ethan," he said, his posture straightening and his chest inflating. "Because I've got something that I want to show you guys." This exchange between Ethan and Steve seemed awkwardly forced – almost as if it had been rehearsed behind the backs of everyone else.

Steve reached into the back pocket of his tattered jeans and pulled out a few pieces of paper, newly printed and crisply folded in half. After taking a few steps over to the nearest wall, he slapped the papers against the chipping paint. His lips continued to curl mischievously as he unfolded the pages, flattening them and smoothing out the wrinkles that had accumulated along the bundle's spine.

"What's this?" I asked, following Steve towards the wall of the garage.

"It's a band constitution," he announced, not bothering to turn around and face me. "To guarantee that no one ever screws up again."

Ethan, Chunk, Victor, and I crowded around Steve in a semicircle. As he held the document in place, I could see the tips of his fingers shaking slightly. I attributed his trembling hands to his nervousness, to his shame for screwing up so badly in Berkeley.

That's surprising, I thought to myself. *I don't think I've seen Steve this shaken in years. Not since he almost choked at that Ventura Theater show.*

I shook myself free from my thoughts and squinted at the words printed on the pages in front of me. My vision was starting to deteriorate by that time, but I hadn't taken the plunge into wearing glasses yet. I thought I could see fine.

I didn't know how clouded my vision actually was.

Call Field Constitution, the first paper said, each word of the title bolded dramatically. It was an intimidating legal-looking form with itemized articles and numbered statements. I took a cursory glance at each of the bulleted paragraphs and tried to wrap my mind around some of the convoluted clauses in front of me.

"My dad's lawyer helped me draft it," Steve casually said. "He says it's pretty ironclad. Just like my dad's divorce papers." He forced out a strained laugh, like a high school actor playing the part of a bitter, jilted lover.

It didn't really make sense to me why Steve would go through all this trouble just to penalize himself. *Did he really doubt his own self-control that much?* I wondered. *That's a lot of work just to corner himself with a contract...*

"What's this part here?" Victor asked, pointing to Article Thirteen of the document.

"Ah," Steve sighed contentedly. "This is the most important part of the constitution. It says that if I ever do anything like that again, if I ever miss a show – technically, if *any of us* misses a show for *any reason at all* – then that member of the band will be expelled from the partnership. That person will have no legal rights to the band's name or future business decisions. Basically, if I screw up again – or if *any of us* screws up – then that person is out of the band. Forever."

In my arrogance and my hubris, I saw this as a prime opportunity to take back what I emphatically saw as mine. I had no doubt that Steve would slip up again, just like he had done at our Gilman show. Though it obviously crossed my mind how bizarre it was for Steve to set his own mousetrap, I was brash enough to think that this contract was exactly what I needed to regain control of my band.

I've let Steve run the show for too long, I thought to myself. *Now it's time to corner him. He either gets his act together or we kick him out. It's a win-win, right?*

I was foolish back then.

So foolish.

Even thinking about it today, two decades later, I want to tell the twenty-year-old version of me to throw down the pen and hire a lawyer. I want to shake that arrogant kid by his shoulders and tell him to wise up. I want to slap him across the face and warn him about what would happen only a few months later.

Unfortunately, I let my pride get the best of me. I guess my vision was clouded in more ways than one.

Hindsight is 20/20, as they say.

And I seriously needed a pair of glasses.

To be fair, all of us *did* read through every single sentence in that contract. There were sections about professionalism, monetary penalties for tardiness, and language forbidding the consumption of intoxicating substances (amongst other seemingly trivial minutiae). As far as I could see, most of the clauses demanded professional conduct – which wouldn't be a problem for me. I certainly wouldn't be imbibing alcohol or ingesting anything intoxicating before a show; being onstage was too important, too holy, for me to desecrate. In my clouded eyes, Steve was the only one whose erratic behavior might land him in hot water.

As I looked around the group, I saw nodding heads and quizzical expressions. We all seemed to be weighing the consequences of signing any kind of legal document, but nothing in the contract seemed applicable to me – or Chunk or Victor or Ethan, for that matter. Each of us exchanged furtive glances, but no one raised any objections.

Victor was the first to sign. With a shrug of his broad shoulders, he walked over to the case of his bass guitar, popped it open, and pulled out a black ballpoint pen. Then, neglecting to make eye contact with anyone else, he marched over to the contract, flipped to the last page, and scrawled his signature on a preprinted space.

Ethan was next. As Victor handed him the ballpoint pen, our lead guitarist's fingers twitched nervously and he took a deep breath. Ethan stole one last look at Steve, grimaced, and then placed his hand firmly on the contract. Without looking up, he slowly signed his name, sluggishly looping the letters in his autograph. When he was done, he handed the pen to Chunk.

Chunk scrunched up the right side of his face, his cheek folding in on itself. He tapped the pen on the wall rhythmically, somewhere between a waltz and a shuffle. Unlike Victor and Ethan, who had been so quick to put their signatures on paper, Chunk seemed reticent – as if he was weighing pivotal outcomes in the palms of his hands.

"We *all* need to sign it?" Chunk asked, his fingers casually tapping the wall.

"Yup," Steve said. "Unless we all put our names on it, it won't keep us accountable. It's hard to enforce anything, unless we all agree to it in writing."

For a split second, I thought Chunk might not sign the contract. The pen retreated away from the paper, and he started to turn towards me. Thinking better of it, though, Chunk stopped, turned back to the wall, and started to write his name.

"When we're all done, I'll have this notarized," Steve informed us, his eyes carefully contemplating Chunk's hands as the pen moved asymmetrically across the page. "You know, to make it official."

Because I never went to law school, I *still* don't know too much about legal documents – and I knew even less when I was a twenty-year-old college student. While I should have seen some fiercely flashing red flags, I was simply blinded by my arrogance. I wanted to hold Steve accountable for his actions, and this seemed like the safest way to do that.

I studied the document, squinting intensely as I tried to decipher the legalese on the pages. All the while, my mind kept playing out fantasy scenarios in which Steve was surreptitiously booted from the band and I stepped in as frontman. I envisioned myself as a counterpart to Joan Jett, when she took over the lead vocals for the Runaways once Cherie Currie quit the band. After the Gilman show, it didn't seem so far-fetched to me anymore. After all, I was the songwriter for Call Field. And the Gilman show proved to everyone that I could sufficiently serve as a lead singer.

What's the worst that could happen? I asked myself.

Steve seemed to sense my hesitation. "Are you having doubts?" he asked, left eyebrow raised haughtily.

"So, just to clarify," I asked, my eyes thinning into slits, "this is a *legally binding* contract? It's something that will hold up in court?"

"That's right," Steve confirmed. "Like I said, my dad's lawyer is the one who helped me put it all together. He told me he's confident that it will *serve its purpose*." With those last few words, he gave me an expression that can only be described as a cross between a sneer and a grin – disdain and glee, wrestling in tandem.

Some small part of me must have felt a sense of uncertainty or suspicion, right? I wasn't *that* foolish, was I?

"Of course, if you don't feel *comfortable* with it," Steve added nonchalantly, "you don't have to sign the contract. That's fine." He held the ballpoint pen in his hand, waving it back and forth like a metronome. His smug expression was absolutely infuriating, as if he was challenging me to a game of chicken without uttering a single word.

And I took his bait.

Without any further discussion, I snagged the pen from Steve's hand, whipped through the sheets of the document, and hastily scrawled my signature on the last page.

Game. Set. Match.

Without knowing it, I had signed my own death warrant.

CHAPTER FIFTEEN
"Surf's Up"

This is the point in the story when things start to fall apart – when the gears start to jam and the paint starts to chip. It began slowly, building momentum like a terrible virus, and kept deteriorating until my whole life broke apart in one terrible night.

At the time, though, I was ignorant to the forces metastasizing around me. There were simply too many distractions – love, school, homework, recording, publicity – for me to recognize the shadows creeping up behind me.

In the months leading up to the album's release, Lowercase Records went to work on the post-production elements of *A Different Slant of Light*. There were photoshoots and music videos and interviews and every kind of publicity that you can possibly imagine. When I wasn't writing research papers or crafting literary analysis essays for my UCLA classes, I was practicing songs and reviewing proofs and trying to spend time with Lani. It was absolutely exhausting.

In the midst of all this, I didn't go home to see my parents for a few months. The record label rented us a practice space in the basement of their headquarters, so the boys ended up resettling in Los Angeles. As a result, there was a paradigm shift: we all felt ourselves migrating away from our childhood homes in Ojai. Ethan and Steve found a seaside bungalow in Malibu and relocated their lives to Los Angeles County. Victor and I were still rooming together, renting a ramshackle apartment in the general vicinity of Westwood, so that we weren't too far removed from school or the Lowercase Records building in Santa Monica. Chunk even moved in with us for a while, when he got tired of commuting all the way from UCSB.

Of course, I didn't actually spend much time in our shared rental: Lani occupied most of my days and nights, so I pretty much lived at her apartment – and only came back to my own place to sleep each night.

I feel incredibly guilty about it now, but I didn't call my mom and dad much during this time. After a few semesters, it's pretty common for college students to pull away from their parents and spread nascent wings of independence; after all, with so many distractions (academic and otherwise), it's easy to forget the foundations of your childhood. I won't make excuses for my behavior, mind you. I just have to admit that my family didn't enter my preoccupied mind. I was consumed by school and music and young love, so I simply forgot where I came from.

When I did remember to call (or when my mom managed to catch me on the telephone between my multitudinous obligations), I always felt distracted – like I had more pressing business than casually gabbing with my parents. Of course, as my mom relayed to me week after week, my dad seemed to be battling a never-ending succession of sicknesses. With almost every call, Mom relayed stories of vomiting and fatigue and flu-like symptoms. Yet, despite perpetually staving off some illness or another, my father refused to see a doctor.

"Maybe Dad should go to urgent care," I suggested. "Hasn't this been going on for a long time now…?" My voice trailed off, the implications becoming thinner than wisps in the wind. I was probably checking my watch, afraid of being late for class or band practice or a date with Lani.

"You know your father," my mother sighed, resigned to accept her husband's stubbornness.

I wish I would have said something, that I would have pushed harder. But I was young and dumb and distracted. Realistically, it wouldn't have made much difference, anyway: my father was so thickheaded back then that it was almost impossible to coerce him into something he didn't want to do.

I'm pretty sure I inherited that stubbornness from him.

As January folded into February and March angled into April, we found ourselves geeking out over all the typical rock and roll rites of passage. We did a photoshoot for the album cover on a beach in Malibu, recorded scenes for a music video on the Santa Monica Pier, and started making the rounds with press and promotion. There were radio station visits and newspaper interviews and magazine shoots – and we thoroughly enjoyed the thrill of each new experience. Of course, the novelty eventually settled into routines and redundancy; just like anything else in life, repeating an adventure over and over tends to ruin the relevancy and freshness of the façade.

Despite the fact that we felt like real live rock stars, some ominous undercurrents began subtly shifting beneath the tame waters of our lives. We had always considered ourselves a democracy, a functioning organism with four (later five) interconnected limbs. The record company, however, took a different stance. In their eyes, we were simply an inorganic product – a commodity to be molded and sold for the biggest financial gains. As such, they took some infuriating liberties with the finishing touches of the album.

Take the cover art, for instance. When we did our photoshoot in Malibu, I expected that Lowercase Records would use some Beach Boys-inspired shots of the full band wading into the ocean or staring off towards the sunset or something equally egalitarian. When we received the final album cover mock-ups, though, they looked like this:

Notice anything amiss with the album cover? Oh, right…

IT WAS A SHOT OF STEVE.

ALL. BY. HIMSELF.

We had spent years working as a group, envisioning ourselves as an actual collection of human beings – a *band*, if you will – but the album art told a different story. Ethan, Chunk, Victor, and I were completely cropped out of the cover. From all outward appearances, it looked like Steve was a solo artist utilizing the faux front of a group name, like Bright Eyes or Bon Iver or Dashboard Confessional or Iron & Wine. Steve's visage stared forth from the cover like a male model on a magazine cover, the luminescent sunset behind him framing his form like a sepia-toned halo.

Needless to say, I was upset about it. A little bit. Or, maybe, *a lot*.

I hated it.

Unfortunately, when we confronted Lowercase Records, their stock answer boiled down to one thing: sales. The marketing executive at the label, a rigid German gentleman named Günter Wüste, simply folded his hands together in a pyramid and stared at us over the top of his flawless Cartier glasses. He was an impeccably dressed man, always clad in a crisp black suit and a red necktie, and he generally had no patience for the underdressed artists on the Lowercase roster.

"You simply don't have *the look*," he explained to us, the pedantic throes of his voice seeping impatiently across his oak desk. In quick succession, he pointed his stiff finger accusatorially at me, Ethan, and Chunk, offering his impressions. "You're too fat, you're too thin, and you look like an unkempt lumberjack," he told us. When he settled on Victor, he paused for a moment and considered his impending critique. "You *almost* have the look, but you're too… ethnic," he concluded.

However, when Günter's finger pointed at Steve, who was wearing a tight-fitting t-shirt and Gucci jeans, his position softened. "Now, *this*," he intoned with relief, "is what a rock star looks like. This boy's face was made for album covers and his body was made for magazine spreads. The rest of you… well, the rest of you look better in the background. Blurry and out of focus."

All of us – except Steve, of course – burned bright red with anger or embarrassment (or a vacillating combination of the two). I opened my mouth, ready to launch into a tirade, when Victor forcefully grabbed my arm and quickly jerked me aside.

"*Let it go*," he quietly hissed at me. "You're just going to shoot yourself in the foot."

I was livid, but I adhered to Victor's advice. I swung around towards the door and stomped out.

It only got worse from there.

When we saw the first cut of the music video for "Incomplete," it was basically *The Steve Öken Show*: there were shots of him flirting with a redheaded model, cuts of him crooning into a vintage microphone, and footage of him frolicking on the sunset-drenched beach. Anyone watching the music video would naturally assume that this was Steve's band playing Steve's songs for admiring crowds of Steve's fans. The rest of us were relegated to background shots and B-roll footage.

It's hard for me to describe how frustrated I was without sounding like a self-absorbed diva. Just as I'd felt the crushing weight of jealousy years ago during Serena's *quinceañera*, I once again felt like creations that were mine – *my* band, *my* songs, *my* album – were being stolen away from me.

While I expected every other member of the band to share my righteous indignation, it turned out that Chunk was the only one who felt the same way. Ethan and Victor, while nonplussed, generally accepted the label's response and were willing to look past the Steve-centered focus. When I made the mistake of venting my frustrations to the two of them during a quick In-N-Out lunch trip one day, I found myself suddenly forced into a defensive position.

"Why do you care who's on the album cover?" Ethan asked me, obviously irritated by my complaints. "It's *your* music that we're playing. It's *your* song that got chosen for the single and the video. Hell, it's basically just *your album* with the rest of us making guest appearances." He scoffed and stormed off, leaving his trash scattered all over the table. As he shoved his way through the glass doors of the fast food franchise, he refused to turn back and face us.

What's going on? I remember asking myself. *Why is Ethan mad at ME? Shouldn't all of his anger be directed at Steve?*

Victor, still navigating uncertain waters as the rookie in the band, seemed torn. As he watched Ethan stomping off, he just shook his head and averted his eyes. "You're playing a dangerous game, Brick," he warned me. "This band is on the verge of a nuclear standoff, and I don't think you'll like the results if this turns into the Cuban Missile Crisis." He glanced up at me for the briefest of moments, some undetectable emotion threaded through his eyes, and sighed. Without saying another word, he got up from the table and followed Ethan outside.

Okay, so *maybe* I could accept that the frontman of our band was getting all of the attention. *Maybe* I could deal with the fact that his face was the only one gracing our album cover. *Maybe* I could get over my limited role in our music video. That was all just ego and vanity. It wouldn't have been impossible for me to gracefully step back from the spotlight and let our fearless leader hog all of the attention. Again.

At least we have control over the music, I assumed. *They can't take that away from me.*

Boy, was I wrong.

During our tracking sessions, I had been thrilled with the band's performances. Under Storf's mentorship, Call Field sounded tighter than ever before. Jimmy knew all the clever studio tricks that helped flesh out our recordings – the stacking of harmony vocals, the subtle placement of keyboards, the extra tambourine and glockenspiel flourishes that bolstered the bare bones of our punk-rock songs. After endless hours in the studio building glamorous castles of sound, we had constructed something impressive: the recordings were pure and raw and harmonious and aggressive – all at the same time.

This is the album that Call Field is destined to make, I thought to myself. *Intelligent punk rock for the twenty-first century.*

There was just one small problem: Lowercase Records didn't feel the same way.

When we got our mixes back from the label, the songs sounded castrated. Or, if not castrated, then at least circumcised – surgically altered without consent. The loud punk guitars were buried in the mixes, which leaned towards clean vocals and cleaner drums. All the anthemic energy and rebellious spirit had been drained from these tunes. My creations, which I expected to become powerful, monstrous, Frankenstein-like beasts, sounded more like the Munsters – like mundane caricatures manufactured for primetime television. The melodies and the lyrics were still intact, obviously, but I felt like someone had turned my edgy Warhol sound paintings into innocuous Hallmark cards.

We protested, of course. Even Steve, with whom I had been feuding for months, joined me against the head honchos at the label. We were like the Justice League of Rock and Roll, facing off against the most boring team of supervillains ever: *The Suits*.

All of us, individually, had listened to the mixes over and over – and we all felt like the balance of the recordings didn't sound anything like *Call Field*. Or *Caulfield*. Or even the *Bookhouse Boys*, for that matter. We scheduled a meeting with the label's top brass, marched into the Lowercase headquarters ready for warfare, and prepared to stand as a united front against those old geezers who couldn't appreciate the musical masterpiece we'd made.

It didn't go very well.

"Lowercase Records owns these recordings," good ol' Günter Wüste coldly reminded us after we'd pleaded our case. "If you don't want to follow our directives, then you can walk away from your contract. But you'll never be able to release this album, and your songs will never see the light of day."

As upset and infuriated as we were, they had us cornered.

You hear stories all the time about the friction between bands and their labels – heck, even the almighty *Pet Sounds* was met with skepticism from Capitol Records – but to actually *live* through that yourself? It isn't a matter of coming to a business arrangement that benefits both parties; it's basically handing over your child and watching another parent dress the kid in ridiculous clothing. Sure, it's still your creation – but it's like your offspring is sent off into public wearing neon green pants and polka dot suspenders. Your child is still alive, but reduced to a caricature of itself.

In the eyes of Lowercase Records, we were a pop-rock band, not edgy alternative rockers with punk-rock roots. After all, this was the era of Faith Hill and Destiny's Child and Matchbox 20 and Creed. Heck, even blink-182 had polished things up for *Enema of the State*. As much as we might have considered ourselves heirs to the legacy of the Ramones and Social Distortion, Lowercase Records wanted us to produce the kind of palatable pop music that would be safe for teeny-boppers and soccer moms.

I'm not going to lie: it felt a little like selling your soul to the devil.

While we stewed on this for weeks on end, our stomachs and souls violently churning with frustration, we found ourselves settling into a state of begrudging acceptance – some of us more quickly than others. Unsurprisingly, Steve was the first to cave.

"In the end," he argued, "it's still our music. It's my voice and Victor's bass and Ethan's guitar and Chunk's drums and Brick's… *whatever it is* that Brick played on this album." The disdain in his voice made me want to punch him in his disgustingly perfect face. Apparently, his anger towards the label had been channeled back against me – like a bitter boomerang of resentment.

That didn't take long, I thought to myself.

It was clear that Call Field was dividing into camps: Chunk and I on one side, Steve on the other, and the remaining band members caught in the middle. All of us could feel the invisible tug-of-war for loyalties, the battle for the future of the band. We seemed to be nearing an inevitable impasse, and the unavoidable showdown was only exacerbated by the label molding Call Field into the sellable product that they envisioned – our own dreams and desires, be damned.

It was actually Storf who managed to talk us down from the ledge (at least temporarily). As things got uglier and uglier with the label, he took the initiative to call a band meeting under the auspices of buying us lunch. One particularly muggy Saturday afternoon in early April, as the California sunshine seemed determined to melt us all, we met Storf at a Malibu seafood restaurant just up the road from Pepperdine University. The six of us – every member of Call Field and Storf – piled onto the benches adjacent to the restaurant and fanned ourselves with plastic menus.

"Here's the deal, guys," Storf explained. "In this industry, ya' have to compromise in order to gain enough power to exert artistic control. It's a bit of a paradox. Ya' start out in full control of yer' music, and then ya' get signed to a label. Of course, the label tries to rip away that control, and ya' have to suck it up…"

"That doesn't sound like compromise to me," I butted in. "It sounds like prostituting yourself for a paycheck."

"Will ya' let me finish, kid?" he shot back with an uncharacteristically impatient scowl.

I was stunned.

Storf scanned the faces around the table, his own distaste mirrored by Ethan and Victor. And Steve, of course. Chunk, at least, seemed to be on my side, though his stoic expression was a bit hard to read.

"As I was sayin' before," Storf continued, undeterred, "ya' play the game by the label's rules for a little while, ya' make some good cash, and ya' establish ya'self as artists wit' good heads. After that, once ya' done and made Lowercase a pretty penny or two, then ya' can flex ya' muscles. But it's only once ya' *establish* ya'self that ya' can fight these kinda' battles with a record label."

"So, if I'm hearing you right," Steve interjected, "we do what they say until we prove ourselves, and *then* we get to do what *we* want?" His eyes shot coldly over in my direction, waiting for confirmation from our musical mentor.

"Exactly," Storf said with a sigh. "I'm glad ya' been payin' attention, kids." He reached down into his basket of battered victuals and picked up an oblong mass of fried food. With a gratified grin on his face, he dipped the fried lump into tartar sauce and took a huge bite.

"What are you eating?" Victor asked, slightly repulsed.

"Fried oysters," Storf said. Except it sounded more like "*Freud oi-stuhs.*"

Right then, I had a weird moment of déjà vu. Storf's lunchtime discussion triggered a memory of *another* father figure talking about "oysters and pearls" in an old café. Suddenly, I had a vision of my dad counseling me during a particularly dark period of my teenage years, talking me through a personal crisis over a cup of coffee. Though separated by half a decade, I was instantly drawn back to that heart-to-heart years before, when my father had consoled me at Ventura's Café Voltaire.

I need to call my father, I thought to myself as I blinked through the hazy fog of memory. *I should see how he's doing.*

But I didn't have time to dwell in the past when the future was at stake. I snapped myself out of my daydream and turned back to the conversation with Storf.

"So, what do you recommend that we do?" I asked, exasperation saturating my voice. "How do we move forward from here and make some kind of career out of this without compromising ourselves?"

"I'm glad ya' asked, kid," Storf smiled back at me. "This is what ya' need to do…"

Storf was pretty adamant about the fact that we just had to "suck it up and make the most of it," to use his expression. As he bluntly explained to us, this was an opportunity that very few people ever have: releasing an album on a major label could open some big doors for us – but only if we played along with the label's demands. Though he wasn't exactly thrilled about the album's neutered final mixes, he also reminded us that this was a *business.* The music industry is one of those rare environments in which art and commerce do battle, and the collateral damage is that artists are frequently forced to – and here's the word again – *compromise.*

"It ain't pretty," he admitted with a sigh, "but it's the only way to make a career outta' writin' and recordin' music."

I shouldn't have been surprised by Storf's candid perspective. During preproduction for the album, he had some pretty cutting commentary about *everything* – from Steve's mediocre guitar playing to clichéd word choices in the lyrics to the importance of showing up on time to recording sessions. He was (first and foremost) a pragmatist, someone who knew the ugly truths about the music industry. To borrow a phrase from Lin-Manuel Miranda's *Hamilton*, Storf had spent enough time in "The Room Where It Happens" – and he knew intimately "how the sausage gets made" with record labels.

Objectively, I understood that Storf was right. But I couldn't shake the nagging feeling that we – Call Field – were "selling out." We were compromising our art and our vision for the sake of a paycheck and widespread media exposure.

But was this deal with the devil worth it?

Looking around at the conflicted faces of my bandmates, I had to recognize that the compromise *was* worth it… at least to them. Steve, Ethan, and Victor all nodded compliantly, but even they seemed wary of what the future might portend. Only Chunk showed any inkling of doubt: as I briefly met his eyes, I sensed a mutual disbelief emanating from across the table. Quickly, though, he looked away, diverting his attention to the subtle battering of waves just across the thin lanes of the PCH.

In the end, it was heartbreakingly clear: we felt like we had no choice but to concede to the label's demands.

When we wrapped up our meal, collecting our soiled dishes and disheveled napkins, the boys and I shook hands with our producer-turned-mentor and started to walk off towards our respective vehicles. As I turned to go, however, Storf put his hand on my shoulder and pulled me aside.

"Ya' got a minute?" he asked quietly, out of earshot of the guys.

"Sure," I answered hesitantly. "What's up?"

Storf's rail-thin frame closed in, almost conspiratorially. The deepening creases on his forehead, on the other hand, betrayed a sense of concern that caused me to automatically tense up.

"I had a great time working with ya' in the studio, kid," he told me. "Ya' got some great intuition with songwriting, ya' got chops on a buncha' instruments, and ya' got a great work ethic."

"Thanks," I said, my voice muted and uncertain.

"But…" he started to say, his voice trailing off.

"But *what*…?"

Storf gave me a look of tentative disapproval and reached into the folds of his suede jacket for a packet of cigarettes. He pulled out the box, tapping it delicately like a tambourine, and turned towards the horizon. When he angled back to face me, a blanched cigarette protruding from his cracked lips, he sighed deeply and shrugged his shoulders.

"I think ya' might be settin' ya'self up for a fall, kid," he mumbled gently. He snapped open his lighter, lit the tip of his cigarette, and inhaled.

"What do you mean?"

"Well, kid…" he began sympathetically, deepening the lines of worry in his creased brow. "Ya' got some problems in tha' land a' Call Field. And I don't think ya' can maintain this trajectory wit'out the band implodin' or fallin' apart." He took another drag off his cigarette and exhaled in the direction of the shimmering ocean waves.

I didn't know how to respond. The coastal breeze suddenly kicked hard against us, and I felt a chill rising from my naked wrists up to my neck. I wrapped my arms around my chest to keep warm, trying to find some tentative comfort in the cold.

"Duly noted," I said, puckering my lips intently against my chittering teeth. "Any advice that you can give me?"

Storf studied his cigarette.

"Ya' know, kid, I been in this business a long time. Longer than most a' the suits back at yer' label." Storf flicked the end of his cigarette, little flakes of ash fluttering delicately off the burning tip. "I seen bands come an' go. I seen trends fade in an' out. It ain't a pretty sight when a great band wit' great songs and great chops self-destructs on the periphery of success." He tapped me gently on my shoulder and then gestured skyward. "An' right now, I think ya' might be flyin' too close to the sun, kid. Those wings made of wax won't last if ya' can't keep 'em attached to ya' shoulder blades."

My head dropped in shame, like a schoolboy scolded by the principal for a classroom infraction. I was embarrassed – but also angry and insolent. Part of me wanted to keep my head low and just play it safe. Another part of me, however, felt like a boxer rearing up for a fight.

"Thanks for the advice, Jimmy," I said as I shook his hand in the frigid coastal air. "I'll do my best to keep those wax wings from melting away."

I turned towards my car and marched off, stiffening my shoulders in desperation and defiance against the encroaching chill of the twilight.

CHAPTER SIXTEEN
"Pacific Coast Highway"

Everything should have been smooth sailing for the band from that point on: we had a major label contract, a single that looked like it might get some serious radio play, a music video on the way, and a headlining tour coming up in a few short months. But, despite all of these awe-inspiring accomplishments, there was a dangerous infection festering just beneath the surface.

Storf wasn't alone in recognizing the impending cataclysm of the band. While we were listening to the final mixes of *A Different Slant of Light* on a weekend drive from UCLA to Zuma Beach, Lani pointed out something that should have been clear to anyone intimately involved with the band.

"You're not happy, are you?" she asked me, her gentle voice comprised of equal parts caution and concern.

I didn't answer her at first. By this point, Lani knew me better than I knew myself. If she could sense that something was off, it wouldn't have been the mysterious work of a mind reader.

"No," I mumbled back to her, feeling a sense of defeat creeping up my throat.

She pursed her lips in the adorable way that manifested when she was problem-solving; I had seen it many times when she was writing articles for the *Daily Bruin* or crafting papers for an English class. "If you're not happy, then why don't you do something about it?"

I kept my fingers glued to the steering wheel, my eyes fixed on the road ahead of me. As the car crept forward on the long, clear passage of the Santa Monica Freeway, I couldn't bear to look at anything other than the blacktop lanes beyond the windshield.

"What could I possibly do, Lani?" I asked.

"Well, you could try to get out of your contract with Lowercase Records," she suggested softly. "Or you could confront Steve. Or you could kick him out of the band. Or…" Her voice, as soft as hibiscus petals, trailed off.

"Or… what?"

Lani sighed. "Or you could quit the band, Bri," she finally said.

My immediate, knee-jerk reaction was to slam on the brakes, pull over to the side of the road, and go running from the car. I didn't do that, obviously. But I was tempted.

"That's just crazy," I shot back.

She squinted her beautiful chestnut-brown eyes and scrunched up the left side of her mouth. "Is it *really* crazy, though? If you're not happy… if this is causing you more frustration than joy…"

"Which it currently is," I admitted.

"If that's the case," she continued, "then you should seriously consider walking away. Or running away. Or hiking away."

"But it's such a pivotal piece of who I am," I pleaded – more with myself than with her. "What am I, if I'm not a songwriter or a bass player or a keyboardist or a member of a band?" Those questions lingered in the air like invisible cigarette smoke.

"You're Brian Richard Smith," she said. "You're a three-dimensional human being who isn't defined by any one, singular thing." She reached over and spread her small hand across the center of my chest. "You're a handsome man with a good heart and a remarkable mind. And you're the person I love more than anyone else in the world."

Damn, she's good, I thought to myself. *She really is smarter than me.*

"If you're not happy," she concluded, "then just leave."

Just leave. This hadn't ever seemed like a possibility for me. I'd spent so many years defined by rock music, and I couldn't fathom an existence without songs and bands and writing and recording. The idea of leaving those things behind, of starting a new life without that seemingly pivotal piece of my identity was frightening…

But it didn't seem impossible with Lani by my side.

We drove on, crawling up the freeway until we reached McClure Tunnel, that conical connection to the Pacific Coast Highway. As we emerged from that cylindrical cavern, the coastline seemed to burst forth from the horizon, the cresting waves of the ocean calling out to us.

We crept through the blustery traffic until we reached our sand-dune destination. Though it was a busy Saturday afternoon, and tourists seemed to be filling every available parking spot, we managed to snag a vacant space only a few short blocks from the shoreline. We grabbed our gear from the trunk of the car and soldiered on through the white sands towards the beautiful breakers that shimmered in the distance.

Glancing around at the many beach bodies that graced the summery sands that afternoon, it struck me once again how mismatched Lani and I must have seemed from an outsider's perspective. I was this lumbering, overweight oaf with painfully pale skin who struggled to make it through the coarse grains of sand that coated the shoreline; beside me, however, was this petite goddess with sun-kissed skin and flawless features who seemed to float across the dunes.

After we laid out our wrinkled beach blankets and set up a wavering umbrella, Lani reached deep into one of her bags and brought out a large bottle of sunblock. Without saying anything, she tossed me the bottle and gestured for me to apply it to my body.

"Don't you need any?" I asked her.

"Please," she said, rolling her eyes, "I have built-in sunblock." She stretched out her lithe arms and twisted them in a circular motion for me to see. "I have a little more leeway, courtesy of my Polynesian ancestors, so I can wait five minutes before I lather up. You, my love, are not so lucky. In sixty seconds, you'll be burnt and blistering." She gave me a mischievous smile before laying down on her towel and adhering a pair of sunglasses to the smooth slope of her nose.

It was true: Lani's skin was darker, an elegant shade that offered her more protection from the dreaded, unseen ultraviolet rays of the sun. I, on the other hand, could only stand a few hours exposed to sunlight before it wreaked havoc on my pale epidermis. If I spent more than twenty minutes under blazing sunbeams, I turned a lobster-ish shade of red. Lani, however, seemed invincible. Like the melatonin that painted her perfect skin, she was strong – impervious to the little pricks and perforations that tormented her ghost-white boyfriend. Even then, my future wife was much less vulnerable to the slings and arrows of outrageous sunburns. She had the strength (inside and out) that I lacked.

I looked down at the little pink-and-white bottle in front of me and examined it closely. I'm sure the bottle read SPF 75 or SPF 100 or SPF 1,000 – some incredibly high form of protection that Lani had instinctively packed before we left Westwood. Methodically (and begrudgingly), I slathered the white goop all over my arms and legs and chest and back. I'm pretty sure I looked like a walking donut covered in sunscreen-scented frosting.

For a long time, we sat side-by-side in the overwhelming embrace of the indelicate sun. We held hands, talked about classes, and continually flipped our bodies over like hamburgers on a grill, until thick beads of sweat came rolling down our backs.

On her, it was sexy. On me, it was slimy.

Casually, she propped herself up, dusted the stray grains of sand from her legs, and reached her hand out to me. "Come on," she urged me with a flick of her wrist, "you need your Vitamin D and I need to cool off."

I took her hand and let her lead me in the direction of the roaring ocean ahead of us. As we made our way through the fiercely formidable beach, I felt myself tightening up. We crossed the invisible border demarcating the transition from hot, dry sand to the smooth coat of cool, clumpy coastline. As we stepped closer and closer to the water, I pulled my hand away from hers and planted my feet.

"What's wrong?" she asked.

"It's the ocean," I told her, my heart vibrating uncomfortably. "I've got a… thing… about going in."

"Seriously?" she asked, her forehead creased skeptically. "I've seen you in a swimming pool a bunch of times before."

"But the ocean…" I started to say. "It's… *different*. It's too… unpredictable."

"It's just water, Brian." As if to prove her point, she kicked a rippling wave that crested in front of her. "You have nothing to be afraid of," she reassured me.

Still, though, I couldn't shake the interminable anxiety that wrapped its fingers around my chest. Something about the uncertainty of the waves, the instability that they created – it was enough to drown a man in fear.

"You go ahead," I told her. "I'll watch you from here."

Lani looked at me in disbelief, as if she couldn't understand or comprehend my reservations. We were simply too different. She was a lithe, amphibious siren who felt equally at home on the sand or in the waves; I was a timid sailor who could barely handle exposure to the sun, let alone submit myself to the anarchy of the ocean.

"Alright," she finally acquiesced, "it's your loss." She turned away from me and walked towards the vast expanse of the horizon, her tan legs seamlessly submerged.

I pulled back a few more steps, leaving a growing distance between us. Eventually, I sat down in a stiff, unyielding plot of shoreline and watched her wading into the waters – braver than I could ever be. Like a spectator, I remained on the course sands of the beach, unable to bring myself to take a single step into the wild, mercurial waves.

It's easy to remain tethered to the shore, I thought. *It's a lot harder to break the invisible clasps that bind us, and dive into uncharted waters.*

It was just a passing thought, some random synapses of my brain making connections and bridging the gap between reality and fiction, between poetry and life. Either way, I realized, the metaphor held true.

CHAPTER SEVENTEEN
"Heroes & Villains"

Just as the Beach Boys' narratives focus on the clash of musical titans – usually portrayed as an unending battle between Mike Love and Brian Wilson – the fate of my band depended upon the impending showdown between me and Steve. Obviously, this is *my* story, so I'm going to look like the hero of the tale (or so I hope). If you speak with Steve, however, you'll probably hear a different perspective, one in which I might look a bit more culpable – perhaps even a tad villainous.

Like everything else, the truth probably lies somewhere in the middle.

Am I an unreliable narrator? I'd like to *think* that I'm pretty dependable when it comes to truthfully relaying what happened all those years ago… but memory is a flawed mechanism – a malleable device that can be molded and shaped to better suit the delusional narratives we tell ourselves as consolation for our missteps and our mistakes.

I am only human, after all.

As we march forward in the pages ahead, just know that this is where things get complicated. This is the part of the story when the tightly woven fabric of my life started to unravel, thread by tenuous thread. By the time that the summer of 2000 had ended, I was left with spools of scorched strands… and very little bound together in the aftermath.

CHAPTER EIGHTEEN
"Solar System"

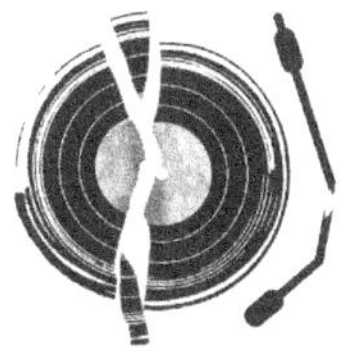

It was shortly after that beach visit with Lani when we received copies of the final, finished record delivered to our doorsteps. As I ripped through the thick tape and flimsy cardboard of the FedEx package, my fingers were shaking uncontrollably. I brushed away the pointless padded puff of packing peanuts and unveiled the album.

There it was: *A Different Slant of Light*.

I can't adequately describe the singular experience of holding that album in my hands for the first time. It was the final product of so many months spent rehearsing and recording and mixing and mastering – not to mention the years' worth of practicing and writing and learning and living. As my eyes scanned the glossy pages of the CD booklet, it felt like gazing upon a newborn baby, a tiny creature that had spent endless months gestating and forming within the womb of my brain and the placenta of my heart.

I studied those liner notes religiously, fawning over each and every detail: the titles of the songs and the names of the musicians and the locations of the recording sessions and everything else that was printed on that stapled set of square pages. On the back flap of the booklet, our names were printed in bold and coupled with the instruments we played. If you've seen the CD booklet, you know that it looked something like this:

***Steve Öken:** vocals and guitar
***Ethan Hidalgo:** lead guitar and harmony vocals

***Brian Richard ("Brick") Smith:** bass, piano, keys, guitars, harmony vocals, and other assorted instruments

***Charles ("Chunk") Smith:** drums, percussion, and harmony vocals

***Victor Wu:** bass and harmony vocals

Technically, our names were in alphabetical order – with the exception of Steve, of course, who received top billing on this miniature marquee. I couldn't help but scoff when I saw my name buried right in the middle of everyone else's. It felt frustratingly fitting, as if I was hidden in the middle of the pack, tucked away from the spotlight and neatly edged out to the periphery of the frame.

There were a few fictitious fabrications on that list. Victor didn't *technically* join the band until after the album was completed, but it seemed like good karma to include his name in the credits. I figured that when we recorded our second album, Victor would have the opportunity to lay down some bass and vocals. It seemed like a safe assumption.

Of course, as you know, we never made it that far.

The big inaccuracy (for me at least) was the fact that Steve's credits listed "vocals *and guitar*" next to his name. That irritated me to no end. Sure, Steve played lackluster rhythm guitar in our live shows, but Ethan and I had to record all of his parts on the album. Early on, Storf had told us that Steve's playing wasn't up to snuff, so Ethan and I had spent countless hours recording all of the strumming and palm-muting and soloing that Steve never could have nailed.

Steve literally did not play a single guitar note on the album… but he still proffered the illusion that he was a multitalented musician whose skillset extended beyond the limited sphere of the microphone. Just like he'd proven countless times since our very first show, he had no problem taking credit for other peoples' work – especially when it was *my* work.

Mind you, I still wasn't thrilled about the picture of Steve that took up the vast majority of the album cover, flanked by the band's name on top and *A Different Slant of Light* on the bottom. Though it was Steve's face that was front and center, Ethan had been right: these were *my* songs and *my* album title. I had to keep repeating that line in my head over and over to prevent myself from strangling our lead singer.

When I flipped the jewel case to the back, the titles of my tunes reflected back at me through the thin plastic sheen of the packaging. They were all there – the opener "Time Bomb," followed by our *Twin Peaks* homage "Sherilyn" and our first single, "Incomplete (Just Like Your Smile)." After that, the mood vaulted through peaks and valleys with "Wurlitzers & Women" and "Sam Cooke's Soul" and "Don't Want to See You Tonight" completing the first half of the album. The second half of the record started with "Beautiful Girl from Heaven" and continued on with "Stop & Talk" and "(Won't You Be My) June" and "Barbed-Wire Skies." The final song of the album *should* have been the slow, elegiac "Patterns in Snow" – but there was one last recording that made its way onto *A Different Slant of Light…*

"Stars."

The worst song on the record.

The only song that I had no hand in writing.

The song that ultimately nailed the coffin shut for Call Field.

Over the course of our years together as a band – first as the Bookhouse Boys, then as Caulfield, and finally as Call Field – we had amassed an impressive archive of material. Yes, I singlehandedly wrote most of the songs in our musical arsenal, but we had a few killer outtakes that would have been nice additions to *A Different Slant of Light.* Heck, even my amateurish attempt at a rock anthem, "Different Seasons," would have been a better way to end our album.

Steve, however, felt the need to flex his atrophying muscles. Of course, as I'll explain momentarily, he had his reasons to add "Stars" to the record. However, no matter the personal stress he was under at the time, I wish that the rest of us would have bucked and told him that we wouldn't record it. Even if we *had* stood our ground, though, Steve couldn't be swayed: he made sure that we fell in line and recorded his sole solo writing credit. As painful as it was to put our name on his crappy composition, Steve was too driven and too stubborn to back down.

In fact, when it came time to mix and master and sequence the album, Steve just had to have the last word – literally, in this circumstance. Call Field placed "Stars" as the final track on the record, the closing song on the album that *I* had meticulously crafted with Storf and the band. Despite the fact that I had been Call Field's guiding songwriting force for so many years, writing or co-writing all of our songs, it wasn't my melody or my words that closed the album.

It was Steve's.

It should have been a warning to me that the tide was shifting, that the band was headed in a different direction…

Without me.

I've already told you about most of Call Field's songs and how they were written: "Time Bomb" and my teen crush on Serena, "Sherilyn" and my *Twin Peaks* obsession, "June" and the awkward love triangle with Lani and her ex-boyfriend – and, of course, "Incomplete" and the story of how my whole life incrementally inched towards the moment I wrote that song. I had a hand in composing every single track on *A Different Slant of Light*.

Except one.

After we'd finished (or *thought* we'd finished) recording the album, we conducted some post-production "proofreading" by listening back to the tracks with Storf and bouncing some rough mixes. During one of these sessions, Steve came to the studio with a stack of photocopied pages in one hand and an acoustic guitar case in the other. As he passed out the papers to us, his hands were trembling – whether in frustration or fatigue, I didn't know.

When I reached out and took the wrinkled photocopy from Steve, it seemed like I was suddenly looking at someone I didn't know. With a handful of exceptions, I couldn't recall Steve ever seeming so vulnerable, so fragile. Judging by the deep wrinkles that sagged under his eyelids, I assumed that he must have been up all night. He didn't look intimidating as much as he simply looked *tired*.

I studied the creased paper and saw lines of handwritten chords and lyrics. A quick scan down the page showed that it was a pretty simplistic song – only three or four chords and some straightforward, confessional lyrics. As we each read through the lead sheet in front of us, Steve cracked open his guitar case and pulled out his Gibson acoustic. He took a few tentative strums and then started to sing.

"The stars are out tonight... and so are we," he began, his gravelly voice more tender than I'd ever heard it. *"The moon is alive tonight... and so are the trees..."*

I couldn't help but cringe as he continued making his way through the song. The chord progression (a descending *G* chord that walked down to a *D/F#* and then to an *Em*) cycled through itself over and over, never really leading anywhere. And the lyrics…

Oh, God, the lyrics.

I would call it bad high school poetry, but that would be an insult to teenage poets everywhere. Bad *middle school* poetry, perhaps? The whole thing was riddled with unoriginal rhymes and pathetic platitudes and inept imagery. Basically, it was an amateurish mess without much redeeming value. The chorus was basically Steve crying "I miss you" over a clichéd chord progression that seemed to simultaneously plagiarize U2's "With or Without You" and Green Day's "When I Come Around" – but failed to evoke the pathos of either one.

But, regardless of its fatal flaws and withering weaknesses, Steve demanded that we record it. Immediately.

Storf had been listening disinterestedly from his leather swivel chair, but he flipped around to face us when Steve finished the last note of his impromptu performance. He crinkled his eyebrows in concentration, as if solving a calculus problem, and delicately folded his callused hands in on each other. I wasn't sure what I could say without sounding like a complete jerk, so I watched Storf for a cue.

"So, why the sense of urgency?" Storf finally asked, wetting his lips and tapping his stubbled chin. He was clearly much more diplomatic than I could have been.

"It's something I need to do," Steve said. He looked away from our faces towards the glass partition that separated us from the soundproof foam walls of the isolation booths. "Something *we* need to do. Serena left me and I…"

"Wait, wait, wait…" Ethan interrupted. "Did you just say that *Serena left you?* Like *dumped* you?" His mouth was parted slightly, awestruck by the nascent news.

"Yes," Steve answered curtly, his eyes drilling holes into Ethan's skinny frame. "That's what I just said, isn't it?"

I felt my face unwillingly flush scarlet. The implications of this breakup launched a million thoughts into swirling orbit around my brain.

Though I tried to keep my head down, I couldn't help but steal a few looks around the room. Ethan seemed flabbergasted, while Chunk just cocked his head in surprise. Storf, situated in his leather command chair at the mixing board, could not have cared less. This kind of schoolboy spectacle was beneath him, apparently.

"So… what happened?" Ethan delicately asked. Steve wouldn't acknowledge the question, and Ethan suddenly looked incredibly uncomfortable, like an intruder reading a locked diary. "I mean, if you don't want to talk about it…"

"No, it's fine," Steve grumbled. He kept his focus on the ground, unwilling to make eye contact with any of us. As his lips moved into various scrunched-up positions, I got the feeling that he was mustering the courage to divulge some damning revelation.

What he told us next was earth-shattering, a seismic shock to our little musical ecosphere.

"I cheated on her," Steve mumbled.

"You did *WHAT?*" I bellowed. As much as I wanted to restrain myself behind a curtain of stoicism, my heart betrayed me. Like it or not, I still felt protective over Serena – even though she had broken my heart years ago and ultimately chosen Steve over me.

I should have felt vindicated. But I just felt betrayed.

"I *cheated* on her," Steve repeated, his words more cruel and cutting this time. His eyes slowly crept up to meet mine, challenging me like a boxer ready to pounce in the ring. "It was stupid and now I'm paying for it."

The silence in the room made us all uncomfortable – except (of course) for Storf, who felt no need to engage in our adolescent drama.

Ethan did his best to ease the tension, to slice his way through the fog of uneasiness that permeated the room. "If it was just a one-time mistake," he started to say, "then maybe she'll forgive you…"

Steve scrunched up his mouth again. "Here's the thing…" he said, guiltily stretching out each word. "It wasn't just one time. It was a few times."

Once again, silence descended on the room like a claustrophobic curtain.

Only Chunk had the courage to ask what we were all wondering. "How many times, Steve?" he cautiously uttered.

"Thirteen…" Steve muttered with his eyes closed, as if channeling the inner strength to face off against an invisible Goliath.

"Wait," Storf chimed in from across the room. "Ya' cheated on yer' girlfriend *thirteen* times?" His jaw crept open in disbelief.

"Well, thirteen *and a half* times, technically…" Steve started to say.

"You cheated on Serena *THIRTEEN AND A HALF TIMES?*" Chunk shouted with equal measures shock and disgust.

"I didn't do it all at once," Steve shot back. "It was thirteen and a half times over the course of… like… five years. That's only like two or three times a year."

All of us – even the ever-stoic Storf – were speechless.

"Jesus," Steve muttered defensively. "It was a few mistakes a year. I'm not an asshole."

"I beg to differ," I chimed in.

In all the years that I'd known Steve, I'd received countless glaring stares from him. This infernal instance, however, made all of the other fiery faces seem like cinders in a dying fireplace. Steve's seething, vibrant anger had burned into something else: unabashed hatred.

"Either we record this song or I walk," Steve demanded through gritted teeth. "I don't think you understand that this is not a request. We *will* learn this song. And we *will* record it. Today. End of story."

Steve wasn't kidding around. As I scanned the room for reactions, the boys all seemed taken aback by Steve's ominous tone. Storf, on the other hand, simply raised an eyebrow and offered a resigned shrug.

Begrudgingly, we learned "Stars" and recorded it over the next few hours. Though we had *thought* we were finished with the album – that we were ready to pop the champagne and celebrate – we found ourselves in the precarious situation of recording *yet another* song… which felt a lot like running an additional 1600 meters after finishing a grueling 26.2-mile marathon. We were tired, but we soldiered on for the sake of our lamentable leader.

Adding insult to injury, however, was the fact that the soundtrack to our musical cool-down mile was incredibly inconsequential, amateurishly derailing Call Field from the more meticulously crafted songs that fleshed out the album. I know it sounds arrogant, but my compositions were light years beyond what Steve had brought to the table.

You have to know your strengths: I was the writer and Steve was the singer. Neither of us could do the other's job nearly as well. But Steve refused to accept his station as a second-rate songwriter. Maybe he felt like he had something to prove to the rest of us; realistically, though, he probably just wanted to make some grand gesture to show that Serena had made a mistake when she dumped him.

I tried to imagine myself in Serena's situation. If my significant other had cheated on me – *repeatedly* – would a cheap, clichéd love song make me rethink my decision to break up? Would a simple melody and contrite lyrics erase all of the hurt and heartache? Maybe a brilliant song with a lasting legacy might help ease some of that pain. Perhaps a majestic masterpiece could help make things right.

But "Stars" wasn't brilliant. It wasn't a masterpiece. It wasn't even *memorable*. Rather, it seemed more like the pathetic attempt of a mediocre high school student stuck in detention on a sunny day.

Basically, Steve was screwed.

Because we were so focused on learning and recording Steve's song in such a hasty manner (in fact, I think we ended up using the third or fourth full take of the song for the final album), it wasn't until hours later that one of Steve's earlier comments clicked in my brain.

When Steve demanded that we record his song or he would "walk," it sounded an awful lot like an ultimatum, a threat to press that big red button and kickstart nuclear warfare.

Did he really threaten to quit the band? I wondered to myself.

I wistfully imagined Steve missing another show, and Call Field using our lead singer's own "iron-clad" contract to finally oust him from the band. I envisioned myself – along with Ethan, Chunk, and Victor – beginning a new chapter with *me* at the helm of the ship, steering our course to smoother waters. I dreamed of a lifelong career with Call Field: writing hundreds of songs, recording dozens of albums, and playing thousands of shows. I could see it as clearly as a sailor sees the Northern Star illuminating the nighttime sky.

But we couldn't accomplish all of this as long as Steve was holding us back. And with his recent demands, it felt like he was gearing up to enact a musical Cuban Missile Crisis. But was he Russia or the United States? And how would this standoff end? With a peaceful compromise? Or with mutually assured destruction?

As it turned out, there were a few casualties in the impending showdown.

At least I wouldn't go down fighting alone.

CHAPTER NINETEEN
"Mrs. O'Leary's Cow"

I've spent a lot of time leading up to this moment – much longer, in fact, than I anticipated. I thought for sure that I would hastily compose some cursory chapters and quickly rush through the most traumatic moments of my life… Little did I know that exorcising the demons of my past would so thoroughly possess me that I'd spend months and months typing it all out on my trusty laptop.

As it turns out, I'm a bit long-winded. Of course, you've figured that out by now.

In my defense, it was a bit naïve to think that I could sum up the most important events of my life in a matter of a few dozen pages. Life is not a simple, rigid line from Point A to Point B. Instead, it's a complicated labyrinth with twists and turns and dead-ends and secret passageways.

While I appreciate you taking the time to accompany me through this seemingly never-ending journey, I have to warn you that we're about to face the Minotaur of this story – the monster at the heart of the muddled maze.

Spoiler alert: this is the chapter in which everything falls apart.

The night of June 21st, 2000, should have been an evening of smooth sailing and joyous celebration. It was my twenty-first birthday, the beginning of our tour supporting *A Different Slant of Light*, and Call Field's debut performance at the legendary Fillmore in San Francisco. It should have been a moment of magic, of revelry, of triumph…

Instead, it became the worst night of my life.

It was the night that I lost almost everything important to me.

As you've seen in the hundreds of pages leading up to this moment, Call Field had become a minefield: we were all treading lightly on dangerous ground, awaiting an explosion that could cataclysmically corrupt or definitively destroy us. In my foolishness, I assumed that Steve would be the one to carelessly step on the detonator and sabotage everything that we had worked so hard for.

Hubris, man…

It nearly ruined Odysseus, and it almost killed me.

It's worth noting that Steve was violently ill-tempered that night. A few days before we left on tour, he and Serena had another huge showdown over his industrious infidelity. You saw how the scene unfolded when he told us in the recording studio – and we instantly pounced on him. I can only imagine how his conversation with Serena played out.

"Babe," Steve probably pleaded. *"It was only once or twice. I promise to never do it again."*

"It wasn't a couple *of times!"* Serena would've most likely spit back. *"It was thirteen-and-a-half times!"*

God, what a mess.

Again, I'm not sure how you can cheat on someone thirteen *and a half* times (how does that mathematically and/or logistically work out?), but that's beside the point. Cheating is like emotional embezzling. And Steve was the king of white-collar crime in this romantic relationship.

The moral of the story: when faced with a choice between the handsome, magnetic frontman (who will undoubtedly cheat on you) or the less-attractive, introverted bass player (who will remain eternally faithful), the decision should be simple. Always go with the bass player.

Sadly, Serena didn't choose wisely in high school, and she was now reaping the harvest of that damning decision. I, on the other hand, had the great luck of seeing my formerly miserable life inverted into a series of fortunate events – not the least of which was falling in love with Lani.

If you're keeping track, the half-time scores were as follows: Steve and Serena were at low points in their lives, while I was more successful than I had ever been. Unfortunately, the world would turn upside-down in just a few horrific hours. And I would spend years picking up the mess.

When it came time to take the stage at the Fillmore, I assumed that both Lani and Serena would be there to support their respective boyfriends. San Francisco was, after all, only a day's drive away from Southern California. Surely, our significant others (along with our closest friends and family) would be there rooting for us during the opening show of our big national tour?

As it turned out, I had the biggest cheering section that night: my parents drove up from Ojai the morning of the show with Lani in the backseat, caravanning with Uncle Jeff and Aunt Alyssa. My sister, Marina, and her boyfriend, Reggie, planned on meeting us at the Fillmore after they got off work. The convergence of the tour's opening night with my twenty-first birthday ensured that it would be a festive evening; even if I didn't get to blow out candles on a frosted birthday confection, knowing that I would be surrounded by my family and friends on one of the most important nights of my life would be the *real* icing on the cake.

Of course, I wasn't the only member of Call Field with a fan club. Ethan's dad made the trek up from SoCal, as did Victor's parents and his boyfriend. A few of Ethan's Bay Area relatives, including his cousin and his grandmother, were also planning to attend.

The only person without a support crew? Steve.

For whatever reason, Steve's dad had booked a flight back home to the motherland of Sweden, while Steve's mom and her new boyfriend were enjoying a Caribbean cruise for the first two weeks of our debut national tour. And Serena? Well, she was a wildcard. Would she show up after their big blowout? Or was she finally over Steve and his infidelity? We wouldn't know until we hit the stage.

Looking back years later, the contrast seems striking: I was loved and supported by my family, while Steve was very much a lone wolf navigating the frozen tundra of his life in isolation. And though I wouldn't have mustered an ounce of pity at the time, I didn't realize just how profoundly that loneliness had affected him.

Certain people are just unknowable.

That goes for fiction and for the folks in your real life.

In my eyes, Steve seemed to have it all – good looks, golden vocal cords, rich parents, and a girlfriend who just happened to be my first crush – while I was simply struggling to get credit for all of my hard work. I felt vindicated watching Steve get his comeuppance, and there was only a small part of me that wanted to see him make things right with Serena and humbly return to the fold.

But considering how many times Steve had set fire to the bridge between us, why should I have cared at all? Why should I have sympathy for the devil?

Even demons deserve happiness, I suppose.

Like rock and roll tourists, we spent the afternoon before the Fillmore show exploring San Francisco and attempting (in vain) to quiet our nerves. I remember eating at a hole-in-the-wall Chinese restaurant on 19th Avenue, gazing at the Golden Gate Bridge from Baker Beach, and sightseeing along the creaky beams of Pier 39. The city held so much magic and mystery, I could almost imagine myself beginning a new life with Lani and Call Field in the Bay Area. Twenty-four hours later, however, I wouldn't be able to look at the city the same way.

We splintered into separate sightseeing factions over the course of the afternoon: Steve, Ethan, and Victor took a ferry out to Alcatraz, while Chunk and I stayed behind on the mainland. The boat ride was the dealbreaker for me. I refused to sail out onto those choppy waters for a prison tour when the temptation of solid ground seemed much more appealing. Like I said before, I had a "thing" about the ocean back then.

Though the majority of Call Field had abandoned me for a glorified field trip, my cousin stuck around onshore. Chunk might have also felt the enticing tug of adventure calling him from the depths of the bay, but he made a conscious decision to keep me company on *terra firma*.

"Happy birthday, Brick," Chunk told me with a consoling pat on the back. "Who wants to hang out on a prison island with those bozos, anyway?"

While the rest of the band was gone, we talked about the future, about our hopes and dreams and visions for Call Field. While things might have been rocky with the other guys, at least I knew that Chunk was on my side. Blood is, after all, thicker than water. And you know how I felt about water at that point in my life.

At some point, though, Chunk went off looking for a souvenir kiosk – leaving me all by myself in the thick, soupy fog of the San Francisco coastline. I have a vivid memory of walking along the waterfront alone that afternoon with a styrofoam cup of coffee in my hand, the cream and sugar swirling dreamily in a lazy circle. As I stared off at Alcatraz in the distance, the curling waters of the bay sweeping in and out of focus, my dad's old familiar mantra popped into my head: *"Life's too short to drink your coffee black."*

With a twinge of regret, it dawned on me that I hadn't seen my parents in six months. Even though Ojai was only a few hours away from Los Angeles, I had been too busy with Lani and school and the band to visit them. I felt a slight pang of guilt, but I nudged that nagging feeling out of my mind.

Despite my mixed emotions, I had a moment of clarity there along the waterfront. The swirling coffee in my hand reminded me of the mythological *Ouroboros* – the snake eating its own tail as a symbol of infinity and completion. For a few minutes, it was like some singular sense of serenity had delicately placed its invisible hand on my shoulder, reassuring me that everything would work out fine.

Boy, was I wrong.

A nervous buzz permeated the air in the hours leading up to the show. Though we all tried to play it cool, we knew that this moment in our shared history was remarkable – epic even. Call Field was rocketing its way up the trajectory of fame and fortune, and who knew where the apex might be?

At some point, Storf called us at the Fillmore to congratulate us on the RIAA certification of 100,000 album sales for *A Different Slant of Light*. He half-jokingly told us that we were 20% of the way towards a gold record distinction. It seemed like one heck of a birthday present to hear that Call Field had reached this monumental demarcation. It was, I hoped, just the start of even more triumphant success. If we could sell 100,000 copies of the album in such a brief window, it seemed entirely plausible that a Gold or Platinum certification might be in our future. Our prospects seemed limitless.

As the hours ticked by, we fiddled around backstage, making small talk and finding amusement in the mundane distractions around us. Chunk repetitively twirled his drumsticks in his hands, while Ethan, Victor, and Steve played poker with a bent stack of Bicycle cards. While the trio slapped down spades and handed over hearts, I was changing the thick steel strings on Victor's bass guitar in the green room backstage. As remarkable as his musicianship was, my UCLA roommate's nerves almost got the best of him: his hands were twitching intensely and he felt so ill he thought he might throw up. Poor guy.

As my fingers wound and tightened strings, I found myself daydreaming, staring at the multitude of posters from past Fillmore shows that adorned the walls. There was such extraordinary history in this place – it was like stepping back in time to the days of Bill Graham and the "swinging sixties." And here we were, poised to take our place in the pantheon of rock royalty.

After I finished winding the strings on Victor's bass, I decided to explore the historic venue. I was completely lost in thought, roaming the narrow lavender hallways of the Fillmore's darkened backstage area when I passed a withered old man who wheezed as he walked towards me. He was pretty nondescript: he must have weighed about a hundred and eighty pounds, though his slouching posture made him seem much more frail. Even with the enveloping shadows, I could see that he clutched a shiny red apple in his wrinkled hand. The pitiful fellow was enrobed in an oversized leather jacket that draped over baggy Levi's jeans, and the top of his head was hidden by a blue baseball cap with *Cal* embroidered across the front. His sallow skin hung off his emaciated frame, folds of flesh creating jowls on his clean-shaven face and neck. He looked old and pathetic, like a scrawnier version of Mr. Magoo.

When he shuffled within a few feet of me, he stopped. "Do you know where I can find the headliners for tonight's show?" he asked in a tender, raspy voice that sounded vaguely familiar.

"Are you looking for Call Field?" I asked, my eyes scrunching in the dim light to make out the old man's face.

And then it hit me.

"Oh, my God!" I shouted. "*Dad...?*"

"*Junior!*" he croaked, his gruff voice immediately muffled by an ensuing series of coughs. He wrapped his arms around me, pulling me weakly into an enervated embrace. His trembling mouth mustered up enough strength to utter three weakened words: "Happy birthday, son!"

It had been *half a year* since I'd seen my father – since New Year's Day, in fact. While six months might not seem like a lot of time, my father had somehow shriveled up in that period – like a reverse butterfly, folding its magnificent heft into a tightly constricted cocoon. He had lost a *lot* of weight – probably close to a hundred pounds – and he had shaved off his copper-colored beard, that signifier of age and wisdom that he had sported since I left Ojai for UCLA.

He was a different man – like a sunken shadow of his former self.

What happened to you, Dad? I remember thinking to myself.

My father, who now seemed so stooped and bent, looked up at me with shimmering eyes that hid nervously behind his horn-rimmed glasses. "I look a little different than the last time you saw me, don't I?" he asked.

"Well... uh..." I stammered. "You shaved. The last time I saw you, you had a Wookiee's worth of hair on your face."

"Yeeeep," he sighed. "And I shaved off a few pounds, too." He took a step back and made a sweeping gesture to the space between us – to the ghostly, uninhabited place where his bountiful gut should have been.

"How...? Why...?" I was nearly speechless, unable to fashion a full sentence.

"Well, I've been *sick*, son," he said quietly. "I've had this never-ending cycle of colds and flus and aches for months now, and it's been wreaking havoc on my poor old body. I mean, it's an effective way to lose weight... but I wouldn't recommend the diet." He chuckled to himself softly – before his voice caught, and his throat exploded into a succession of short, violent coughs.

"Have you seen a doctor, Dad?"

"Ah…" he muttered, shaking his head delicately, "now you sound like your mother." He grimaced and shrugged. "I'll be fine. It's just one of those yucky bugs that's hard to kick."

I started picking at a hangnail on my right thumb. "But that's a *long* time to be sick, Dad… Shouldn't you see someone…?"

"I haven't been to the doctor for *sixteen years*," he reminded me, smirking like a mischievous schoolboy with a slingshot up his sleeve. "So, why would I start now?"

He had me there. My father might have been brilliant and insightful, but he was also as stubborn as a mule. Knowing that I couldn't change his mind, I simply sighed in defeat and offered one last, unenthusiastic question.

I glanced down at his right hand, which trembled delicately as it encircled a glossy red apple. "What's up with the fruit?" I asked him.

My dad looked down at his hand and awkwardly juggled the apple between his fingers. "They've got barrels full of them up by the front door," he told me, gesturing with his left thumb. "It's a longstanding tradition for the Fillmore. I think it's something Bill Graham started a few decades back."

My father, I thought, *the quintessential rock and roll encyclopedia. An* ill *encyclopedia, mind you, but an encyclopedia, nonetheless.*

"Are you sure that you're well enough to be here?" I asked with one last, desperate appeal.

Flashing a Cheshire grin, he looked up at me with a twinkle in his eyes. "You couldn't keep me from seeing you tonight, here at the *Fillmore,* on your *twenty-first* birthday," he said hoarsely, "even if it's the last thing that I ever do."

He gave me a wink, and the matter was settled.

"Besides," he added, holding up the glossy crimson apple in his shaking right hand, "*an apple a day keeps the doctor away*, right?"

After my dad departed back into the audience to find the rest of our family, I kept to myself, investigating the edges of the darkened halls and trying to soak up the rock and roll history of the legendary Fillmore. Meanwhile, the opening act, Ventura's Army of Freshmen, were blasting their way through a killer set of power pop tunes that elicited enthusiastic cheers from the crowd. AOF's lead singer was rapping and singing about being "Bulletproof in Baggy Jeans" and lamenting the "Hellhole" of minimum-wage employment. It was catchy stuff. The band was on the verge of releasing their debut album and they were in top form, warming up the crowd for the opening night of our first nationwide tour. It felt like a serendipitous steal to snag the Freshmen before they rocketed to larger fame and fortune. The stars seemed to be aligning for us.

Shortly before our scheduled set time, the venue's stage manager came sauntering through the halls to find us. "Call Field!" he yelled out. "You're up!"

I walked back to the green room, attempting to appear nonchalantly confident in the midst of such a momentous moment. As I passed through the doorway, I did my best to read my bandmates' poker faces for any tells that might reveal how they were actually feeling. Chunk was tapping his feet at a ridiculously rapid pace, Victor had his arms wrapped around his chest like a straitjacket, and Ethan was picking away at the cuticles on his fingernails. I swear you could see the sweat dripping off of Ethan's forehead as his eyes tightened up into fine slits.

Steve, on the other hand, seemed more focused, more intense than the rest of the band. "It's game time," he said, thrusting his hand forward into the space between us.

Ethan, Chunk, Victor, and I formed a crude circle beside him, all of us flinging our fingers forward in unison. Hands collapsed on top of other hands, sweaty palms soaking onto twitching wrists.

"*Cooper…?*" I suggested, thinking back to those old *Twin Peaks*-inspired days of our youth, when Call Field had been Caulfield – or even further back, when we played our high school talent show as Marina & the Bookhouse Boys, and we'd had our first taste of stardom.

"No," Steve answered coolly. "This is the beginning of a new era. I say we change things up a bit."

The rest of us shuffled in our spots, feet nervously tapping and sliding and squeaking on the well-trod floorboards. No one thought to challenge Steve's commandment. It was eerily quiet for a moment.

"What did you have in mind?" Chunk asked.

Steve's lips curled up conspiratorially. "*To the future*," he suggested. "Because that's where we're headed."

We all looked at each other and nodded in acquiescence. Only Chunk seemed to hover beneath the shadow of doubt, his face calmly contorted in a skeptical expression. Finally, though, he relented.

"*To the future!*" we simultaneously shouted, our hands reaching to the ceilinged beams above us.

And then we proceeded forward through the darkness towards the brightly illuminated stage.

When I think back to that night's show, it all bleeds together in my mind, with flashes of feeling bursting through my clouded, overcast memory. To be fair, the concert itself was only about sixty supercharged minutes of my life – and the hours that immediately followed were far more haunting. Bear with me, in case I forget a few details. After all, the concert was only the beginning of that never-ending evening.

As we walked onstage, we were greeted by a thunderous applause – a wilder, more welcoming entrance than Call Field had ever received. We took our places behind our respective instruments, wincing at the intense illumination of the floodlights that shined down into our faces. As I made my way over to my 88-key Alesis keyboard, I glanced around the stage, taking in the scene. I couldn't make out a single face in the crowd through the blinding beams. Nevertheless, I was stunned by the sheer volume of cheers that emanated from the crowd.

These people are here to see us – to see CALL FIELD, I remember thinking. *We're not the appetizer for some main-stage marquee musicians. We're the main course.*

Right about then, I heard Chunk's drumsticks clicking off our four-count for the first song of the evening. We were off to the races.

As usual, we opened with "Time Bomb" – that musical call-to-arms that had signaled our arrival at so many shows before. While we'd played plenty of venues over the years, the audience's enthusiasm was amplified exponentially at the Fillmore. Maybe it was the release of the album a few weeks earlier. Maybe it was the gradual ascendency of "Incomplete" on popular radio. Whatever the case, though, we were met with an intensity unmatched by any show we'd ever played.

There at the Fillmore, almost four hundred miles from our humble home in Ojai, a packed ballroom full of folks shouted along with Steve's growling tenor. Kids bopped up and down like human pogo sticks. Fists pumped up and down in time with Chunk's drums. And I soaked in every single moment.

As we made our way through the setlist, from "Time Bomb" to "Sherilynn" through "June" and into "Stop & Talk," the energy in the room kept escalating. This felt like a new beginning for the band, a long-awaited promotion into the big leagues of rock and roll. To top it off, it was also my twenty-first birthday – and it felt like I was entering a brave new world as I crossed the threshold into a bold new year.

Of course, my experience was also a bit tempered by the fact that I was now relegated to a less-visible backing role – behind a keyboard *Fortress of Solitude*. I had spent so many years performing onstage with my bass guitar in hand, it felt awkward standing stationary behind that Alesis keyboard and attempting to stay engaged in the show. Sure, I had a microphone in front of me so that I could chime in on harmony vocals, and I was adding that extra layer of pop sheen as I clamped down on the keys; however, I just didn't have the Elton John charisma that elevates a supporting keyboardist to a featured figure on the stage. A few piano players can pull off that kind of showmanship (Ben Folds, Billy Joel, and Elton obviously come to mind), but it's hard to look like a rock star when you're standing still behind an unmoving piece of musical furniture.

I felt more like an upholstered armchair than the roaring engine of a race car.

Yes, this was Call Field – the same band that I had been playing with since I was a kid in high school. But it was also something new, an untamed stallion of rock and roll on the verge of stardom. And, as someone who was no longer riding in the saddle, it felt a bit foreign and strange. I was an alien in my own flying saucer.

It wasn't until we got to "Incomplete" that I finally settled into my groove as Call Field's keyboardist. The minute Ethan hit the chiming notes of the song's intro riff, the audience erupted into a crazed, madcap reception. The band beckoned the room's spectators with the tune's bouncy intro hook, and the audience's anticipation echoed that ecstasy.

Nothing could have prepared me for the flood of emotions that I felt when we got to the chorus. As Steve wailed *"I get lost sometimes in the melodies of my mind,"* the audience belted out every word. There, at the legendary Fillmore auditorium in San Francisco, young men and women of all different races, creeds, and colors were singing along at the top of their lungs, screaming the lyrics to a simple pop song that I had written less than a year before. I couldn't help it: I got choked up, tears welling in my eyes and my chest inflating proudly. I barely managed to make it through the song without fumbling a few notes on the keyboard.

We've made it, I thought to myself. *After all these years of hard work, Call Field has made it.*

It also dawned on me that *I* – Brian Richard Smith, Jr. – had made it. That lonely, socially awkward kid who became a tormented teenager had somehow grown into a successful, talented musician living a fantasy life. I had an amazing girlfriend, my band was taking off, I was going to one of the best universities in the world, and I finally – *finally* – felt like that overwhelming cloud of depression that had haunted me for so many years was evaporating under the elevation of beautiful blue skies.

I could do this for the rest of my life, I thought. *I could be a professional musician and songwriter and producer. I could make my living playing rock and roll for admiring crowds. I could do this forever…*

After we finished "Incomplete," we waved at the crowd and walked offstage, expecting that to be the end of the show. We had played almost every song from *A Different Slant of Light*, as well as some odds and ends from our early punk-rock days, and we didn't think we had much to offer beyond that hour-long setlist of material. Backstage, though, in the blinding darkness of the wings, we could hear a buzz emanating from the audience.

"Is that… is that what I think it is?" Ethan asked, eyes askew and neck craning towards the stage.

We turned to face the distant lights and listened intently, our eyes wide with wonder. There was a rhythmic thumping and a muffled chorus of voices that bled through to our space backstage.

Duh-Duh-Duh, we heard from our vantage point. *Duh-Duh-Duh.*

We took a few steps closer to the stage we had just left, sweat coursing down our bodies and pooling in spots on the black floorboards.

DUH-DUH-DUH. DUH-DUH-DUH.

We inched closer and closer until the words were clear enough to discern.

"ONE-MORE-SONG!" they chanted. *"ONE-MORE-SONG!"*

I couldn't believe it. An encore. They wanted us to do an *encore*. At the Fillmore. In San Francisco. On the first show of the first leg of our first nationwide tour.

It couldn't get any better than this.

Besides the fact that we now had a room full of people stomping and clapping and chanting for us, we also had *our* people in the audience. Mom and Dad and Lani and Marina were all out there somewhere – as were Uncle Jeff and Aunt Alyssa and who knows how many other friends and family. This was a monumental moment for each of us, and even though we might not have been able to see them through the blinding floodlights, the members of Call Field got to share it with the people we loved the most.

Except Steve. No one had shown up to see him.

Anxiously, we walked back out onto the Fillmore stage – and we were met with deafening applause. It was like being real, live rock stars: the voluminous volume, the enchanted audience members staring at us in awe, the glistening sweat on the faces of our fans. It was a wild spectacle for our ragtag band of college kids.

As he strapped on his guitar, Steve turned around to face us. "What should we play?" he asked, barely audible over the thrumming audience.

Ethan, Chunk, Victor, and I all looked at each other. At first, no one offered up a suggestion; we were all too awestruck by the sheer surreality of the moment. It was Ethan who finally spoke, breaking our momentary paralysis.

"What about a Ramones cover?" he suggested.

Without waiting for any of us to consent, Steve immediately started playing the intro chords for "I Wanna' Be Sedated" – and the crowd went wild.

We plunged ahead into the song, Chunk thunderously thumping the beat while Victor battered his bass with swift downstrokes. Ethan's lead guitar snaked in-between Steve's power chords, floating like a buzzing musical salve. Steve howled into the microphone, spit and sweat festively flying off of his face.

As the boys beat on forward, I found myself struggling to squeeze in a keyboard part. From the safety and comfort of my Alesis, I held long block chords with a simulated Hammond organ setting, trying my best to pad the song without coming across as cheesy or uninspired. It was strange, though, trying to navigate through a perfect punk song while playing the *least* punk-rock instrument onstage. It occurred to me at that moment that I had somehow relegated myself to an extraneous accoutrement in the shadow of the band.

I was not one of the spires reaching towards the rafters. Instead, I was like the load-bearing base at the foundation of the beams. Once again, I had become a brick. Or, technically, a capitalized, proper-noun *Brick,* as it were.

When we came to the last crashing chord of "I Wanna' Be Sedated," the crowd instantly erupted into riotous applause. It was clear from their cheering and stomping that they weren't quite ready to let us go. We all sensed it, but no one knew what to do or say next.

"Should we play another cover?" Victor proposed.

"Maybe some Weezer?" Chunk suggested.

Steve, however, just gave us an impish grin. "Follow my lead," he commanded, before whipping around and facing the audience.

I turned back to look at Chunk, who seemed visibly concerned.

"*Just go with it,*" I mouthed to him, "*whatever it is.*"

"Thank you, San Francisco, for making this the best night of my life," Steve rasped into the mic. "I've worked so hard to get here, and this is a moment that I will never forget."

The crowd hollered back an overwhelmingly loud response, and we reveled in their reaction. Steve and the boys beamed proudly as they basked in the audience's unadulterated love.

But something wasn't sitting right with me.

This wasn't just Steve's *night to remember,* I thought to myself. *He's not the only one who worked hard to get here.*

"We've got one more song for you tonight," Steve promised the crowd. "And here it is."

At that point, Steve stepped on a guitar pedal, cutting the crackling hum of distortion and replacing it with an uncharacteristically clean, shimmering tone. He started strumming gently, a familiar-sounding open *G* chord issuing forth from his amp and reverberating through the venue.

Oh, no, I thought to myself as I recognized the familiar walk-down chord progression. *Please don't let him play that…*

Much to my dismay, Steve started singing the terribly trite opening line. *"The stars are out tonight… and so are we…"*

That's right: "Stars." The painfully mediocre song that he had composed for Serena in a vain attempt to win her back. Steve opted to play the worst song on our album to close out the best show of our lives. With obvious irritation, Chunk mechanically thumped on his kick-drum and tried to keep time with Steve's inconsistent waltz. Victor joined in with single whole-note beats on his bass, while Ethan picked an arpeggio on his Gibson's strings. As Steve soldiered on, strumming his mediocre ballad in the center of the Fillmore's stage, the kinetic energy filling the room dropped to a stillborn, muted hum.

What is he trying to prove? I asked myself. I turned back towards the drum kit and gave Chunk a quizzical look. He just solemnly shook his head and continued tapping his snare with battered Vic Firth drum sticks. Looking over at Victor and Ethan, I was a bit surprised to see the two of them fully focused on our fearless leader. *Don't they realize just how bad this song is?* I wondered. *And how bad it will be for our careers?*

Steve didn't seem to care, though. He just continued strumming his guitar lightly and cooing into the microphone. And, while I clearly had Chunk in my corner, I was shocked that Ethan and Victor actually seemed to be *enjoying* themselves while they played along. Finally, after much delaying and handwringing, I started tinkling along on the keys, coaxing the Alesis to emit a glossy sheen for that turd of a tune.

There was a reason that we didn't put "Stars" on our setlist that night: the song has the strength and momentum of a turtle in rush hour traffic. The lyrics are putrid, the chord progression is amateurish, and the melody is maudlin. And yet, for all its terrible flaws, Steve deemed it worthy to play at the Fillmore.

The Fillmore.

I thought about all of the photos I had seen backstage: Jerry Garcia and the Grateful Dead, John Fogerty and Creedence Clearwater Revival, Jimi Hendrix, Led Zeppelin, Pink Floyd… None of those legends would have dared play something as trite as "Stars" on that historic stage.

As I tediously tinkered along on my Alesis, an epiphany washed over me. *As long as Steve is leading this band,* I realized, *we will never be anything more than a second-rate pop-rock act.*

I looked up from my keyboard to scan the faces in the crowd. There were some star-struck young women in the front fawning over Steve, but I saw throngs of folks heading for the exits. A few audience members listlessly checked their watches, yawned, and started making idle conversation with their friends. Even Steve's acolytes, Ethan and Victor, started to look bored onstage as they played a supporting role behind our lead singer.

"Stars" was meant to be a power ballad, but there was nothing powerful about it. It was banal drivel with little redeeming quality. And the only person who couldn't see that, apparently, was Steve.

One of us needs to go, I thought to myself as I seethed over my keyboard. *It's either going to be Steve or me.*

When the house lights finally came on and the band left the stage, it was an anticlimactic conclusion to the evening. Despite the incredible momentum we'd accumulated over the course of our set, it felt like we fizzled out with our final song. We should have ended our performance with a musical home run, but our lead singer chose to wrap up the show with a self-indulgent bunt – not the grand slam that we needed. As T.S. Eliot might say, Call Field finished the concert "not with a bang, but a whimper."

The mood backstage was a cauldron of chaos and cacophony. Steve, riding high on what he assumed was his ultimate moment of glory, schmoozed with pretty young blonde girls who had maneuvered their way into the VIP area. He barely even acknowledged the presence of his bandmates as we rolled cables and packed up equipment for the load-out.

Ethan and Victor, periodically glancing over their shoulders and generally looking conflicted, simply watched from a distance.

Chunk and I, on the other hand, were fuming. We exchanged a few heated looks as I helped him load his drums, and I could see that his hands were shaking uncontrollably.

"You okay?" I asked him.

"No!" he grunted, his arms vibrating with increasing intensity. "I can't believe the nerve of that jackass!" He gestured with his head back towards the green room door, where Steve was busy entertaining starstruck suck-ups and sycophants.

"This is definitely *not* how I expected my birthday to end," I confided, heaving his cymbals up into my sweaty arms. "This was supposed to be our big moment of victory, you know?"

"What a dick!" Chunk reiterated, his venerable voice quaking with frustration. "He didn't even *mention* us! He didn't say our names, he didn't introduce us. And he sure as hell didn't sing you 'Happy Birthday' out there."

It hadn't dawned on me until Chunk pointed it out, but he was right: Steve had all but ignored us in front of the audience. It was like we were hired guns for some sanctimonious solo artist.

"Someone needs to say something!" Chunk announced indignantly, his voice rising to a crescendo.

"Just let it go," I told him, doing my best to bite my tongue and repress my rage. "It's like you told me a while back – *it's not worth it.*"

God bless my cousin. Though Chunk was undoubtedly a quiet guy, he was also a man of conviction. And he wasn't going to let this go without a fight. He turned away from me and let the gravitational force of his anger propel him towards our lead singer.

"Hey, Steve!" Chunk yelled out over the clutter of backstage bodies and equipment. "You forgot to mention Brick's birthday back there!"

"Did I…?" Steve answered with unfiltered contempt. "I guess that was an oversight of an insignificant detail."

Ouch. I'd been reduced to an *insignificant detail.*

"That's kind of funny," Chunk shot back, "because you also forgot to mention *our names* onstage. Are we also *insignificant details* to you?"

I swear that time stood still in that moment. It was like all sound and sensation stalled, and the whole world orbited this satellite confrontation between Chunk and Steve. Resentment had been building for quite some time now: the indignation that had been threatening to surface for years had ascended from the dormant depths and erupted in one cataclysmic explosion of emotion.

Steve started taking large strides towards us, his face an iron mask of anger. "You're not the one out front and center!" he yelled back. "*I'm* the one up there selling it, elevating us to something more than a mediocre garage band!"

Chunk bolted upright, like a bear pulling itself up from its haunches and preparing to slaughter an enemy. "*Mediocre garage band?*" he fumed. "You're just a marionette, pretty boy! You couldn't write a song to save your life, and it's this *mediocre garage band* that's pulling your strings and making you dance!"

"*I'm* the one carrying all the weight out there!" Steve shot back. "You think your ugly faces would bring anyone out to a concert? You think your fat asses would sell records if it wasn't for me?"

My cheeks were burning crimson now. *How dare he say that? How dare he dismiss us so casually, without any respect or regard for our talent and our work?*

Steve continued berating Chunk – and, by default, the rest of the band. "Did you see the way that the audience looked at me tonight? Do you think we would have *anything* if it wasn't for me? You think we'd have fans? A record deal? Shows? It's *all* me!"

Chunk laughed at him, taking a few huge steps forward and straightening his posture to the rafters. It was like watching Bruce Banner mutate into the Incredible Hulk, his anger transforming him into an intimidating size and shape.

"I wouldn't be so sure of that, pretty boy," Chunk spat out. "You don't have the brains or the talent to make it by yourself." He gestured in my direction. "The only reason you've made it this far is that Brick's been writing all the songs for you!"

Steve's face scowled with indignity, and his lips curled in arrogance. "Please! It was *my* song that brought the house down at the end of the night!"

I scoffed loudly enough for Steve to hear, and he immediately twisted his whole body towards me.

"What is it, fat boy?" he seethed. "Have you got something to say?"

"Fat boy?" Something about the way he snarled at me triggered my repressed rage. I felt a fuse lit inside me, the fiery flame igniting the twisted wire in my chest. "Call me fat one more time and see what happens!" I yelled at him.

Victor and Ethan, seemingly immobilized until that point, raced towards the impending brawl, both of them wearing confused and frightened expressions. They looked like traumatized bystanders, their bodies twitching nervously as the capricious powder-keg threatened an inevitable explosion.

"Everyone is watching us," Victor hissed, gesturing behind us to the rest of the backstage area.

I looked around and saw that Victor was right. Stagehands and roadies and other unknown spectators had all spun around to watch Call Field turn on itself like a gathering of punk rock cannibals. The pretty young blonde girls that had been draped over Steve like rumpled bedclothes hurriedly made their way out of the room, looking disillusioned and uncomfortable as they gripped their handbags tightly. I couldn't help but wonder if they were hoping to become numbers fourteen-and-a-half and fifteen-and-a-half in Steve's dirty laundry list of infinite infidelity.

"Guys, guys," Ethan pleaded, stepping between Chunk and Steve. "This is really unprofessional."

Chunk spat out an angry laugh. "You know what's *really* unprofessional?" Chunk asked, wheeling around towards Ethan. "Pissing all over the band that's been carrying your dead weight for half a decade."

"*Dead weight?*" Steve echoed Chunk's words back to him. "You heard what the record company said. *I've* got the look and *I've* got the voice! It's *my* picture on the album cover! This is *my* show and the rest of you are just riding my coattails!"

Despite my best intentions, the fire had crept too far along the fuse in my chest for me to remain calm any further. I finally entered the fray.

"You are *nothing* without us, Steve!" I yelled. "Those are *my* songs that you're singing! *My* words and *my* melodies! Call Field is nothing without *me!*"

Maybe I could have explained my position a little more delicately.

Maybe I overstated my role in the band.

Maybe I should have followed my own advice and kept my cool.

It was too late, though. Our fault lines were exposed and the tectonic plates had shifted. The seemingly solid earth that stabilized the band had been ruptured, and seismic convulsions were threatening to consume us.

As soon as I spat out my response, Ethan and Victor whirled around on me. Their expressions had transformed from hues of nervous confusion and equivocated anxiety to a downright vengeful shade of resentment. It was no longer Steve against the rest of the band: it was suddenly the Smith cousins against everyone else.

"That's where you're wrong," Steve said, his lips curling into a fiendish smile. As he turned to face me, I watched an arrogant calmness course through his body like a vitriolic vaccine. "You're nothing but concrete. You're just the floor that the rest of us stomp on. No one in the audience cares about you. They're watching me and Victor and Ethan run laps around that stage, entertaining the world while you and your two-dimensional cousin plant your flat feet in the background."

Chunk's anger was boiling over now. He could see the fault lines cracking, could recognize the chasm expanding between us. Suddenly, our musical brotherhood felt like a split group of Yankees and Confederates, neither side backing down from the impending civil war.

"In fact," Steve added with his ghoulish smirk, "you've made yourself obsolete." He looked back at Victor, whose arms were crossed tightly across his chest. "We have a *real* bassist now, one who can play a hell of a lot better than you ever could. You're just a useless keyboard player in a punk band. You're like a tuxedo in a swimming pool – completely unnecessary."

"*A tuxedo in a swimming pool?*" I laughed incredulously. "You can't even spit out a decent insult unless someone else writes it for you! You might be a pretty puppet with a good voice, but you're just dangling there unless someone feeds you the lines. *I'm* the one who pulls the strings, Pinocchio. You can't write a song to save your life!"

"What are you talking about?" Steve whined. "When I played 'Stars' tonight…"

"'Stars' is a piece of garbage, Steve!" I shot back. "Your stupid power ballad *killed* our momentum tonight. But you wouldn't have noticed that because you were too busy drooling over yourself to pay any attention to anyone else."

"I'm in the spotlight with my guitar," Steve started to answer with a slight tremor in his voice, "but you – "

"You and your guitar," I snorted. "You couldn't even strum well enough to make it onto the album! I had to record all your parts for you, you pathetic piece of trash."

Steve actually laughed at me, the brief traces of trepidation in his voice suddenly evaporating in the heat of the moment. "You think *I'm* the 'pathetic piece of trash?' If I'm so pathetic, how come I got the girl? You've been pining away for Serena all these years, crying from the sidelines, wishing it was you that was *sleeping with her*." Of course, he used a much cruder phrase, but I'll let you fill in the blanks yourself.

I was engulfed in rage, my hands shaking uncontrollably and my legs trembling. But Steve wasn't done yet.

"She didn't pick you," he snarled. "She picked *me*. Over and over again, she picked *me* over you."

"And look how well that turned out for her, you cheating bastard," I spat. As much as I tried to put up a steely, stoic front, Steve had found my Achilles' heel and plunged his verbal knife in.

"Serena didn't pick you because you're not good enough for her!" Steve roared, continuing to twist that burning blade. "You're fat and soft and weak. You mope and cry and write all these self-absorbed songs about girls and other petty *stuff.*" Once again, he used a cruder word to describe things, but I'm pretty sure you can use your imagination.

I thought my legs were going to collapse right underneath of me. My kneecaps started to wobble and I felt light-headed. The luminescent bulbs overhead suddenly seemed uncompromisingly blinding. I was shaking, swaying where I stood.

Steve saw me foundering, and he continued launching insults.

"And you know what, Brick? You're not good enough for *Call Field*, either. You might think that you're the backbone of this band, but you're just a pothole in the road. All you do is make Call Field sound weaker and softer."

Chunk must have sensed my frailty, because he stepped up next to me and placed his hand on my shoulder, steadying me as my body threatened to collapse. I turned my head halfway, just enough to read the expression on his face, and saw him glaring at Steve with unvarnished, unmitigated hatred.

"And that's because you're weak," Steve added. "You're soft. You're just a big, fat failure. You have nothing to offer Serena. You have nothing to offer me. And you have nothing to offer this band."

The sturdy foundations of my legs seemed ready to topple at any moment, but the incendiary fire in my chest ignited a kind of hatred that I had never felt before. Consumed in flames of resentment and betrayal, my body seemed simultaneously ready to collapse and catapult explosives at the enemy in front of me.

My hands balled up into tightly tethered fists. "It's taking everything I've got to stop myself from punching you right now…" I told him, gritting my teeth so hard I thought they might chip.

"DO IT!" Steve goaded me. "PUNCH ME, YOU PUSSY!"

It had all led up to this. Years of competition and rivalry had all been prologue to this precise moment. From that first meeting on the football field in the summer before our sophomore year of high school to

Serena's *quinceañera* to graduation tryouts to writing "Incomplete" to recording Call Field's major label album – it had all been building up to this critical climax. I spent years waiting to oust Steve from the band, to lash out at him with all the volcanic fury that had been swelling inside my heart for the better part of a decade. And the time had finally come.

But it wasn't me who threw the first punch.

It was Chunk.

With more force and fury than I thought possible, Chunk cocked his right arm back and launched his fist forward. As his knuckles connected with Steve's face, I heard a sickening smack that reminded me of sandbags dropped on a tile floor. Our arrogant lead singer pivoted to his right like a drunken dancer, wobbled, and then collapsed.

He hit the ground. Hard.

Ethan and Victor charged over, pushing past me and Chunk and dropping to their knees beside Steve's limp body. Ethan put his arm beneath Steve's neck and cradled our lead singer's head. Victor, however, looked like a confused bystander, unsure of how to proceed. When I glanced back at Chunk, he was trying to appear stoic – but the panicked glint in his eyes betrayed him. The twitching spasms around his temples revealed a mixture of shock and vindication, two conflicting forces that battled for control of his facial expressions.

"WHAT THE HELL, MAN?!?" Ethan screamed in our direction.

I was completely speechless, motionless – shocked by this unexpected twist of events. I had always assumed that *I* would be the one to go toe-to-toe with Steve, that it would be yours truly who finally erupted and entered a steel-cage death-match with our lead singer. Who would have expected that my cousin – quiet, unassuming Chunk – would finally be the one to snap?

Meanwhile, Ethan was gently slapping Steve's face, desperately trying to revive him from unconsciousness. "C'mon, Steve… C'mon, Steve…" Ethan repeated over and over. "Wake up, man!"

I glanced over at Victor and saw him starting to panic. Consumed by this cacophonous chaos, he got up from his awkward stance on the ground and began to nervously pace back and forth.

Finally, Steve started to stir, his eyelids flittering open, and his mouth soundlessly moving up and down. The left side of his face was a brilliant shade of crimson, amorphous bruises starting to form where Chunk's knuckles had collided with Steve's jaw.

When I glanced over at Chunk, I saw that his fingers were still curled up into tight fists, his fingernails biting into his palms.

And I just stood there.

What's going to happen next? I wondered, shock flooding every limb of my body. *This night can't possibly get any worse.*

And then it did.

CHAPTER TWENTY
"It's Over Now"

Just as the molasses-caked gears of time started to unfreeze and resume their normal speed, a piercing cry rang out from the far corner of the loading dock.

"BRIAN!" A familiar voice called out. *"OH, MY GOD, BRIAN!"*

I whipped around and saw Lani sprinting for me, her petite frame moving faster than I thought possible. As I ran over to meet her, I noticed her face was pale and stained with small, dried rivers of black. Mascara streaked down from her glistening eyes, leaving shriveled lines of makeup on her cheeks. I pulled her into my arms, her body convulsing and shaking hysterically.

"What is it?" I asked, a different kind of panic filling my chest. I threw my arms around her and held her tightly, her frame quaking uncontrollably.

"It's your dad..." she cried, her words barely breaking through her muffled sobs. *"Something's happened with your dad..."*

Lani quickly filled me in on everything. Halfway through our set that night, my dad had started hyperventilating and complaining about a pain in his chest. He begged my mom to take him back to Marina's house in San Rafael, saying that he needed to lie down or else he might pass out. My mom, Lani, Marina, and Reggie panicked – as would be expected – so they immediately ushered Dad out of the Fillmore and into Marina's car.

"We asked him if we should drive him to the hospital," Lani explained through breathless tears. "But he wouldn't let us. We made it across the Golden Gate Bridge but as soon as we passed the hills in Sausalito he told us to pull over so Marina veered off to the side of the road and helped him out of the passenger seat and he rolled out onto the ground and then he vomited all over and then he just collapsed…"

"Oh, my God…" I gasped, my heart beating sharp staccato rhythms in my chest.

"He was still breathing, but he wasn't moving," Lani rushed on, "so I ran over to the closest roadside emergency phone and dialed 911 and then ran back to the car. It took a few minutes for the ambulance to get there, but once they loaded him up, they took him to the nearest hospital." She paused, trying to catch her breath. "South San Rafael General Hospital. Your mom and Reggie went with him in the ambulance, but Marina and I came back to get you. Marina's out front with the engine running, but we need to leave *right now!*"

My eyes looked searchingly at my bandmates. This was the worst convergence of disasters in my life: my father in critical condition, my band falling apart on the opening night of a meticulously plotted national tour, and the most important friendships in my life suddenly jeopardized by physical violence and long-standing resentment. My eyes darted between Lani and the guys in the band.

"I've got to go," I said, my voice cracking with panic. I grabbed Lani's hand and prepared to dash off towards the direction of the street.

Just as I turned my heels to leave, however, a familiar, gritty voice called after me.

"Are you sure you want to do that?" Steve asked. He was conscious now, slowly stumbling to his feet and delicately rubbing his jaw. "I didn't give you permission to go."

"*Permission*…?" I shot back impatiently. "Why the hell would I need *permission* to leave?"

There was an eerie silence, like the unbreakable stillness before a hurricane strikes.

"If you leave," Steve said quietly, "then you're out of this band."

As if he'd been waiting for this moment all along, Steve walked over to his electric guitar case, popped it open, reached down, and pulled out a stack of folded papers. Slowly, methodically, he flipped through page after page in the packet until he found what he was looking for. As he held it up for me to see, I recognized the familiar bullet points and scrawled signatures.

It was the band constitution.

"According to this *legally binding* document," Steve said, condescendingly enunciating the latter cluster of his words like a college professor about to lecture his students, "if *any member* of the band misses a paid performance *for any reason*, he will be removed from the band partnership and forfeit all rights to the usage of the band name." He smirked at me like a jovial jackal toying with its prey. "If you leave now and miss tomorrow's show, you are out of this band. Forever."

So, it had all come down to this.

Years of friendship and camaraderie and music and tension and jealousy had led to this strange moment in a strange city at a stranger time than any of us could have imagined.

I squeezed Lani's hand tightly. "Go wait in the car with Marina," I whispered to her. "Tell her to keep the car engine running."

Lani's forehead scrunched up in worry. "Are you sure, Brian?"

My eyes cast back towards Steve, at his cruel smirk and vindictive posture. "I'm sure," I whispered in her ear with a resigned sigh. "This is going to get ugly."

Lani nodded and kissed me on the cheek, her eyes glazing over as she turned away from me. Her flip-flops slapped sharply against the hard concrete as she ran back in the direction of the street, the vibrations echoing back and forth across the hallway. Soon, the sound faded and Lani was gone.

I turned back to face Steve and jammed my hands into the pockets of my jeans, like a wolf placing a muzzle over its own mouth.

Maybe if I keep my hands tied down, I thought to myself, *I won't be tempted to throw a punch.*

"I need to leave," I told them as calmly as I could. I don't know what depths of my subconscious spurred me on, but my father's words raced from the recesses of my memory through my mouth and out into the world: "*Some things are more important than rock and roll.*"

No one said anything. Perhaps my bandmates were letting the weight of my demand sink in, allowing my words to settle in their minds like fog upon the shoreline.

For a brief moment, I felt a glimmer of hope as Victor reached out his hand and placed it delicately on Steve's arm. "Clearly, we've reached an impasse," Victor said. "Why don't we just table this until the morning and not make any hasty decisions?"

Steve shrugged off Victor's hand and swatted it away like he was waving off a housefly. "This isn't a *hasty decision*," Steve scoffed. "I've been waiting for this moment for a *long* time."

Victor, my college roommate and trusted confidant, recoiled like a beaten child. He took two steps backward and stared warily at the ground in front of his feet.

I turned to Ethan, hoping my oldest friend – the shy kid who had bonded with me and Chunk in middle school so many years before – would intervene, would say something on my behalf. But he wouldn't even look at me.

Ethan. Victor. Steve. None of them had my back when I needed them the most. None of them would come to my defense. None of them would stick their necks on the line. As the realization washed over me like a fiery incantation, I could feel the lava in my veins rising to the surface. I was angrier than I had ever been in my life. I stared at Steve, my eyes hard and seething, my fingers quaking.

"*My dad is sick!*" I yelled at him. "He's in the *hospital*, for God's sake!" My eyes stung, and tears threatened to cascade forward.

"It doesn't matter," Steve whispered coldly, an icy smile on his bitter lips. "You have to make a choice."

My eyes searched around the room, turning again from Steve to Ethan to Victor to Chunk. Only my cousin's expression mirrored mine. It was clear to me then that Victor and Ethan wouldn't rush in to defend me now – or ever again, for that matter.

Chunk took two bounding strides forward, his massive frame towering over Steve. *"You can't do this!"* Chunk bellowed at him. Despite Chunk's hulking presence, I could see the panic clinging to my cousin's countenance, feral and unyielding. His arms shaking, he slashed his hands through the air and snatched the contract out of Steve's tenuous grip. He turned to me, seemingly for approval or affirmation, then flipped around to stare at Steve.

With one seamless, fluid movement, Chunk tore the contract in half. The pages fluttered downward like molted feathers, and the room was eerily still. Wisps of paper softly floated to the ground, making a barely audible scraping sound before they rested lifelessly on the concrete floor.

Steve started to cackle, his laughter vicious and cruel. "That's just a photocopy," he said with a malicious snicker. "My lawyer has the original signed copy in his office."

When I looked up at Chunk, he was quietly crying. Tears soundlessly filtered down the folds of his cheeks as he set his jaw firmly in place.

I turned to Steve, fighting back the tears in my own eyes.

"How did we get here?" I asked him. "How did it come to this?"

Steve's unflinching gaze was locked on my defeated face. "You brought this on yourself," he said. "After all those years of thinking you were so much better than everyone else, that just because you wrote the songs that you were somehow more important…" He took a few steps forward and poked a bruised finger into my chest, letting his words flutter in the air – like the band's torn-up contract that had descended impotently to the ground only a few seconds before.

"You can't do this without me," I muttered, my voice cracking with uncertainty.

"Well, Brick, this is the moment when you realize just how wrong you've been. You're just an unnecessary appendage to this band. You're not the heart. You're not the brain. You're the appendix. If you miss the next show, then you're out. You'll be legally, surgically removed from this band. And we won't even notice that you're gone."

I turned away from Steve and once again searched the faces of my bandmates, looking for some kind of reassurance or support. But there was nothing. Ethan and Victor refused to meet my eyes. They looked sheepish, embarrassed – almost scared, in fact – but they obviously didn't reflect the deep-seated loathing and despair that overwhelmed me in that terrible moment of betrayal.

I couldn't believe it. I had been presented with an unjust ultimatum that left me at the mercy of fate's cruel whims. What choice did I really have?

I glanced over at Chunk. He took a deep breath, looked back at me, then nodded. And, with my cousin's tacit approval, I made my decision.

"I'm done with you," I said. "I'm done with *all* of you. I quit."

There may or may not have been a number of expletives strewn about my sentences, but the gist remained the same.

I was finished.

I was finished with Call Field.

I was finished with Steve – and Ethan and Victor, for that matter.

I was finished with my old life.

Unflinching in my resolve, I turned my back to the group and stormed out the door into the cruel night.

I wished that I had something to destroy – to tear, to smash, to punch, to crush – a symbolic gesture that would emphasize the significance of my departure. As it was, I had to settle for the heavy stomping of my boots against the concrete floor and the echo that trailed behind me like so many wasted years of my youth.

CHAPTER TWENTY-ONE
"Break Away"

As I launched myself into the bitter nighttime air outside the Fillmore, I felt weightless, ungrounded, untethered from the earth. Gravity had shifted in a mere matter of minutes, and suddenly the world seemed very different than it had only an hour before. But the sobering sense of panic that was rising in my chest smothered any other concerns.

Once again, my father's words echoed back to me: *some things are more important than rock and roll.*

It didn't take long to find Marina's car. She was parked in the yellow loading zone in front of the Fillmore, her hazard lights flashing in lazy legato beats. As I ran to the car, Marina rolled down the passenger side window.

"Get in!" she yelled, her voice weary and weathered. She jerked her head towards the backseat, where Lani was fidgeting restlessly.

I flung open the passenger-side door and hopped into the cushioned seat. "Let's get going," I said to Marina as I fumbled with my seatbelt.

Just as she clicked off her hazard lights and released her parking brake, a voice rang out into the darkened street.

It was Chunk.

"Wait up!" he shouted. His footfalls echoed hard as he pounded towards us. He threw open the rear driver's-side door and jumped into the backseat next to Lani.

"What are you doing?" I asked him.

"You think you can ditch me with those jerks?" he grumbled, giving me a wink and a halfhearted smile. "I'm not going to stick around and play crappy power ballads for the rest of my life."

"Are you sure you want to do this?" I asked him.

Chunk reached forward and slapped me on the shoulder. "If the boat is sinking, it's better to jump overboard than go down with ship, right?"

I gave him a halfhearted smile in return.

Chunk deciphered the mixed emotions on my face without much effort. "It's going to be okay, Brian," he reassured me.

Marina shifted the car into drive. "I guess the matter is settled then," she said. And, with that, we pulled away from the curb and into the cold, foreboding night.

We maneuvered through the maze of 19th Avenue and edged our way towards the formidable, towering figure of the Golden Gate Bridge. Lani reached forward from the backseat and clutched my hand tightly, her fingers intertwining with mine and her thumb rubbing circles in the callused palm of my hand. I did my best to focus on the scenery around us, the exotic restaurants and stores and gas stations and apartment buildings that flew by us as Marina wove her way through the mystery that is San Francisco.

As we entered the verdant grounds of the Presidio, it felt like we were transported to another city, another world – as if we were navigating our way through the dense forest greenery of Endor rather than the urban hub of Northern California. When we emerged from the clearing and crossed into Fort Point, the claustrophobic woods gave way to an endless expanse of water that stretched out indefinitely into the western and eastern horizons.

The silent, gentle lapping of waves against the rocks seemed so vague and distant, like painted images from a Thomas Kinkade portrait. It was jarring to quickly cross from the hurried and hungry streets of San Francisco into the Presidio's pristine expanse of greenery, from the rocky cliffs of Fort Point to the rusted rafters of the Golden Gate. It felt like entering portals into other worlds and other lives.

In a way, I was at my own awkward precipice, crossing over from a life of almost-rock-stardom with my band – excuse me, *former band* – and venturing into some strange, surreal reality defined by urgency and ambulances and hospitals.

I stared out the window, my eyes tracing constellations in the sky. The steel beams of the Golden Gate arched skyward and stretched to the heavens before curving back down to the asphalt of the road. Up and down, up and down, the beams loped in alternating patterns like still-frames of cascading waterfalls.

This will be my life now, I thought to myself, *with interconnected peaks and valleys, all bound by the coiling beams that bind my past, present, and future…*

I snapped back to reality when Marina's right hand abruptly slapped the steering wheel, followed in quick succession by the unintelligibly loud honk of her car's horn.

"*COME ON, COME ON!*" she protested aloud as her eyes darted back and forth between the cars in front of her. "Move it, people!"

She was weaving in and out of traffic, fluidly etching her way across the three or four open lanes of the northbound freeway as she jammed her foot on the gas pedal. Throughout it all, Marina's worried expressions manifested in periodic slaps against the steering wheel and blunt elbows hammering against the driver's-side door. Apparently, I wasn't the only nervous wreck.

Lani squeezed my hand and leaned her head against my forearm. "Not exactly how you wanted to spend the last few hours of your birthday, is it?" she asked.

My birthday. That reliable signifier that annually marked the first day of summer, heralding the end of the school year and the beginning of ceaseless sunshine. Of course, it also meant that we were in June, halfway through the year, and I hadn't seen much of my parents at all during the months prior – months in which my father had apparently been spiraling into a whirlpool of poor health and prospective illness.

A new year. A new beginning. A new life.

Everything I was – everything I had been – was left behind in the rearview mirror.

CHAPTER TWENTY-TWO
"Our Prayer"

I hate hospitals. Always have. Probably always will. No matter how kind the nursing staff might be, how competent the doctors, how clean the facilities, there's always the lingering scent of death and decay that no amount of bleach can scrub away. As Marina, Chunk, Lani, and I made our way through the winding white halls of South San Rafael General Hospital, I couldn't help but gag from the caustic antiseptic smell that overpowered every other odor.

When we first arrived at the hospital, I was struck by the vaulted ceilings: the impossibly high walls gave the distinct impression that the building's architecture was making a vain attempt to reach for the heavens. I had no time to stop and ponder the symbolic significance, however, as we spun through the revolving doors at the entrance and frantically rushed over to the reception desk.

"He's on the eighth floor of the hospital," the receptionist calmly informed us. "Room 814. If you take these elevators up to floor eight, the room will be to your right, just past the nurses' station."

"Thank you!" Marina shouted as she bolted away from the foyer.

The rest of us followed close behind, swooping into the nearest available elevator, which beckoned us with its open doors. I swear, I've never been in a longer elevator ride: the hospital seemed to mock us as our claustrophobic metal cabin crept up the shaft at a leisurely pace. When we finally heard the long-awaited ding, and the sliding steel doors casually opened onto the eighth floor of the hospital, we dashed forward into the corridors looking for number 814. Skidding down the glossy tile, we would have completely missed the room had it not been for my mom.

"Over here!" she shouted over the stillness of the hallway. She lurched forward into the doorframe, waving at us as we whipped around and trailed back to the correct location. She put her hand over her chest, as if to still the panic in her heart. "Thank God you made it," she sighed.

We nervously crept into the room, greeted by an assortment of tinny beeping sounds and wheezing machines. The white noise and the white walls washed over me as I hesitantly shuffled forward. I squinted as my eyes adjusted to the timid thrust of halcyon lights in the dimly lit room. Each footfall seemed louder than I expected, each breath exponentially more deafening than I could have imagined. When my mother embraced me, I squeezed her tightly in my arms and stared over her shoulder at the hospital bed.

There was my father, stretched out underneath crumpled white sheets, his chest rising and falling in slow succession like a morbid waltz in 3/4 time.

"Is he okay?" Marina asked anxiously.

"He's okay for now," Mom told us with a constricted breath. "The ambulance ride was scary, but they moved us out of the ER pretty quickly. They want to do some CT scans and figure out what's going on with him, but there was some kind of highway crash in Novato that took priority, so they moved us out. Something about triage, they said, and being understaffed tonight. God, what a mess…"

Marina enfolded her in an embrace, and Mom immediately started sobbing. I instantly felt like an awkward little kid again, watching my big sister step up to comfort our mother while I just stood uselessly on the side. I snapped out of my self-pity, however, when Lani reached out and threaded her fingers through mine. Though I was more scared than I'd ever been in my life, having Lani there by my side helped ease my well-founded fears.

As I looked around, I thought to myself that Dad's assigned room seemed more like a luxury suite than a squished cubicle. It was much more spacious than any other hospital chamber I had ever seen, with comfortable chairs, a wardrobe, and a private bathroom replete with a full shower. The partially drawn blinds revealed a gorgeous view of a nearby forest. It was breathtaking.

As far as hospital rooms are concerned, this was the Ritz Carlton.

Though it had only been a matter of hours since the showdown at the Fillmore, everything that had transpired after the concert felt like a distant memory. There we were, gathered in the tidy confines of a San Rafael hospital room – while Steve, Ethan, and Victor were an hour's drive away in San Francisco, doing God knows what in the aftermath of the band fracturing apart.

The road had forked and split, leaving me in a spinning whirlwind of uncertainty.

I don't know how many hours passed before my dad woke up. He was medicated with some narcotic or another, so his typically jovial disposition was strangely subdued. Despite it all, however, he hadn't lost his sense of humor. As he looked up at us with glazed eyes, his glasses no longer glued to the bridge of his nose, he gave a little smirk.

"All this fuss over little old me?" he asked with a timid laugh before falling into a coughing fit.

"Dad! You're awake!" Marina cried, tears starting to make their way down her cheeks.

"I think I'm awake," he muttered. "Where am I?"

"You're in a hospital, Brian," my mom told him, stroking his hand gently.

"A hospital…?" he repeated back, blinking absently. "That must have been some concert if I ended up in the hospital." His ragged breathing echoed throughout the room, but a smile crept across his chapped lips. "Did I spend too much time in the mosh pit?"

My dad. What a comedian.

We spent a few awkward hours perched uncomfortably by his bedside, impatiently waiting to hear an update from the doctors and nurses who seemed to perpetually dash back and forth between the patients scattered throughout the halls. At some point or another, the hospital staff wheeled my dad off to get CT scans and administer a battery of other tests. The rest of us solemnly hunkered down in the waiting room, desperately looking for ways to occupy our time in the middle of this medical madness.

My mom, God bless her, couldn't stop pacing up and down the hallways. At one point, a nurse kindly asked her to stay out of the corridors, because she was obstructing the hospital staff's pathways. Uncle Jeff and Aunt Alyssa, who arrived shortly after the nurses wheeled away my father, were munching on some fast food. Since this was back in the days before cell phones became ubiquitous electronic appendages, there was a bit of confusion when they arrived at Marina's house and found no one home; so, while the rest of us stayed with Dad, Reggie volunteered to drive back and let Jeff and Alyssa know that we were waylaid at a hospital on the edge of town. Chunk was engrossed in a cheap, frayed Stephen King paperback, vainly trying to take his mind off the clumsy catastrophes of the prior evening. Marina and Lani were engaging in some sort of conversation in the far corner of the waiting room, my sister gesticulating wildly with her hands in frantic motions as she talked.

Unable to sit still, I found myself wandering the room, studying the surroundings. I dragged my hand across the sea-foam green walls, tracing the embossed patterns that looked like anarchic waves – white demarcations that some interior decorator had undoubtedly stamped with random assertion on the plaintive surface. It seemed to me that the walls were engaged in an eternal struggle between land and ocean, a cosmic cacophony of entropy and equivocation.

I was so trapped in my own thoughts that I didn't even hear Lani approach me. Silently, she slipped her hand through my arm, locking us together as we stood side-by-side. Though my eyes didn't leave the strange swirl of shapes in front of me, I suddenly felt tethered, grounded by her presence. We stood there, our feet planted in place like roots of a double-trunked tree, until we heard the swishing sound of a door open behind us.

There was a rush of urgent footfalls as our small crowd of family hurried over to the short, bespectacled man in a lab coat who had broken the stillness of the room. He surreptitiously glanced down at his clipboard, his almond fingers reaching up to push his glasses back from the bridge of his nose. He didn't seem very old at all – maybe forty-ish or so – but he exuded a sense of confidence and certainty that only accompanies years of wisdom and experience. He scanned the group of nervous faces surrounding him, finally settling his steady gaze on my mother's frail form.

"Mrs. Smith?" he asked, speaking directly to my mom.

Mom's voice cracked like a porcelain teacup. "Yes…?"

"I'm Doctor Saagar," he said, fingers flanking his metal clipboard. "I've just reviewed your husband's charts and scans, and I need to talk with you about a few things."

"Of course," my mom answered nervously.

"Would you prefer to speak in private?" he asked, glancing quickly at the half dozen people who formed a semicircle around her.

"No, no," she said. "We're all family here."

Lani squeezed my fingers. In this moment of uncertainty, she had officially been ordained as family. I just wish it could have been under better circumstances.

"In that case," the doctor said, taking a deep breath, "one of you might want to take notes."

Without a word, Lani rushed back to her purse, rifled through it, and returned with a pen and small pad of spiral-bound paper. She looked up at Dr. Saagar and gave him a nod.

"Ready when you are," she announced, sounding more like a dutiful reporter than an anxious girlfriend.

Dr. Saagar turned his attention back to my mother. "The scans show that there's a tumor, roughly the size of a baseball, blocking your husband's digestive tract," he explained. "We'll have to wait for confirmation until the bloodwork comes back, but there's a distinct possibility that we're looking at colon cancer."

Cancer. My dad might have cancer.

Though I wasn't looking at her, I could feel Lani shudder. Just a few years before, she had been through a breast cancer scare with her mother; I could only imagine the thoughts that must have been running through her head after my dad's diagnosis. She never wavered in her concentration, though: her attention remained fully focused on her notepad, her pen dashing off ink-stained scratches at lightning speed.

I knew that my dad hadn't been feeling well for awhile, but he was confident that the rest and relaxation of summer would help him kick whatever bug he had been unable to shake over the previous months. I didn't realize – in fact, *none* of us realized – that these manifestations were symptomatic of something more life-threatening.

Cancer.

"Because the tumor is so enlarged," Dr. Saagar explained, "he's probably been fighting this for quite some time now. When was his last physical examination?"

My mom immediately broke down in tears. As she sobbed, the doctor shifted uncomfortably in his place, subtly easing his weight from one sneaker-clad foot to the other.

"It's been more than a decade since his last doctor's visit," I interjected. "Probably close to two decades, in fact."

Dr. Saagar gave me an incredulous look. "It's been *years* since he's seen a medical professional?"

"He's got a… *thing*. With doctors," Marina clarified. "He always has." She averted her eyes from the physician in front of us and turned her gaze to the south-facing window.

"I see," Dr. Saagar said, his face a cool, stoic mask. "Well, unfortunately, his distaste or mistrust of doctors is not an excuse to postpone medical treatment at this critical point in time." The doctor flipped through a few pages on his clipboard, the small scraping of paper echoing listlessly through the room. After jotting down a few notes, Dr. Saagar retrained his eyes on Mom. "Your husband is not in good shape, Mrs. Smith."

My mother choked back a sob, her hands flying up to her quivering mouth. Marina wrapped her right arm around Mom's shuddering frame, squeezing her tightly. "What options do we have?" Marina asked, turning back to face the doctor.

Dr. Saagar flipped back through his chart once more before looking up at Marina. "The problem is that your husband's body has become incredibly compromised," the doctor explained. "His vitals are fluctuating dangerously. His heartbeat, in particular, is alarmingly irregular."

It seemed uncanny to me, in some strangely poetic way, that my father's heart could ever be "irregular." My dad was always such a consistent presence in my life, and a sturdy rock of support for so many other people – friends and family, students and staff. The idea that his heart could betray him just seemed impossibly ironic.

"At this point in time," Dr. Saagar continued, "our best course of action is to immediately prep for surgery. Chemo and radiation might be long-term courses of treatment to battle any cancerous presence we find, but we can only hope that any potential cancer hasn't metastasized. In the meanwhile, the tumor that's causing his blockage has progressed to a point where his body won't be able to process food normally until this is rectified. All the vomiting that you've seen in recent weeks – maybe even months – has been a direct result of this blockage."

My mom pulled her quavering hands away from her mouth. "I think we should do the surgery," she said. "We need to take out whatever's killing him."

Dr. Saagar locked his penetrating vision onto my mother. He looked unswervingly into her eyes and nodded. "Duly noted, Mrs. Smith. I must warn you, though, that there is a distinct possibility he might not survive surgery. This is a risky procedure, even under the best of conditions. Your husband's body, unfortunately, has deteriorated to a dangerous point. You need to decide if this is the right decision before we proceed any further."

My mother looked back at Dr. Saagar and opened her trembling mouth to speak. "It's not really much of a choice, now is it?"

CHAPTER TWENTY-THREE
"That's Why God Made the Radio"

By the time that the hospital staff wheeled Dad back into his room, he had somehow navigated his way through the confused fog of medications and was starting to sound more like himself. He was an exhausted and fatigued version of himself, mind you, but he more closely resembled the man I knew than the frail incarnation I had seen backstage at the Fillmore. His vital signs had improved a little, as evidenced by the staccato metronome beeps and blips that punctuated the silence. Still, though, he floated in and out of consciousness, falling asleep at irregular intervals like a bedridden narcoleptic.

We took turns stationed at his bedside, tapping out when we were too tired or emotional or uncomfortable to continue sitting in the compact, upholstered chairs in his hospital room. During the nighttime hours, when twinkling stars and blinking neon cast diminutive light in the darkness, we kept the room's plantation shutters open; during the daytime, we pulled the cream-shaded shutters closed and dimmed the halcyon lights to a humming luminescence. Not quite day and not quite night, we were living in a perpetual state of twilight, of in-betweenness.

The room was a strange mixture of clean and cluttered: a flurry of cords (not unlike the microphone and instrument cables strewn about our garage back home) stretched out from Dad's body, connecting to a series of mystifying machines measuring unknown rhythms and motions. For a brief second, I was kicking myself for not pursuing a career in the medical field. Maybe if I hadn't been wasting my time studying literature, I could have developed skills and knowledge that would've been helpful there in the cold confines of my father's hospital room. As I sat at a cheaply made wooden desk (a fixture that looked like expatriate furniture from IKEA), I found myself sketching out a succession of words and phrases – none of which helped shed light on the medical mysteries facing my father.

We had been at South San Rafael General Hospital for four days at that point, spending most of our waking hours perched by my father's bed and taking turns sleeping at Marina's house a few miles up Highway 101 on Lucas Valley Road. I had volunteered for the graveyard shift each night, holding down the fort in the wee morning hours while everyone else crashed at Marina's. I was a solitary figure in the night, like a lonesome nighthawk from an Edward Hopper painting (albeit quarantined in a hospital, rather than a midnight diner).

I remember walking up to my father's room that fourth night, ready for my shift and holding a steaming cup of vending machine coffee that I had procured from an adjacent hallway across the eighth floor. According to the push-button description, the coffee was supposed to taste like a Butterfinger candy bar; however, the flavor felt more like bitter midnight than any kind of saccharine sweetness. As I passed the threshold of the doorway, I heard the familiar sounds of a deep, heaving snoring emanating from my father's chest, like the ocean howling at the mouth of a cavernous lacuna. In that moment, it was strangely comforting to watch Dad's chest rise and fall in rhythmic succession, elevating and subsiding in alternating movements. I felt like a little kid, catching my dad napping on the living room couch; that same somnolent growling, though significantly more subdued than normal, reminded me that my dad was still alive and fighting. He hadn't given up the ghost yet.

I crept to the northern wall of the room and gently tucked myself into an upholstered chair. Even though I was a devout night owl back then, I still felt my body struggling against the encroaching exhaustion that had been building for the last few days – heck, the last few *months*. The human body is a flawed machine, an unreliable carriage for our minds and souls. Lamentably, it's the only apparatus we have. I just prayed that the vending machine coffee would help me persevere through the relentless night.

Cradling the styrofoam cup in my hands, I glanced around the room, searching for something to occupy my withering attention. From the hallway outside, I could make out the discordant moans and whimpers of patients from other rooms, the barely audible murmurs of conversation from the on-call nurses at their stations. But by my father's bedside, I found myself distracted by the inhuman beeping of the heart monitor, marking the rhythm of Dad's organs like a meek metronome.

As I glanced away from the heart monitor, I spotted a disheveled duffel bag full of clothes and other goods that had been stashed on a plastic chair next to my father's hospital bed. On the top, a rolled-up magazine protruded from the unzipped bag, reaching its fanned pages upward towards the ceiling.

At least I've got some reading material to help pass the time, I thought to myself as I reached into the duffel bag.

I uncurled the periodical and flopped back down into my chair, smoothing out the wrinkles of the glossy cover. Below the magazine's masthead, Kid Rock glared up at me and pointed an accusatory finger, his half-naked body posed like a redneck Uncle Sam. It was the June issue of *Rolling Stone*, hot off the presses, but someone had already been through it, apparently: a neon-yellow Post-it Note jutted up from the crinkled rear of the magazine. I flipped through page after page, skipping past the pieces on Don Henley and Derek Jeter and Kid Rock, until I landed on the article with the aforementioned sticky note.

Right there, on the seventh page of the *Reviews* section, buried behind critiques of rappers and rockers and pop stars, was one long, thin column devoted to Call Field's new album:

★ ★ ★
Call Field
A Different Slant of Light
LOWERCASE RECORDS
SoCal pop-punkers face identity crisis

all Field can't decide what it wants to be.
Is this crew of Southern California kids a
hard-partying punk band, an ensemble of
radio-ready frat boys, or an aspiring assembly
of alternative rockers? On the group's major
label debut, A Different Slant of Light, Call
Field takes its cues from blink-182 and Weezer
but forgoes the dick-and-fart jokes of the former and Dungeons &
Dragons geekines
of the latter. Alas,
spite of these tri
and-true touchsto
this album co
across as a pale
tation of those
cal forbearers.
its stylistic
comings, however, A Different Slan
songwriting,
CALLFIELD

***

Call Field

A Different Slant of Light

Lowercase Records

SoCal pop-punkers face identity crisis

Call Field can't decide what it wants to be. Is this crew of Southern California kids a hard-partying punk band, an ensemble of radio-ready frat boys, or an aspiring assembly of alternative rockers? On the group's major label debut, *A Different Slant of Light*, Call Field takes its cues from blink-182 and Weezer, but forgoes the dick-and-fart jokes of the former and *Dungeons and Dragons* geekiness of the latter. Alas, in spite of these tried-and-true touchstones, this album comes across as a pale imitation of those musical forbearers.

Despite its stylistic shortcomings, however, *A Different Slant of Light* showcases exemplary songwriting. Disparate pop culture references abound throughout the sun-drenched songs: the band places itself in Johnny Cash's dusty boots in "(Won't You Be My) June," and invokes David Lynch's *Twin Peaks* on "Sherilynn." Still, it's "Incomplete (Just Like Your Smile)" which has the unrivaled potential to wind up as the song of the summer. "I get lost sometimes in the melodies of my mind / where I've tried to find what I need," growls lead singer Steve Öken over chiming electric guitars. Undoubtedly, the song will find a home on MTV in the months ahead and serve as the de facto summertime soundtrack to frivolous days at the beach. The only clunker here is the album's closer, "Stars," a schmaltzy ballad which reminds us that this group of youngsters has quite a bit of growing up left to do.

Like Holden Caulfield, the adolescent antihero that inspired the band's moniker, these young men are prematurely wizened, stuck between childhood and adulthood, waxing nostalgic about days in the sandbox while dreaming of monogamous long-term relationships with bikini-clad babes. It would be cute if it wasn't so quaint. Let's just hope that future albums deliver on the promise of this debut record and that these beach boys find a way to grow up into sophisticated, tuneful young men.

Rolling Stone.

Call Field was in *Rolling Stone*.

My band had made it into *Rolling Stone* magazine.

Correction: my *former* band had made it into *Rolling Stone* magazine. And which member of Call Field was the only one name-checked in the article? Steve.

Because of a song's lyrics that I had once scrawled into the margins of an old copy of *Rolling Stone* magazine, my band had made it into the actual printed pages of *Rolling Stone*. And while *my* words, *my* lyrics were the ones printed in those coveted columns, my name was never mentioned once.

I slapped the magazine closed and threw it across the room. As it gently banged against the sterile hospital wall and fluttered to the floor, I crumpled into my seat and crossed my arms across my chest. And then, like an indecisive lover in a Cameron Crowe film, I changed my mind. As soon as the magazine hit the ground, I jumped out of my chair and ran to retrieve it. I flipped open to the yellow sticky note and read the article again. And again. And again.

As much as I wanted to fume over the continued injustices I had to endure in the shadow of Steve, I couldn't help but feel vindicated by the *Rolling Stone* review. Sure, they had failed to name-check anyone else in the band, but Steve was only mentioned in one clause of one sentence of one paragraph. Yes, it was easy to get distracted by the criticisms of the album's production and style – something which frustrated *all of us* in the band – but side-by-side those insults came a flurry of prevalent praise. In particular, the line about "exemplary songwriting" bolstered my spirits. The rock and roll gods had proclaimed that my writing was *exemplary*.

Yup, your humble narrator had gone from zero to hero, from underdog to top-dog. And I had the proof in print.

As I reread the article again for the sixth, seventh, and eighth times, it felt like my life's work and worth had been validated within the thin columns of those flimsy pages. Even if the album wasn't perfect, my work had *value* and *credibility* and (perhaps) even *significance*. For a few precious, fleeting moments, I felt myself floating.

And then I remembered that my time in Call Field was done.

As petty as it might have been, you know what made me smile the most? The fact that the reviewer had called Steve's sole writing contribution a *clunker*. Steve might have considered me "obsolete," but *he* was the one who couldn't write a single decent song. Even if I had lost the war over control of the band, winning that battle felt good. Really good.

In the early morning hours before the dawn, I was working my way through the rest of the *Rolling Stone* issue, reading about Don Henley's solo career and his turbulent years with The Eagles, when the snoring suddenly stopped. It's funny: you become so accustomed to the onslaught of sibilant sounds that when they disappear, the room suddenly feels eerily quiet. I sat up straight in my seat and craned my neck forward to study my father's frail frame.

His eyes were blinking rapidly, as if his eyelashes were winking away cobwebs that kept him in a comatose cocoon. He was breathing regularly, his chest rising and falling in syncopated rhythm, but he looked like he was sleeping with his eyes open. Eventually, he turned his head in my direction and squinted in the darkness.

"If it isn't my favorite rock star," he whispered, his voice barely audible above the staccato beeping of his heart monitor.

"Hey, Dad," I whispered back, reaching over to give his withered hand a tight squeeze.

He tried to prop himself up from his reclining position, but he winced in pain as his shaking arms fumbled for a substantial surface. "I feel like I need the world's biggest cup of coffee to wake up from this fog," he said. Eventually, he gave up his attempts to change position on the mattress and simply let his head fall backwards onto a half-deflated pillow.

"If it's any consolation," I told him, scooting my chair closer to his bed, "the coffee here is terrible."

He glanced over at the cup in my hands and his eyes folded in on themselves, his vision cloudy and unfocused.

"It's from a vending machine," I told him, swishing the remnants of my drink in the almost-empty styrofoam cup. "It's just a notch up from muddy water."

"That's a shame," my dad grumbled in his dazed state. "Coffee is one of life's most precious commodities."

"Amen to that, Pops," I laughed.

"And life's too short to drink your coffee black," he reminded me.

Although I had heard the phrase countless times over the previous twenty-one years of my life, it had never seemed more relevant than inside the surreal space of a hospital room. My smile faded, and I let my eyes trail down to the nearly depleted cup of coffee in my hands.

"Where is everyone?" my father asked with a wide yawn, his arms stretching outward towards the walls.

I looked at my watch. The numbers on the face read *7:45 AM*. I had been up all night.

"Mom and Marina should be here any minute," I said, stifling a yawn of my own.

As his eyes scanned the room around us, he seemed to gradually emerge from the fog of sleep and medication. I didn't want to broach the topic of his health, but I couldn't think of any other way to proceed than to simply address it head-on, like a steam locomotive staring down missing spikes on a railroad line.

"So, this might have been developing for years?" I asked him, keeping my vision trained on the styrofoam cup between my fingers.

"That's what they told me," he grunted, still trying in vain to prop himself up. "God, I hate this bed. Hospitals are supposed to make you feel better. These beds are supposed to *comfort* patients, but they just end up causing more discomfort."

"Do you want me to call a nurse?" I asked, jumping out of my chair and taking a few steps forward.

"No, it's fine. I've seen more nurses in the last few days than in the last twenty years."

"Are you sure?"

"I'm *fine*," he told me, perhaps a little more forcefully than he intended. His chest deflated, and he sank back into the stiff confines of the bed. "I'm sorry, Junior. I'm just not myself right now."

As I stood there over my father's flimsy frame, my body casting bleak shadows over the bed, I studied him again. The loose flaps of skin that hung from his bony arms, the sunken sallow craters around his eyes, the weathered wrinkles that creased in folds on his spotty hands… When had my vivacious father become so old, so frail?

"Are you okay?" he asked me.

Ironic, considering that he was the one in a hospital bed.

"Yeah," I muttered.

"You seem distracted."

"I'm just thinking, Dad," I whispered back.

"We tend to do a lot of that in this family. Thinking."

"You can say that again," I chuckled softly.

His fingers suddenly darted into the air. "Did you see the *Rolling Stone* article?" he asked me, his eyes aglow. He hiccuped abruptly, and his body shuddered. It seemed inconsequential at the time, but it was jarring, nonetheless.

I sighed. "I may have read it," I admitted, "a few dozen times."

"*Is that amazing or what?*" he said, his voice more animated than I had heard in ages. "My son… my SON is in *Rolling Stone* magazine!"

"It's not exactly the *cover* of the *Rolling Stone*," I added, half-singing the old Dr. Hook & the Medicine Show song.

"Don't be so modest!" His eyes darted around the room, searching for something. "I had a copy here somewhere…" he started to say.

Another few hiccups escaped from his jerking body.

I reached back to my upholstered seat in the corner of the room and snatched the issue of *Rolling Stone*. Delicately, I placed it on the bed beside his left arm, careful not to disturb the web of wires that spread out like plastic veins across the sheets.

He grabbed the magazine and held it up for me to see. "This! This is something huge! Do you know how many people would kill to have their name in *Rolling Stone*?" Yet again, he hiccuped sharply, and his body quaked.

"But my name wasn't actually *in* the article," I pointed out. Despite my father's unerring optimism, I still felt deflated.

"That's just a technicality," he shot back, dismissing my concerns with a wave of his bony hand. "Your band…"

"It's not my band anymore, Pops," I interrupted.

He continued on, undeterred. "The band that *you* started, Junior, and the songs that *you* wrote have done something remarkable, something that very few people ever accomplish."

Hiccup.

"You have made it into the world's foremost rock and roll magazine!" he exclaimed. "And they called your songwriting *exemplary!* That's incredible!"

Hiccup.

I couldn't help myself: I was swayed by my father's pride. A wrinkle of a smile formed at the corner of my lips and I felt my chest swell a little. Even at the ripe old age of twenty-one, I found myself bolstered by my father's approval.

"Thanks, Dad," I mumbled.

"Seriously, Junior, you can die happy now," he told me. "Heck, I think that *I* can die happy now."

Another flurry of hiccups immediately followed.

Just as quickly as it had blossomed within me, I felt the self-satisfaction and pride of my accomplishment suddenly wither in the face of reality. "But it's not mine anymore," I sighed.

"What do you mean?" he asked.

Hiccup.

"I mean that the band isn't mine anymore," I reiterated. "I walked away. I quit."

"Okay, sure," my dad conceded. "But that doesn't mean those songs don't belong to you. You made them, you shaped them. They're your children. No matter what happens, those songs will always be yours."

I found myself rubbing the bridge of my nose. "But what good are a bunch of songs if I'm not actually *playing* them?" I asked. "What am I, if I'm not a musician or a songwriter?"

My father drew in a long breath.

Hiccup.

"Those are questions you'll have to answer for yourself, Junior."

Hiccup.

"You have many years to unravel the thread of your identity," he told me. "One little tear in the fabric isn't enough to destroy the entire tapestry."

Hiccup.

Though he might have been right, I couldn't conceive of my life in those terms. Back then, I saw things as an either/or dichotomy: I was either a musician or I wasn't. I either had a band or I didn't.

"You don't understand, Dad," I muttered to the wall. "This is bigger than me. I have to make choices now. I have to decide if I want to go crawling back to the band and beg for forgiveness, or if I want to say 'screw it' and move on with my life. I either have to give up my self-respect or fight to keep my dignity."

There was a pregnant pause in the conversation. My dad looked up at me from his prostrate position in the hospital bed and studied me like a weary god rendering judgment.

Hiccup.

"You don't have to choose," he told me, his voice like parched leather. "Your life doesn't have to be incomplete." He looked down at his hands, away from my line of sight.

It started small. The hiccups had been building slowly, like small whitecaps cresting upon the shoreline at irregular intervals.

Then it exploded.

Suddenly, an invisible torrent shook his body like lightning splitting a tree down to its earthen roots. Then it reached a crescendo, an invisible force mounting him like a wave, shaking his body in violent fits.

And then he started convulsing.

CHAPTER TWENTY-FOUR
"'Til I Die"

Watching someone die is nothing like in the movies. There's no gentle seeping out of the ghost, no dramatic sigh as life escapes from the lips of the recently deceased.

Death is violent.

Death is uncomfortable.

Death is frightening.

The soul doesn't whisper forth quietly: it rages and rattles the walls of flesh that bind and anchor it.

I remember watching my father's body convulsing on the hospital bed, the heart monitor accelerating from a series of increasingly frequent beeps to one long, sustained siren. At first, my brain couldn't process what was happening: how could someone who seemed so present – so *alive* – one moment suddenly find himself in a life-or-death battle?

The hospital staff rushed in to answer the clarion call blaring from his monitors, a sudden blur of blue scrubs and white tennis shoes squeaking across the tiled floor. They pressed their hands upon his chest, eyes darting to the shrieking machines that wailed like banshees into the night. All the while, my father's body quaked and shook like a toy in a petulant child's hands.

It was like watching someone succumb to demonic possession. But instead of a mythical devil entering the body, it was the absence of life that shook and shattered my father's frail frame. All the while, I stood motionless, staring impotently as doctors and nurses rushed around the room. A flurry of cream-colored coats flashed around me, and a nurse forcibly ushered me out of the hospital room so that I wouldn't interfere with their work.

It didn't feel real– *couldn't* feel real – as I watched the doctors and nurses open up the defibrillator paddles in one fluid motion and strap them to my father's chest, as the cacophony of voices and commands mixed in the austere hospital room with an achingly familiar cry (*oh my god*, I realized, *is it my own scream I'm hearing?*), as a doctor's stiff arms found their way to Dad's sagging chest and pushed, pushed, pushed against the blackness that threatened to devour him, as Marina and my mother came rushing through the hallway, their styrofoam coffee cups dropping to the waxen floor in slow-motion, and suddenly I was on the ground, clawing with my curled fingers at the edges of the wooden frame of the doorjamb, someone's white-garbed arms blocking the entrance, Marina trying to reason her way through anyway, my mother sobbing and emitting sounds like a wounded creature, and my breath bumbled in my bubbling throat, caught in a concrete force of air that silenced me, winded me, a sense of panic rising uncontrollably in my chest, my arms shaking, vibrating, pulsating, and hysteria seeping into my veins until I was no longer myself, I was a primal animal, all teeth and sobs and swift, violent motions trying to stay the inevitable reality that everything was changing, life was changing, and there was nothing I could do to stop the oncoming storm of macabre clouds and lethal lightning and terrible thunder because I was just a powerless creature without any agency, without a magic wand to stave off the inevitable reality that his life was ending – the life of my father, the best man I had ever known, the one person who had always believed in me, supported me, cheered for me, embraced me, and guided me through even the darkest of my days, a miniature god who wielded words like Zeus's bolts and who used to lift me up like Hercules and who could navigate any torrential current better than Odysseus, a giant of a man who taught me how to play guitar and fasten a necktie and mow the lawn and scrub the dishes, a fevered force of humility and gratitude that commanded the attention of everyone in the classroom or the backyard or the dining room, a singular figure whose gentle hand urged me forward even when I was frozen in fear or halted by heartbreak – and now I could feel the curtain of pitch-black despair descend over my cowering head, the light draining from my eyes, and he wouldn't be here to guide me through it, wouldn't be able to hold my hand like he did when I was a child, wouldn't be there to pull me in tightly to his chest or write me letters or listen to my songs or talk to me about anything – God, what I wouldn't give to just speak with him about the most ridiculously trivial details of pop music, about Brian Wilson and the Beach Boys and their complicated history and the debates about Mike Love and the future of the band and whether or not they would ever get back together, if it's possible to reconcile those broken bonds, those shattered windows of relationships, if the rearview mirrors of our lives are irreparably damaged or if there's salvation for even the most twisted of souls, the ones that seem irredeemable, and though he had lived his life by the book, had dedicated decades to helping others, he would never see his reward, never smile serenely at his retirement party, never get to live for himself, never visit Hawaii or write his book or record his album, never get to see my wedding day or witness the birth of a grandchild or complete another brilliant thought –

He was gone.
My father was gone.

CHAPTER TWENTY-FIVE
"A Young Man Is Gone"

How do you continue standing when the foundation of your existence has crumbled, dissolved, faded into nothingness?

I remember my body draped across the tile floor, limp and lifeless and curled inward like an infant impotently floating in its mother's womb. But someone must have pulled me to my feet, dragged me from the scene of my father's death. And then I was in another room, sobbing into my shirt, inconsolable in my despair. Lani had wrapped her arms around me and was cradling my trembling body as I wept. At some point, we were ushered out of the hospital, and we reluctantly drove back to Marina's house. When we arrived at her place, I collapsed in the guest room, sprawled out on a twin bed, lying on my side and howling into the muffled surface of a pillow.

While I was cowering and quaking in that spare bedroom, the world outside those walls continued on undisturbed. Cars flew down Lucas Valley Road, speeding off to work or school or lovers or doctors, while neighbors walked dogs on the sidewalk or jogged on the street or chased after wayward basketballs in pristine driveways. So much movement, so little friction to stop the gears of a swiftly fractured reality.

Just because your world implodes in trauma and suffering, it doesn't void the existence of other lives, other paths, other journeys. While I was struggling to make sense of my loss – to navigate the intractable, winding rivers of grief – the world was continuing on around me.

Almost as if my father had never existed at all.

Try as we might, it's impossible to intellectualize death in the aftermath of a personal tragedy. We are wounded animals in these times, aching in agony, grasping for stability and security as we descend into the quicksand of mourning. In our grief, we sink, sink, sink – but we flail with our arms and legs, desperately searching for a solid surface to anchor ourselves so that we can make sense of the desolate, shuddering aftermath.

One moment, you're talking and laughing and joking. Then, within seconds, it all changes. The familiar voice that you've known for years is suddenly silenced. The smile that greeted you every single day after school is rigid and uninhabited. The warm breath that you felt on your neck with every embrace is a cold, motionless void.

Gone, gone, gone. All of it. Forever.

You can rage, you can sob, you can protest all you want. But death is an indifferent, unrepentant harvester, claiming life after life with a gleaming scythe.

In the wake of such loss, there is a vacancy, an emptiness that possesses you. You feel barren and lifeless, even though you can sense the warm pulsing of blood through your tired veins and the exhausted breath seeping in and out of your mechanized lungs.

Grief is a strange shoreline. Pain washes over you in waves and then recedes unexpectedly. Sometimes, you feel like you're drowning. Other times, you feel desolate and bone-dry.

After you lose someone you love, someone whose life has shaped yours beyond even your own comprehension, it doesn't ever get better – it just gets easier. Slowly, slowly, the pain subsides in incremental notches until the stinging sensation of sorrow becomes a bruised numbness and a hollow vacuum.

Your heart drifts slowly towards the shore. Though you feel unanchored for so long, adrift at sea with no tether to the ocean floor, you see promising land on the distant horizon. Like Gatsby's green light, you know it's almost within reach. If you're lucky, you might find outstretched hands to pull you ashore. You will stand on solid ground soon.

It's just a matter of time.

At that point in my life, though, I couldn't see any lighthouse or illumination leading me ashore. I felt submerged, like air was escaping from my ribcage and bubbling up to the inimitable surface of the ocean. It was simply too much for me to handle.

In a matter of days, I lost almost everything.

I lost my father.

I lost my best friends.

I lost my band.

I lost my career.

Even though it's been over two decades now, I still feel my chest tighten and my lungs constrict when I think about those days. Sometimes, the littlest trigger, like a hospital bed or styrofoam cup – even an orphaned issue of *Rolling Stone* – is enough to bring me to the precipice of a panic attack. After my father's death, I crumbled, receded into myself, faded from the light into a shroud of darkness.

Those shadows hovered over me for a long, long time.

CHAPTER TWENTY-SIX
"Summer's Gone"

The days after my father's death were impossibly hard to navigate. Everything around me seemed blurry, as if the world was permanently warped with the watery distortion of tears in my eyes. I felt like the wind had been knocked out of my lungs by the swift fists of fate, and I was constantly left gasping for breath in the aftermath.

Thank God for Lani. She was my mast during those unmoored days. Every time I collapsed, she was there providing stability. Every time I broke down, she threw her arms around me and pulled me back up.

It was my mother, though, who became our driving force in the days leading up to my father's funeral. I don't know how she was able to compartmentalize her grief, but she transformed into our family's bold matriarch overnight – feeding us, hugging us, even delegating tasks for us to tackle before Dad's memorial service. While Mom spoke with the crematorium and called around for venues to hold a funeral, she assigned duties for the rest of the family: Marina assembled a bulletin board with decades worth of photos, Uncle Jeff called every known relative and acquaintance to break the devastating news, Aunt Alyssa prepared casserole after casserole in our claustrophobic kitchen, and Lani ran an endless gauntlet of errands to the supermarket and beyond.

I was left with the daunting task of writing my father's obituary.

"You're the wordsmith, little brother," Marina reminded me. "This is your forte. This is your realm."

Under different circumstances, I might have felt flattered. But this responsibility weighed heavily on my aching Atlas shoulders.

How do you sum up a man's life in a matter of paragraphs? I wondered to myself. *How do you capture a man's complexities and victories in a handful of simple sentences?*

I had never written an obituary before, but I somehow channeled all of the disparate, throbbing emotions in my heart and composed a simple column of formulaic paragraphs. Lani was the perfect guide for me: at some point in her journalism classes and internships, she had written a few mock memorials. As I strung words together like Christmas lights on the skeletal limbs of a naked tree, she sat patiently beside me, listening and reading and offering gentle suggestions.

"It's beautiful," she told me when I finally typed out my closing sentence. "Your father would be so proud right now."

I gave a halfhearted smile in the dim glow of the computer screen, tears trickling down my oily skin. I sobbed and she held me, her hands weaving their way across my back and through my hair. I crumpled into her arms and let the waves of grief course through my shuddering body.

My father's funeral was, by all accounts, a celebratory event. Of course, I shouldn't have been surprised: he was, after all, a well-loved member of the Ojai community and a revered teacher at Sespe Creek High School. With this in mind, Mom called up Principal Gardner at Sespe Creek and arranged for us to rent the school's auditorium for Dad's memorial service.

In my naiveté, I assumed that a few dozen people would attend, mostly out-of-town family and some Sespe Creek staff members. Imagine my surprise, then, when throngs of people showed up to pay their respects, filtering into the SCHS auditorium and crowding into the tiny seats of the theater. In addition to my father's family and friends and coworkers, hundreds (and I mean *hundreds*) of his former students filled the seats around us. Although I had taken my dad's AP English course only a few years before – and I knew fully well how remarkable a teacher he had been – I didn't anticipate how dramatically he had impacted the lives of his former students.

When you're sixteen or seventeen years old, forced to spend an hour each day in a stuffy classroom covered in posters of poetry and an odd assortment of kitschy knickknacks, you don't really think about how the middle-aged teacher in front of the class will leave a long-lasting legacy in your malleable mind or your harrowed heart. And yet, as I scanned the aisles around me in that ancient auditorium, I saw several decades worth of students coming to pay their respects to my father. Of course, there were the teenage tykes in jeans and converse who had only recently been enrolled in my dad's English class. But I also saw grown adults – men and women with children in tow – who had been my father's students before I was even born. Something about "Mr. Smith" (as they knew him) had reverberated for them in a profound way; even years later, they felt so indebted that they came from miles around to pay their respects.

When the memorial service began, I was front-and-center in the theater, flanked by Lani on one side and my mother on the other. Principal Gardner, that old patriarch of Sespe Creek, walked up to the podium first and began a lengthy diatribe about how Dad embodied the best qualities of Sespe Creek High School. As Dr. Gardner attested, my father was selfless and talented and compassionate and brilliant and noble and kind.

The school district's superintendent, Dr. Arroyo, followed Principal Gardner, his ghostly gray hair radiating in the spotlight onstage. In broad statements and vague compliments, Dr. Arroyo described how my father had worked for the Ojai Valley School District for three decades. From behind the podium, the superintendent did some quick math, explaining how thirty years of teaching with 150 pupils each year meant that my father had positively impacted the lives of some 4,500 students. He then gestured around the auditorium, his arms sweeping grandly over the hundreds of men, women, and children who had come to honor my father's memory.

As I glanced behind me at the packed theater – every single seat filled with a warm body, and dozens more lining the walls or sitting cross-legged in the carpeted aisles – I felt a lump forming in my throat. In that moment, I couldn't help but feel proud of Dad – the man whose balding head and husky frame had towered over me for so many years. He wasn't just *my* father, a family man with a small sphere of influence; rather, he was a miraculous *mensch* whose *mitzvah* had wide-reaching implications, far beyond what I could have imagined at that point in my life.

We were celebrating the life of a giant, and I felt like a dwarf beside his memory.

Throughout the service, Lani stabilized my shaking hands, channeling strength into my entire body with every gentle squeeze. We watched as former students and colleagues crept onto that decrepit stage and rhapsodized about how my father had dramatically changed their lives. It felt like I was just barely learning about a man whom I had known so intimately my whole life. How could I have failed to realize how monumental my father had been? How could I have seen him in such two-dimensional terms, as someone who belonged to me and my family and not the greater community?

Each of the speakers relayed a story about my dad and some long-lasting piece of wisdom he had imparted. One former student explained how he had admonished his class to "not let the dishes pile up in the sink" when they were behind on their homework. Another related a story about my father's pep talks, quoting him that "wishing on a star only works in Disney films, while the real world requires you to build your own rocket ship." Yet another former student described how Dad would borrow a lab coat from the Science Department and conduct an "essay autopsy" after a timed writing session ("Cause of death? Lack of textual support."). These "Smith-isms" (as one former student called them) were touching and funny and incredibly insightful. I couldn't help but wonder what my father might have said and done, if he'd only been blessed with time to finally write that novel he'd dreamed up or record that album he'd always talked about.

But we would never read his novel.

We would never hear his album.

All we had left of him were stories and memories and photographs.

All that remained were shadows of a great man whose towering presence was gone.

When it was my turn to take the stage, I wasn't sure that I would have the strength to face a single human being – let alone an audience of this magnitude. I walked up the stairs with quaking legs and quivering arms. At this point, though, I wouldn't have Lani to hold my hand.

I was facing the crowd alone.

As I made my way to the back of the stage and unsnapped the clasps on the guitar case that waited for me behind the proscenium curtains, I pictured my father sitting in our garage during one of our weekly jam sessions, tenderly holding his precious acoustic guitar in his thick hands. He had loved this instrument so much, had considered it one of his prized possessions – and yet he gave it to me on the day of my high school graduation. It was the 1961 Martin D-21 guitar he bought on his fifteenth birthday, the one he tucked away into his closet while Marina and I were growing up. It was also the same instrument which helped birth so many of my songs, the guitar that I used in the recording sessions for *A Different Slant of Light*.

The room was eerily quiet when I stepped towards the microphone. I had been on this stage many times before, between talent shows and assemblies and other school events, and yet I couldn't shake the feeling that I was standing on those trembling floorboards for the first time. With the floodlights blinding me and obscuring my view of the audience, I cringed and searched desperately for a familiar face in the front row. I could feel a sense of panic swelling like a mylar balloon in my chest, the air in my lungs vanishing and leaving me breathless.

I stepped up to the microphone, my lips only inches away from its perforated metallic surface. "A few months ago," I began, my voice echoing back through the theater, "my dad told me the song that he wanted played at his funeral. I just didn't think…" I choked up, my throat throttled as I stood in front of that jam-packed auditorium. "I just didn't think it would come so soon…"

An uncomfortable silence permeated the room as I struggled to collect myself.

I took a breath and lifted my head back to the microphone. "My father was obsessed with the Beach Boys and their songwriter, Brian Wilson. Dad loved this song, and he wanted people to remember him as someone who was kind and compassionate. And he hoped that living the mantra of *love and mercy* would make his life meaningful in a way that death would not."

My hands were quaking so intensely, I felt like the living embodiment of the San Andreas Fault. I felt like I might break, like I might crumble on that very stage. But it was then that I saw Lani below me, her black dress drifting from her legs to the floor, her eyes staring up at me with a look of tenderness that I'll never forget.

"*You can do this*," she mouthed to me silently.

Lani gave me the strength I needed to make it through the song. With my father's guitar clutched tightly in my hands, I started playing those old familiar chords, the sound of the strings reverberating through the room. As my fingers moved delicately across the frets, I could remember sitting next to my father just a few months before, watching that Brian Wilson concert in Northern California – the night that I wrote "Incomplete." My father was there with me that night and so many nights before, teaching me how to read and write and think and strum and sing – and even how to knot a stupid necktie. My father was there for all of those pivotal moments in my life. And now I would be here for him in his death.

I opened my lips and began to sing.

My voice wavered at first, unsteady as a drunkard on an empty street, while I sang about crummy movies and violence and suffering and the helplessness that accompanies moments of despair. The cavernous high school auditorium, even with hundreds of people filling its ancient seats, was eerily quiet. As soft and delicate as those plucked guitar strings might have been, I could still hear each somber note filtered through the theater's speakers.

I took a deep breath and thought of my father as I began to sing the chorus. "*Love and mercy...*"

As I made my way through the song, I felt myself growing more confident, channeling a menagerie of emotions into my performance. I thought of my father telling me to "sing the hell out of it" in this very same auditorium when I was auditioning for my high school graduation ceremony. With those encouraging words echoing from my memories, my voice sailed through the rafters, coursing through the pillars and beams, reflecting off the particle-board walls and into the ears and hearts and minds of everyone in that building.

I made my way through the verses and choruses like a sailor navigating familiar channels and harbors. And when I reached the final lines of the final chorus, it felt like an invocation: *"Love and mercy..."* It was an invitation for everyone in that room to exercise compassion and wisdom.

It was exactly what my father would have wanted everyone to hear at his funeral.

Love and mercy, I reminded myself as I was singing, *was what we all needed to make it through the tempestuous days and the unyielding nights of our lives.* Though the song's lyrics aren't as poetic and rich as Bob Dylan or Tom Waits or Robert Hunter or Van Dyke Parks, there is something powerful in the simplicity of Brian's words. After all, *love* and *mercy* are the two qualities that can help bridge gaps and create closure – forceful rivers that might otherwise seem untenable to drowning hearts.

When I finished the last few lines of the song, repeating *"Love and mercy"* over and over, I felt a weight lifted from my shoulders. The pain and anguish fluttered away from me like the sounds of my voice wafting towards the walls, my heart filled with a newfound calm and clarity. It was as if my father was waving to me from the shoreline as I drifted out to sea, and I was at peace with the inscrutable, enigmatic burden of living.

For a moment, everything was okay. But only for a moment.

As the last ringing notes floated away into the theater and dissipated like sea foam, I stood motionless and watched the audience absorb the words and music that Dad loved so much. A surprising number of people lifted tissues and handkerchiefs to swollen eyelids, mopping up the tears that had been coursing down their faces. I don't know if it was from the song or my performance or simply the sheer weight of loss that we all felt, but I'd like to think that I made my father proud in that moment.

In the end, Dad got exactly what he wanted: a funeral that celebrated his life and left the congregants feeling uplifted. From beyond the veil, Brian Richard Smith, Sr. reminded everyone that love and mercy can help souls find solace in even the darkest of times.

After scanning the faces in the front row, glimpsing Lani and my family smiling up at me through the tears in their eyes, I turned away and walked off to the wings of the stage. When I placed my father's guitar into its plush case, delicately laying it down like a coffin into firm soil, I felt like I was turning the final page of a book.

It was the last time I would perform onstage for twenty years.

CHAPTER TWENTY-SEVEN
"(Wouldn't It Be Nice to) Live Again"

Cemeteries and funeral homes have been trained to speak of the deceased in the present tense, as if the dead have merely stepped out of the room and will return before your steaming cup of coffee turns cold. It's a subtle rhetorical trick, but an effective one: it gives the illusion that our lost loved ones are still with us – still present, despite their obstinate (and eternal) absences.

I think it's bullshit.

Dead is dead. It's heartbreaking and frustrating and maddening, but it's the truth. As much as I would love to believe that the deceased are magically hovering around us, watching over us and protecting us against illnesses and bad decisions and traffic collisions, the truth is that once someone dies, they are gone.

The end.

I hope that I'm wrong. I pray that there's some heavenly afterlife in which we are reunited with everyone we've ever loved. But my brain knows these longings of the soul are nothing more substantial than empty wishes. I desperately want to believe that I'll see my father again, but I also recognize it's simply a child's naïveté pumping false hope through my grieving heart.

When we spread my father's ashes in the San Francisco Bay a few days after his memorial, I knew that his soul was already long-gone. The grey skies of the city echoed the colorless depths of my own wounded heart, and the icy wind felt more like a reflection of my spirit than some malicious meteorological force. After Dad's funeral, we drove up north with Marina, retracing our miles back to the county in which he died. It was me, Lani, Mom, Marina, Reggie, Uncle Jeff, Aunt Alyssa, and Chunk – the same caravan that had driven up north only a few weeks before to see Call Field's show at the Fillmore. Even though only a dozen days or so had passed since that terrible night, it felt like another lifetime. In some ways, it *had* been a different life – the final chapters of my childhood, before destiny's cruel claws ripped the book from my hands.

We had talked about spreading Dad's ashes back home in Southern California, but it seemed more appropriate that the remnants of his flesh should spend eternity in the cool waters of the San Francisco Bay. After all, he was a Berkeley graduate who got his teaching credential and MA from Stanford, and those were the years that he marked as the true beginning of his life. It seemed weirdly appropriate that Dad's story would end where it began: orbiting the Golden Gate bridge in Northern California. Sometimes, fate seems strangely circuitous, like the ancient Egyptian figure of the *Ouroboros* – the serpent swallowing its own tail.

In sharp contrast to that mythical snake, I was doing the exact opposite of swallowing: I was vomiting violently over the rails of our rented boat. Unlike that fabled symbol of eternity and continuity, I was unraveling and falling apart. When I should have been softly mourning and wrapping myself in the comforting blankets of home, I was sadistically ill and throwing up into the waters of the San Francisco Bay. Though it might have been disgusting, it wasn't shocking: I hadn't spent any time sailing and I didn't have my sea legs – nor did I have the foresight to take a dose of Dramamine before stepping onto the boat.

Poor Lani kept rubbing my back in circular motions while nausea flooded my body in torturous waves. It was like I was expelling everything inside of me, reaching deep down into the bile buried at the bitter bottom of my stomach. It all came up in ruthless, roiling rhythms, coarsely coursing through my chest and throat into the darkened waters below.

Yet the boat continued on, burrowing into the bay, piercing deeper into the fog that enshrouded us until we were completely surrounded –

enveloped by the thick, soupy sheets of moisture that persistently hover above the San Francisco Bay. As we reached the standard 100-yard threshold off the coastline, Mom hugged the canister of ashes to her chest, giving Dad one last embrace before setting him free into the uncertain eternity of the water below. With tears streaming down the heavy lines of grief on her face, Mom unscrewed the top of the canister, closed her eyes, and poured the ashes over the starboard side of the ship. A thin, ghostly trail of dust spilled forth, almost indistinguishable from the fog that encircled us. It all happened so quickly, like sped-up footage of sand seeping through the chambers of an hourglass. The powdery remains of my father's flesh quickly disappeared into the darkness.

And he was gone.

Little children dip their fingers into fountains and streams, searching for something magical within the slippery, unyielding instability of water. They make wishes and throw spare change into the depths, as if the acquiescing liquid could grant them their hearts' desires. Wishes are like petite prayers, tossed overboard or into the heavens, little intangible dreams to which we cling for some sense of hope and reassurance. As we grow older, though, we recognize the impotence of these actions: God doesn't reward us for our interrupted innocence.

You can throw a penny into a wishing well, but nothing will come of it. You've simply lost a penny. That little copper-coated circle is not a shiny shell containing a magic trick. It's only a lifeless trinket that crosses through our fingers and into our pockets and then is discarded, never to be seen again.

We are all pennies in the cosmic illusion of a wishing well. Our lives are over in a flash and then we disappear into the shallow depths of repurposed water. When our burned bodies are swallowed by the sea, we're gone forever.

I hate it when people say that "everything happens for a reason" or "it's part of God's plan." The truth is simply that terrible things happen in life. My father didn't die because he was a pawn in a deity's architectural design. He died because he was too stubborn to go to the doctor, which prevented any early detection of the cancer that ultimately spread throughout his body and culminated in the heart attack that claimed his life. You can't wish away a genetic predisposition to cancer, but you can take steps to identify and treat tumors before they metastasize. My dad's neglectful manner towards his health, his heavy-handed refusal to see a doctor, and his inability to prioritize illness over work are what led to his premature passing.

Nothing more, nothing less.

I burned through the stages of grief following my father's death. My initial shock and denial eventually gave way to an irrepressible anger and desperate bargaining which shook me to my very core. As much as I loved Dad when he was alive, I couldn't help but resent him for leaving me so soon. I only had him for twenty-one years.

Twenty-one years.

Twenty-one years is not enough time for a child to spend with his father. The seed that was planted with my parents' marriage sprouted into a seedling, then blossomed into a sapling when my sister and I were born. But that tree was ripped from the soil before it could fully grow thick roots and firm branches.

I felt robbed.

It's been over two decades now since my father passed away, which is roughly the same number of years that he and I spent together on this planet. By the time that Sam is in middle school, my dad will have been gone for more years than he and I shared. Each day, it gets easier to move on with my life, but I still feel maimed by his memory. His intangible spirit cannot be exorcised from my heart.

Some ghosts need to be clutched tightly, incorporeal as they might be. Once their subtle silhouettes are gone, they're as good as forgotten, as empty as the caskets we purchase to store their remains. And though we can never bring them back, never force them to materialize through the sheer determination of our will, it's impossible to stop trying.

It's the paradox of haunting.

CHAPTER TWENTY-EIGHT
"Busy Doin' Nothin'"

In the weeks following my father's death, I felt like a vessel trapped in the fog. For every fathom forward that I moved, a curtain of white hid everything beyond my immediate vision. During this time, I inched along the coastline of my life, marking every day that passed in cups of coffee consumed and packs of cigarettes smoked. I didn't even like the taste of tobacco, but going through the movements like the automated arms of an analog clock helped keep me focused. It gave me a reason to step outside the walls of my house and breathe in the unfiltered air through the filtered tip of a cigarette.

People forget sometimes that the mechanical aspect of smoking is something akin to a religious ritual: the user finds a sense of solace in the rote, repeated actions that satisfy our innate human desire for structure and order. At a time when I felt like the world was suffocating me, when the cold fingers of claustrophobia were creeping around my neck, the only time I left the house was to step outside the front door and smoke.

In my grief and sorrow and despair, even something as simple as driving to the store for a loaf of bread felt like an impossible task. I felt weighed down, like invisible anchors of lead were draped from my quaking shoulders. And yet, at the same time, I also felt ungrounded – as if there was nothing tying me to the soil, and I might float, float, float off into the vast expanse of the atmosphere above me. I was simultaneously bound by gravity and unbound by grief.

I ate.

I drank.

I smoked.

I slept.

Around and around the face of the clock, I watched the arms move. But I was the pin at the center of those mechanical limbs, fixed in a finite place while the world continued spinning around me.

Eat.

Drink.

Smoke.

Sleep.

Eat.

Drink.

Smoke.

Sleep.

Eat.

Drink.

Smoke.

Sleep.

Eat.

Drink.

Smoke.

Sleep.

Repeat.

And repeat.

And repeat.

A week passed.

And then another.

And another after that.

The hours bled into days
which wept into weeks.

I
was
unmoored.

I
was
drifting.

I
was
lost
at
sea.

I
was
a
long,
long
way
from
the
shore.

CHAPTER TWENTY-NINE
"Guess You Had To Be There"

According to my friends and family, "Incomplete" received a lot of attention during those lost months of grieving. And when I say "a lot," I mean the song popped up every few hours on commercial radio and in regular rotation on MTV. A few suburban broadcast stations named the song the "summer rock anthem of 2000," and Call Field (comprised of my ex-bandmates and a few sidemen) apparently played a whole bunch of festivals, including shows on the Warped Tour – in addition to the multitudinous tour dates that we had already booked.

To be fair, radio stations were pretty desperate for decent music at that point: the summer of 2000 was dominated by vapid pop songs like Britney Spears's "Oops… I Did It Again" and NSYNC's "It's Gonna Be Me," so anything that was halfway-decent rock and roll was going to be touted as a "rock anthem." In mid-July, "Incomplete" peaked on the Billboard charts at #19, sandwiched between Bon Jovi's "It's My Life" and Sinead O'Connor's "No Man's Woman."

Not too shabby for a little song that I wrote all by myself in the middle of a cold October night.

While other songwriters and musicians might celebrate the fact that one of their compositions had created such a notable wave in popular culture, I was too broken to appreciate the song's success.

I was angry and hurt.

I felt betrayed.

Remarkably, I even came to resent the song itself.

It's silly, in retrospect, to think that I could have felt such animosity for a three-and-a-half-minute pop song (especially one that had been the crowning achievement of my musical career). But the fallout from that summer's meltdown left me grappling with my own form of suburban small-town PTSD.

In the aftermath of my father's death and my exodus from Call Field, I was a shadow of my former self, a broken marionette that dangled lifelessly from its strings. To coin a phrase, I was living through PRRSD: "Post-Rock & Roll Stress Disorder." While my PTSD – or PRRSD, as it were – experience pales in comparison to soldiers returning from war or victims of domestic abuse or survivors of horrific trauma, I was in the throes of an intense anxiety that derailed everything else in my life.

Death will do that to you.

After all, grief is a mystifying force. It makes even the simplest situations seem insurmountable.

When people hear the phrase "nervous breakdown," they usually imagine hysterical histrionics and catatonic comas. The truth of the matter, though, is that it's much less theatrical. Melancholy manifests in a variety of vicious ways, but – for me, at least – it feels more like drowning on dry land. In some ways, it's like the 31 Flavors of Sadness: *This one tastes like despair! That one tastes like defeat! Here's a double-scoop of desperation and disenchantment with whipped cream and a cherry on top!*

Looking back now, I consider this time my "sandbox summer." Just like Brian Wilson exhibited extremely erratic behavior after the *Smile* album fell apart, I became a hermit – albeit one without mountains of sand installed in my living room. I put on a lot of weight during that time, swelling from 250 to upwards of 275 pounds (and counting). I smoked too much, ate too much, and slept too much. I struggled to leave my parents' house. Heck, I barely managed to leave my *bedroom*. When I did finally muster the strength to step outside, I felt like a vampire melting under the harsh light of the sun. The only time I felt safe was when my eyes were closed and the light switch for my brain had been turned off.

And – during the nastiest nadir of that summer – I wanted to flip that light switch off permanently.

I know I said early on in my story that I had an unremarkable childhood, that I was a pretty normal kid – but a few hundred pages later, it's strikingly clear that something was *always* wrong with me. In addition to being an overweight and sensitive child, bullied by a few malicious jerks like Marcus Huskey, there was something else going on: a looming despair that always seemed to creep into the edge of the frame, the subtle vignette of depression that darkened every picture.

Healthy, well-adjusted kids don't fall to pieces when something terrible happens. They don't hide from the world when they enter into a foreign classroom. They don't shut down when their crushes fail to reciprocate affection. And they don't turn emotionally comatose when they lose a parent.

All along, there was something wrong with me.

I just didn't know it at the time.

With the vantage point of four decades under my belt, coupled with my experience teaching for almost twenty years, I realize now that I spent my childhood in the grips of an undiagnosed anxiety disorder. The tension that rose in my chest every single time I faced a new obstacle or a new environment wasn't just an anomaly: it was a misfiring cylinder in my brain threatening to shut down the entire engine.

For years, I chalked it up to me just being a "weird kid." However, I'm beginning to realize that my damaged DNA was manifesting monsters inside my preadolescent body all along. In that summer-school Chemistry class with Serena so many years ago, our teacher taught us about genetic predetermination and predisposed character traits; I didn't think much of it at the time, but years later I'm able to see the trajectory of those characteristics, from laborious lift-off to stratospheric ascent to astonishing apex to cataclysmic crash-landing the summer that my father died.

It's almost like watching crystals form in a high-pressure vacuum, compressing and changing from rough carbon to something gleaming and shining and indestructible. The conversation I had with my father right after Serena's *quinceañera* also hinted at something else: that depression and mental illness might have been genetically inherited. Multiply all of that with my weight and my general sensitivity, and it's no wonder that I was preternaturally prone to depression.

Looking back now, it's obvious to me that I was headed for a fall.

Something inside of me broke when my father died. The simple, mechanical cogs that keep us moving through our clockwork days just stopped whirring and clicking. Grief jammed the gears.

Mental illness is an indiscriminate predator. It doesn't care if you're weak or strong or fat or thin or brilliant or dull. It strikes in the dead of night and the blistering zenith of day. The deep, interminable melancholy that clouds every moment, every thought, hovers just outside the edges of the pictures that we frame and place on our mantels or on our desks. It's always there, an invisible parasite feeding on the frayed corners of our souls. Sometimes, it nibbles on our hearts like a minor nuisance; other times, it devours us and spits out our bones in the parched desert.

The summer after my father died was a particularly long, scorching drought.

There wasn't much left of me to go around.

CHAPTER THIRTY
"Brian's Back"

I remember dreaming of a desolate landscape, a barren sea of sand and stone. No matter how many miles I walked, though, I was still alone. There wasn't a single soul in sight. My footfalls were impossibly heavy, kicking up dust and dirt as I made a pathetic trail through the Death Valley terrain. It stretched on for hours, but it seemed like I barely made any progress at all. I just kept moving, but I wasn't going anywhere.

Right foot. Left foot.

Right foot. Left foot.

Repeat for eternity.

Suddenly, the earth started shaking. It quaked gently at first, but the movements became heavier and heavier. It felt like the entire world was convulsing, and I was unbound from the ground beneath me. As the soil's seizure shuddered in epileptic fury, a chasm cracked open at my feet. Immediately, the empty space before me stretched wider and wider, threatening to swallow the valley whole. My foot slipped and I panicked, flailing desperately to find purchase in the stubborn silt. Sand sifted through my hands, but my fingernails couldn't anchor my body to anything substantial. My arms attacked caked dirt, my lungs filled up with dusty fumes, and I slipped down into the untenable abyss. Just as I was about to be consumed by the unfathomable depths of darkness…

I opened my eyes.

"You need to get up," Lani commanded, forcefully shaking me

awake from the depths of slumber. "It's time to go outside."

I responded with a half-grunt, my face smothered by the pillow that clouded my sight and muffled my voice. I pulled the blankets up over my head and tried to burrow deeper into my mattress.

It was a mid-August morning, roughly seven weeks after my father died. The oppressive sun beamed in through the slanted window shades that someone – most likely Lani – had inconsiderately drawn open. I felt like a vampire melting in the tyrannical sunlight, my very skin warning that I might disintegrate into ashes and dust at any moment.

"It's too early," I mumbled, wrapping myself in the safe cocoon of cotton sheets. "Let me go back to sleep."

Even though I couldn't see her, the subsequent silence gave me the distinct impression that Lani was irritated. When she did speak, it was with the cold voice of an embittered victim.

"It's almost *noon*, Brian," she said, audibly annoyed.

I'm sure if I had looked up, I would have seen her eyes rolling. As it was, I simply clenched my eyelids shut and refused to pull my body out from under the sheets.

"Seriously, Brian, you need to get up and take a shower," Lani commanded. "You smell like dirty gym shorts and your hair is greasier than a Volvo's carburetor." She yanked the sheets off of my body, jarring me out of my cocoon, and I felt the first puncturing shiver of cold as my uncovered skin was exposed to the air.

Despite Lani's unyielding demands, I wouldn't back down – or get up, as it were. I grabbed the duvet cover out of her hands, scowled at her, and violently pulled the sheets up around me. Doing my best to batten down the hatches of my bedsheets, I clenched my fists tightly around the smooth cotton fabric and refused to budge.

"You need to get up and shower, Brian," she repeated, her voice controlled and deliberate. "*RIGHT. NOW.*"

Once again, I can only guess the reactions that might have spread across Lani's face. I just know that I obstinately clenched my eyes and covered my head. I do remember hearing the slightly muffled sound of an exasperated sigh, though, which makes perfect sense considering what happened next.

"Don't say I didn't warn you," Lani murmured in an exasperated singsong voice. There was a strange, rippling aquatic sound, like the noise you hear when you step into a bathtub, coupled with what sounded like ice cubes clinking in a plastic cup.

The next thing I knew, I was soaked with ice-cold water.

"WHAT THE HELL!" I screamed, jumping up out of my now-drenched sheets. My skin shuddered viciously – in sharp contrast to the searing anger coursing through my veins. On the ground in front of the bed was a big plastic tub that only seconds before had contained several gallons of water. Chunks of ice, sluggishly dissolving into lazy liquid, lay scattered in my bed and on the floor. I turned to Lani, angrier with her than I had ever been. "WHAT ARE YOU DOING?"

Lani gave me the hint of a forced, resentful smile. "I can see now that you're up out of bed. That's a good start, Brian." She shoved a handful of clothes into my bare chest, the jeans and shirt unfurling towards the ground. A pair of socks tumbled from my hands and fell onto the floor, quickly sopping up some of the water that had started soaking into the carpet.

I shivered again, a chilled wave shooting up my spine as I stood quivering in front of the woman that I loved. In that moment, though, I'm pretty sure I thought that she was the embodiment of all evil in the world. In my eyes, she was like a demonic Shamu, cruelly dousing me in my own bedroom.

"Why would you do this to me?" I asked, my voice weaker and more desperate-sounding than I had anticipated.

Once again, Lani sighed, the breath from her delicate lungs seeming to contain all the exhausted wisdom of the universe. "Do you know what today is?" she asked me.

I scrunched up my eyes, trying to pry some bit of information from the blurry recesses of my brain. Try as I might, I was drawing a blank.

"I don't know," I finally admitted. "What day is it?"

Her nostrils flared, as if she was holding back plumes of fire behind her clenched teeth. "It's August 14th, Brian," she whispered darkly. "It's your father's birthday."

All the color drained from my face. "You mean it *would have been* my father's birthday," I whispered back to her.

"It doesn't matter if your father isn't here with us. It's still his birthday." Lani pulled the glasses off her face and rubbed the bridge of her nose. She squinted forcefully, her voice muffled behind the folds of her fists. "We're not going to erase his memory just because he's gone."

I fell back down onto the sopping-wet bed behind me.

"Oh, no, you don't!" Lani grunted, wrapping her hands around my right arm and yanking me back to my feet.

I have to admit: for a twenty-year-old girl who was barely five feet tall, she looked rather intimidating. As much as I wanted to lay back down on my bed (soaking wet as it might have been), I was too timid to fight against the furious little fairy that stared me down from her Louis Vuitton glasses. Like a simpering puppy dog, I got up and stood there waiting for the next command.

"What are you waiting for?" Lani asked. "Get your ass in the shower."

I took a step forward, my knees feeling like they might buckle beneath me. Little droplets of water made their way down my arms and legs, pulled by gravity to the pools that collected on the floor. All the while, Lani stood there, fixed in her position, with her arms crossed sharply across her chest.

"Why are you doing this to me?" I asked again, feeling exhausted and defeated. My body resumed its quivering – whether from the ice bath I'd just unwillingly taken or from my own feeble heart, I can't say – and I started to cry. Masculinity, be damned: I was a broken shell of a man, my heart as thin and delicate as a cracked eggshell. I collapsed to my knees, placed my head in my trembling hands, and sobbed.

Lani stood stock-still for a minute, frozen in her stoic, statuesque pose. Like the ice on the floor, however, she started to melt – and found herself drawn to the ground in front of me.

"I love you, Brian," she whispered to me as she nuzzled her head into my shoulder. "But I don't want to watch you bury yourself."

I craned my neck to look up at her. Despite her diminutive height, she seemed so much stronger than me, so much more grounded in the weight of reality. As she returned my look, however, her eyes started to well and glisten. Finally, a crack in her icy armor.

Lani wiggled from her knees to the ground, and she stroked my naked back with her left hand. We sat there for a minute, tears falling and mingling with the water that coursed down my skin. Drop after drop filtered its way to the carpet.

The circular caressing on my back stopped, and Lani slipped her right palm under my jaw. Five slender fingers lifted my chin to face her, Lani's chestnut-brown eyes locked on my own.

"When I was in high school," she sighed, "and my mom had breast cancer, it was the scariest thing I'd ever seen. She went through hell with chemotherapy and radiation, and I watched her wither into a skeleton…" Her voice caught, and she stopped speaking for a second as she wiped the corners of her eyes. "I thought I was going to lose her. And I remember that never-ending sense of dread that seemed to simmer just beneath the surface of everything. After every bedside conversation, I thought *this might be it. This might be the last time I ever see my mother alive.*"

Lani looked away from me and gazed off towards an imaginary island in the distance, where the past and present mingled in the recesses of memory. She took a deep breath, and her eyes trailed back to me.

"But you know what, Brian?" she continued on. "Though my dad and I were ready to plan for a funeral, my stubborn mother refused to die. Her hardheadedness always got under my skin when I was little, and it would frustrate the hell out of me. But this time… this time, that annoying characteristic – the stubbornness that used to drive me *crazy* – is what kept her going. She wouldn't give up. And now, just a few years later, she's in remission. She's still alive."

Lani placed the palm of her hand along my scruffy cheek, caressing my sandpaper skin with her velvet fingertips.

"I'm not going to watch you die, Brian," she whispered. "Beneath that big body of yours, I see your soul withering and wilting. I see the Brian Richard Smith that I love disappearing right in front of me. And it's destroying me."

Unexpectedly, she leaned over to kiss me. As she pressed her nose against mine, I could smell that sweet, familiar scent of hyacinth and tangerines. Just like we had done in her dorm room so long ago, we were sharing breaths, bonded by the adamantine spirit that passed between us.

"I don't want to spend the rest of my life – or even the rest of this *week* – watching you kill yourself from the inside out." She traced her thumb across my chapped lips. "I love you. And I will always love you."

"I love you, too," I whispered to her.

"But loving me is not enough," she said. "I need you to *love yourself.*"

Something about the way she uttered those simple words cut deeply. The self-destructive weeks following my father's death left me drowning, but Lani knew me better than I knew myself. If I really cared about my own well-being, I needed to do something – to raise my arms against the unyielding waves, swim to shore, and crawl onto dry land.

"What do I do?" I asked her. It was more of a rhetorical question than one which anticipated any real answer. Nevertheless, Lani offered up some sage wisdom.

"You need to go out for a walk," she told me. "Laying around in bed all day isn't doing you any good. Get up off the floor, take a shower, go shopping… Just take a step forward and move on with your life. It doesn't mean you're forgetting about what happened. It just means that you're not going to punish yourself for surviving."

With her slender golden arms, Lani pulled me in tighter. I nuzzled into her, my shaggy hair pressed against her chest.

"Seriously, though, Brian," she said, scrunching up her nose. "Take a shower. You reek."

After Lani left, I did exactly what she recommended: I pulled myself up off the floor, took a scathing hot shower, and scrubbed the grime off my skin. It felt purifying, as if I was washing away the film of despondency and defeat that had built up in sedentary layers during the weeks of my self-imposed exile. I scrubbed the dust and dirt and sweat off of my arms and legs and chest and everywhere else I could reach, until I felt clean and refreshed. It was a bizarre kind of baptism for a drowning man, but it would have to do.

As I walked out of the shower and dribbled water onto the bathmat, I looked up at myself in the mirror. For the first time in months, I really studied the figure that I saw there before me. He looked like me: he had the same ghostly pale shade of skin, the same auburn hair draped over his skull, and the same Bermuda Triangle of moles framing his face. But the man I saw in the mirror looked more like the image of my father that had been seared into my memories: his hair was starting to thin and he was uncomfortably bloated, with a round belly protruding over the edge of the white towel that wrapped around his waist.

During my weeks and weeks of solitary suffering, I had swelled into a caricature of myself, folds of skin inflating over what had once been muscle.

It was eerie. I felt like I was looking at Pops, but with my face superimposed over his body. I saw his sagging arms, his thick thighs, his thinning hair.

I didn't look like myself. I looked like my dad.

I was losing myself in the memory of my father.

And we all know how his story ended.

Surprisingly, I was able to get a walk-in appointment with my general practitioner that afternoon. It could be that his office staff took pity on me, considering my father had just passed away; perhaps, I just got lucky with someone else's last-minute cancellation; or, maybe, the universe was looking out for me. In any case, I soon found myself sitting on the crinkly waxen paper of an elongated table in one of the doctor's examination rooms. My eyes scanned the area around me, eventually settling on a wooden pamphlet holder adorning the wall; titles like *Living with Type I Diabetes*, *Screening for Breast Cancer*, and *A Brief Guide to*

Bipolar Disorders occupied my attention as I waited impatiently. I was shifting my weight, leaning uncomfortably on one side of the table, when I heard a brisk knock.

Without any delay, Dr. Náftis swung open the door and entered the room. Dr. Náftis was a trim, well-kept gentleman with dark olive skin, someone whose charismatic presence demanded undivided attention. A forced smile weighed heavily upon his lips as he held out his arm and squeezed my shoulder.

"I'm sorry about your father," he said quietly, his voice intentional but soft. There was a slight hint of a Greek accent in his speech, and I couldn't help but wonder if he had Zeus's lightning bolts shoved in his back pockets.

"Thank you," I muttered. It had only been a few seconds, but I could already feel myself tearing up. I was a walking raw nerve.

"How are you holding up?" he asked me, setting his clipboard down on a countertop and scooting onto a rolling chair.

I'm normally a pretty private person. I don't share much of my darkest self with others, especially in an environment as sterile and uncomfortable as a doctor's office. Between Lani's icy pep talk and the genuine look of concern Dr. Náftis gave me over the tilted frames of his glasses, I recognized that something had to change.

I was at a crossroads. And it was time to choose my path.

I needed to do something.

I swallowed hard and started to speak.

"I'm not doing well, Doc," I told him. "I'm not doing well at all."

I laid it all out for him, choking back the rising anxiety in my chest and letting the whole unfettered truth spilled from my lips like water from a fountain. Although it probably only lasted ten or fifteen minutes, it felt like an eternity as I spewed forth every truth, insecurity, and fear that had been dammed up inside my brain for the last two decades of my life.

I told him that I constantly felt an unfathomable weight strangling my every thought.

I told him that I couldn't bear the prospect of facing anyone else on my worst days.

I told him that I had a hard time simply getting out of bed in the aftermath of my father's death.

I told him that I had thought about killing myself.

Dr. Náftis listened to every rambling word. As I spoke, he leaned in closer, his hands forming a crooked steeple on his lap.

Finally, I breathed out the last of my confessions and lowered my head. The room was so quiet, I could hear every ticking movement of the analog clock's mechanical arms. Undeterred by the oppressive silence, the clock continued its defiant movements.

Tick... tick... tick...

"Thank you for sharing all of this with me, Brian," he said in a gentle voice, his right hand slowly reaching out to touch my shoulder. "It's clear to me that you're in the throes of a deep depression, and that you have been for quite some time."

Depression.

Just putting a name to it had a profound effect on me.

I rolled the word around on my tongue, finessing the sounds as I said it out loud. "*Depression.*"

The darkness had a name.

Sometimes, simply naming the monster cripples the beast. It might not deprive the demon of its powers, but it can rip the sharp teeth from its vicious mouth.

I felt a firm grip on my shoulder. As I looked up, Dr. Náftis was staring at me, his eyes boring straight into me like I was nothing more substantial than cellophane.

"But, Brian, it's bigger than that," he said carefully, in measured tones. "I'm not a psychiatrist, but it sounds like you might have some kind of social anxiety disorder, too. You could very well be suffering from something else, too, like agoraphobia. This pressure you describe when you go out into public – your inability to communicate in a 'live setting' – this is actually more common than you might think."

Social anxiety disorder? I thought to myself. *Is that a thing?*

Dr. Náftis continue elaborating. "And some of what you're describing sounds like it checks the boxes for a variation of bipolar disorder, particularly with the extreme depressive episodes that you've had recently."

"Bipolar disorder?" I asked, scrunching my eyes into slits. "Does that mean that I'm not… normal?"

"*Normal* is a relative term," he explained. "Think of bipolar disorder as something like a grandfather clock. The pendulum swings far one way and then swings just as far in the opposite direction. When you think of '*normal*,' what you really mean is *healthy*. Mental health might mean staying centered, staying consistent. Not swaying too far in either direction. When someone suffers from a bipolar disorder, however, they can feel extreme highs and extreme lows. Maybe they *never* feel grounded or stable."

His words resonated deeply. I felt *exactly* like the pendulum he described, swinging back and forth between highs and lows. And I rarely felt like I was actually stable.

"There's something else that you should keep in mind," he continued. "Even if you're able to keep a level head during normal circumstances, stress can trigger or escalate your reactions. Sometimes, encountering tragedy or trauma – like losing your father – ignites a powder keg inside of you. And that's what worries me about you and your circumstances."

I shifted in my seat uncomfortably. Though I'd certainly *heard* of mental illness, I'd never envisioned myself as someone who suffered from such an affliction.

Depression. Bipolar disorder. Social anxiety.

This wasn't who I was… right?

Dr. Náftis loosened his grip on my shoulder. But he didn't release me. "This is important, so I want you to listen carefully," he commanded. "And I need you to answer me honestly."

"Okay," I whispered back to him.

"You're expressing *suicidal ideations*," he explained. "That's not something to be taken lightly. And I need to ask you some serious questions."

This part is hard for me to talk about. As much as I would like to paint a vivid motion-picture scene for you, dear reader, I just can't. It's difficult enough to simply *admit* these things, let alone describe the memory casually as if it was nothing more substantial than a gentle crest of water on a delicate shore. You'll just have to read between the lines.

Dr. Náftis asked me if I ever thought about harming myself.

I told him that I did.

He asked me if I thought about killing myself.

I told him that I did.

As I spoke, I felt like I was tottering on the edge of a bottomless abyss. For a second, I wavered on that emotional cliff, thinking about taking a step forward into the empty space before me. At the same time, I also thought about leaning backwards onto solid, corporeal ground. In that moment, I could have gone either way.

The room felt hazy, unstable. The white walls that washed over me seemed less like sturdy beams and more like unsteady sand. It would be so easy to end it, to dive forward off the cliff into never-ending darkness. No more pain. No more suffering. But I also knew, deep down inside, that it wasn't the right choice. I needed to find purchase in the dusty earth. I needed to pull myself up.

"Are you ready to accept help?" Dr. Náftis asked me.

I thought about my father.

And my mother.

And Lani.

And Marina.

And Chunk.

Even as I kept my eyes trained on the abyss, I knew that it was time to make a difficult decision. The quicksand of darkness had enveloped me, threatened to smother me, and I realized that I needed to accept any rope that was offered.

I took a deep breath.

"Yes," I whispered. "I am."

Dr. Náftis looked at me with his kind eyes and nodded. "Then let's get you the help you need."

That conversation was a turning point for me. In that moment of suffering and suffocation, I took the lifeline that Dr. Náftis offered. He recommended that I see a psychiatrist, that I start trying out different forms of medicine (pharmaceutical *and* holistic), and that I make some dramatic lifestyle changes.

"The elephant in the room," he calmly told me, "is your weight. You're morbidly obese, Brian. According to my charts, your weight and your BMI put you into very dangerous territory."

I shuffled uncomfortably on the examination table.

Obese, I could understand. But calling me *morbidly obese...*? How could I be "morbidly" *anything* at twenty-one years old?

Dr. Náftis sensed my hesitation and continued elaborating. "If you take nothing else from your father's passing," he said, "it's that stubbornness and self-destructive patterns of behavior – even dietary ones – can be fatal. Your father was a large man. And if you want to live longer than he did, you'll need to make different lifestyle choices. If you want to make it past your early fifties, you need to change your path. And change it *now*."

I looked down at the soft rolls of skin that sagged and folded over my belt. "I know, sir," I told him.

"When you stepped on the scale today, Brian, you weighed..." He referred back to his notes, tapping his ballpoint pen against the metal clipboard he clutched in his hands. "Hmmm... Two hundred and eighty-three pounds."

I grimaced, my face contorted in distress, as if I could wish away the weight that had accumulated around my stomach and chest and everywhere else on my engorged body.

"You're about one hundred pounds overweight, Brian. I know it seems like a tall order, but I'd like you to lose sixty or seventy pounds."

"*Sixty* pounds?" I echoed back in disbelief.

"Or seventy. That would be even more ideal, Brian." Dr. Náftis looked over at the plastic rack of brochures that tilted forward from the wall and grabbed a few.

Involuntarily, I found myself shaking my head back and forth, my denial manifesting itself in the horizontal twists of my neck. "But how do I lose all that weight?" I asked. "Is that even *possible*?"

"I won't lie to you," he said, "it won't be easy. You'll need to make some serious lifestyle changes and start a strict regimen of reasonable dieting and regular exercise."

"But how do I *do* that, Doc?"

"It starts one step at a time," Náftis told me. "You know: *right foot, left foot, repeat.* You literally take one step after another and continue for an extended period of time. I'd like for you to start with…" he paused, calculating his recommendation. "Let's start with an hour a day, Brian, and see how it goes from there."

An hour a day.

I had a long road ahead of me.

I spent the afternoon running errands and shopping for a few things. When it was time for lunch, I felt that deep gravitational pull to Carl's Jr. – but I refused. Instead, I swung by the supermarket and picked up a prepackaged salad from the produce aisle… along with three dozen red roses for my frustrated, water-dumping girlfriend. With all the gusto of a lonely vagabond, I ate that supermarket salad in my car, the red roses sitting complacently on the passenger seat. As I scooped up leaflets of lettuce with a small plastic spork, I looked around the half-empty parking lot. To be honest, that lunch didn't exactly give me the emotional or physiological fulfillment I needed: every crisp, crunchy bite of lettuce tasted like bland sadness and cardboard defeat. It would have been so easy to just pull up to a drive-through… but that kind of thinking is what got me in trouble in the first place. It was time for me to draw a line in the sand. Or parking lot, as it were.

Since sugar and alcohol were no longer viable options for my lackluster lunch, I decided to reward myself with a different kind of dessert: music. With that terminus in mind, I polished off my pathetic salad, pulled out from the supermarket parking spot, and drove west. Just fifteen minutes up the 33 and down the 101, my destination awaited.

Salzer's Records.

Driving south on the 101 freeway towards Victoria Avenue, I saw the familiar sign for my old music-store stomping grounds. When I was a kid, Salzer's was my dad's favorite shopping detour: he regularly frequented the venue for new cassettes or vinyl records. And as an adolescent, I used to spend hours with Chunk and Ethan browsing through the racks and racks of CDs – searching for the next musical holy grail to add to my burgeoning collection.

After clumsily and crookedly parking in a spot outside the store, I walked up to the industrial-looking structure of the record store. When the doors crested open, I felt like Charlie Bucket entering Willy Wonka's chocolate factory. The shelves of vinyl and CDs and books and shirts and other assorted memorabilia instantly reminded me of my not-so-long-ago younger years. I'm pretty sure the clerks at the cash register were even blaring Weezer or the Ramones.

It felt like home.

I waddled through aisle after aisle (because waddling was a much more accurate description of my ambulatory prowess at that point), passing the Allman Brothers and the Beatles and blink-182 before facing the Grateful Dead and Jimmy Eat World and the Old 97's. Somewhere around Pearl Jam or the Ramones, I heard a gruff young voice behind me. And then a finger tapped my shoulder.

"Um… I'm sorry to bother you," the voice began after clearing its throat. "Are you…?"

I clenched my eyes tightly.

This is it, I thought. *My first celebrity sighting, and I'll have to explain that I'm no longer "the bass player" in Call Field, that I left the band and quit music and had a nervous breakdown.*

I took a deep breath and I turned around to face the kid who had tapped my shoulder.

He wasn't much younger than me – eighteen, maybe? – but he already had a full, bushy black beard that crawled halfway down his hickory neck. He was dressed in varying shades of black, from his Misfits baseball cap down to his ink-dark Converse. Underneath his denim jacket, he wore a graying shirt bearing the familiar skeleton logo of Social Distortion. He looked at me strangely, his eyes squinting and searching.

Yup, I assumed, *undoubtedly a local punk rock kid who remembers seeing Call Field in some dungeon of a coffee shop back when we were in high school. Just what I need right now.*

The kid blinked twice before he spoke.

"You're Mr. Smith's son, right?"

Mr. Smith's son.

There I was, caught up in my arrogant fantasy – and I wasn't even recognized for being a rock star. In this kid's mind, I was defined only by my relationship to my late father.

"You're Mr. Smith's son," he repeated, eyes aglow with recognition. "You played that Beach Boys song at his funeral."

"It wasn't *technically* a Beach Boys song…" I started to say, before realizing that such musical minutiae is trivial at moments like this. "But, uh, yeah… that was me."

He reached out his hand and I shook it.

"I'm sorry for your loss," he told me, quietly and soberly.

"Thank you," I said, softly releasing my hand from his grip and pulling it back, like a turtle retracting into its shell.

He took a deep breath and scrunched up his eyes in concentration. "Mr. Smith was the best teacher I've ever had. He changed everything for me. Before him, I hated English and I hated school." He fiddled with his fingers, picking at rogue hangnails as he spoke. "I graduated in June, and now I'm starting at Ventura College. I never got the chance to tell him, but I don't think I would've finished my senior year of high school if he hadn't been there to help me through everything that was going on in my personal life."

I started to tear up. It had been weeks and weeks since my father had passed away, and yet this kid's statement scratched across the raw, exposed wounds in my heart.

"I know you must be grieving…" he started to say.

I nodded, but I couldn't muster the strength to say anything out loud. I was literally speechless. The wordsmith had no words to forge.

"It can't be easy for you right now," he continued tentatively. "I lost my own father last summer, and it still hurts like hell. That's part of the reason I was such a mess last year." His voice caught a bit and his body twitched, as if he could shake off the coat of grief that he wore. "But Mr. Smith helped fill that void for me. No one can ever replace my dad, but your father helped me pick myself up when I was in pieces. I owe him for that."

I couldn't help it. My eyes welled up, the edges of my eyelids stinging intensely, and I just cried.

Right there, in the middle of the stoic CD racks at Salzer's Records, I wept.

Then something unexpected happened. This kid, only a few years younger than me, wrapped his burly arms around me and held me tightly. Around us, the casual shoppers in the store stopped and stared uncomfortably before averting their eyes and pretending we weren't there.

And I cried in the arms of this stranger, someone whose life was only tangentially related to my own, bound by the common cord of my father's life.

"I miss him," I whispered between sobs. "I miss him so much."

The kid patted me softly on the back. "It'll get easier," he told me. "It'll get easier."

And somehow – inconceivably – it did.

I left the record store that afternoon without buying anything. Music, the guiding source of inspiration in my life for so many years, no longer seemed relevant. In my mind, at that instant in time, rock and roll became something I never thought it would be or could be: trivial.

When I'd driven off from my parents' house at Lago de Paz Court that morning, I expected an uncomfortable visit with my doctor and an uneventful afternoon – maybe running some errands or picking up a couple of CDs or even taking a long walk along the beach. What I didn't anticipate was confronting my father's legacy.

My head was swirling like a whirlpool as I pulled out of the Salzer's parking lot, and I felt like a swimmer fighting against an intractable riptide. Taking an endless succession of deep breaths, I drove onto the 101 freeway and headed north towards the Ventura mall. With Dr. Náftis's orders on my mind – and my chance encounter with my father's student at the record store echoing in my chest – I parked by the Sears entrance and walked up the stairs to the sports equipment section.

There, amidst all the random weight sets and ellipticals and stationary bikes, I saw it: the key to my new life.

A treadmill.

A NordicTrack Pro, to be specific. It was shiny and polished and beautiful. And it was going to save my life. I took a tentative step onto the floor model and felt the friction of the tread underneath my Converse. Forward and backward, I shuffled my feet, moving with the gentle traction of the machine.

I thought about what Dr. Náftis told me: *"Right foot, left foot, repeat. You literally take one step after another…"*

One step at a time.

Moving forward, I would take my life one step at a time.

Maybe there was hope for me yet.

I found the nearest sales representative, a middle-aged man in a dark blue polo shirt, and whipped out my credit card.

"I need to buy a treadmill," I told him. "And I want that one over there."

An hour later, as I pulled up to my parents' house – now just my *mother's* house – I was closely followed by the Sears delivery van. I saw a couple of silhouettes peeking through the winking windows, figures that soon rose from their seats and headed towards the front door.

The delivery guys parked, walked around to the back of their van, and started to unload my new purchase. My mother, wide-eyed and confused, opened the front door and walked up the pathway towards the street. A rather stern-looking Lani trailed behind her, arms crossed skeptically and held tightly to her chest.

"What is that?" my mother asked hesitantly, her eyes scanning the strange scene unfolding on her front lawn.

"That is going to be my first step forward," I told her. "Literally and figuratively."

Lani squinted in the twilight, her eyes bunched up as she tried to decipher the print on the side of the box. "Did you... did you buy a *treadmill...*?" she asked.

"I did."

My girlfriend, the newly anointed queen of ice baths, was completely surprised. Her expressions canvassed through a cycle of emotions, her furrowed brow betraying a mixture of confusion and concern.

I reached into the front seat of my car and pulled out the bouquet of supermarket flowers I had purchased a few hours before. Sheepishly, I walked towards her and stretched out my hands with the penitent offering.

"I'm sorry," I told her. "You were right. About everything."

Lani couldn't suppress a grin beneath her bitter expression. "I'm *always* right, Brian. You should know that by now." A smirk escaped her lips as she took the flowers from my hands.

"Lani…" I began to say, shuffling my feet and taking another step towards her. "Things are going to change. *I'm* going to change."

She scowled at me, but her lips were quivering. "Good," she said, "because I am *not* going to waste my life watching *you* waste away yours. Do you understand me, Brian? I will not throw away the best years of my life waiting for you to get your crap together. You and I – we're a team. And you need to pull your own weight." She scrunched up her eyes and looked down at my sizable waist. "No pun intended, of course."

I took another step forward until she craned her neck to look up at me. With a slight twitch, I pulled Lani into my chest and rested my trembling chin atop her head.

"You're not going to waste your life on me," I told her. "I promise you. And I will spend the rest of *my* life proving that to you."

"I'm counting on it, mister," Lani said, a sparkle of tears in her beautiful chestnut-brown eyes.

And I kept my promise. Every morning, I would wake up at a reasonable hour, drag myself out of bed, throw on a pair of XXL Champion running shorts, lace up my New Balance shoes, and step onto my brand-new NordicTrack treadmill.

Right foot. Left foot.
Right foot. Left foot.
Repeat for an hour.

Day in and day out, I walked on that treadmill. Religiously.

I won't lie. It was *really* hard at first. My body felt so encumbered by the excess weight that I had gained, I simply didn't feel right in my own skin. But I also dramatically changed my diet: I cut out beer and soda and fast food, trading in burgers and fries for fruits and salads.

At times, I felt like Andy Dufresne from *The Shawshank Redemption*, chipping my way out of a jail cell. Each night, a little progress; each week, a little more. Except I wasn't carving out a tunnel for escape: I was shedding the pounds that weighed down my body, and jettisoning the emotional baggage that weighed down my soul. Like that mild-mannered accountant held captive in Shawshank Prison, I was searching for freedom – from my old life, from my self-doubt, and from the psychological jail I had created for myself.

Slowly, slowly, slowly, the weight started to come off. At first, it was only a few ounces at a time: I would nervously check the bathroom scale each morning, stepping a hesitant toe onto the cold metal of its surface. After a few weeks, I dropped a couple of pounds… but then it became a dozen pounds. And then a *few* dozen pounds. It just took a little motivation. And a lot of work.

Right foot. Left foot.
Right foot. Left foot.
Repeat for an hour.
The human body is a remarkable machine.

It probably doesn't come as a surprise, but Lani and I made up. Even though I had driven her to the brink of a breakup – and been doused with an ice-cold baptism, as a result – she took me back. Thank God for that. I wouldn't be who I am today without her.

I know that I've spent most of this book idealizing Lani and describing her as perfect, but that's not a fair representation of who she is – or who any of us are, for that matter. None of us is perfect. We each have our flaws and imperfections and demons and ghosts and vices. Lani, while a better human being than most everyone in my life, had reached her breaking point with me. As she so coolly informed me during my involuntary ice bath that morning, I needed to pull myself together or she wouldn't stick around.

I really had no choice.

We had a long talk that night about where we were headed, what we saw happening with our lives in the years beyond the horizon. I may or may not have informally proposed marriage to her during that conversation, but she and I have been debating that for years. She still argues that I made the comment jokingly, but I'm pretty sure that my suggestion of eloping was serious – even if it was delivered casually. A few years later, though, I got exactly what I wanted: Lani agreed to put up with me, for better or worse, in sickness and in health, 'til death do us part.

When the night ended, Lani drove back to Los Angeles with the promise that I could come visit her the next weekend. I hadn't felt so tentative about our relationship in ages, but I knew I had to re-earn her trust somehow. It's strange to think that a relationship can stretch out so far that you circle back to the beginning. After months and months of tidy, comfortable happiness in a committed relationship, I suddenly felt like I was that nervous, insecure kid sitting on the unmade bed of my dorm room, aching for the girl across the hall.

Nothing was promised. Nothing was guaranteed.

The following weekend, after a long drive down the 405, I found myself walking up to her doorstep with another bouquet of flowers, sweating profusely in the Westwood heat. I rang her doorbell, tugged at the collar of my shirt, and let a cool trickle of sweat trail down the back of my newly shorn neck. When Lani opened the door, she was a revelation: a petite goddess in a sundress and flip-flops.

"Hi, stranger," Lani said softly. She stood on the tips of her toes, straining to stretch up and give me a gentle peck on the lips.

"Hi," I whispered back. I sheepishly handed her the bouquet.

"You know," she said with a hint of skepticism in her voice, "you can't just buy me flowers to get back in my good graces. I'm not some doe-eyed vixen in a romantic comedy."

"I know," I nodded back nervously.

She studied the flowers dutifully, squinting as she investigated the waxen petals. "They are kind of beautiful," she admitted begrudgingly.

"Not as beautiful as you," I said.

"Cool it, Romeo," she grinned. "Let's just put these in a vase and then we can eat. I'm starving."

Lani wasn't the inspired cook then that she is now, but she made one heck of a salad that night. I realize how absurd it is to remember something as mundane as a homemade concoction of lettuce and trimmings, but (like I said) I was at a crossroads in my life at that point. I had already boarded the veggie train earlier in the week, lumbering down the track to healthier eating. But I was still resentful of my new diet.

As I shoveled green leaves into my mouth, every subtle little taste and texture seemed a revelation to me – the crunch of pecans; the contrast of pungent gorgonzola; and the crisp, tart, sweetness of Granny Smith apple slices. In the days leading up to our date, I had come to think of my new existence as something tedious and tiresome, and eating romaine lettuce day in and day out only reinforced that idea. But with Lani, things not only *felt* better, they *tasted* better, too.

Salad is like life: boring unless it's done right.

Lani and I talked for hours that night, taking our sweet time to work through the healthy dinner that she had prepared for us. She went on at length about her internship at the *Los Angeles Times* (which had kept her occupied most of that summer), as well as her parents' restaurant back in Maui and her little sister's college applications. For the first time in a long time, I listened – *really listened* – to what this beautiful woman had to say. She asked me about my re-enrollment at UCLA, which was going a little more smoothly than I had anticipated: it turned out that my planned leave of absence was easier to revoke than I assumed. I confided in her that I was nervous about starting school again, and she listened patiently as I rattled off my long list of concerns. The look in her eyes seemed full of compassion and empathy – mingled with a mild amount of skepticism, mind you.

It was during this conversation that we received an unexpected phone call. Lani was mid-sentence, describing her work on the *Daily Bruin*, when the familiar, tinny sound of a telephone ring interrupted us. Lani dropped her fork onto her napkin with a gentle thud before dashing over to the phone.

She picked up the phone and murmured sweetly into the receiver. "Lani speaking," she answered. Suddenly, her eyebrows perked up. "Oh, hi!" she squeaked, glancing over in my direction. Lani tilted her head, as if she was studying me while she listened to the voice on the other end of the line. "Yeah, we're fine," she said. "Do you want to speak with him?"

I cocked my head quizzically to the side. *Who would be calling me here at Lani's apartment?* I wondered.

"It's for you," she said, handing me the phone as its cord stretched taut across the table. "It's your mom." Lani gave me an inquisitive look as she passed off the telephone receiver like a baton.

I cautiously took the phone and cradled it against my right ear. "Hey, Mom," I said. "Is everything okay…?"

"I'm sorry to bother you two during dinner," she said, a hint of timid urgency in her voice. "I just needed to check in with you about something."

"You're scaring me," I admitted, a sense of panic beginning to well in my gut. "What's going on?"

"Everything is fine, Brian," she calmly explained. "It's just that I was going through the mail tonight, and… well… you have a rather sizable check here that's addressed to you."

"A *check*…?" I asked. "For me? What does it say?"

"I'm not entirely sure what it's for, but a few other pages are attached with a bunch of song titles. And there's an acronym at the top of the paper that says A-S-C-A-P. Does that mean anything to you?"

ASCAP? I wondered to myself. *That's weird.*

"That's the acronym for the American Society of Composers, Authors, and Publishers," I explained to her. "Lowercase Records told us that we might receive some royalty payments after the album was released."

"Oh," she muttered into the static of the line. "In that case, I think this might be a royalty check."

Great, I thought, *another reminder of my former life*. I didn't want to think about it at all. Even if it was a paycheck that I had rightfully earned for the songs I'd written and recorded, the windfall felt like blood money to me – tainted, contaminated cash that would only soil my soul as it padded my pocketbook.

"To be honest, I don't want to deal with it, Mom. I don't care if it's a thousand bucks. It feels dirty to me."

"It's quite a bit more than a *thousand dollars*, Brian…" she started to say.

"You know what I mean, Mom," I interrupted. "I don't really care about the money." I felt my chest starting to seize up, that familiar sense of panic and anxiety rising from my ribcage to my throat. "I… I just can't deal with it right now."

There was dead air on the other end of the telephone line. I could hear my mom breathing softly into the receiver, little wisps of air crackling into static.

"It's a lot of money," my mom said. "I mean *a lot*."

At the time, I didn't really have a solid foundation in accounting or money management. Heck, even a few hundred dollars in my pockets made me feel like a millionaire.

But I didn't want to deal with it.

"Is your name still on my checking account, Mom?" I asked her.

It was more of a rhetorical question than anything else. I already knew the answer: my only checking account, the one I'd started after my *bar mitzvah* at the ripe old age of thirteen, still had my parents on it. I might have legally been an adult, but I felt more like an oversized kid, living at home and stealing food from the refrigerator. I couldn't even write a single check without my parents – I mean my *mom* – knowing about it.

"I believe so," she answered.

"Okay," I sighed. "I have a favor to ask."

"What did you have in mind?"

"Can you just *do something* with it?" I asked her. "I don't want to see it and I don't want to think about it."

"But I don't think you understand, Brian…" she started to say.

"Please, Mom?" I implored. "*Please*…?"

I could hear the subtle cues of her confusion as her breath quietly crackled on the line. "Fine," she finally said. "What do you want me to do with all the money?"

"I don't know," I said, exasperation seeping through my voice. "Can you pay off some of my student loans?"

There was a pause on the other end of the telephone. "I think I can pay off *all* of your student loans with this money," she said.

"*All* of my student loans?" I echoed back.

"*And then some*," she added cryptically.

Yikes, I thought to myself. *That must be a* really *big check.*

"So, after I pay off all of your student loans," she continued, "what should I do with the rest of the money?"

"Ummm… Is there enough there to start paying off Lani's student loans, too?" I asked.

When I glanced over at my girlfriend, she was animatedly waving her arms like she was trying to spell out a sentence with semaphore. I ignored her and turned my back to the dinner table.

There was another pause on Mom's end of the line, her breath barely audible above the subtle analog hiss of static. "There's definitely enough here to pay off all of Lani's student loan bills, too. But what about the rest of the money after that?"

How much money would be left after that? I wondered.

I vaguely remembered Storf saying that songwriters earned something like 9.1 cents per song per album, and how that adds up over time when you compose a lot of melodies and lyrics and sell a decent amount of records. I did some quick calculations in my head: nine cents times ten or so songs times a hundred thousand records… The math just made my head spin. I stopped myself before I pulled a final number out of my brain's foggy mental abacus.

"Do you want me to put the rest into an interest-yielding CD account at the bank?" my mother offered.

I chuckled to myself. "That's funny."

"What's funny?" Mom asked.

"The CD thing," I said. "Putting money from CD sales into a CD account."

The silence on the other end of the line led me to believe that my mom wasn't quite as amused by my observation. *I* thought it was funny.

"But, yeah," I told her after a long sigh. "Just do whatever you think is best, Mom."

There was another soft crackle on the other end of the line, like my mom was scraping a Kleenex across the receiver. I'm pretty sure that she was softly crying and dabbing her eyes. "You know, I'm really proud of you, Brian," she whispered, her voice catching. "And I love you. Tell Lani that I say hi."

"I will, Mom. And I love you, too."

Something subtle, like a stifled sob, escaped from my mother's lips before the receiver's click cut off all sound.

Lani stared at me in disbelief. "Did you just tell your mom to *pay off my student loans…?*" she asked me incredulously.

My lips pulled back into a sheepish expression. "Maybe…" I nervously admitted to her.

She cocked her arm back and threw a napkin at me. "I told you that you can't just buy my affections, you jerk!"

I was completely caught off-guard. "I'm not trying to buy your affections!" I pleaded with her.

"Then what are you trying to do?" she shot back angrily.

My face flushed scarlet and I could feel the heat rising from my neck up to my temples. "It's not like that at all!" I entreated. "Will you just hear me out?"

Lani scowled at me with self-righteous vindication. "Then *what is it like*, Brian?" she spat out.

I stood before her with my palms up, like a priest supplicating on the steps of a church. I spluttered and stuttered for a moment before I could answer her. "I… I… I've been thinking about my future, Lani," I explained. "About *our* future. I keep running through all of these scenarios in my head, thinking about where I want to go and how I want to get there and who I want to spend the rest of my life with."

"*Whom*," she mumbled, still scowling. "You're supposed to say, 'with *whom* you want to spend the rest of your life.' Not *who*. It's *whom*."

Like I said, Lani has always been smarter than me. She was back then, and she still is now.

"All grammar aside," I continued on, undeterred, "it always comes back to you. You're the person who I… sorry… *whom* I want to spend the rest of my life with."

"You can't end a sentence with a preposition," she said with a scowl.

"Fine," I sighed in exasperation. "You're the person *with whom* I want to spend the rest of my life." As I spoke, I took a small step towards her. "Can I end my sentence with a *proposition* instead of a preposition?"

It was almost imperceptible, but her expression softened just a little right then, and the sharp creases on her forehead eased into smoother skin. Her arms, however, remained firmly crossed in front of her chest.

I took another small step forward. "I love you, Lani. I love you more than I've loved anyone else in my entire life. And I will continue to love you for as long as I live. I know that sounds like a trite Hallmark card, but…"

Lani dropped her arms and rushed up to me, her fingers wrapped around my neck, pulling my head down towards her and pressing her sweet lips against mine. It felt like our first kiss all over again.

When she finally pulled her lips away, she kept her left hand curled around the base of my skull. "I am not your prostitute," she scolded me. "You can't buy my love just because you have money all of a sudden."

"A *prostitute*…?" I nervously asked, half-grinning and half-squinting. "Does that mean I'm going to get lucky tonight?"

"It means that *I love you*, you idiot." Her lips curled into a puckish smile. "And I'll love you forever."

The next morning, I woke up early – before the sun had even crested over the horizon of the Hollywood hills. Lani was snoring softly, her smooth cheeks turned away from me, her lips gently parted as the breath flowed in and out of her chest. As quietly and delicately as I could, I sat up and let the cushion of the mattress slowly rise beneath my rather sizable frame. Though Lani was never much of a late sleeper (even in college), I wanted to give her a few more valuable minutes of snoozing before the sunlight nudged her awake.

As stealthily as I could, I made my way to her kitchen, squinting as my eyes adjusted to the darkness of near-dawn. I turned on the coffee pot and waited as the familiar hiss of the machine signaled its awakening from robotic slumber. In a drowsy daze, I filled up the water reservoir, measured out coffee grounds from a tin can of Folgers, and dumped the gritty grains into the coffee filter's lacy tarp.

As I waited for the steaming liquid to drizzle into its carafe, my eyes scanned Lani's apartment. Groggily, my gaze meandered from the framed photo of Maui on the wall to a copy of the *Los Angeles Times* that sat half-opened on the tile countertop to the thin vase that propped up the flowers I had brought her the night before.

In her cupboards, Lani had a small collection of coffee mugs from her parents' restaurant in Paia, the Hulabilly Diner – a fan-favorite tourist pitstop which sat just a stone's throw away from the Maui coast. I picked up one of the mugs and slowly twirled it in my hand as I waited for the coffee to finish brewing. The logo was a mashup of Hawaiian-rockabilly couture, featuring an acoustic guitar with a lei draped over the neck, a set of cartoonish tikis emerging from lush foliage, and a stylized banner with vintage 1950s fonts scrawled across the base.

It struck me then that the picture was a perfect summation of our relationship: I was the oversized acoustic guitar and Lani was the beautiful floral lei. Though the juxtaposition might have seemed jarring, maybe even odd, it all worked somehow.

The image also reminded me of the Beach Boys – my father's band, the soundtrack to my youth. Though my father was gone, he still loomed large in my subconscious as I grappled with the grief that had defined my life that summer.

"Life's too short to drink your coffee black," he used to say.

As I curled my fingers around the steaming mug and dribbled in a fair amount of milky-white creamer, that old aphorism once again manifested from the recesses of my memory. Slowly, mechanically, I swirled my spoon over and over in a circular pattern. The slight silver utensil rotated clockwise, trailing a comet's tail of cream and sugar through the small pool of black coffee. I was in a haze that felt vaguely like a fugue state, going through mechanical motions while my mind clouded over in a fog. Strangely enough, there was something comforting in the routine: it was as if my brain was on autopilot, and my body naturally navigated through the overcast shapes and figures to find substantial footing.

And still, I heard my father's voice repeating in my head: *"Life's too short to drink your coffee black."*

As much as I tried to stifle it, a grin spread lazily to my lips. While my chest still felt tight and awkwardly constricted, I knew that my father wouldn't want me to dwell on his loss. He didn't want me to suffer. He would want me to continue living, to enjoy the subtle sweetness in an otherwise bitter world.

The vast black waters of grieving can drown a man. I know, because I felt the weight of those waves all summer long. Finally, though, I felt like I was emerging from the water – soaked, but still breathing. In a brief moment of clarity, I knew that I was going to be okay.

CHAPTER THIRTY-ONE
"When I Grow Up (To Be a Man)"

Though my father guided me and helped shape me from the rough clay of my childhood to the finely detailed molding of my teenage years, he missed some of the most important events in my life. He wasn't present for so many formative experiences in the following years, and his absence cast a large shadow over the ensuing decades.

My father wasn't there for my college graduation, when I proudly marched across the stage at UCLA with my diploma pressed tightly to my shaking chest.

My father wasn't there to see Lani's first printed article in the *Los Angeles Times*, with her epic maiden name stretching out across the page in the ink of the byline.

My father wasn't there to pat me on the back when I received my teaching credential from Pepperdine University. He wasn't there to take me out for a beer when I got hired at Oxnard Shores High School. He wasn't there to ask me about my first day at the front of a classroom. He wasn't there to hear me talk about how it felt to have rows full of wide-eyed students look to me for guidance and direction. He wasn't there to congratulate me when I received my first "Teacher of the Year" award (or my second or my third, for that matter).

My father wasn't there the day that I formally proposed to Lani – as I bent down on one knee and placed a sparkling diamond on her left hand – and he wasn't there the evening that she and I got married under the picture-perfect Maui skyline, complete with cool, crisp colors of orange and auburn and violet and crimson adorning the horizon.

My father wasn't there when Lani and I announced to our family that we were expecting our first child – a baby girl. He wasn't there the day that Lani gave birth – when, after twenty hours of hard labor in the hospital, we welcomed Samantha Brianna Kamele'alania Smith to the world. He never got to see the beautiful baby girl whose middle name, Brianna, was a testament to how much he – Brian Richard Smith, Senior – shaped my life.

My father wasn't there for these memories, or for so many more…

My father wasn't there.

There are so many things that I wish I could have shared with him, experiences that would have brought him so much joy. I wish he could have heard Brian Wilson's finished *Smile* album – completed 37 years after it was abandoned by the Beach Boys. I wish he could have seen Brian and Al Jardine and David Marks reunite with Mike Love and Bruce Johnston for the Beach Boys' fiftieth anniversary tour in 2012. I wish he could have seen Brian Wilson's sold-out *Pet Sounds* show at the Hollywood Bowl in 2015. I wish he could have heard Blondie Chaplin sing "Sail On, Sailor" in Santa Barbara with me and Mel – almost four decades after Blondie quit the Beach Boys.

On a broader scale, I wish my father could have witnessed the election of Barack Obama – the first African-American president of the United States. I wish he could have seen the national legalization of same-sex marriage. I wish he could have played with apps on a smartphone or browsed Facebook for old college friends or streamed his massive record collection on Spotify.

Most of all, though, I wish he could have seen Sam growing up these last few years. Samantha Brianna – the little girl named after him, the little girl whose compassion and curiosity and confidence and contemplation would have undoubtedly entertained him beyond words. Sam, with her sandy skin and hazel eyes and her bright smile, would have brought my father so much joy and happiness.

I know it, because that's what she brings to me.

Sam's *other* middle name, *Kamele'alania*, is a tribute to her Hawaiian heritage. According to Lani, *Kamele'alania* translates roughly to *"the melody of calm waters"* – a very apt description of our beautiful little girl. For so many years, my life was turbulent, full of violently clamoring waves and whispers of withdrawing tides, but Sam has brought serenity and resolution to my life. In the same way that teaching has given me focus and direction, parenting has provided me with a sense of purpose that threads itself through every fiber of my stitched-up soul. That Hawaiian name, *Kamele'alania*, perfectly encapsulates the peace and joy that I have searched for my entire life.

Even in the aftermath of such tremendous loss and devastation, Sam helped me heal and grieve and move on from the darkness of my youth. The fact that she's also named for my father – and, by extension, me – only reinforces the idea that the present and past are inextricably bound together. My life is like that ancient image of the *Ouroboros*, the eternal cycle of the serpent eating its own tail, illustrating how every generation is connected with the ones that precede it. In that regard, my story ends where it begins: with my father and my daughter.

When Samantha was born, my life finally started to feel unbroken.

To feel whole.

To feel complete.

BRIDGE

As specters sang from faraway horizons,
Fireworks exploded in the sky.
We watched it all from underneath the pier,
Before we had to leave and say goodnight.

CHAPTER THIRTY-TWO
"Soul Searchin'"

For the first time that I can remember, Veronica was literally speechless. And I mean the *mouth agape, tongue-tied, struggling for words* kind of speechless. While that might not seem so dramatic for a normal human being, anyone who has ever met Veronica Jones knows that the girl can *talk*. After who-knows-how-many hours of listening to my story, I expected her to pummel me with follow-up questions. Instead, she sat motionless, studying the tile in front of her while her long black hair obscured my view of her face.

When she did finally open her mouth to speak, it was a muted response. "Wow," she whispered, barely audible over the hum of my computer. She sat still, penitent in her posture, and shifted uncomfortably in her seat.

"So… what happened next?" Veronica asked cautiously.

"Well, after I became a teacher, everything became a very comfortable pattern," I told her. "And my life has been pretty much the same ever since. It's a lot like running on a treadmill. Kind of predictable and tedious, but comfortable."

"And not much else has changed for you?"

I crossed my arms in front of my chest and sighed. "I mean, life is always evolving and changing. But all of my attention has been on Samantha and school. There hasn't been much time for anything else."

"Sam *is* pretty darn cute," Veronica added quietly.

"It's all from her mom's side," I said. "It would be hard for Sam to *not* be adorable with Mel's genetics."

Veronica let loose a small smile – the first that I had seen from her in hours. Slowly, though, her expression darkened again, like a somber cloud encroaching on blue skies.

"Do you miss it?" she asked.

"Miss what?"

She shifted again in her seat, leaning forward on the desk. "*You know*," she prompted with a restrained tone. "Playing music. Writing songs. All that rock star stuff."

"Honestly?"

"Honestly."

I paused for a second. "So many years have passed that it's hard to say. On most days, I've got my head down and I'm just trying to get through the week." Without thinking, I brushed my fingers against the stubble on my chin. "But…"

"But… what?"

"But, sometimes," I sighed, "when I pass by a coffee shop and see some kid strumming an acoustic guitar or playing a piano, I get this subtle sting in my gut." I looked down at my slightly trembling hands. "I guess, on some level, I do miss it."

Veronica's only response was a crooked smile. I could almost see the gears turning behind her dark eyes, a plan formulating in her razor-sharp mind.

"So, what if…?" she started to say.

Veronica didn't get to finish her question. At precisely that moment, when Veronica seemed ready to pose some grand hypothetical scenario, the school's alarm blared through the intercom.

"*ALL CLEAR*," the disembodied voice announced. "*Our lock down has been lifted and we are ALL CLEAR. Please proceed to lunch.*"

I turned to Veronica with quiet conviction. "You heard the announcement, kid. You better get going."

She didn't move at first – she just gazed off into the distance, as if she was watching the sunrise cresting behind the whiteboard.

"Okay," she murmured back as she gathered her things. Silently, Veronica crept towards the door, her bursting-at-the-seams backpack slung over her shoulders.

I had just walked over to my computer to check my work email when I heard her voice from the doorway.

"Mr. Smith…?"

"Yes, Veronica?"

"Thank you," she said. Those two simple words contained all the earnest emotion she could muster.

"Thank you?" I echoed back. "For what…?"

"Thank you for sharing all of that with me. I know you don't like to talk about yourself, but…" Her voice transformed from a river to a creek. "I'm grateful that you told me. So, thank you."

I gave her an exhausted smile. "You're welcome, Veronica."

And, with that, she turned and disappeared out the door.

CHAPTER THIRTY-THREE
"Be Still"

In usual Veronica fashion, that was not the end of the conversation. Although I had the temporary buffer of winter vacation to offer a quiet intermission from Veronica's inquisitive interrogation, I inevitably found myself fending off queries and comments when we returned from our two-week break. Veronica didn't let up: she peppered me with questions before school, at lunch time, during passing periods – and even occasionally during AP English, while the class was diligently doing group work or tackling other independent tasks. When Veronica started to ask about the fates and fortunes of my bandmates, though, I had to admit to her that I didn't know what they were up to these days.

"So, you don't know what happened to *any* of the guys in the band?" she asked in disbelief one day during lunch.

"Not really," I told her. "Chunk is the only one I've kept in contact with." I stopped myself to correct my grammatical error: "Sorry. Chunk is the only one *with whom* I have kept in contact."

"Mel would be proud of you," Veronica said with a snicker.

I rolled my eyes. "*Anyway*, Chunk is family, you know? He's bound by blood and all that. After everything collapsed with Call Field, he finished up his undergraduate degree and eventually earned an MBA from Loyola Marymount University. Believe it or not, he actually bought a comic shop not too far from LAX. And he's been happily running his store for the last decade."

"A *comic shop*…?" Veronica asked in disbelief. "That's kind of a strange follow-up to a career as a rock star."

"As I've explained before, Veronica," I sighed. "We weren't rock stars. We were barely rock *meteors*. Maybe even just rock *asteroids*."

"Whatever," she mumbled, rolling her eyes. "Okay, your cousin runs a comic book store. Is that even a thing anymore?"

"Well, the last time that I checked, superhero movies were raking in billions of dollars at the box office." I shuffled some papers on my desk, trying in vain to wish away the teenage girl who relentlessly pummeled me with questions. No such luck. "Though brick-and-mortar stores might have a hard time surviving in the age of Amazon and online shopping, Chunk has somehow managed to stay afloat and make ends meet."

"Do you see him often?" she asked.

"As a matter of fact," I said, "I just saw him over break. Chunk and his wife and their kids live in Marina Del Rey, just close enough to come home and visit for holidays and family gatherings. They drove up for the last night of Hanukkah and stayed through New Year's Day. We probably see them once a month or so."

Veronica tapped a pencil against her chin like a metronome filled with no. 2 carbon lead. "But you have no idea what happened to the other guys?"

"None at all."

"You haven't tried Googling them or anything?" she pressed on. "No private investigators?"

"Nope."

"Huh," she muttered faintly. "That's interesting."

"Is it, Veronica?"

"Yes," she said. "It is."

Time marched on. I had an endless supply of essays to score, tests to grade, and lessons to plan. Day in and day out, I kept my nose to the grindstone – taking my life one small step at a time. Of course, there were always the demarcations of time passing: weeknight workouts and weekend dinners, playdates and parties, formidable term papers and preparation for first-semester final exams... The days floated by undisturbed, like cumulus clouds drifting lazily through the firmament.

By the time that MLK Day weekend was nearly upon us, I didn't think there would be any further developments in the world of Call Field. Veronica's questions – while not entirely halted – had slowed down to a leisurely crawl. Foolishly, I assumed that she would drop the whole unnecessary obsession with my musical history.

Of course, I was wrong.

Let's talk about teachers' assistants. Once upon a time, teachers would accumulate TAs like trading cards, stockpiling them without much thought and usually underutilizing these proactive students. However, in a pedagogically progressive move, our small school district created a CTE Education pathway with a "student teaching" course of study. Basically, we take kids with a vague interest in teaching and transform them into mini-student-teachers. Of course, this also necessitates a series of benchmarks for the "student teaching" class – including graded assignments for one-on-one tutoring, small-group facilitation, and full-class instruction. In short, we teach our TAs how to teach and then grade them on their teaching.

Phew.

So, why do I mention all of this educational mumbo-jumbo? Well, dear reader, I'm hoping to front-load information so that you can understand how Veronica Jones ended up teaching a lesson on poetry for my AP English Language course, shortly after first-semester final exams.

Commence scene.

Veronica was positioned at the front of the classroom, her perfectly manicured fingers twisted around a smart-board pen. Embracing her moment in the limelight of my classroom, she was dressed to the nines in a black pencil skirt that draped just below her knees, a puffy white blouse, and a jet-black blazer. She even forewent her usual contact lenses for a pair of professorial black-rimmed spectacles. The seventeen-year-old kid who frequently sported her ubiquitous BYU hoodie had suddenly transformed into a precocious corporate lawyer. If it wasn't for the little tells that gave her away – rocking back and forth on her high heels, leaning forward on the podium like it was supporting the entire weight of her 110-pound frame – she could have passed for a full-fledged teacher. In fact, when a clueless office assistant came into the class to deliver a call slip, the pimple-faced boy walked right up to Veronica and handed her the paper. The class snickered while the poor, bewildered kid walked away in confusion. It was the kind of bizarre high school memory that's so peculiar you can't invent it. Sometimes, truth actually *is* stranger than fiction.

So, there she was: Veronica Jones, student extraordinaire, in her mock-adult getup. Never mind the fact that no other female teacher on campus ever looked so decadently decked-out (except begrudgingly for Back-to-School Night). As she manipulated the wireless keyboard and mouse on the podium, the LCD projection behind her showed the familiar-looking desktop image of Samantha in costume Gryffindor robes. It seemed like any other lesson in my classroom – except that I was seated at a desk, taking copious notes, while my TA stood front-and-center.

"Today," Veronica announced casually to the class, "you will call me '*Ms. Jones*.' If you refer to me as 'Veronica,' I will throw an eraser at you."

The class tittered in glee with the novelty of the moment. The Queen Bee of English AP had a new hive at her disposal.

"So, *Ms. Jones*," I interjected in an attempt to move things along, "what will you be covering in class today?" I had my trademark blue Uniball pen poised over a photocopied rubric, and I was ready to jot down notes and observations.

Veronica looked over at me and gave me her trademark mischievous smirk. "I'm glad you asked, *young man*," she answered puckishly. With a few swift clicks, she logged into her Google Drive and navigated her way to a folder labeled *AP English Benchmark Presentation*. "Today, we're going to analyze rhetorical devices in a piece of nonfiction… well, *mostly nonfiction* writing." She held up a stack of photocopied papers in her hand and waved it above her head like she was hailing a cab.

I made a quick note to myself: *Student-teacher is dressed professionally and prepared with materials for her lesson.* So far, Veronica's presentation was off to a good start.

"However," Veronica intoned slyly, "we're not going to look at some old, boring historical speech. On the contrary, class, we are going to analyze something completely different today." She swiftly clicked a few more buttons and started to open a Google Doc file. "Today, we are going to analyze… *song lyrics.*"

The LCD projection behind Veronica was suddenly filled with a series of familiar looking stanzas, heralded by a bolded title:

"INCOMPLETE (JUST LIKE YOUR SMILE)"
CALL FIELD

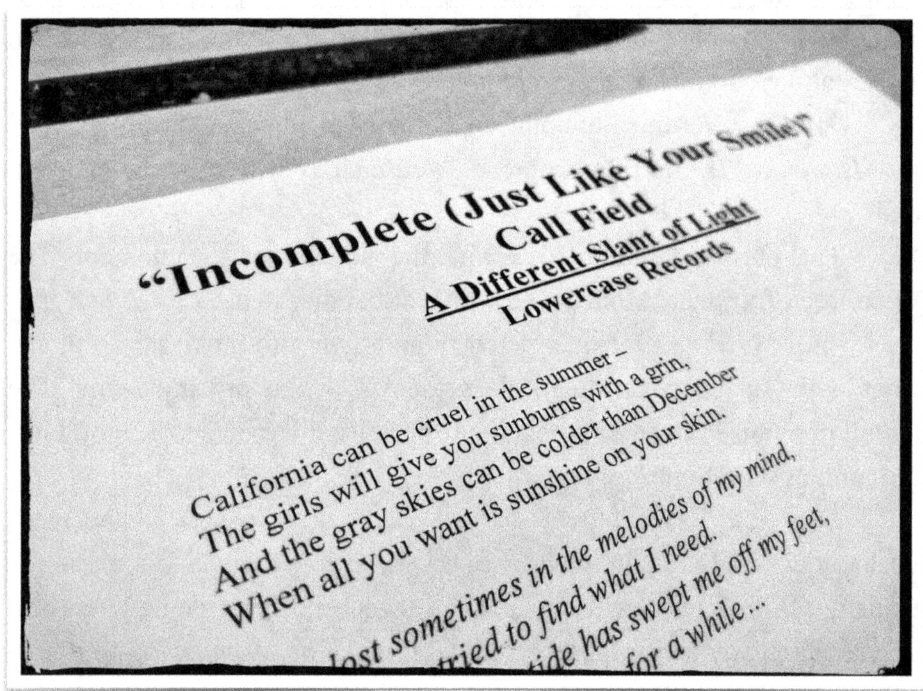

Needless to say, I started to panic.

Damnit. Damnit. Damnit. Damnit. Damnit. Damnit. Damnit.
DAMN. IT.

Veronica stepped forward from the podium to the empty space at the front of the room. "Because Mr. Smith – our *Captain, My Captain* –

loves music so much," she dramatically drawled, "I thought it would be fun to analyze a rock song from his youth."

I don't know how well I was hiding the terror that sprouted from my heart and flowered in my face, but Veronica seemed to be savoring my discomfort.

"It's a song that's near and dear to his ancient heart," she explained, "one that he's probably spent countless hours analyzing himself over the years." Her eyes scanned across the class and then lingered on me sadistically. "Isn't that right, Mr. Smith?"

Although I felt like I was on the verge of a panic attack, I faked a smile and muttered a forced response. "Please go on, Veronica," I squeaked.

She scowled at me. "Today," she reminded me, "it's *Ms. Jones.*" She grabbed a whiteboard eraser from the perch behind her and held it over her head, threatening to launch a fuzzy projectile in my direction.

The class erupted in laughter.

"I beg for your forgiveness, *Ms. Jones,*" I apologized with a gently mocking tone. "Please proceed with your lesson."

"As I was saying," Veronica continued, "this set of lyrics harkens back to the days before any of us were born, way back in *Anno Domini* 2000. Back then, a young punk band from Southern California called Call Field…"

"Who the heck is Call Field?" one of the kids in the back of the class interrupted.

"I'm glad you asked," Veronica said with a wicked smile. At a leisurely pace, she sauntered back to the security of the podium. "They were a group of suburban punk rockers who hailed from a town not far from here. Ojai, I believe. Isn't that right, Mr. Smith?"

I nodded uncomfortably, the spittle in my throat threatening to make me gag.

Veronica gesticulated elaborately, like an actress in a silent film. "This group, much like blink-182 and the Ramones, blended pop-punk music with some more melodic influences… like the Beach Boys." She fiddled with the wireless mouse as she studied the LCD projection behind her on the board, opening Spotify and typing *Call Field* in the search engine. Within seconds, the landing page for the band opened up – with "Incomplete" listed as the top track.

My cheeks felt red-hot to the touch, and I could feel a cold trickle of sweat threatening to dart down my neck.

Veronica soldiered on, unaware of (or indifferent to) my discomfort, her fingers counting out pieces of paper in small stacks. "As we listen to the song, please annotate the set of lyrics that I'm handing out." She left the security of the podium and made her way around the classroom, passing out a handful of collated papers to each row. "As usual, be sure to highlight or mark up anything that stands out to you."

After she had completed her rounds, she circled back to the podium and fiddled with the mouse. As Veronica clicked *play*, those old, familiar octave chords came blaring through the speakers. Within moments, Steve's voice echoed through the classroom.

"California can be cruel in the summer…"

The next three and a half minutes were among the most uncomfortable of my entire life. Imagine someone passing around naked baby photos of you to a class of sixteen- and seventeen-year-old high school students. It's a special kind of hell to be exposed so explicitly to a crowd of teenagers.

As much as I wanted to crawl into my own skin and disappear, I was trapped. I had spent years trying to forget that part of my life, shoveling dirt on top of my musical grave. Here I was, though, watching teenagers excavate the skeletal remains of my youth. As much as I respect and admire Veronica, I was decidedly *not* thrilled with her at that point.

Finally, after the *a capella* break and final chorus that wound down the song, it was over. My undershirt was soaking up the sweat that had been beading on my back and chest for the last few minutes, and I secretly prayed that armpit stains weren't leaking through to my collared shirt and necktie.

"Now that we've had a chance to listen to this rather beautiful and poetic song," Veronica announced, "let's take a moment to annotate." Her eyes roamed the room, assessing the reactions of the students.

Although a few kids stared at the ceiling while thoughts percolated in their heads, the vast majority of the class scribbled away frantically on their photocopied lyrics. After two minutes or so had passed, Veronica chimed the bell that I kept on my desk, calling the class's attention to the front of the room.

"Before we begin our full-class discussion," Veronica instructed, "turn to a partner sitting next to you for a *think-pair-share*."

As directed, the students turned to their classmates and the room erupted in a buzz of conversational analysis. If I hadn't been so distracted by the absurdity of the scene, I would have been proud of Veronica and the rest of my students for maintaining such a productive academic environment – especially with a guest teacher. As it was, however, I felt like I was barely preventing the panic in my chest from exploding like a sweaty atom bomb.

The student immediately to my right, a petite brunette girl named Brenna, turned to me and delicately lifted up her copy of the lyrics. "Would you like to join us, Mr. Smith?" She gestured to the girl seated next to her and shrugged her shoulders.

"Uh…" I stammered momentarily. "Sure, Brenna," I finally answered, before scooting my desk over a few inches. "What do you and Riya think?"

Riya, the future valedictorian of her graduating class, leaned forward in her desk and placed her annotated lyrics in the center of our huddle. "This is *not* my style of music," she admitted casually, "but I like the lyrics. It's an interesting twist on summer. A bit paradoxical in its juxtaposition of pain and summertime, as you see in the opening lines." With her green gel pen, she gestured to the opening salvo of the song.

"But there's a dramatic shift in the second verse," Brenna interjected, pointing a manicured fingernail at the lyrics in front of us. "While the first verse talks about 'sunburns' and 'cruelty,' the next section uses the word 'salvation.' That's some pretty loaded diction."

"I'm not familiar with this allusion in the second verse," Riya said. "*Pet Sounds*…? What's *Pet Sounds*…?"

I chuckled nervously to myself. "It's an album by the Beach Boys," I explained, looking into the faces of these two teenage girls for some glimmer of recognition.

They gave me blank stares in return.

"*Rolling Stone* magazine named it the second greatest album of all time," I said. "Right behind *Sgt. Pepper's Lonely Hearts Club Band.*"

Once again, I was met with blank stares.

"You've really never heard of it?"

Both girls shook their heads.

Man, I felt old.

"Sooooo…" I mumbled, trying to change the subject. "What else did you two notice in these song lyrics?"

"I like the reference to ghosts in the second-to-last part," Brenna said. "The section about specters singing and 'faraway horizons.'"

"It's an interesting contrast," Riya added. "You usually think of horizons as promising hope. Like Gatsby's green light or something. But then you've got this image of specters haunting the speaker of the poem. It seems like a bit of an oxymoron. Like a haunted hopefulness or something."

"*Haunted hopefulness,*" I echoed back. "I like that, Riya."

"Thanks, Mr. Smith. I was thinking…"

The distinct, piercing sound of my classroom chimes interrupted our conversation. Veronica, having returned to the podium at the front of the room, held the mallet slightly aloft like a musical conductor in front of an academic orchestra.

"It's time to reconvene, everyone," she commanded in a singsong manner.

The sound of desks screeching on the floor reverberated throughout the room. Sitting alongside Brenna and Riya as a casual audience member instead of a director, I marveled at how well-trained these eleventh-grade AP English students – *my students* – behaved. When you've established norms and procedures with your pupils, it's easy to forget how chaotic a classroom can be. It was a nice ego boost during that half-hour of panic, a brief respite from the adolescent nightmare that I was enduring during Veronica's lesson.

"My dearest AP students," Veronica sang out, "what observations do you have for this genius piece of musical poetry?" She looked over at me and raised an eyebrow, like she was throwing a gauntlet at my feet.

Let the games begin, I thought.

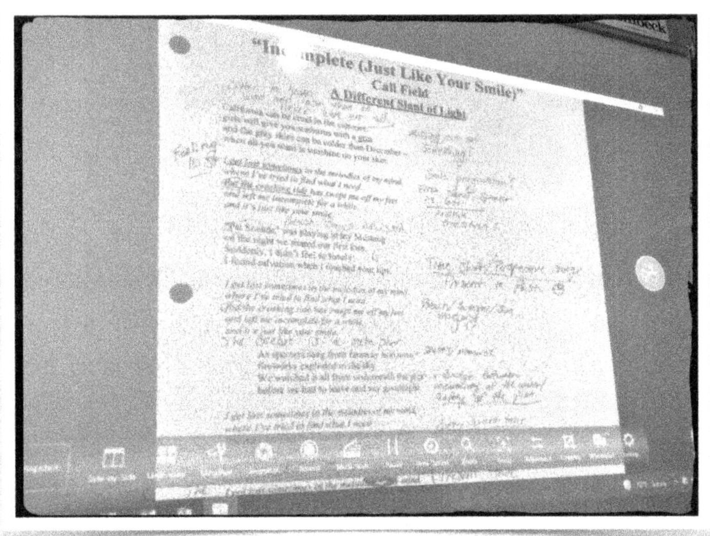

Surprisingly, the class was able to cull some remarkable analysis of "Incomplete" during that class discussion. Like Riya and Brenna, other students latched onto the paradoxical juxtaposition of images, the connotation of loaded diction like "salvation," and the dramatic shift from present tense to past tense in the final chorus. They even made arguments about the cacophonous alliteration in the opening line, "<u>C</u>alifornia <u>c</u>an be <u>c</u>ruel," discussing how that simple repetition mirrored the conflict in the first verse. My students astounded me with their insight – a pride that was only compounded by the fact that they were analyzing something I had written so many years ago (unbeknownst to them, of course).

At the same time, these marvelous students of mine also picked up on some of the song's deepest flaws.

"What is it with adolescent boys and their unrealistic expectations of women?" noted one raven-haired student, Esperanza.

"Seriously!" chimed in another girl, Lakendra. "Boys can be so two-dimensional!"

A copper-hued hand darted up in the air, fingers wiggling rapidly.

"Yes, Alexandria?" Veronica prompted, adjusting her glasses dramatically. My TA was clearly savoring her role as a temporary teacher – and tormentor, in my case.

I held my breath.

Alexandria – or *Alex*, as she was usually known – was a preternaturally insightful young woman, wise beyond her sixteen or seventeen years of age. She was also, as our class had come to see that year, capable of distilling a discussion down to its prime, essential elements.

Alex lowered her hand and rested it calmly on her desk, palm down on the scarred wooden surface. "I think it comes down to a misperception," she said. "No human being – especially a teenage girl – can provide *salvation* to another person." A small chorus of girls cheered from behind her.

I was just about to concede that the adolescent version of myself – the haunted young man who had composed that song so many years ago – had only a limited knowledge of himself and the world around him, when a soft-spoken blonde student named Jacob raised his hand. Veronica smirked and called on him to speak.

"I don't want to start any gender wars," he said nervously, "but who are we to say that this person didn't *feel* like his relationship had been a kind of 'salvation' for him?" A few muffled groans sparked up in various corners of the classroom, but Jacob continued on, undeterred. "I mean, I think Alex is right. You can't *literally* be saved by a teenage girl. But maybe – in some grand, hyperbolic way – that relationship gave him a new sense of hope. Hope for himself. Or for the world. Or maybe just for future happiness." He paused, his monologue dancing in the stillness of the room's subsequent silence. "That makes sense, right?"

Scattered conversations instantly erupted between the aisles of desks. Normally, I love it when my students feel so passionately engaged in a discussion that they're unable to hold back their opinions. This time, though, the chaos and critiques brought more anxiety than unmitigated joy.

"Hold on, hold on," Veronica called out to the class. "Let's not lose sight of our lesson."

Still, side conversations continued, unabated.

Perhaps sensing that the class was slipping away from her, Veronica turned in my direction. "And what do *you* think, Mr. Smith? I believe you're pretty familiar with this band, are you not?"

The class instantly hushed. Something about a teacher's authority can have that kind of predictable power on a group of well-trained teenagers. Whether I liked it or not, all eyes were on me.

"Yes, Veronica…" I started to say – before she scowled and pointed at her black-rimmed glasses. "Sorry… yes, *Ms. Jones.*"

"That's better," she chided.

"This song came from a very youthful, inexperienced point of view," I argued. "The person who wrote these lyrics had a very limited perspective of the world. As a result, his conception of salvation was a bit restricted in scope."

A few heads nodded in agreement. Esperanza and Lakendra and a handful of other students didn't seem entirely sold on my argument, though, so I doubled down and explained further.

"Remember our discussions when we were reading *Catcher in the Rye*…?" I asked. "We talked about how Holden Caulfield is an *unreliable narrator*, a character whose understanding of a situation is limited by his own tunnel vision and perception of the world. I think the person who wrote this song –"

Veronica coughed loudly and grinned at me.

"As I was saying," I continued, frowning bitterly at Veronica, "the person who wrote this song created a *somewhat*-unreliable narrator in the lyrics. Whether or not this song is autobiographical –"

"And I believe that it is," Veronica added craftily.

" – the fact remains that the writer painted a portrait of the world as seen through his own eyes – the eyes of a young man whose reverence for the girl that he loves breathed a new kind of life into him, inflated his lungs and his heart so that he could finally find a sense of meaning and purpose in his life. Thanks to his relationship with her, he found the completion that he so desperately craved. And *that*, I would argue, should be valued more than the artistic missteps he might have taken with his emotional immaturity."

The class was stubbornly silent for a second.

"Mr. Smith?" another student quietly called out from his seat.

"Yes, Nick?" I answered, turning around to face the unobtrusive young man who had said my name.

"Aren't we supposed to use the present tense when we're discussing works of art? Like 'the writer *paints* a portrait… *inflates* his lungs…' Isn't that the way you taught us to discuss pieces of writing? Like they're time capsules trapped forever in the present tense?"

I was awestruck. In discussing my own song, I had lapsed into the past tense, speaking about "Incomplete" as if it was my own personal history – which, technically, it was – even though the lyrics themselves would forever remain trapped in amber and preserved in the present tense.

"You're right, Nick," I admitted. "Literature and poetry – even in a set of song lyrics – is always happening *right now*. Thank you for catching that."

Nick smiled in that serene way students have when they intellectually best their teachers, catching those seemingly inconsequential errors that expose their teachers' imperfections.

"Of course," Veronica added, with her mischievous smile on full display, "he did learn from the best."

From my peripheral vision, I saw a hand shoot up to my right. "Miss Jones?" Brenna called out.

"Yes?"

"Is there a music video for this song?"

Veronica's smile widened further into a Cheshire grin. "Why, yes, Brenna. There *is* a music video. And it's a really good one, too. You should check it out on YouTube."

I lowered my forehead into my palms and prayed that God would take me right then and there.

CHAPTER THIRTY-FOUR
"Think About the Days"

I'd like to say that I strutted out of my classroom that afternoon feeling vindicated and validated, but I had a nagging feeling in my gut that wouldn't go away. Something about Nick's comment stuck with me: that my words would always be happening in the present tense, as if the past and present were inexorably entwined.

Would I ever be able to escape my haunted history? Could I ever divorce myself from the young man that I used to be? Was I doomed for eternity to ask rhetorical questions about my fate?

My messenger bag was all packed and I was just about to shut down my computer when Veronica bounded into my vacant classroom like a toddler bouncing on a trampoline. It had only been a few hours since her student-teaching lesson, but she was already back in jeans and her trusty BYU sweater, looking less like a lawyer and more like the unpretentious teenage girl I had come to know and respect.

"You better watch out, Mr. Smith," she taunted me. "I'm gunning for your job!"

I stifled a laugh. "It's a good thing you're going into dentistry and not teaching," I told her. "Or I'd be out of work."

"You could always go back into the music business," Veronica said. She gave me a piercing, arrogant look – the kind that can only be administered by teenagers who think they own the world.

"I thought I was going to have a panic attack, Veronica," I admitted. "You really caught me off-guard. Though I shouldn't expect anything less from you, I suppose."

"Oh, get off it, old man," she teased me as she curled her arms around herself. "Don't be so ridiculous! Did you see how much they loved your song? They were picking it apart as if it was *Shakespeare*, for goodness' sakes!"

"Well, *Shakespeare I am not*," I said.

"Although you do share a similar hairline," she jibed.

I held my palm up to my heart. "*Et tu, Brute?*"

"You're such a dork, Mr. Smith," she said with a melodramatic rolling of her eyes.

I threw my messenger bag over my shoulder and walked towards the door. "So, what brings you back to campus, Veronica? I'm heading out now, so make it quick."

Veronica followed like a pouncing puppy, bouncing behind me as I flicked off the classroom lights, locked my door, and walked out into the hallway.

"I almost told them," Veronica admitted giddily. "They *loved* your lyrics, Mr. Smith. I had to bite my tongue so I wouldn't announce to the whole class that it was *your* song we were discussing."

I stopped dead in my tracks and clenched my eyes shut. "I am *so glad* that you didn't do that, Veronica. So. Glad. Considering how close I was to having an anxiety attack, I'm pretty sure that my heart would have flatlined if you had told a class full of teenagers about something I've been trying to forget for twenty years."

When I opened my eyes, Veronica was snickering in front of me. "You know it's just a matter of time, right?"

"What do you mean?"

"We live in the twenty-first century, Mr. Smith," Veronica laughed. "Once Brenna or Jacob or Riya or any of the other kids in your class snoops around on the internet, they'll find the same information that I did. Your days of anonymity are over, Mr. Rock Star."

Veronica was right.

My days were numbered.

Driving home, I kept replaying the morning's events in my mind. My hands gripped the steering wheel so tightly that my knuckles whitened, and I could feel the sandpaper friction between the palms of my hands and the plastic wheel cover.

How long do I have? I wondered. *Days? Weeks? Months? Or only hours?*

I tried to tell myself that I was overreacting. After all, I was a grown man with forty years' worth of experience and a lifetime of healing between my former life and the one I lived now. Would it *really* be that bad if a handful of high school kids knew my secret?

By the time that I arrived home, my heart felt like a seesaw, vacillating wildly between peerless panic and calmer confidence.

As I walked from my car to the front porch, I caught myself absentmindedly jangling my keys, a nervous tic that I've never been able to shake.

Before I opened the door, I closed my eyes and took a deep breath. It was a simple coping mechanism that my therapist, Dr. Valencia, taught me when I returned to UCLA after my dad died. As he explained to me, having little tricks like these in your psychological toolkit can help keep a full-pledged panic attack at bay. Sometimes, just by taking a second to pause and focus on your breathing, you can "reboot" your brain. It doesn't *always* work, mind you, but it helps out in some scenarios.

As I stepped into the entranceway of my humble abode, I expected a clatter of household noise: a television or a radio or Sam's voice reverberating through the halls. Instead, I was met only with complete silence. So, my curiosity piqued, I set down my messenger bag and crept around to the dining room.

She didn't say anything, but I could see the back of Mel's head hunched towards a computer screen. She ran her fingers through her long black hair and sighed audibly.

"Hey," I said from the kitchen, as I set my keys on the counter.

"Hey," she mumbled back, her eyes still focused intently on the screen.

I walked up behind her and rested my chin on the top of her head. "What are you working on?" I asked, encircling her with my arms.

She tensed up and stretched her neck. "Ugh. The kid who wrote this article doesn't know an assumption from his ass. How can anyone expect me to fix writing *this bad* on such a short timeline?" Mel took off her glasses and rubbed the bridge of her nose.

I quietly studied the top of her head. "You've got a few gray hairs back here," I told her.

"Thank for reminding me, *jerk*," she scoffed. "Way to kick a girl when she's down."

"I'm sorry," I said sheepishly. "Is there anything I can do to help?"

Mel blew out a puff of air from the corner of her mouth. "Make sure that Sam is finishing her homework," she told me. "And start putting together a salad for dinner. I've got a *lot* of work to do tonight."

As much as I wanted to lay my burdens at the feet of my wife, I realized that this wasn't the right time. A key ingredient for successful marriages? Working as partners, taking turns picking up the slack. Though I wanted to dwell in my self-absorbed drama with an enraptured audience to hear my woes, I needed to do my household duties for the evening.

One of the strangest parts of adulthood is watching the people around you change and grow and evolve into new incarnations of themselves. As I worked my way around the kitchen, I couldn't help but smirk. The girl who once doused me with ice water to wake me up from the dark depths of my doldrums was now the mother of my child, the wife with whom I would share the rest of my life. And that very same woman was now muttering profanities at the computer screen in front of her.

As I promised Mel, I flipped on my "domestic daddy" switch: I helped Sam with her homework, set the table, prepped lunches for the next day, and fixed up dinner (with my limited culinary capabilities, of course). While Sam read a copy of *Charlotte's Web* on the living room couch, Mel's nimble fingers click-clacked across the keyboard, working the wordsmith magic of a career-long copy editor. Although the *Oxnard Breeze* is a far cry from the *Los Angeles Times* or the *Daily Bruin*, Mel brought the same level of professionalism and productivity with her wherever she went. She was – and is – the smartest woman I know.

By the time Mel wrapped up editing and uploaded her revised drafts to the newspaper's editor-in-chief, dinner was all set up and ready for consumption. I gathered Sam from the living room and dragged her to the dining room table, where we commenced our dinnertime routine. After some light conversation, I finally got the nerve to bring up Veronica's shenanigans during AP English a few hours earlier.

"So, a funny thing happened at work today…" I began. I told Mel the whole story, paraphrasing as much of the discussion as I could remember. I even brought up the debate about teenage boys and their melodramatic impressions of girls.

"I kind of feel like I should be personally offended," Mel laughed. "If you ask me, *salvation* seems a pretty apropos term for the redemptive magic that I worked on you."

Meanwhile, Sam sat there throughout the conversation, digesting every last word and observation.

"Wait… wait…" Sam interrupted at one point. "You were in a *band*, Daddy? Like a *real* band?"

"Samantha," I whined in mild exasperation, "you *know* that. I've told you that before."

"I know you played music, but I thought it was just, like, around the house or something. You made a *music video*? Really?"

"Yes, Sam," Mel chimed in. "Your dad was a rock star before you were born."

"I wasn't a *rock star*," I interrupted, gesticulating awkwardly with my hands.

"Were you *famous*?" Sam asked.

"No, Samantha," I told her. "I was never famous. I was the guy in the background while the lead singer got all the attention."

"Where is he now?" Sam asked.

"Who, sweetie?"

"The lead singer."

"I have no idea, whatsoever," I told her. "And I don't mind if it stays that way."

I didn't think much of it at the time, but Mel shot me a strange look right then – an expression that seemed equal parts concern and confusion and dramatic irony. And she bit down on her lower lip – the telltale sign that she felt conflicted about some mysterious subject.

She knew something that I didn't.

CHAPTER THIRTY-FIVE
"Amusement Parks USA"

The last few days before semester grades are due always make me feel like a sprinter desperately trying to cross the finish line. I gave my freshman a final exam on *The House on Mango Street*, had my Advanced Placement students take a mock AP test (including a timed essay about the extinction of plastic lawn flamingoes), and did everything I could to stay awake in the midst of a sleep-deprived, somnambulant week. Finally, after a Herculean amount of grading essays and scoring Scantron sheets, a three-day weekend was finally upon us.

Words cannot express the relief that I felt.

The 72-hour extended weekend after finals is always a welcome respite from the insanity of 60-hour work weeks and unrelenting stress. Exhaustion tends to pile up on educators like mounds of filthy laundry: little by little, the hampers of our souls get filled to the brim – then wind up overstuffed and overflowing. I can't speak for all teachers, but I find myself sleeping twelve hours a day during that fleeting Saturday, Sunday, and bonus Monday. This year was no different.

As luck would have it, Samantha's birthday fell on that Sunday, right in the middle of the three-day weekend. We didn't anticipate that our daughter would be born at the end of January, but Mel went into labor two weeks earlier than anticipated. Although Sam was born underweight – she was a tiny little thing, not even six pounds in total – she managed to catch up with her peers and has consistently been one of the tallest kids in her class each year. But the unintended side effect of her premature birth is that her birthday almost always falls in the middle of final exams. This year, at least, we had a long weekend to celebrate with our precious daughter.

And, because Mel and I are suckers for nostalgic childhood cartoons, we've made it an annual tradition to visit the House of Mouse for Sam's birthday.

Yup. Disneyland.

I know that folks have hurled all kinds of criticism at the "Happiest Place on Earth" over the years, but I will forever defend Disneyland as a charming, enchanting escape from reality.

Sam loves it, Mel loves it, and I love it. The end.

Plus, it was still cheaper than throwing her a big birthday party. We are, after all, operating on the salary of a public-school teacher and a small-town newspaper copyeditor.

I'll spare you a laborious recounting of our day at the park, but you should know that the biggest revelation for me was Sam's unexpected passion for the Haunted Mansion. During her first few trips to Disneyland, Sam was absolutely *terrified* of my two favorite rides, Pirates of the Caribbean and the aforementioned Haunted Mansion. To be fair, all that death iconography can seem daunting for toddlers and tykes: those singing skulls and symbolic signifiers of slain souls, not to mention the creepy sound effects, can be a bit overwhelming for sensitive kids. So, imagine my surprise when Sam bravely announced that she wanted to go on the Haunted Mansion for the first time. And the second time. And the third time.

In fact, I'm pretty sure that Sam would have willingly joined those 999 grim, grinning ghosts and permanently moved into the Mansion, if the park would have let her. Go figure.

Somehow, my timid little girl – the same one who bawls every time a beloved character dies in *Harry Potter* – had become accustomed to the looming shadow of darkness and death. Miraculously, she was well on her way to becoming a Disney-level existentialist.

However, the most important part of the day (as far as this story is concerned, anyway) occurred that evening, as we were dining at one of the restaurants in Downtown Disney. We were all exhausted after a long day of walking the park – and Sam was almost ready to fall asleep face-first in her plate of spaghetti – when a familiar song started pouring forth from the restaurant's family-friendly radio station…

"California can be cruel in the summer…"

Once again, the ghosts of my past were circling me in the most unexpected, inopportune moments. The spirits and souls in the Haunted Mansion have got nothing on me.

This time, however, my chest didn't seize up. Nor did my palms instantly turn cold and clammy. Maybe I was just desensitized after Veronica's traumatizing lesson the week before, but "Incomplete" – that cursed relic of my past – didn't seem to hold as much sway over me as it had for the prior two decades. I looked over at Mel, whose expression was one of mingled curiosity and amusement.

With a careful, deliberate thoughtfulness, she turned towards Sam. "You hear that song on the radio, honey?" she asked our daughter, eyeing me peripherally.

Sam bopped her little head, her slight body swaying lightly – as if the song was slowly possessing her, like a minuscule medium at a musical seance. "What about it?"

A grin spread across Mel's lips. "Your daddy wrote this song," she said. She winked at me, still gauging my reaction.

"*You* wrote this, Daddy?" Sam asked.

"I did. Almost twenty years ago, in fact."

"No. Way. *Seriously…*?" Sam stared at me incredulously, as if I had sprouted Maleficent's horns atop my balding head.

I merely nodded.

"Is that you singing, too?" she asked, the volume of her voice rising to match the intensity of her disbelief.

"Nope," I said. "That was the lead singer for the band."

"But *you* wrote the song?" Sam pressed on. "All by yourself?"

"All by myself."

"And it was on the radio?"

"It's on the radio right now, isn't it?"

Sam's eyes widened as if she was discovering a secret Amazonian tribe in the middle of a verdant jungle. "Did you know about this, Mom?" she asked, still in shock.

"Of course, sweetie," Mel answered. "He wrote it about me."

"*HE WROTE IT ABOUT YOU?*" Sam bellowed. She looked like her overstimulated little brain was about to explode.

Right around then, a waiter trooped up to our table to check on us. "Is everything okay?" he asked politely.

Sam whipped around in a frenzy and turned to the waiter. "*DID YOU KNOW THAT MY DAD WROTE THE SONG THAT WE'RE LISTENING TO ON THE RADIO RIGHT NOW?*"

The poor young man cocked an eyebrow in confusion, turning to me and Mel for some affirmation of Sam's wild claim.

"It's true," Mel laughed. "You're looking at the songwriter and bass player for the band Call Field, whose music we are currently enjoying in your fine establishment."

The waiter, still fighting off well-placed doubt, eyed us skeptically. "Call… Field…?" he asked suspiciously. "I don't think I've ever heard of them before. Are they still around?"

Before I could say anything, Mel chimed in with an answer. "Actually, they hit it big in the summer of 2000 and broke up a little while after that."

The waiter snapped his fingers together. "That's why I don't recognize the name," he announced, seemingly vindicated. "That's the year I was born."

Once again, I felt incredibly old. How could a full-grown adult have been born the year that our album was released?

Aging sucks.

Mel gave her best saleswoman pitch to the waiter. "Well, you should check them out on Spotify," she said. "Or, better yet, buy the album from your local record store. You won't be disappointed."

God bless my brilliant, brazen, and beautiful wife.

The twenty-year-old waiter nodded and smiled, quite possibly distracted by Mel's charming speech and captivating presence. He muttered something about iTunes and then moved off to another table in his section.

As I turned back to look at my daughter, she still had an awestruck expression on her face.

"*Woooooow…*" Sam whispered, her eyes peeled open in shock. "My dad is *famous*."

"*Kind of* famous," I reminded her. "Or, at least, I used to be."

CHAPTER THIRTY-SIX
"Lay Down Burden"

It still seems strange to me that my life might be defined by a three-and-a-half-minute pop song that I wrote when I was twenty years old. In the canvas of my life, "Incomplete" is one long, broad stroke of the brush. In sharp contrast, the many lives that I've touched in my teaching career seem like thousands of tiny, almost imperceptible specks of pointillism. Only after I've retired will the painting of my life make sense, as I step back and look at the grander image formed by the myriad classes and multitudinous students I've taught over the years.

That interaction with our waiter on Sam's birthday reminded me that art can often end up seeming inconsequential. As the years pass and bygone eras subside into new generations, a trivial pop song that ended up on the radio twenty years ago seems less and less important.

I can't help but think back to that chance encounter with my father's student at Salzer's Records, as I was emerging from the fog of my nervous breakdown. That kid didn't care that I was the bass player in a rock band with a music video on MTV. He only cared about my father's impact: the love and support Dad gave this young man during a tumultuous season of his life. My father's intangible encouragement provided much more sustenance and meaning than a frivolous pop song on the radio.

That was Dad's gift to so many of us – his children, his friends, his family, his colleagues, and his students. It might not have been as flashy or dramatic as a music video in regular rotation on MTV, but it was significantly more meaningful in the long run.

When we got home from Disneyland late that night, Sam and Mel went straight to bed and fell asleep almost immediately. I, on the hand, couldn't shake the feeling that something important was happening inside of me, something that I couldn't name or identify.

But it was changing me, nonetheless.

While my sleeping beauties drifted off to slumber, I unloaded all of our bags from the car and started unpacking the spare change of clothes I had brought with me. Inexplicably, I found myself walking into my office, flipping on the dim lamplight, and staring at the empty space where my Stuttering Surfers vinyl record used to hang. The wall seemed naked without that black circle mounted there, like a tarnished canvas that had been wiped clean of its paint.

Fun fact: the word *phonograph* roughly translates from Greek as "an image or writing of sound." That particular "writing of sound" – that little slab of vinyl – was a fragile fragment of my father's life. It was the only music that he ever captured in a studio. Dad's sole audio artifact was a scratchy, worn vinyl copy of The Stuttering Surfers' first recording, that priceless commodity which had been shattered into dozens of pieces after it unexpectedly tumbled from the wall.

I looked over at my oversized music collection, the hundreds and hundreds of albums released by artists – living *and* dead – the documents of their lives preserved forever in the almost imperceptible grooves of spinning vinyl, in the reflective coating of CDs. These albums captured the hearts and souls and words and melodies and artistry of so many human beings – fathers and sons, mothers and daughters, brothers and sisters, friends and acquaintances. For a brief second, I felt like a suburban folklorist, a collector of the past, like a 21st-century version of Alan Lomax. The most important artifact, though – the treasured centerpiece – was missing.

Without my father and his words and his voice, my colossal collection of music felt incomplete.

That's the thing about life: we only have a limited number of years to make an impact on the world around us. Some of us create vast, impressive records of our lives; others survive tedious decades without leaving behind much documentation of any sort. We are all fragile balloons, hoping to remain tethered to the ground, even as the threat of floating away from earth looms above us. And sometimes we burst unexpectedly, before we have enough time to dance in the wind or bathe in the sunshine. Our hearts stop, leaving only a withered, lifeless shell behind.

My dad never got to write his book. He never got to record a full-length album. He was too camera-shy to step in front of my mother's lens for photographs. Because of this, I only have a handful of souvenirs to remind me of my father's existence.

But the most important one, the one that provided me with the deepest connection to that tenuous thread of my father's life, was gone.

Would I have much more to show for my own life?

CHAPTER THIRTY-SEVEN
"Endless Harmony"

The rest of the weekend was relatively uneventful. I remember sleeping quite a bit the next day, lying in bed until seven or eight in the morning (Sam let us sleep in for once!), and even squeezing in a midday nap. It was a glorious departure from my usual 5:00 AM wakeup, and I felt like I was recharging my batteries – knowing that I would shortly return to the inevitable stacks of insurmountable grading. While I couldn't avoid my usual domestic duties of yard work and washing dishes and folding laundry, that weekend helped me recover from the emotional marathon of the first term's end. When the time came to return to work on Tuesday, I felt reinvigorated – ready to take up my sword and shield (or pencil and laptop, as it were) against the second half of the school year.

I was not, however, ready for the curveball that life – and, specifically, *Veronica Jones* – was about to throw my way.

Veronica played coy the following week, describing her three-day weekend as "productive." I assumed she had done whatever it is that teenage girls do when they're not shackled and chained to a high school campus. Not to stereotype, but it would be easy to imagine someone like Veronica lounging by the pool with cellphone in hand, scrolling endlessly through social media while a battered Jane Austen novel lay half-propped-up on an adjacent towel. The reality of Veronica's free time was much less leisurely, however, as I would soon discover.

"I've been working on this project for a while, and all the threads are *finally* coming together," Veronica explained on Friday morning. "It's not locked in yet, but I have a good feeling that it's all going to work out." She seemed to be suppressing the world's largest Cheshire grin, but she refused to budge when I asked her about her mysterious undertaking.

"That sounds like a pretty intriguing project," I said. "When is the big unveiling?"

"You'll just have to wait and see," she answered, hiking up her backpack and heading out of the classroom with a pink inter-room pass in her right hand. "I'm off to chat with the principal. See you this afternoon!"

"This afternoon?" I asked, confusion etched into the lines of my forehead.

She turned back to face me for a brief second, smirking mischievously as she walked out the classroom door.

I don't put much stock in superstitious premonitions, but something in my gut told me that Veronica's covert plans didn't bode well for my future. The rest of the day, my stomach was in knots. I even found myself jumping skittishly at the slightest footfalls in the hallway.

What's coming? I wondered to myself. *And how exactly can I get out of it?*

After school let out and the masses of students eagerly fled from campus for the promise of the weekend, I entertained a brief feeling of relief. Veronica hadn't shown up, and I assumed that my fears had been unfounded.

As it turns out, however, they were *very* well-founded.

I had my messenger bag slung over my shoulder, the compartments filled to the brim with in-class essays analyzing a Langston Hughes poem, and I was ready for two days of sleeping in and catching up on work. I had just started walking to the door when it suddenly flung open, like the wind was trying to rip it from its hinges. For a moment, I envisioned a telekinetic Sissy Spacek in *Carrie*, and my heart leaped into my throat.

"Jesus!" I yelped, my arms spasming involuntarily.

"You shouldn't take the Lord's name in vain, Mr. Smith," called out that oh-so-familiar teenage voice. "You never know when you might need Him in your corner."

"I'm sorry, Veronica," I panted, still recovering from the shock. "You scared me to death just now."

Veronica just chuckled. "You don't have anything to fear," she said with a hearty laugh. And then she ominously added one word: "Yet."

I stood stock-still, catching my breath as this tenacious teenager tormented me. "How can I help you, Veronica?" I asked.

That Cheshire grin returned to Veronica's face. "Well, Mr. Smith…" she began. "Remember that project I was telling you about?"

"You mean the secretive one that you mysteriously alluded to earlier today?"

"That's the one," she answered. "I've been talking with Principal Mandaragat and with my drama teacher…"

"Mr. Franklin?" I asked.

"Yup," she said, "and they're completely on-board."

I didn't like where this was heading. "On-board for what, dare I ask…?"

Veronica took a deep breath, as if she was building up the nerve to cross a rickety bridge suspended above a river of ravenous crocodiles. "Remember when we played the Winter Spectacular, and you commented that the auditorium was in bad shape?"

My mind traveled back to that December's talent show performance, recalling the flaky fabric of the curtains and the stage's creaking floorboards. "Sure," I answered hesitantly. I still had no idea where this conversation might lead. "What about it?"

"Do you remember what you suggested to fix up the theater…?" she asked.

"Refresh my memory," I said.

"You told me about Neil Young and his annual benefit concerts –"

"The Bridge School Benefit concerts," I interrupted.

"Right, the Bridge School concerts," she echoed back. "And then you suggested that someone organize a benefit concert to raise money for repairing the theater."

"Okay," I admitted. "I *do* recall that conversation." I squinted at her, trying to predict her next move like a boxer waiting for his opponent to throw a follow-up punch.

At this point, Veronica could hardly contain her excitement. "Well, *that* is what I've been planning for the last month and a half. A benefit concert."

"And you want me to help out in some capacity…?"

Veronica smirked back at me. "You guessed it. And since *you* came up with the idea…"

"You mean, I *suggested* the idea," I corrected her.

"Whatever," she said dismissively. "It's still your idea, whether you claim responsibility for it or not. And Oxnard Shores High School *really* needs your help." She bit her lip, preparing for the big question. "Will you help me?"

I sighed. "I suppose I don't have much of a choice, do I? You're going to insist that I still owe you for your dad's dental services…"

"Actually," she interjected, "I think you owe it to yourself."

Her response caught me off-guard. What kind of precocious high school kid talks like that to the adults in her life?

Veronica Jones. That's who.

"Owe it to *myself*…?" I asked. "What do I owe myself, pray tell?"

"A chance at redemption, Mr. Smith."

Redemption. Now *that's* a loaded word. A lot like *salvation*, come to think of it.

I exhaled in exasperation. "So, what exactly did you have in mind, Veronica?"

The light hiss of wind whipping through the hallway seemed extraordinarily loud while I waited for her to answer. As confident as Veronica was, even she knew that there was a lot riding on this conversation. She fidgeted with her backpack and twisted her keychain in her hand.

"I have a favor to ask of you," she finally blurted out. "A really big one. Like *epically* huge."

"*Another* favor? You know, kiddo, you're going to owe me a lot of babysitting hours by the time that you graduate…" I stopped myself from venting and just sighed. "Dare I ask what this favor entails?"

"It's another music performance…" she tentatively began.

I could feel the light condensation of perspiration starting to form on my forehead. "Let me guess," I croaked out. "You want me to play guitar for you at this benefit concert that you're organizing, so that you can woo the crowd with your singing and go down in history as the philanthropic savior of Oxnard Shores High School?"

"*Not exactly…*" she said, dramatically drawing out the words as if they were taffy. "I was thinking of something… bigger."

"*Bigger* than playing guitar for you…?" I asked, not quite understanding where this was leading. "Did you want *me* to sing at this thing…?"

"With all due respect, Mr. Smith," she said slowly, "while I would love to see you do the solo coffeeshop thing, I don't know how much of a draw you'd have all by yourself. We need to raise money for our school. Like a *lot* of money."

"But what could I do that would…" My voice trailed off as the gears started whirring and aligning in my brain. Suddenly, it all made sense. A light clicked on in my head and a chill ran up my spine. "Oh, God," I murmured. "You don't mean…?"

As a smile crept across Veronica's lips, I couldn't help but feel a sense of all-consuming terror, like I was staring at the Joker or Pennywise the Clown – demonic forces determined to upend my world and unleash mass mayhem in my life.

"It's time for you to do your civic duty, Mr. Smith. It's time for Call Field to get back together."

Now it was *my* turn to be speechless. My heart palpitated so violently that I thought it would burst out of my chest like the Xenomorph from *Alien*. My jaw mutely opened and closed.

Veronica's request was absurd – *impossible* even.

"I haven't spoken with most of those guys in years," I told her, immediately producing an uncomfortable laugh. "Apart from Chunk, I haven't seen anyone else in the band since…"

"Since that night in San Francisco?"

"Exactly," I said. "Even if Chunk agreed to come out of retirement and play drums for me, I would still have to recruit Ethan and Victor and… and Steve."

"That would be the ideal lineup," Veronica agreed, casually nodding her head. "After all, we want this to be a big show with a big headliner that would yield big money for our school."

"Listen, Veronica," I pleaded, "even if I agreed to participate in this thing – which, for the record, I am *not* doing right now – I would still have to convince three other people whom I haven't seen in *decades* to reunite and do something monumentally complicated for me."

The beads of sweat were amassing on my forehead and temples and neck. Even *I* could tell that my voice sounded frantic and unhinged. Veronica, however, remained as cool as could be.

I kept venting, trying to poke holes in her plan. "The last time I saw Ethan, Victor, and Steve," I reminded her, "we were ready to kill each other. How in God's holy name would I be able to coerce them to talk to me – let alone play a concert in a high school auditorium? How would I convince them, Veronica?"

She simply flipped her backpack around, unzipped it, and rifled through her assortment of color-coded folders before locating what she was looking for. She gazed up at me in vindication, an *I-told-you-so* look spreading across her face.

"You won't need to," she told me calmly, pulling out a collated pile of papers. "Over the last month, I've been in contact with all the guys in Call Field."

Veronica handed me a stack of printed e-mail messages. I thumbed through page after page, surveying the correspondence between this teenage girl from my present and the ghosts of my past.

"You see, you don't need to convince them," Veronica explained. "They've already agreed to play the show."

FINAL CHORUS

I get lost sometimes in the melodies of my mind,
where I've tried to find what I need.
But the crashing tide has swept me off my feet,
and left me incomplete for a while...
And it's just like your smile.

CHAPTER THIRTY-EIGHT
"Isn't It Time?"

Veronica had been a busy, busy bee over winter vacation. While I'd kept my nose to the grindstone and my feet on the treadmill, little Miss Jones was diligently working on this massive musical undertaking all by herself. Well, *mostly* by herself.

Unbeknownst to me, Veronica had been tirelessly calling and e-mailing all of the former members of Call Field in the weeks following our school's Winter Spectacular. Though I'm sure it must have been awkward for my ex-bandmates (including my loyal cousin) to hear from a complete stranger – and a *teenage* one, at that – they all ultimately agreed to listen to her sales pitch. Of course, as you've seen by now, Veronica is preternaturally skilled at the art of persuasion. With every correspondence, she enthusiastically explained the purpose of the benefit concert and how the proceeds would be used to fix up the theater at Oxnard Shores High School. Somehow, using her wit and charm and rhetorical skills, Veronica managed to convince Chunk, Ethan, Victor, and Steve that it was their "civic duty" to do this show.

Yes, even Steve.

Of course, the afternoon that she sprang all of this on me, I was considerably less calm than I am now as I type out my play-by-play recollection.

"YOU DID *WHAT*…?" I asked, panic flooding my voice.

Veronica refused to let my terror deter her sales pitch. "I simply pulled some strings and arranged a reunion concert with some of your old acquaintances," she explained in a maddeningly calm manner. "It was surprisingly easy, actually. I got Chunk's phone number from your wife and Chunk got me the contact info for Ethan who got me in touch with Victor and Steve. Everything else was simply a matter of e-mailing and calling until I got the responses that I needed."

It took me a second to process all of this. "Wait," I called out. "My *wife* was in on this?"

Veronica nodded her head in a pitying sort of way. Her reaction made me feel like a fourth-grader who failed to grasp the subtle nuances of the multiplication table. "Your wife was the first person that I approached," she told me. "It was the night of the Winter Spectacular. In the green room, while you were walking around with Sam."

God, I felt stupid.

"I think I'm going to have a long talk with my wife when I get home…" I said.

Veronica flinched. "Don't be mad at her, Mr. Smith," she pleaded. "This was all my idea and she just helped me follow through with it." She paused before adding an addendum: "Although…"

"Although… *what*…?" I asked.

"*Although*…" Veronica continued, "she did tell me that you needed something like this to break you free of your routines. She said something like, *'a man can't live his whole life on a treadmill and not go anywhere.'* I'm paraphrasing, though."

"I happen to like my treadmill, thank you very much."

"Look," Veronica argued, "bands get back together all the time. Didn't your precious Beach Boys reunite just a few years ago?"

"Yes, but that lasted for exactly one summer tour. After that, they split up into warring factions all over again."

"Okay, bad example," she conceded. "What about blink-182?"

"They had to replace founding member Tom DeLonge with Matt Skiba from Alkaline Trio," I snapped back condescendingly.

She squirmed. "Fleetwood Mac?"

"They fired Lindsey Buckingham and hired two other musicians to take his place."

Her lips curled into a frustrated sneer. "The Eagles?"

"Glenn Frey just passed away a few years ago."

"Dang," she yelped. "What about the Grateful Dead?"

"Well," I answered caustically, "Jerry Garcia died in 1995 and three of the four remaining members are on tour with John Mayer and Oteil Burbridge. Phil Lesh, the original bass player – *my counterpart, I will remind you* – refuses to participate in any further reunions."

"Grrrr…" Veronica snarled in frustration. Her eyes darted across the room, searching for some artifact to anchor her argument. Suddenly, she froze. Her eyes locked onto something behind me, and a triumphant smile spread across her face. "*Twin Peaks!*" she yelped.

"What…?"

"*TWIN! PEAKS!*" she yelled victoriously, pointing at the faded poster next to my desk.

I glanced backwards towards the image of Dale Cooper in the Black Lodge, and turned back to face a triumphant-looking Veronica. "That's not a *band*," I reminded her.

"Minor detail…" she mumbled with a dismissive wave of her hand. "Wasn't there a space of, like, two decades before they brought it back?"

"Twenty-six years," I said.

"So, they brought back an entire *television show*, with a bunch of different actors and writers and stuff, after *twenty-six years…?*"

"Yes," I acknowledged.

"And was it a disaster? Did it go down in flames like the Hindenburg?"

"No," I begrudgingly admitted. "It was pretty well-received by critics and fans."

"Well, there you have it!" Veronica announced. "I think it's a sign. You wrote a song about *Twin Peaks*, used the name 'The Bookhouse Boys' for your first band, and then they brought back the entire TV show. And, by your own admission, it was a success. If that isn't God trying to send you a message, I don't know what is."

"Veronica, that's *totally different*," I argued. "And I don't think that God communicates to mortals using bizarre television shows."

"You're right, Mr. Smith. This is even better than *Twin Peaks*, because you're doing it for a noble cause. And you only have four other guys you have to work with, not a whole bunch of actors and behind-the-scenes crew."

I wanted to scream. "While I appreciate that you're having a blast watching me squirm, you're asking me to turn my life upside down for a… a… stupid concert."

"A *benefit concert*," Veronica reminded me. "A chance for you to do some good for your community using an underutilized talent." She over-enunciated each word, like a lawyer lecturing a jury.

Silently, I fumed. I wrung my fingers together manically, as if I could squash the proposition out of existence using my bare hands.

"You're killing me, kid," I finally said.

All throughout our conversation, Veronica had been twiddling with her keys, spinning them around and around in a circle with nary an end in sight. Suddenly, though, she gripped the keychain tightly in her closed fist.

"You know that this isn't just a benefit concert, right?"

"What do you mean?" I asked.

Veronica scrunched her mouth up, like she was biting the inside of her cheek. "Remember when you chipped your tooth at the beginning of our October break?"

"I know, I know," I grumbled. "I owe you because your dad saved my teeth from destruction and despair. *Blah, blah, blah…* I've heard it before, Veronica. And it's getting stale."

She scowled at me. "It's not that," she said in an eerily calm, quiet voice. "Although I still maintain that you will be indebted to me for quite some time."

"Then what is it?" I whined at her.

"Okay, do you remember what you asked my dad when he explained that you would need a root canal?"

"Vaguely," I muttered.

"Well, let me recount it for you," Veronica said, with a slightly condescending tone in her voice. "My dad said you would need a root canal, and you asked if you *had* to do it – as if your tooth would magically repair itself. Like you could simply *will* yourself to heal or something."

"That's not what I meant…" I started to say, before Veronica cut me off.

"You asked what would happen if you refused treatment," she reminded me. "My dad told you that the infection was something you couldn't just ignore, that it wouldn't just go away. He said the infection would spread, causing more pain and further damage to your mouth and jaw. And that it could, theoretically, cause an infection capable of killing you."

I stood there silently, not sure where Veronica was going with all of these didactic dental details. "So, how does this relate to Call Field?" I finally asked.

Veronica shifted in place, crossing her arms across her chest like makeshift armor. The girl was ready to do battle.

"Mr. Smith, I think that there has been something missing from your life for a long, long time. Like a… a cavity in your heart, you know? It's an empty space that used to be filled with something substantial. Definitely something stronger than tooth enamel."

Veronica turned her face to the right and gazed off into the distance. As she did so, I was left looking at her profile, recognizing just how young and naïve this teenager really was. She reminded me of a female Don Quixote astride an invisible Rocinante – with a BYU sweatshirt, of course, instead of a lance. I couldn't help but imagine that she was dreaming of far-off battlefields and decaying windmills.

"This reunion concert…" she continued. "It might be the best way to get you off the redundant treadmill of your life. And I think it can help you take back a piece of your history that feels stolen."

I shifted in my place, suddenly feeling like my feet weighed a thousand pounds each. As I did so, Veronica turned back to face me.

"Think of this reunion as a root canal, Mr. Smith… It's like a *root canal for your soul.*"

I couldn't help myself: I laughed louder than I probably should have. "Did you really just say, *'a root canal for your soul?'*" I asked her.

Veronica met my eyes with a fierce resolve. "Why, yes. Yes, I did. You, Mr. Smith, are in dire need of a root canal for your soul."

You've got to hand it to Veronica. The gal was sharp. As reticent as I was to dive deep into the dark recesses of my past, I couldn't help but smirk at the sheer absurdity of the situation.

"I can't believe that you just used a root canal as a metaphor, Veronica," I said, trying to stifle whatever semblance of a grin was creeping towards the surface of my face.

"A wise man once told *me,*" Veronica said, standing proudly in place, "that a wise man once told *him*, 'you can make anything a metaphor, if you're creative enough.'"

Even though he'd been dead for twenty years, my father's wisdom still came back to haunt me. I have a feeling that he and Veronica would've gotten along smashingly.

When I arrived home that afternoon, I had already spent the entire drive back to my house stewing on Veronica's improbable proposition.

Could this really be happening? I wondered to myself. *Is this some strange fever dream, and I'm going to wake up feeling relieved that it was all just a twisted fantasy in my incapacitated brain?*

But it wasn't a dream. This is the kind of experience that you can't fabricate or invent. It's simply too strange to be fiction.

Of course, I still needed to have a conversation with Mel about her secretive plotting with Veronica. *How could* my wife *have been scheming behind my back all this time?* I wondered.

As I dropped my bag on the tiled floor of our front hallway, I wasn't sure if I was angry or amused or simply amassing a cancerous anxiety that was sure to metastasize at any moment. I made my way to the kitchen table, stomping a bit more loudly than usual. Once again, I saw Mel's back curving like a parabola over the dinner table.

"Hey, honey," she called out, not bothering to look away from her computer screen. "Can you get dinner ready? I've got one more article to edit before I'm done for the night."

I trudged over to the table and threw myself into one of our antique oak chairs. Without warning, I placed my hand on the back of her laptop screen and pushed it closed.

"Uhhh… *I'm working here*," Mel said, surprise and irritation intricately intertwined in her voice.

I ignored her comment and plunged right in. "You won't believe what happened to me today," I began, feeling the force of my indignation welling inside of me like molten lava. "Veronica Jones asked me for the most fascinating favor this afternoon. She said she's been covertly communicating with some ghosts from my past…"

Mel didn't act shocked or excited or angry or hopeful. Her face went blank, like an unpainted canvas. She did have one key tell, though: as she clasped her hands together and placed her elbows on the countertop, she bit down on her lower lip. For as long as I've known her – from that golden era in the UCLA dorms to the present day – Mel's lip-biting tic always gives her away. It's good to know that some things never change, I guess.

"So, Veronica finally got around to telling you about her plan, I see." Mel scrunched her eyes and removed the glasses from the bridge of her nose. "How do you feel about that?"

As much as I wanted to scream from my bowels to the rafters, I felt disarmed by Mel's question. She's smart enough to know when it's time to play the amateur psychologist, deflecting attention away from herself back to the person with whom she's conversing.

Still, I needed to vent.

"I feel like I'm being forced into something I don't want to do!" I bellowed in complete exasperation.

Mel let her hands sink back down to the table. As she did so, her fingers began tapping quarter notes on the top of her laptop. Her eyes moved away from me, focusing instead on the window to our backyard.

"Something you don't *want* to do?" she asked. "Or something that you don't feel *ready* to do?"

"BOTH!" I yelled back, leaping to my feet. I could feel my temperature rising and anger escalating. I don't often let my temper get the best of me, but this was a rare circumstance, indeed.

Desperate times called for desperate emotions.

Mel, however, refused to match my rage. With a calm demeanor – *maddeningly* calm, I should add – she motioned for me to sit next to her. I wanted to flip the table or smash her laptop or throw a vase across the room. But, like a penitent puppy, I obeyed.

"I can tell that you're… *upset*," she said quietly.

"That's an understatement!"

Mel leaned forward, her right hand stretching out to cover mine. She was like a horse-whisperer, taming the wild creature in front of her while never losing her cool. The *English-teacher-whisperer*, if you will.

"Can you tell me why you think you're so upset right now?" she asked, her voice as soothing and tranquil as the current in a creek.

As scarlet as my face might have been, I could feel the boiling resentment in my chest simmer down. I wanted to be angry. I wanted to vent. I wanted to scream and shout and thrust my fists into the air. But I couldn't answer Mel's question.

"I don't know why I'm upset!" I yelped back at her, my face flustered. "Now I'm just angry that I'm angry!"

The world stood still for a second. Then, Mel snickered and snorted, her whole body quaking with laughter. Her hilarity was contagious: within seconds, I was shaking my head and giggling myself. I gripped the top of a chair, steadying myself against the onslaught of laughter that coursed through my body.

"Mom… Dad…" Sam's tiny face appeared in the hallway, half-obscured by the doorframe. "Is everything okay…? I thought I heard screaming and then…" She surveyed the room, unsure of how to interpret the scene before her.

"We're fine, honey," Mel said, wiping the tears of laughter from her eyes. "Mommy and daddy were just having a discussion about something…" *Giggle*. "Something…" *Giggle*. She waved her hands in the air dismissively.

"Something ridiculous," I interjected. "You have nothing to be worried about." I walked over to her, sank down on one knee and kissed her on the cheek.

She looked at me, skeptical and confused, and then wrapped her arms around me.

"Why don't you tell me all about your day, Sam," I said, hugging her tightly. "I can't wait to hear about what you did at school…"

Mel and I didn't really have a chance to finish our conversation until Sam was all tucked in and ready for bed. That's one cold, hard truth about parenting: you learn how to drop all of your problems and concerns until your child is asleep and unable to eavesdrop.

So, there we were, basking in the exhaustion of the post-bedtime routine with a kitchen full of dirty dishes and half-packed lunch bags. Mel didn't seem too eager to broach the topic, so I waited until I couldn't resist anymore.

"When were you going to tell me?" I asked, my hands submerged in sudsy sink water.

Mel continued to rustle plastic bags and Tupperware, the telltale signs of parental lunch-packing. "To be honest," she said softly, "I didn't think it was going to work out."

"How so?" I rinsed off a soapy plate and delicately placed it in the dishwasher.

"Well," she began, "I know Veronica is a go-getter…"

"That's an understatement," I scoffed.

"Yes, I've clearly learned that over the last few months," Mel chuckled. "But even a motivated overachiever can't move mountains. Especially a high school kid with a limited skillset."

"I think we both underestimated Veronica Jones," I grumbled.

"She's a good kid," Mel said. "And she really looks up to you."

"No, she doesn't," I said. "You should hear the sassy way she talks to me. I think she's a little too familiar and comfortable with me."

"She's only sassy with you because she likes you so much."

"I find that hard to believe," I said with an eye-roll.

"*Trust me*," Mel said, wrapping a turkey sandwich in cellophane and dropping it into a square Tupperware container. "When she first started planning it out –"

"When was that, by the way?" I interjected.

Mel made a sound like a tire releasing trapped air. I couldn't see her expression from my vantage point at the kitchen sink, but I could just imagine my wife furrowing her brow and biting her lower lip.

"I think it was right around Christmas. You know that Winter Spectacular thing? Veronica broached the topic that night and then just plunged ahead, full-steam. By the time that New Year's rolled around, she had it all mapped out in her head with a timeline for contacting everyone involved and reserving the school's theater and asking local businesses to sponsor the event. She even had a rudimentary spreadsheet with all the costs associated and the potential profit margin. It was pretty impressive, all things considered."

"Wait, wait, wait... Since *Christmas*...?" I asked in disbelief. "You've been keeping me in the dark for a *month* now?"

"You sound surprised," Mel answered, slightly offended. "To be fair, though, I had to stew on it for a little while. I weighed your insecurities and your anxieties against the potential for your personal and spiritual growth. Plus, I honestly didn't think it would work out."

I dropped the sponge in the sink and grabbed a hand towel. "What do you mean by *'personal and spiritual growth'*...?" I asked with a slight scowl.

"Well, Brian," Mel sighed. "You've been in a holding pattern these last few years. You're a devoted father and husband, a dedicated teacher... But I feel like you need something else in your life. Something that's been missing for a while."

"I'm content with the way things are," I said.

"You might be *content*," Mel responded, "but I don't think that you're truly *happy*. On Maslow's hierarchy of needs, you've got a guitar-shaped pothole blocking your path to self-actualization."

I twisted myself around and gripped the curved edges of our granite countertop. "You really put all that thought into this?"

"I think you forget, dear husband, that I'm smarter than you."

Touché.

"So, you really think I should do this?" I asked her.

"Without a doubt," Mel answered. "It's time for you to get some closure."

She stepped away from Sam's *Star Wars* lunch bag and made her way to my side of the kitchen. Slowly, calmly, she wrapped her arms around my waist and stared up at me with those blisteringly beautiful brown eyes. I rested my chin on the top of her head and kissed the arrow-straight part of her hair.

"I'm so proud of you for everything you've accomplished," Mel told me. "You're always there for Samantha. And for me. And you're a remarkable teacher who inspires his students to do ridiculous things like organize a reunion concert for a band that broke up twenty years ago."

I chuckled softly. "Veronica said that this would be a *'root canal for my soul.'* What a nerd."

"Spoken like a true future dentist," Mel added. "Cheesy analogies aside, it's been two decades, Brian. I think it's time for you to put your ghosts to rest."

I could feel her hot breath through the cotton of my t-shirt, and I lay my cheek against her scalp. "How did I get so lucky?" I asked.

"You wrote me a hit song," Mel answered. "And I'll always be your number one fan. For the rest of my life."

I squeezed her tightly and gave her a kiss on the forehead.

"But the next time that you mess with my laptop while I'm working," she whispered sweetly, "I'll throw all of your CDs and vinyl records in the dumpster. Don't test me."

"Yes, ma'am," I said with a laugh.

I had a feeling that she was only half-joking.

CHAPTER THIRTY-NINE
"Beaches in Mind"

That weekend, while I was panicking about the potential disasters that might strike if I agreed to do the benefit concert, Mel decided that we should take a trip to the beach. It was a typically sunny midwinter afternoon (which, in California, tends to feel more summery than summer), and Mel was convinced that we needed to take advantage of the perfect SoCal weather. After all, our Central Coast climate can be unpredictable and temperamental 95% of the time. You know: *the gray skies can be colder than December"* and all that jazz.

"We've been cooped up in the house too much," Mel argued. "We need to get out and clear our heads with some sand and sunshine."

As you know by now, Mel is a convincing woman. While I wanted to put up a fight and just work my way through the stack of AP English essays on my desk, I knew that this was a battle I wasn't going to win. So, I slapped my pen down on top of that daunting pile of paper and sulked off to search for my swimming trunks.

On this particular Sunday afternoon, Mel was determined to venture out to the neighboring city of Ventura and its small stretch of coastline known as Surfer's Knoll. As we pulled into the sandy parking lot, I couldn't help but think about a certain cloudy afternoon at this exact location twenty-five years ago. While the sky on *this* outing was as clear as an empty Coke bottle, I had an achingly familiar memory of that ancient adolescent outing with my high school crush. This was the same place where Serena and I talked about our abandoned romance, where my heart was smashed like the broken glass that littered the sidewalk. That fateful afternoon, I accrued a blistering sunburn, my skin tender and peeling for days afterwards. I shivered with the vague recollection of that pain – on the surface of my skin and beneath the recesses of my heart.

As soon as we laid stake to a particularly clean and trash-free section of beach, Mel slid a bottle of sunscreen into my open palms.

"Put this on, Brian," she commanded. "I like my husband pale, not burnt to a crisp."

I lathered the creamy lotion onto my hands and smeared it all over my pallid skin. Though it felt embarrassing for me to be shirtless and oily in full view of the public, I was willing to suck up my vanity and pride for the sake of my wife and daughter.

"Can you get my back?" Mel asked, pointing to a patch of skin between her shoulder blades that she couldn't quite reach.

I did as I was told, smearing the sunblock all over her neck and down her spine. There was a time when I would have trembled at the thought of simply touching Mel – the *Beautiful Girl from Heaven* who had lived just across the hall in UCLA's dorms – but now the feeling of my fingers across her body was a commonplace comfort. I studied the small of her back, tracing the gorgeous curves of her taut skin and the stretch-mark patches that served as artifacts of her pregnancy with Sam.

When I glanced up at our daughter, who was darting up the beach towards the wet sand where the waves crashed against the shore, I was struck by the notion that Sam is a perfect blend of her parents. Her bronze skin, a shade lighter than Mel but several tones darker than my own bland epidermis, reminded me that we are all compounds of our complex heritage, couriers of intertwined DNA that transform our children into something new – something better and healthier and more refined than their parents.

You might remember from my multitudinous ramblings that Sam has a fascination with mermaids that's evolved into something of an obsession. Starting with Ariel – that hardheaded, scarlet-haired icon for so many children – and carrying on through swim lessons and seashells and Halloween costumes and themed blankets, Sam has been a mermaid-in-training for longer than I can remember. While I always find myself confined to the solid ground beneath my feet, stuck on that treadmill of my life, Sam has no scruples about plunging deep into the uncertain waters and swimming arm-over-arm to stay above the cresting waves.

As I mentioned before, I had a "thing" about the ocean when I was younger. So, it's a strange twist of fate that my amphibious daughter would feel equally comfortable on *terra firma* or in the swelling seas. I have a feeling Sam inherited that bold, aquatic ambidexterity from Mel. She sure didn't get it from me.

As I watched Sam frolic in the water, my father's voice lingered in the back of my mind like a specter in a haunted house: *"Life's too short to drink your coffee black."* As my dad knew, life is a constant balance of yin and yang, of darkness and light, of sea and sand, of coffee and creamer. Sam has blossomed into the perfect equilibrium of her father's sensitivity and her mother's courage. God, my dad would have been *so proud* of Sam – this headstrong little girl who brazenly dashed into the cascading waves with absolute abandon.

But I digress.

As I was saying, I was in the middle of rubbing sunblock onto Mel's shoulder blades when she broke the distilled silence. "Do you know why I suggested that we come here today?"

"Because it's beautifully sunny and you didn't want to be cooped up inside our stuffy house…?"

"No, Brian," she grumbled. And though I couldn't see her face, the condescending tone in her voice led me to assume that she was rolling her eyes. "Why I said we should come *here*. To Surfer's Knoll."

I scrunched my nose in the glare of the sunlight, perhaps hoping that the answer would magically manifest in front of my eyes. Alas, nothing came to me.

"You're gonna' have to help me out here," I confessed. "We've been to this beach a bunch of times over the years, and I'm not sure what you're alluding to…"

Mel twisted back to face me. Though her eyes were barely visible through the tinted lenses of her sunglasses, I tried to read her expression for some sort of clue. She reached out her hand and rubbed the side of my stubbly jaw.

"Because this is where your story began," she said. "We're returning to the scene of the crime."

I gave her a quizzical look. "What do you mean?"

"Think about it. *California can be cruel in the summer…*" she began to sing in her light, airy voice. "*Girls will give you sunburns with a grin…*" She watched me, studying my expression for any semblance of understanding. "This is where your song starts, right…?"

It was strange discussing my first amorous adolescent affair with the woman who superseded Serena in my heart. I wasn't sure where Mel was headed with this conversation, but I learned long ago not to question my wife's motives.

"Yes," I begrudgingly acknowledged. "This is the same beach where Serena Rios broke my little teenage heart and left me anguishing afterwards. Why are you bringing this up now…?"

Mel studied the lines in my face. "Does it hurt being back here?" she asked.

"That's a ridiculous question," I said.

"I'm *serious*," she pressed on. "This place – this beach – was the site of one of your most traumatic teenage experiences, right?"

"Right," I admitted. "But that was years ago."

"*EXACTLY!*" Mel squealed victoriously. "That painful experience, the opening salvo of your signature song, was more than *twenty years ago*. Since then, you've grown and changed more than you possibly could have imagined as a fifteen-year-old kid."

I still wasn't boarding Mel's train of thought. She clearly had a destination in mind, but I needed a roadmap to point me in the right direction. "So…?"

"*So*, if you can put that painful event behind you, then you should be able to play with your old band again and not let it destroy you." She dug her hands into the golden sand and let the grains trickle between her fingers.

"But that's different…" I started to say.

"Different *how*, Brian?" she pressed on. "You've been unwilling to revisit that part of your life for *years* now. I know it was painful and I know it makes you anxious. I get that. I really do." She sighed. "But, sooner or later, you *will* need to confront that part of your history."

"But I'm comfortable with my life right now," I pleaded. "I got my happily-ever-after ending and I'm okay jogging in place. As long as I have you and Sam, I don't need to jump off the treadmill and go running off on unexplored paths. Why is that so problematic?"

"Because your life isn't over yet," she said. "Your story doesn't end with us falling in love and living happily ever after. Our lives are not truncated fairy tales."

"But why should I open myself up to that painful experience again and risk getting burned?"

"Everything with you is a *but*, Brian," Mel said with another sigh. "You have an answer for every suggestion, a comeback for every proposition." She wiped grains of sand from her hands, her eyes darting downward. "You're forgetting something, though."

"And what's that?"

She smiled roguishly at me, her eyes trailing up towards my face. "You won't get burned this time, Brian. You have *me* to watch out for you." She took my hand in hers and started to rub circles on my palm. "And I won't give you a '*sunburn with a grin.*' On the contrary, I'll spray you with sunblock if you start to feel overwhelmed and take you into the shade when it gets too hot."

I couldn't help but imagine Mel dousing me with sunscreen while my bandmates played on without me. I had to stifle an exhausted, defeated laugh. Still, I shook my head.

"What's your motivation behind all of this?" I asked. "You keep pushing me to do something that I don't feel comfortable doing. Why?"

Mel looked straight at me with her piercing chestnut-brown eyes. "Because I love you, Brian. You're a good man. I married you because you're brilliant and talented and kind. But you're stuck on this treadmill, constantly in motion, but never going anywhere. Meanwhile, you have all these ghosts hovering around you that you refuse to exorcise. Ultimately, I think that's preventing you from really, truly finding happiness."

"I *am* happy," I argued. "You and Sam make me the happiest man in the world."

"That's nice to hear. It really is," Mel said with a pitying smile. "But it's a fundamentally flawed way of living. True happiness needs to come from *within* you, not from external forces. For too many years, you've had this cancerous wound eating away at you. And it's time to confront that. Or, to use Veronica's analogy, this can be a spiritual root canal –"

"A '*root canal for my soul*,'" I corrected her. "That's what Veronica said."

"Whatever. No matter what happens to you, just remember that I'll be your Novocaine. I can help you get through any potentially disastrous situation you might encounter." She took both my hands and enfolded them in hers, bringing my fingers up to her chin and kissing them softly. "I love you. And I really, honestly believe that you need to do this. Forget Veronica. Forget Oxnard Shores High School and those stupid decaying curtains. You need to do this for yourself. For *you*."

Her words hovered in the air, suspended like a seagull balancing its weight against the wind. I didn't know what to say. She was smarter than me, wiser than me. How could I say no to her?

"MOM! DAD!" Sam yelled from the water, knee-deep in the ocean's subtle waves. *"I found sand crabs! They're digging under the surface! Come see!"*

Diverting my eyes away from Mel, I turned towards Sam's small frame. "We'll be right there, honey!" I answered.

"Duty calls," Mel mumbled. "We better get back to parenting before our daughter drowns."

I snorted. "Have you *met* our daughter? I'm pretty sure she could beat even the waves into submission."

"That's because she takes after me," Mel said, her lips curling into a smile. "*Obviously.*"

"Obviously," I echoed back quietly.

The truth was, they were *both* braver than me. I didn't have the courage to face the uncertainty of the ocean on my own. But I was about to take one small step towards the shoreline.

My whole life has been a journey from the mountains to the sea, from sandy suffocation to the untamed liberation of the ocean.

And it was time for me to step foot into the water.

I only prayed that the waves would be kind.

CHAPTER FORTY
"Daybreak Over the Ocean"

Despite my smothering trepidation and deeply rooted anxiety, I ultimately agreed to do the show.

I know, I know.

For as many pages as I've spent whining about the impossibility of recapturing youth, of feeling weighed down by my past, you'd think that I would have put up more of a fight. Maybe it was the *mitzvah* of raising money for a good cause that allowed me to mask my mutinous desires; perhaps enough time had passed that the impossible only seemed improbable; or, it could be that all of the forces converging on my domestic life had finally coalesced into this remarkable moment in time.

I still maintain that months of Veronica's boundary-pushing behavior served as a prolonged acclimation period for me. It wasn't like I suddenly jumped from retirement back into the spotlight; on the contrary, I had spent months and months psychologically coping with Veronica's poking and prodding, grieving the loss of my anonymity.

During that time, I felt like I was reassembling the various shards of a broken vinyl record – something seemingly beyond repair that could never be made whole again. It's like the Japanese concept of *Kintsugi*: taking something that has been shattered into fragments and repairing it with traces of gold. Except it wasn't pottery or plaster being repaired and stitched together. It was *me*.

Pretty heavy stuff for a one-hit-wonder punk-rock band from the turn of the century.

As it was, I only had one short weekend to weigh my ancient fears against the potential good that might come out of this reunion concert. As you've just seen, though, it was ultimately Mel who helped push me back onto that musical path. Maybe she was right: maybe I'd been so wrapped up in my career and fatherhood that I had neglected a vital part of myself. For all those years, I had allowed an infection to fester in my heart. And now, as Veronica had so bluntly stated, it was time for a psychological and spiritual root canal.

God, help me.

Monday morning, bright and early, Veronica popped into my classroom, anxious to hear my answer. She had literally sprinted from her zero-period class over to my room in the brisk winter air; by the time she made it across campus, she was simultaneously winded from the run and bouncing with anticipation.

"Sooooooo… What's the verdict, Mr. Smith?" she asked breathlessly.

I stared hard at the young lady in front of me, that reckless and rampaging spirit who had done everything she could to force me out of my comfort zone. With her long, flowing black hair and glistening green eyes, she seemed almost childlike with her expectant stare. Veronica wasn't an intimidating adolescent in that moment: she reminded me of a little girl playing with Disney princesses and Star Wars action figures, plotting ways to save her castle from magically malevolent forces.

For a split second, I had a vision of Sam, all grown up and taller than Mel. Samantha might end up just like Veronica, brazen and brash and boldly devoted to improving the world around her – roadblocks, be damned. In that moment, I didn't see Veronica as much as I saw a vision of my own daughter.

And I knew that I had no choice in the matter.

"Yes, Veronica," I said softly. "I'll do it."

Veronica whooped so loudly that kids literally stopped and peered in from the hallway. And, much like my elementary-school-age daughter,

Veronica bounced and danced in that confident, celebratory fashion reserved for toddlers and cheerleaders. If I didn't feel so attached to the kid, I would have been embarrassed for her.

"THANK YOU, THANK YOU, THANK YOU!" she shouted. "YOU WON'T REGRET THIS, MR. SMITH!"

When I begrudgingly raised my hand for a high-five, Veronica reared her arm back and slapped so hard that the sound echoed across the classroom and into the hallway. I'm pretty sure that every student and teacher at Oxnard Shores High School heard that slap.

I had a weird moment of déjà vu, a familiar feeling that Veronica and I had been here before. As she bounded out of the room, half-dancing and half-jogging, I thought about the events that had led to this moment: my root canal, playing guitar for Veronica at the Winter Spectacular talent show, finally opening up to her and telling her my complicated life story. So far, everything had worked out fine. This new plot-twist had to be just as successful, right?

Right…?

For the rest of the day, I felt my mind drifting back to the topic of Call Field's reunion.

How would it work? I wondered. *How am I going to balance these two disparate realms of teaching and rock music? What will happen when these worlds collide? Will I be destroyed in the impending conflagration? Or will it be a crucible from which I emerge stronger and fiercer than before?*

Once again, I had to ask that grand, unyielding question: *what had I gotten myself into?*

Somehow, I made my way through the mental fog of that Monday morning, navigating through group work and grammar lessons and timed writing assignments with my students. When I finally made it home hours later, Sam was struggling with a math worksheet, while Mel was once again editing at the kitchen table. Since everyone was occupied by obligations, I immediately changed into my running clothes and headed to the treadmill in the garage.

As I laced up my shoes and swiped through the apps on my iPad, I could sense the familiar strains of anxiety creeping up from my bowels. Instead of giving in, however, I chomped down and bit hard against the encroaching tremors. Today would *not* be the day that my psychological neuroses got the best of me.

As usual, I started the treadmill at a five-mile-per-hour speed, letting my tense muscles warm up with each thudding step on the board.

Right foot. Left foot.

Right foot. Left foot.

Repeat for an hour.

With each swift movement, I could feel something unnamable coursing through me. Was it nervous energy? Fear? Or was it something else entirely?

Was it *excitement…?*

My hands shaking, I tapped on my iPad and opened up YouTube. My fingers hovered over the search field, and I silently debated with myself about crossing into this frightening, well-trod territory. Eventually, I plunged in and typed a couple of all-too-familiar words.

Call. Field.

As the results loaded on the app in front of me, I took a sharp, stinging breath.

There, at the very top of the page, was the link for the music video of "Incomplete." Below it were a few random lyric videos and automatically generated audio clips. Once again, I felt my fingers drifting just above the screen, equivocating about whether or not I should tap on the video.

Screw it, I thought. *Just watch the damn thing.*

Click.

As the gritty, grainy footage started to roll, the scene on the screen was simultaneously familiar and barely recognizable. It looked like someone had transferred Call Field's music video from an old VHS cassette: the screen was shaky and tentative, like the camera itself seemed nervous about delving into the unsettled past.

Within seconds, I saw the wide, panoramic view of the Santa Monica pier at sunset while the song's introductory octave chords slid in. A quick cut to Ethan's fingers as he maneuvered his way up and down the frets of his wine-dark Gibson SG. A sweeping shot of the full band playing on the beach, Chunk thrashing the drums with his muscular arms, Ethan swaying back and forth with his guitar, Steve gripping an old-fashioned microphone in his right hand, and the bass player…

The bass player.

Me.

I only stood on-camera for a split-second, but there I was: my long, shaggy hair curled by my jawline and that familiar Bermuda triangle of moles instantly recognizable by anyone who knows me well. A chill darted up my spine from the center of my back. It felt like I was watching my own ghost emerge from the grave.

But I also saw something else.

As the broad shoulders and voluminous body of the bass player's figure swayed on the iPad screen, I felt like I was watching someone else's profile – not myself, but a silhouette of someone from my past.

Like the shadow of my father.

I forced myself to watch the rest of the video, to voyeuristically survey the shapes and shades of my youth. I vacillated between laughing at the dated production quality and feeling nostalgic for a bygone era of my life. What I didn't feel, however, was panic. Or anxiety. Or terror.

My mind, like my body, kept pushing onward.

I would not be trapped in the looking-glass of my past.

I would keep moving forward, one step at a time.

Right foot. Left foot.

Right foot. Left foot.

Repeat for an hour.

CHAPTER FORTY-ONE
"Long Promised Road"

I started with the easiest phone call first: Chunk. It seemed only appropriate that my cousin – my childhood best friend and ground zero companion for my music career – would be the first point of contact. Through all the hard times of my life, Chunk always had my back: he was, after all, the only one who joined me when I jumped ship and left Call Field that night at the Fillmore. Nevertheless, it still felt nerve-racking to call my cousin and invite him on my journey hunting down the translucent ghosts of our adolescence.

As I typed Chunk's number into my cell phone, I could feel my fingers tightening in some strange emotional rigor mortis. And, as the light ringing of the phone buzzed in my ears, the familiar march of anxiety started pressing in on me. When Chunk picked up, I felt like I was stepping across some kind of irreversible threshold.

"Hey, cuz!" he answered. "I was wondering when you were going to call!" He laughed casually and the sound reverberated in the receiver.

"Oh, man…" I sighed. "How long have you known about this, Charles?"

He paused for a second, and I swear that I could hear a single eyebrow raising on the other end of the line. "Well… your student called me the first week of January, I think. It was right after we saw you for New Year's."

"*That long…?*" I whined. "And you didn't say anything?"

He chuckled. "That Veronica kid is a trip," he said. "She made me *'cross my heart and hope to die.'* Those were her exact words. Where in the heck did you find her?"

"Technically, I think *she* found *me*," I answered. "She's brilliant, but she's a goofball."

"She might be a goofball," he said, "but she's a goofball who speaks very highly of you. She told me that you're the best teacher she's ever had. That's not just faint praise, Brian."

If I hadn't been so stressed, I would have been touched by Veronica's compliments. As it was, however, I was too flustered to feel flattered. I had more pressing matters on my mind.

"So, what do you think about her proposal?" I asked.

Chunk made a light grunting noise, like he was shifting in his seat. "I have to admit, I was skeptical at first. I haven't really kept in contact with most of the guys. I mean, I usually send Ethan a Christmas card. Steve, though…" He sighed audibly into the phone. "I haven't spoken with Steve in years. But…" His voice trailed off.

"But what…?"

He laughed. "But that Veronica kid wouldn't take no for an answer. She kept emailing me these essay-length messages, arguing that we needed to do the show. I think she just wore me down, to be perfectly honest."

That sounds like Veronica, I thought to myself.

"You're on board with this? Really…?"

"I've warmed up to the idea over the last few weeks," he said. "At first, I was a little apprehensive about dealing with Steve. But I figure I can always punch him in the face again if he starts to act like a prima donna." He cackled into the phone, obviously entertained by the idea of engaging in fisticuffs with our old lead singer.

As anxious as I felt, I had to suppress a giggle. What's that old saying…? *Comedy is just tragedy plus time*, right?

"So, you think I should do it…?" I asked.

"Brian, I *know* you should do it," Chunk answered. "It's time."

I won't bore you with the details about my conversations with Ethan and Victor. Suffice to say, time had healed a lot of wounds. As much as I'd assumed that my middle school buddy and my college roommate had been carrying grudges all these years, the passing time seemed to have weathered their memories.

"You know, Brick," Ethan told me, "I'm really sorry for how everything went down. You were my friend long before I joined the band, long before I knew Steve or Victor, and I didn't stick by you. I backed the wrong horse. I've harbored a lot of guilt about it over the years…"

"About what?" I asked.

He made sounds like he was smacking his lips together, as if he was trying to conjure an answer from his throat. "I've felt guilty about not being there for you when your dad died. And I'm sorry that I didn't stick up for you when everything went down. Even if we didn't always see eye-to-eye, it was messed-up to choose a stupid band over our friendship. So… I'm sorry."

My conversation with Victor wasn't much different.

"To be honest," Victor admitted to me on the phone, "I eventually came to the same conclusion that you did. Steve was toxic back then. As much as I wanted to cling to him and believe that he was going to be our golden goose, it became clear to me pretty quickly that I was nothing but a supporting player in the *Steve Öken Show*. You might have been the 'brick' of our little structure, but it turns out that I wasn't much more than mortar."

I would be lying if I said that I didn't feel vindicated.

Do you know what it's like to spend years of your life dwelling on your mistakes – only to discover that your mistakes might actually have been the right decisions? As I ended my call with Victor, I felt strangely liberated, like the weight of the world had been lifted from my Atlas shoulders.

There was only one last roadblock in the way.

Steve Öken.

At first, I simply couldn't bring myself to call him. You might think that I'm a coward, but (to be perfectly honest) I'm okay with that. Every single time that I picked up my phone and prepared to dial Steve's number, I found myself on the verge of a panic attack that left me hyperventilating.

So, I took the easy way out instead: I emailed him.

Now, you would *think* that writing an email would be the less-stressful alternative to a phone conversation with the guy who stole your teenage crush, coopted your garage band, and decimated your music career… but I swear that I spent more time writing, rewriting, editing, and revising that email than ten uncomfortable phone conversations would have taken. As I hunched over the laptop screen, my fingers dashing across the keys, I could feel my anxiety rising like seawater against the hull of a boat.

It felt an awful lot like retracing my steps back to the scene of a long-forgotten crime.

For a split second, I just considered deleting the entire message and abandoning ship. But my fingers hovered over the keyboard before I finally made my decision.

Screw it, I thought.

I hit send, and crossed the rock-and-roll Rubicon.

There was no going back now.

Less than twenty-four hours later, there was a message in my inbox from (you guessed it) Steve Öken. Although Steve had *supposedly* agreed to play the show – Veronica and her printed emails stated as much – it was different seeing a message *addressed to me*. I felt nervous, like a high school kid receiving an admissions envelope during college-application season, but I clicked on the message anyway – and received my first contact from Steve in twenty years.

Brick! It's so good to hear from you, he wrote. *I never thought I'd have the chance to see you again, so it's kinda crazy to hear from you after so many years…*

My eyes scanned through paragraph after paragraph, anticipating some sort of nasty revelation or snarky comment… but there was nothing, not a trace of the venom I thought would be coursing through his veins (or his sentences, for that matter). The way things had ended with Call Field, I just assumed we would be lifelong enemies watching the bridge between us burning down from both ends. Now, however, it seemed like we were both cautiously walking towards each other on the charred, skeletal remains of that same scarred structure.

It wasn't impossible, mind you, but pretty darn improbable. Implausible, even.

Steve had tried reaching out to me some time after my dad passed away, but I didn't bother responding to him. I was too raw, too broken to speak with him after everything that had transpired between us.

But now, things were different.

It was hard to put my finger on it, to identify what exactly had changed, but the answer was a prime example of Occam's razor: "the simplest explanation is usually the best one."

We had all grown up.

CHAPTER FORTY-TWO
"The Nearest Faraway Place"

I spent the next week emailing back and forth with Chunk, Ethan, Victor, and Steve – the five of us catching up on twenty years' worth of life events. All of us, it turned out, had remained in Southern California. We all found occupations outside the music industry. We all got married. And we all ended up with children. It was so bizarre to think that our little motley crew of punk rock kids had grown up and turned into fully functioning adults.

Obviously, I'd spent countless days with Chunk's family over the years, so I knew all about his comic shop and his wife and his kids. Ethan had been receiving those annual Christmas cards from Chunk, too, but all that history felt like late-breaking news to Victor and Steve. I guess that happens when you let half a lifetime slip away from you.

As it turns out, Ethan ended up in San Luis Obispo, just 130 miles north of our hometown in Ojai. When he left the band after the conclusion of that ill-fated summer tour in 2000, he finished up at Cal Poly San Luis Obispo, graduated with a degree in agricultural science, and subsequently earned a reputation as *the* go-to golf course grass-maintenance guru. He married a Cal Poly classmate, and the two of them had nested in a little creekside craftsman bungalow a few blocks from downtown SLO. They had three kids (one girl and two boys) and a Golden Retriever named Bungalow Bill (whom they named after the Beatles song from the *White Album*).

Victor took the award for the most unusual career path. After studying computer science and working for a few years as a web designer for a start-up (something to do with security and coding, as far as I could tell), he made a ton of cash – and then quit the tech industry altogether. I guess he simply wasn't happy staring at a computer screen all day. In the aftermath of that decision, Victor did a great deal of soul-searching; he broke up with his longterm boyfriend and went back to school for a doctorate in Film and Media Studies at USC. As if that wasn't enough of a sharp left-turn, his story gets even stranger. Remember all those sketches he used to do in our dorm room, with the anthropomorphic dinosaurs in boho hipster clothing? Well, purely for his own amusement, he started a web comic about doctoral life called *The Didactic Dinosaur*. At first, he just published for fun – a few panels here and there, when he wasn't too overwhelmed with his doctoral thesis. Somewhere along the line, though, *The Didactic Dinosaur* really took off. So, Victor ended up dropping out of grad school to pursue animation full-time. Before he left USC, though, he found true love: during his last year as a Trojan, Victor met his future husband, a British cinematographer who had recently moved to the United States. The two of them own a house in Calabasas and just recently adopted a little girl from China.

As for Steve… well, his story is a bit more complicated than the rest of us. After that backstage showdown at the Fillmore on the opening night of the tour, our former lead singer soldiered on with a slowly atrophying version of Call Field. When Chunk and I exited the band, he recruited some musicians from the LA punk circuit to take our places. And, when Victor left, Steve refused to give up the ghost: instead, he hired a session player from the Valley to fill in on bass. The tipping point, however, came when Ethan finally quit the band. During that final incarnation of Call Field, which toured the United States in the spring and summer of 2001, Steve was the only remaining member of our group to continue playing under the band's moniker. For the first time, Steve found himself floundering, ultimately watching his counterfeit incarnation of Call Field whittled down to an acoustic trio that eventually devolved into just Steve with an acoustic guitar.

In the end, Steve got exactly what he wanted: the band was entirely his. But it wasn't the crowning culmination he thought it would be.

I imagine it must have been pretty humbling for Steve to tour all by himself, playing songs that *I* had written without anyone to prop him up in the spotlight. Despite his good looks and his golden voice, the crowds started dwindling with each successive stop. During that time, he started drinking too much and consuming a wide variety of illicit substances. By the time that August of 2001 rolled around, Steve was in rehab, cleaning up the mess that he had made of his life.

I need to be honest here. Part of me wanted to boast and celebrate Steve's imminent downfall, to rejoice in the fact that this stubborn singer, this arrogant asshole, had finally received his comeuppance. But the fleeting sense of vindication I felt was soon replaced by pity. For so many years, I had wanted Mr. Perfect Lead Singer to get thrown overboard by a mutinous crew. As it turned out, though, he ended up drowning alone in the offshore waves.

While he was in rehab, Steve met a beautiful bleach-blonde surfer girl from Malibu. Big surprise there. Within days, the two of them struck up an intense romantic relationship – disregarding the disapproval and chastising of the facility's staff, of course. This gal, Gwen, was the woman whom he would end up marrying – the same woman who would give birth to his two children… before becoming his ex-wife. After several years of adolescent adultery, of being the bad boy who frequently cheated on his girlfriend(s), Steve found himself on the *other* end of the equation: a man whose wife had left him for a younger, more attractive replacement.

It was like the universe had played a game of cosmic karma and Steve had folded his cards with a losing hand. In the end, our lead singer reaped exactly what he had sown: bitterness, betrayal, and bereavement.

Steve hit rock bottom. Hard. So hard, in fact, that he ended up losing almost everything that mattered to him.

And yet, because of these rather humbling circumstances, Steve was forced to grow up *really* quickly. Once he managed to take some steps on the stairwell of sobriety (which, apparently, took a few rounds of falling off the wagon), Steve had to rebuild everything from the bare concrete of his life. Sure, he had his father's money to fall back on, but he was now a man in his 20s with two small children and very few professional prospects. After a series of humbling odd jobs, including a stint as a used-car salesman, Steve ultimately ended up in construction.

For someone who had spent so many hours teetering at the top of a metaphorical steeple, Steve was now forced to work with the very literal bricks and mortar that served as the foundation for each building. But, he stayed with the expanding company – and, over time, was promoted to foreman, then administrator, and ultimately vice-president. He was comfortable now, financially stable and sharing custody of his two kids with his ex-wife. He was even in a serious, long-term relationship with a new woman, a gal with her own kids and an ex-husband of her own. Though Gwen was still in the picture, haunting pick-ups and drop-offs with the kids, Steve had found a new sense of docile domesticity with his life. What a profound change from the wild, untamable antagonist of my youth!

Life had humbled all of us, saddling us with the dignified weight of responsibility and accountability. While I had spent years envisioning my former bandmates and friends as time capsules forever trapped at the turn of the century, they had been growing substantially in isolation, working through their own twisted and thorny paths of adulthood.

None of us were rock stars anymore.

None of us were superheroes.

None of us were anything other than ordinary.

We were simply grown men with roles and responsibilities that we were trying to navigate as we went along, boarding our own vessels towards uncertain shores that we hoped would provide us with more solid ground. We were refugees and sailors and captains and fathers.

And all of us felt like something was missing from our lives.

CHAPTER FORTY-THREE
"Do It Again"

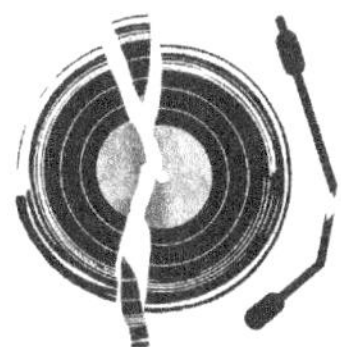

It all seemed to happen so quickly. After two painful decades of punk-rock purgatory, how could I have come so far in such a brief amount of time? At the beginning of the school year, my soul felt infected, like a bad toothache. Any little reminder of my past, of my tragic tenure in a rock band, caused a sharp pain – an unwelcome stabbing sensation that I couldn't shake. Veronica's constant prodding seemed to excavate the wound, though, clearing out the contaminated tissue like so much necrotic pulp. When the time came to heal those gaping holes, I found a cavernous emptiness that needed to be cemented and filled.

It was time for that spiritual root canal.

There's always a multitude of tasks to complete before any big concert: booking facilities, contracting a sound man, promoting the event, posting fliers in local businesses, and too many other detailed duties to list. As the sheer weight of these responsibilities started to creep in from the periphery of my vision, I started to panic a little bit. Fortunately, Veronica reassured me that she had everything covered.

"It's okay, Mr. Smith," she promised. "You just focus on getting the band ready, and I'll handle the rest."

I had a hard time believing that a seventeen-year-old kid – even one as precocious as Veronica – could pull off a project of this magnitude. Of course, as I had learned over the course of the preceding months,

Veronica was born to defy expectations. Which meant, of course, that I needed to fulfill *my* end of the bargain.

I had to get the band back together.

The first hurdle was figuring out where to practice. When we were kids in middle school and high school, my parents' garage had always been our refuge from the world, our musical safe haven. Two decades later, however, that was no longer an option: a few years after my dad passed away, my mom sold the house on Lago de Paz Court and moved into a beachfront property in Oxnard that they had purchased for a significantly cheaper price back in the 1970s. Back then, the house sold for something ridiculously economical, far less than $100,000; in today's market, adjusted for inflation, it's worth close to two million dollars. For years, it was just an investment, a rental property that provided a little extra income for my public-school teacher parents. Little did they know that it would become my mother's second lease on life, a new chapter for her after the trauma of losing her husband.

Part of the reason that Lani and I settled in Oxnard Shores was so that we could be closer to Mom. Lord knows, in the aftermath of loss and grief, you cling to the artifacts of family that you have left. So, when Lani and I went looking for a house to buy in the mid-2000s, we ended up settling on a place just a few blocks over from my mom's house. A few years later, after Sam was born, it didn't hurt that Grandma Smith lived right around the corner; in fact, Mom ended up becoming our daughter's go-to caretaker when Sam was in preschool.

Anyway, the moral of the story is that our old space on Lago de Paz Court was no longer available. Where, then, could a reunited pop-punk band with amps blasting at rocket-ship level volumes practice without disturbing the neighbors?

Once again, Veronica had it covered.

"I talked with Mr. Franklin and Principal Mandaragat, and I got permission to use the school's auditorium to practice," she explained. "I booked it for you to use every Saturday until the concert. That way, you'll have plenty of time to get used to the stage before the night of the show. Like home-court advantage for a concert. Or something like that."

It wasn't ideal, but it was uncannily appropriate. In some ways, Oxnard Shores High School had become a second home to me over the last fifteen years. Lord knows, I spend almost as many hours on campus during the school year as I do at home. Just as my personal and professional lives were colliding, it seemed apropos that my band would start to settle in at my home-away-from-home.

Nevertheless, it would be impossible to gauge how things would work out until Chunk, Ethan, Victor, Steve, and I stepped foot onto the Oxnard Shores stage – instruments in hand and ready to rock.

The day of our first practice began with me standing outside the auditorium's foyer, twirling a set of borrowed keys between my quaking fingers. I was so anxious that I showed up an hour early, just in case any of my once-and-future bandmates decided to roll up before our mutually agreed-upon 11:00 AM start time. As I waited, I found myself fretfully pacing back and forth across the sidewalk, falling prey to nervous tics like picking at my cuticles or scrolling through the digital mountains of email on my iPhone. But it was a good thing that I arrived so early, because my first bandmate showed up at 10:30.

"*Ho-ly crap*," a gravelly voice shouted from the empty street. "Is that you, Brick?"

I looked up, the ascending sun gleaming in my eyes, and saw the familiar blonde hair and muscular frame of Call Field's lead singer.

Steve Öken.

He jogged up, his face instantly recognizable but more wrinkled and weathered than it had been the last time I saw him. Though life hadn't necessarily been kind to Steve in the ensuing years, he *still* looked like a fashion model. Instead of Abercrombie & Fitch, though, he was now J. Crew. Steve might have aged, his gaunt face framing sharper features than in the 1990s, but he still had the appearance of a handsomely distinguished, aging athlete. The bastard.

Instinctively, I felt my jaw tighten, my fingers forming into fists. For a split second, I felt like a thin silhouette of myself – as if I had reverted back into that anxious fifteen-year-old boy hiding in the shadows during Serena's *quinceañera*. Just as I had done twenty years ago, I found myself bitterly resenting the picture-perfect figure approaching me from the empty street.

Despite my own jealousy and insecurity – which clearly hadn't *entirely* evaporated in the span of time since our showdown at the Fillmore – Steve honestly seemed happy to see me. As soon as he stepped foot onto the sidewalk, he threw his arms around me and pulled me in for a hug.

Yes, you're reading that correctly.

Steve Öken *hugged* me.

"*God damn*," he said. "I barely recognize you, Brick." Steve gave me one last squeeze and released me from his grip. He pulled back, but kept a hand locked on my arm as he looked me up and down. "Where's the rest of you? The last time I saw you, man, you were…" Steve's voice dawdled in the subtle drift of the wind, his thoughts left unfinished in the crisp morning air.

"Morbidly obese…?" I offered, shrugging my shoulders.

He cackled, deep from the recesses of his gut. "I was trying to think of a politer way to say that… but you were always better with words than me."

I thrust my hands into my pockets, my body tightening and constricting. Steve took a step back and ran his fingers through his course sandy-blonde hair.

"I've shed a lot of skin over the years," I said, my eyes trained on his. "Literally and figuratively. I've let a lot of things go."

Steve looked away from me, garnering oxygen with a deep breath. "Look, Brick," he said, his voice not much louder than a whisper. "I wanted to tell you that I'm sorry. I've spent a lot of time thinking about how everything fell apart… I mean, we were like kids back then."

"We *were* kids," I agreed with him.

"And even though a simple apology can't make everything better… I'm sorry." When he looked back at me, his eyes were welling up slowly. Without warning, he walked forward, threw his arms around me, and gripped my body tightly.

We were no longer two adversaries locked in an eternal struggle.

Instead, we were reunited friends, locked in an earnest embrace.

Behind that flawless face and that chiseled jaw, there was a man in a lot of pain – something I had taken for granted for all those years. I might have shaped Steve into a villain over the course of my life's narrative, but he wasn't some two-dimensional monster plotting to destroy everything I held dear. He was simply a flawed human being who had made some terrible choices – and whose life had suffered as a result.

And *that* is something no crystal ball could have predicted.

As much bitterness as I had harbored over the years, I didn't rejoice in his suffering – but I also didn't feel the urge to mingle his tears with mine. Instead, I held him tightly against me, the same way that I hold Samantha when she cries over a skinned knee or a bloody nose. In that moment, I didn't feel like Steve's rival or his partner or his equal. I felt like I was his father, holding together the shattered and broken pieces of a grown man. He wasn't much different than the collected shards of vinyl that had only recently scattered across my office floor.

High school is a fever dream of fragile hope and tentative despair. Though we might have felt overwhelmed as we walked over the cracked slabs of sidewalk that guided us from class to class like a tarnished Yellow Brick Road, we were just children marching nervously along the prescribed route in front of us. In sharp contrast, the years *after* high school and college can be cleansing, offering opportunities for redemption with each new step along an uncharted path. Still, though, it's easy to stay trapped inside that gilded cage of adolescence, savoring the bars that separated us from the rest of our lives. And when we look back at our younger selves, it's not much different than a butterfly staring longingly at the chrysalis from which it emerged.

You cannot reenter that wilted womb of youth. All you can do is hold its delicate shell within your nostalgic hands.

When Steve gripped me in a breathless bear hug, I recognized the sharply different trajectories our lives had taken. While he had been the golden boy – the quarterback, the heartthrob, the superhero of our quaint, small-town high school – he had fallen on hard times. He could no longer leap tall buildings in a single bound or throw a football faster than a speeding bullet. Adulthood had been his kryptonite, disarming him and robbing him of his superhuman powers. Now, here he was, a divorced father of two children trying to make his way through an uncertain world. He couldn't recapture the glory of his youth: that lingering magic had long since faded into the ether of yesterday. The man who once swung from the spires was now relying upon a brick (or *Brick*, as it were) to avoid collapsing on the cold, hard concrete.

"I'm so sorry," Steve said penitently, his shuddering breaths exhaled into the collar of my shirt.

"I forgive you," I told him.

And I meant it.

Ethan, Victor, and Chunk all arrived a few minutes later. Instantaneously, I felt like I was living in a distorted dream, a pathetic revenge fantasy in which bloodshed was replaced with tears shed, and broken bones replaced with broken spirits. It wasn't *Kill Bill* as much as it was *Reduce Bill to a Sobbing Puddle in Front of His Old Nemesis*.

Of course, Steve tried to shake it off and project that nonchalant demeanor that we knew so well, running up to embrace his old bandmates like he had done with me only moments before. Chunk immediately sensed that something was wrong, though, as he gestured discreetly when Steve's back was turned.

I just gave him a noncommittal shrug as a response, mouthing the words, *"I'll tell you later."*

Chunk nodded his head, his eyes sternly studying the surreal scene that surrounded us.

We spent a long time talking that afternoon – a *long, long* time. Though we'd been emailing back and forth for a while by then, it felt different to be reunited in the flesh after so many eons apart from each other. Initially, our postures were stiff and cautious – arms folded, legs locked in place. Slowly, though, the ice between us began to melt and slide off our rigid frames. We weren't going back in time, but we were thawing the calcified frost that had kept us apart for so many years.

In some ways, it felt like a subtle, interpersonal melding of metal. Each of us would edge our way into the conversation, contributing an anecdote here and a joke there; the circle of our bodies, which had seemed so spacious and jagged when we started talking, became a smaller, bolder ring. The distance between us – emotionally and physically – was slowly diminishing.

We were working our way back to who we used to be.

But we also refused to compromise what we had become.

Steve still established himself as the epicenter of our little solar system, but all of us orbiting him kept a comfortable distance from his gravitational pull. Whereas before, we might have found ourselves sucked in by the all-consuming force of his oversized presence, we each remained a few steps away, resisting the dramatic draw of his personality. His invisible charisma hadn't completely dissipated, but it wasn't the dominating power that it had been when we were kids. The sun at the center of our universe – the blinding sphere that had once threatened to engulf us as it expanded to a supernova – was reduced to a dying star. As a result, the rest of us no longer felt eclipsed by his light.

Over the course of the next hour, we traded stories of victories and defeats. Unlike when we were kids, though, there was no divisive arrogance or one-upmanship; instead, we all listened patiently, respectfully. We didn't jockey for position as much as we simply kept pace with each other. This was a brave new world, one of children and spouses and mortgages and full-time jobs. And we had to learn how to navigate alongside each other in the process.

Finally, when we reached a comfortable lull in the conversation, I took the initiative to move us along.

"Well, gentlemen," I said. "Shall we get started?"

As I looked around me, I saw the faces of my once-and-future bandmates nodding, even as their expressions mirrored my own mixture of excitement and trepidation.

This was going to be interesting.

Walking out to the stage and grabbing our instruments felt singularly speculative, like relearning how to waltz after spending years with your legs in a cast. Everything felt tentative: the hum of the amps, the clatter of drumsticks dropped on the wooden stage, the shuffling of footsteps on floorboards. Over the years, Call Field had played more shows than I could possibly count; and yet, that moment on stage felt more like a blind date than a faded marriage.

Would it work?

Would we share the same chemistry we once had?

Would we even remember how to play our instruments?

We were about to find out.

CHAPTER FORTY-FOUR
"Strange World"

As it turned out, my fears were unfounded.

Despite the stilted small talk of the afternoon – the cautious gestures and hesitant voices, the little telltale signs that this might be an unmitigated disaster – we abandoned our anxieties as soon as the music started.

The minute that Chunk took his spot behind the drum kit, offering a swift snap of the snare, it felt like someone had flipped a switch and kickstarted the time machine into our past. The muscle memory came back and worked its way through our arms and our fingertips, filtering the movements through the vibrations of guitar strings and plectrums and amplifiers and cymbals.

Thump. Thump-thump-thump.
Thump. Thump-thump-thump.
Thump. Thump-thump-thump.

We hadn't discussed what we would play first, but Chunk's insistent, deliberate drums inspired me to start tapping out a shuffling rhythm, riffing around a *D major* chord on my Alesis keyboard. To be honest, I was just kind of fiddling around with The Beach Boys' "Help Me, Rhonda," the song I saw my father belt out in our backyard on his fortieth birthday. That was the night that I decided I wanted to play guitar, the night that set the course for my entire musical trajectory. In some subconscious way, I was going back to the beginning to find inspiration for the next chapter.

Just as we had slowly come together as friends and bandmates, gradually joining forces and uniting in a shared mission, each successive chord felt like we were excavating the graves of our youth and exhuming the coffins of our adolescence. The song built methodically, purposefully, starting with the foundation of Chunk's drums and continuing with the bouncy piano that breezed forward from my keyboard amp.

At first, I felt rusty and unsteady. Slowly, though, I began to lock in the rhythm, moving in syncopated time with Chunk's drumming. We smiled at each other as our two instruments swayed together like flags in the wind.

My fingers danced over the keys in front of me, replaying that shuffle in swinging 4/4 time and caressing the notes on my keyboard like fingertips on the cheek of an infant. I was sending a musical invitation to my brethren onstage, waiting for them to join me and my cousin in our off-the-cuff jam. Would they answer the call?

Intuitively, Ethan started weaving an intricate lead guitar line into the fold, the hypnotic notes echoing in the spaces around us. The sounds issuing forth were fluid and natural, swimming around each other in a clean, striking pattern.

Steve started strumming his Fender Stratocaster, the sound filtered through the distorted crunch of his Marshall stack. He had been the weakest musician amongst us when we were kids, unsteady and uncertain, always hovering on the perimeter of the rhythm and threatening to veer dangerously off-course. Surprisingly, Steve had come a long way in the last few decades: he was no longer the vapid, off-kilter guitarist whose strumming had to be buried in the mix – the musician whose parts all had to be rerecorded by his bandmates during our sessions with Storf. Instead, his playing served as a rock-solid foundation for the rest of the band, locked in tightly with Chunk's drums and my piano.

Victor, the last member to join the band, finally followed suit. As he nervously looked up at the rest of us, he started thumping away on a walking bass line that mimicked the comforting, commonplace chord changes of our favorite classic rock songs.

And then Ethan started sliding up the neck of his guitar with those instantly recognizable octave chords. We were no longer jamming on "Help Me, Rhonda" – we were plunging into the old, familiar territory of Call Field's best-known song.

We were playing "Incomplete."

When we recorded our signature song, way back in the spring of 2000, we tried our best to emulate blink-182 and Social Distortion and the Ramones – and, of course, the Beach Boys. Because of the cold, calculating hands of the record label, however, the final mixes on *A Different Slant of Light* stripped away the raw roadhouse architecture of the band for a lush, pristine mansion that sparkled more than pounced. But as we locked in together at that precise moment on a dilapidated high school stage, the band felt truer to itself than in any other incarnation. Somehow, undeterred by the fog of atrophy that accompanies years of absence, we were able to reach out our hands and resurrect the beautiful grit at the song's center.

We found the musical core of heartache and longing and frustration and passion – and channeled it into a unified front, raising arms against the shadow armies of doubt. Despite my reservations, the last twenty years of our lives slipped away in a flurry of rhythms and notes and melodies and harmonies.

We still had it.

The magic was still there.

Now, I don't believe in time travel. As far as I'm concerned, it's simply unfathomable that a souped-up DeLorean or lightning-fast rocket ship can bend the laws of science. However, in that moment, I felt a piece of myself twist and turn through the years into a replica of my past. For a split second, I was transported back into the teenage version of myself – all acne and braces and shaggy auburn hair. And, though the bodies around me were obviously older, wizened doppelgängers of their former selves, I swear that the rest of the band felt it, too.

When I closed my eyes, I could picture us in that messy garage at my parents' house in Ojai: a handful of hungry high school boys desperately trying to act cool in the oppressive heat of youth. As we did so, we transformed back into the Bookhouse Boys – that nascent incarnation of the band that had made its debut on the stage of Sespe Creek High School so many summers ago.

And when Steve started singing the all-too-familiar first line of the song, *"California can be cruel in the summer,"* we were transformed again: the Bookhouse Boys evolved into Caulfield, and we were precocious teenagers, finding our way in the dark together, fumbling through the motions of adolescence and ego. The band soldiered on in the shadows, making its way through each of the verses that echoed the trials and tribulations of youth.

When we arrived at the first chorus, Steve began belting out that aching refrain: *"I get lost sometimes in the melodies of my mind..."* As a lovelorn teenager, I had written those words about Lani, the woman who would one day become my wife. When I first crafted the song in the middle of a sleepless late-October night, I imagined that it was about the turmoil of releasing yourself from the grasp of loneliness and isolation, finding comfort and completion in the arms of the girl that you loved. Now, though, those words seemed to echo the weight of the band's fractured breakup: all four of us had felt *incomplete* for the last twenty years, longing for the sense of communion and completion that our musical brotherhood provided.

Gathered together for the first time in two decades, we were letting go of the guilt and grief that anchored us to an overwhelming weight – the burdens of the past, present, and future. We were enveloped in a swelling sense of solace, reveling in the sonic spells that we conjured with our instruments. As Steve's voice navigated through the nostalgic terrain of the song, it sounded like a primordial howl, casting incantations that enchanted us all. And, when the vibrations coursed through our bodies, it felt therapeutic, cathartic, as if the ghosts we each carried – on our shoulders and in our hearts – were exorcised from our fragile frames and released skyward, floating away like mylar balloons on the winds of a clear blue firmament.

Once again, we were Call Field, the young pop-punk band with major-label dreams and a hit song on the radio. We had worked our way through the past – stripping back the years, note by note.

The transformation was complete.

CHAPTER FORTY-FIVE
"Saturday Night"

After so many years spent dwelling on the past – of ruminating in the ruins – it was hard to believe that the pieces of the puzzle could fit together so cohesively and coherently. When you're playing music in a band with other living, breathing human beings, it's always a gamble: you might clash with another musician's style or sensibility or tone or any of the other countless factors that comprise a musical identity. Some musicians never find the artistic partners they need or deserve – and, thus, labor away in obscurity for the remainders of their careers. Chunk, Ethan, Steve, Victor, and I were lucky: we found capable musical soulmates at an early juncture in our lives.

Think about it. Of all the high school bands that exist at any given point in time, how many of them last? How many record an album? How many sign a major-label deal? How many go on tour? Heck, how many even get to play a single show? The fact that our little Call Field cohort managed to check off so many items on that pie-in-the-sky wish list is pretty miraculous.

After we finished up our first practice on that golden Saturday afternoon, we were all basking in the revelatory glow of our reunion. After twenty years and a fiercely fractured ending, it seemed like a bankable impossibility that all five of us could coexist in the same room together, let alone pick up our instruments and continue where we left off. This rock and roll reunion – personal *and* professional – was more providential than I anticipated.

If my life story was a made-for-TV movie, this would be the part of the film in which the lovable hero, reunited with his musical sidekicks, starts his victory lap. There would be hugs and dramatic gestures, and all hard feelings from the past ninety-three minutes of the film would be forgotten in the triumphant final act of the narrative. The band would get back together, re-sign a lucrative major-label record deal, hit the road for a sold-out tour, and top the charts with their incredible underdog comeback story. And then our humble hero would live happily-ever-after with his beautiful wife and daughter, enjoying the remarkable success that he has earned through his Job-like suffering and interminable optimism. Fade to black, roll the credits, and toss back the last few handfuls of popcorn. The end.

There was just one teeny-tiny problem…

I was still on the verge of having a panic attack.

I don't pretend to understand the profound complexities of the human brain or the emotional limitations of the mortal soul. While I'm sure any qualified high school physiology or psychology teacher could lecture endlessly on the irreparable damage that can be done to the human psyche, it's still a mystical profundity that defies my understanding.

So, while everything seemed to be threading together smoothly on the surface, I was quietly, inexplicably fraying underneath.

From a removed, objective perspective, you might be thinking to yourself, "Come on, dude. Pull it together and stop shivering in shame." While you'd be forgiven for entertaining such thoughts, it's just *not that easy*. If, however, you're someone like me – someone who has struggled with depression, bipolar disorder, or any other kind of mental illness – I'm sure you get it. Pulling yourself up by your bootstraps is a lot harder to do when your boots are tantalizingly just out of reach – or simply seem glued to the ground.

For the rest of you out there reading this book, *God bless you*. And may you never have to encounter the disarming disadvantage of silent suffering that clouds your vision and blurs your best intentions.

John Steinbeck once wrote that "A journey is a person in itself; no two are alike… we do not take a trip; a trip takes us." While he was clearly in the thralls of *wanderlust* when he wrote those sepia-toned words, the same paradigm applies to mental illness. No two experiences with a bipolar disorder are identical: it is a singular spiritual journey that each of us must encounter alone. And, to co-opt Steinbeck's conclusion, "we do not take a trip with melancholy; melancholy takes a trip with us."

Depression is the subtle vignette that darkens the corner of every frame. It takes even the sunniest of days and shrouds the light in shadows, reaching its chilly hand into the recesses of your heart. It mocks you, laughs at you, taunts you with its nihilistic view of life.

And I was still in thrall to this bitter beast.

Even in the midst of a seemingly flawless and trouble-free reunion with Call Field, I was struggling. Part of my frustration stemmed from the fact that I was simply out of shape (musically, that is). While I had obviously taken an extended sabbatical from rock and roll after I left the band in June of 2000, the other guys had all continued to play their instruments and grown even more formidable in the interim. Though I might once have been the mastermind behind the band, I suddenly felt like the rookie, the new recruit. It was as if Chunk, Ethan, and Victor – and, surprisingly, even Steve – had all continued running marathons over the last decade and a half, while I had only been jogging lightly on a treadmill. Sure, I would strum a ukulele most nights when Mel and I sang lullabies to Sam, but that was barely enough to keep my muscle memory intact. The rest of the guys, on the other hand, had skillfully evolved with their musicianship – growing more polished and professional while I withered away in mediocrity.

I'm sure that in Veronica's mind, this reunion would be a simple matter of retrofitting the jagged edges of a jigsaw back together. She didn't realize that the central section of the puzzle – your humble narrator – had shrunken and atrophied in the two decades that passed after I left Call Field. That puzzle piece no longer fit.

The part that confused me so much was the discrepancy between the comfort I felt while I was playing and the unmitigated anxiety that came after practice was all over. How could I be fine when standing behind a keyboard, but have heart palpitations while I was lying in my bed at night? It just didn't make any sense to me.

So, I did what any teacher does when confronted with this kind of trial: I put in more hours of work.

The Saturday night after our second successful reunion rehearsal, I was determined to fight back against the prevailing forces of darkness that threatened to defeat me. I went upstairs into my office and grabbed the dusty Martin D-21 acoustic guitar that perpetually perched motionless on its stand.

And I started strumming.

I felt rusty at first, like the Tin Man in *Wizard of Oz* after Dorothy pours some oil on his rigid joints. My arms didn't move as smoothly as they used to: they lacked the natural fluidity that had come to me so effortlessly as a college student, writing song after song in my dorm room. Although it doesn't take much physical strength to drag a plectrum across six coiled strings, there is a certain level of finesse required; in that regard, I was clearly out of practice. My hands moved like blunt instruments, instead of the fine-tuned fingers that could have deftly wielded a musical scalpel once upon a time. Still, though, I refused to give up. I would not let my atrophied skills – or my shaky voice – deter me from the task at hand.

Slowly, diligently, I worked my way through the Call Field catalogue, clumsily revisiting the melodies from yesteryear like a high-school French teacher subbing in an Algebra class. Even though I had been the mastermind behind those familiar songs, the composer who spent hours painstakingly crafting chord progressions and lyrics in isolation, I struggled as I tried to remember the nuances of the music. It felt so strange, like trying on old clothes that no longer fit. And yet, I had to remind myself, I was the sole tailor for all those ancient threads – the one who had sewn everything together, stitch by calculated stitch.

I was midway through a floundering rendition of "Sherilyn" when I looked up and saw Sam standing in the doorframe, staring straight at me. She had Cinnabunny clutched tightly in her right arm and a weathered copy of a paperback book in her left. Though I tilted my head questioningly after she appeared, Sam just watched me.

"Are you okay, kiddo…?" I asked. I let my left hand drop from the neck of the guitar and flexed my fingers like an arthritic grandfather.

"I'm just listening," she said, inelegantly plopping down beneath the threshold of the doorjamb, where the soft carpet of the halls met the wooden floor of my office. "You never play Grandpa's guitar. But you're playing it now." She dumped Cinnabunny on the ground of the hallway, just within reach of her slender arms. "And I want to listen."

I scowled for a second, annoyed by the intrusion into my private practice time. But it was hard to maintain my sour attitude with Sam adorably seated before me. Darn kids and their cuteness.

I took a deep breath through my nostrils and exhaled through my mouth. "What do you want to hear?" I asked her.

She scrunched up her face in a studious frown of concentration. "Ummm…" she mumbled, slowly relaxing her expression. "Can you play the one we heard at Disneyland?"

"In case you're wondering, 'Incomplete' is the name of the song," I told her. "If you're going to make me play it for you, Samantha, you should know the title."

Sam glared at me in her own cute little way. "It's not *my* fault that you never told me the names of your songs," she said. "Just play it."

"'Play it, *please*…?'" I corrected her. "Remember your manners, missy."

"Can you play it, *please*?" she echoed back with more than a touch of sarcasm in her voice. Clearly, Mel's been a profound influence on our diminutive daughter.

I cleared my throat. "Fine. Just remember that I'm still working out the kinks, okay?"

"Okay," Sam said, repositioning herself on the dividing line between the carpet and the wooden floor.

With my left hand, I reached out to the tuning pegs on the headstock, twisting the low E string until it was back in tune. The fingers of my right hand clutched the guitar pick tightly, the triangular edges poking into my palm.

Here we go, I thought to myself.

I started strumming that familiar *D major* chord and opened my mouth to sing. *"California can be cruel in the summer…"*

For the next three and a half minutes, Sam sat silently, transfixed by the song. As I made my way through the verses and choruses, I watched her watching me, her eyes hyper-focused on the chord positions I shaped with my left hand on the fretboard. When I hit the final closing chord, Sam sat bolt-upright and clapped with all the power her little hands could muster.

"You should be a singer, Daddy!" she told me, her little eyes widening enthusiastically.

I laughed at the prospect. "I don't think so…" I snorted. My thoughts traveled back to the night of Serena's *quinceañera* and Steve's commentary about my singing abilities (or lack thereof). Sure, I'd come a long way since my childhood crush's fifteenth birthday, but I still recognized how absurd Sam's suggestion was. "No one wants to hear me sing, sweetie," I told her with a sad smile.

"No, *really*," Sam argued. "You can *actually* sing, Daddy! You should be, like, a professional singer! Like on the radio and stuff."

I slid my hands onto the wooden waist of the guitar. "It's not quite that easy, Sam," I started to explain. "It's a lot more complicated than you might think…"

"All I know," Sam interrupted, "is that you sound like a singer. A *real* singer. And you already had a song on the radio before. But you should sing it, not the other guy."

I could see that arguing with my newly-nine-year-old daughter wasn't going to end in anything but a stalemate.

"I'll think about it," I told her.

"You should," Sam said. "Because who knows what will happen next?"

I ran my hands along the rosewood top of the guitar and pulled my eyes away from her. "*I* sure don't know what's going to happen next," I admitted, staring off at the empty wall space where my Stuttering Surfers record used to hang. My right hand slid onto the bridge of the guitar and traced circles along the edges of the string pins. "No one does."

CHAPTER FORTY-SIX
"She Knows Me Too Well"

The next few weeks were a blur. In addition to all of the usual teaching insanity – grading, lesson planning, etc. – I was now devoting hours each weekend to the resurrection of my long-lost band. Each Saturday at noon, the five of us would meet at the Oxnard Shores High School theater, set up our equipment, and run through the songs that we planned to play at the benefit concert. All the old favorites were there: "Sherilyn," "Time Bomb," "June," and pretty much every other song on *A Different Slant of Light*.

It felt strange to be pursuing this deliriously dichotomous double-life – a regimented white-collar job during the working week and raucous rock and roll on the weekend. Even without the stereotypical consumption of mind-altering substances or the diversion of beautiful young women (or men, in Victor's case), the discrepancy between my two worlds felt striking to me.

And yet...

Slowly, these two dramatically different circles gravitated towards each and began to intersect, the Venn diagram of my life gradually overlapping larger portions of each ring. Unexpectedly, the two lifestyles became more similar: our time playing rock music became more tempered and precise, while my day job felt more liberated and unchained. I could sense that I was becoming more "punk rock" in my classroom and more "professional" at band practice. It was truly a strange contrast, but somehow the two disparate aspects of my life began to delicately inform one another.

As the weeks flew by and the concert imminently hovered on the horizon, my anxiety still kept rearing its ugly head. However, instead of a ferocious pit bull, it seemed more like a mildly threatening mastiff. Of course, the fact that the beast still remained (regardless of its ferocity) worried me. Even with Call Field's seemingly surefire success, I couldn't shake the shadows of my anxiety and depression. I felt like a paper doll, stitched together by obligations. Responsibility, after all, is a powerful thread.

Each night, I would lie awake, staring at the ceiling, while Mel's light snoring inevitably crept over from her side of the bed. While my beautiful wife slept peacefully, I had to conduct breathing exercises to calm my mind and body. That all-too-familiar sensation of an asphyxiating balloon expanding inside my chest would threaten to suffocate me each night, and it was only through a combination of preventative meditation and prescription medication that I'd eventually wind down and force myself to sleep.

I was simultaneously elated and terrified, thrilled and tormented. Those beastly bipolar tendencies, the same ones that I had grappled with since I was a chubby little child gripping Star Wars action figures in my hands, refused the exorcism that I had been trying to execute for so long.

For the next few weeks, though, I would breathe a sigh of relief every time that I slipped a guitar strap over my neck or placed my fingers on a keyboard. Instantly, the weight would lift from my Atlas shoulders – temporarily dispelled, but hovering over me like a vulture, waiting to strike the second that I tucked my instruments away.

It was a battle I felt destined to lose, a tussle with death and destruction in the darkest depths of Hell. And there I was, nary a pitchfork or bifurcated tail in sight.

Finally, after countless days of practice and panic, the week of the benefit concert arrived. As photocopied flyers for the show started cropping up around campus like slim white weeds in a concrete garden, I started fielding an endless array of questions from my students and my colleagues.

"Wait… *you* have a band?" a fellow English teacher asked me in the copy room one day, as the whirr of mechanical gears spit out papers with ink tattooed on identically duplicated pages.

"I *used to* have a band," I explained calmly, staring down at the collated collection of handouts stacked between my palms. "We're just reuniting for this one benefit concert thing that the school is putting on."

"Cool," he said. "What kind of songs do you cover? Country? Blues? Classic rock?"

I snorted a little at his ignorance. "Almost entirely originals," I explained.

"Oh," he muttered in surprise. "Well, what do you sound like?"

"People have described us as a cross between the Ramones and the Beach Boys," I told him. I neglected to mention the fact that *Rolling Stone* had called my songwriting "exemplary" – or that the magazine had described Call Field as caught in the throes of an "identity crisis." I really didn't want to get into those details with my curious colleague.

"Huh," he mumbled, eyes drilling through me in disbelief. "You don't strike me as the punk music kinda' guy…"

If you only knew, I thought to myself.

"Advance ticket sales are going really well so far!" Veronica reassured me a few days before the show. "Even if we don't sell a single ticket at the door, we'll still make a few thousand dollars profit!"

"Did you say *a few thousand* dollars…?" I asked. With all of my teaching and parenting responsibilities, I had happily abdicated all the promotional duties to Veronica and her crew of ASB friends. Despite Veronica's eager assessment, the prospect of raising more than a few hundred dollars seemed like a stretch to me.

Who would want to see a bunch of old, washed-up 1990s has-beens? I wondered to myself.

Veronica gave me another one of her mischievous grins. "This is a *big deal*, Mr. Smith. I don't think you realize what's happening here."

"Clearly, I don't," I told her. As I spoke, I thought of the audacious anxiety creeping at the corners of my consciousness. "And maybe that's for the best."

Eventually, the buzz spread beyond the confines of the Oxnard Shores High School campus. Two days before the show, a complete stranger approached me at the supermarket. There I was, examining organic bananas in the produce section, when a large, bespectacled man stopped me in the aisle.

"You're Brian Smith, right?" he asked, stretching out his hand.

Apprehensively, I reached out for a handshake. "That's me," I admitted. "And you are…?"

"John Silverman," he told me. "My daughter is in your AP English class."

"Brenna's dad!" I said as the realization struck me. "It's nice to meet you, Mr. Silverman. Your daughter is a great kid. I'm very grateful to have her in my class this year."

"Brenna talks about you all the time," he told me. "She just raves about all the things you do in your classroom. And what's this I hear about a concert…?"

I briefly recited some talking points about the benefit concert and explained how we were raising money to repair the high school's theater. Though I tried to downplay my role in the event, Mr. Silverman saw right through me.

"Well, you've got quite the fan club, apparently. My daughter made me buy *front-row* tickets for the show. And they weren't cheap!"

I immediately blushed crimson. "At least it's for a good cause," I offered sheepishly. "And I think it's tax deductible. Or so I've been told."

Mr. Silverman laughed and shook his head. "The things we do for our kids… Am I right?"

"*The things we do for our kids…*" I echoed back. "You are *absolutely* right about that."

By the time that Friday rolled around, I was one big ball of stress. As much as I felt prepared for our performance, I couldn't shake the nagging feeling that everything might self-destruct at any moment. Somehow, I made it through the end of the workweek (though I *did* force my AP students to write an in-class essay, just so that I could avoid standing in front of the room for more than a few minutes at a time).

Teachers can be pretty sneaky and manipulative, when they need to be. Just in case you were wondering.

The sheer terror of performing once again – not to mention the fact that I'd be facing students and colleagues, along with my friends and family – had nearly crippled me on the inside. All the while, I felt like I'd maintained a decent game face for the sake of outer appearances… but appearances can be pretty darn deceiving.

That's the thing about anxiety: it makes mountains out of molehills, turning casual tasks into inexplicably impossible roadblocks. Intellectually, I know how absurd and melodramatic that sounds. Still, though, that's how I felt.

When I finally got home from work that afternoon, I was taking so many deep breaths that my insides felt like an accordion.

"Are you excited about your big concert, Daddy?" Sam asked at dinner that night.

I hemmed and hawed. "I suppose so," I answered. "I'm just a little…"

A little what? Panicked? Tormented? Terrified?

"I guess I'm just a little nervous," I finally said.

"Don't be nervous!" Sam told me. "You're going to do great!"

Mel didn't say anything, but I could see her studying me clinically, like a doctor checking for symptoms in a prospective patient. Her eyes casually drifted from me to Sam and back, but I knew that she was absorbing every little detail. I had a feeling I would hear about it later.

"It's just been a long time since I've done anything like this," I explained. "And I'm not sure how I'm going to feel about it when I'm onstage."

Mel slyly reached across the table and grabbed my hand. "It's going to be just fine," she whispered to me. "*You* are going to be fine."

I could only pray that she was right.

Later that evening, when Sam was curled up in bed and snuggling with Cinnabunny, Mel decided to broach the topic with me again. We were in the middle of the kitchen, making small talk while we unloaded the dishwasher and put away steaming silverware and piping-hot plates. The dishes were bitterly burning from the washer's recently completed clean cycle, and each piece of porcelain and glass was scalding my fingertips.

"How are you feeling?" Mel asked me gently, as utensils clumsily clattered into the drawer. "Like, *really* feeling?"

I kept myself preoccupied with the never-ending series of coffee mugs and conical glassware. "I'm okay," I murmured without looking up at her.

"I call B.S., Brian Smith," she said, slapping a towel on the kitchen counter. "You don't need to lie to me. I know you better than you know yourself."

"Then why do you even bother asking me?" I shot back – a little more aggressively than I intended. I couldn't help it. I was on edge.

She pursed her lips and wiped her hands on a dishtowel. "Because I want to hear it from *you*. I want you to *tell me* how you feel. That's what spouses do."

"Fine," I said, closing the glass cabinet door that housed our massive mug collection. From the corner of my eye, I could see a familiar Hulabilly Diner mug staring back at me. "I feel like I'm on the verge of having a panic attack and I'm frustrated that I don't have complete control over my emotions and I think that I want to crawl into a cave and never reemerge."

"That's oddly specific," Mel said, her fingers tapping on the counter. "Crawling into a cave and giving up on life… Isn't that a Johnny Cash thing?"

"Maybe…" I sheepishly answered. "Nickajack Cave, I think." Once again, I was wrapped up in the minutiae of music history, rather than focusing on the topic at hand. I quickly rushed out a retort. "But that doesn't make it any less true."

"Do you want to talk about it?" she asked, wiping away some stray hairs from her forehead.

"Not really," I said. I mopped my own brow with the sleeve of my pajamas. "But I have a feeling that you're going to make me."

Mel laughed. "You know me too well, my dear husband," she said. "But I would much rather have a conversation with you than have to dump a bucket of ice water on your head." She scrunched her nose at me and stuck out her tongue.

"I still can't believe you did that," I mumbled with a scowl. I kept shaking my head as if I could free myself of the ice-cold memory.

Mel's smile faded slightly, but her lips still bore the semblance of a mischievous grin. "I was at my wit's end with you," she explained. "So, I resorted to drastic measures. I needed something to snap you out of your fog. And it worked."

"*Boy, did it work...*" I said with a sigh.

"I'm no psychologist," Mel said. "But it's clear that you need some healthy coping mechanisms to calm your mind. And calm your body, too." She took the dish towel in her hands and whipped me with it.

"Ouch!" I squealed. "Maybe my *wife* needs some healthy coping mechanisms to avoid physically abusing her husband."

Mel laughed again. "You are such a pansy sometimes, Brian." She took a step forward and placed her right hand on my chest, just above my nervously beating heart.

Something about that simple, gentle act helped calm my nerves – momentarily at least. "Do you think I can do this, Mel?" I knew it was a dumb question, one meant more rhetorically than actually seeking an answer. But I felt the need to ask it, nonetheless.

She looked up at me and smiled knowingly, wisely, in the way that women have when they've completed so many circles around the sun.

"You just have to make it through the next twenty-four hours," she reassured me. "And then it'll all be over. You can go back to your normal life." She paused, glancing over at a framed family portrait that hung on the wall. "Or not. That's for you to decide."

It felt good to hear that simple reassurance from her. And to know that I still had choices left to make.

CHAPTER FORTY-SEVEN
"I Get Around"

The day of the concert had finally arrived. After years of silent solitary suffering and months of incessant harassment from Veronica and weeks of dutiful practice with my old bandmates, we had approached the end of the race, at last. Still, though, it reminded me of when I ran a half-marathon a few years ago: though you might make it through miles and miles of running, it doesn't guarantee that you'll be able to cross the finish line. Despite everything you've done to make it that far, you still have to force your aching body to run one last sprint before you snap through the ribbon that waits for you at the end.

I spent the morning of the show doing what I normally do on Saturdays after breakfast: running on the treadmill.

Right foot. Left foot.

Right foot. Left foot.

Repeat for an hour.

I'm pretty sure that I was watching an episode from the final season of *Game of Thrones*, deeply invested in the fate of Westeros and its many contenders for sovereignty. However, as much as the fire-breathing dragons and vicious ice zombies should have been all-consuming for my fatigued mind, I still found myself preoccupied by that night's impending performance – which, at this point, was only a few hours away.

With each flashing footfall, I found myself thinking about the experiences that had led me here: my father's 40th birthday party, those early days of practicing in the garage with Marina and the Bookhouse

Boys, my brief fling with Serena and the ensuing heartbreak that followed, the introduction of Steve into our musical ranks, meeting Mel at UCLA, all those hours in the studio recording *A Different Slant of Light*, and the self-destructive blowout that led to the band's violent schism.

That convoluted plot-line could put even George R.R. Martin to shame.

Everything that followed in the "real world" – beyond the blinding lights of the stage – had led me to realize the truth in my dad's wisdom, that "some things are more important than rock and roll." With my father's death, my marriage, my relationship with my daughter, and my teaching career, I discovered a new world of complexity and fulfillment – and, with it, a validation of my father's sage advice.

But what about when rock and roll co-opts the "important things" in your life? What do you do then?

With these separate, disparate worlds colliding, I would have to find my pace, my rhythm. I would need to learn how to move forward on the perpetual treadmill of my life. And that night on the Oxnard Shores High School stage would be a pivotal turning point for me.

Until then, though, I needed to keep on moving.

Right foot. Left foot.

Right foot. Left foot.

Repeat for an hour.

CHAPTER FORTY-EIGHT
"Don't Worry, Baby"

Of course, it wouldn't be a Call Field concert without a little bit of unforeseen drama. Four hours before showtime, I saw my iPhone screen light up with an incoming call from Steve. I figured he was calling to wish me luck or offer help loading the equipment.

I was wrong.

"I've got some bad news, Brian," he murmured weakly into the phone, defeat reverberating through every one of his words. "We need to talk. Like right away."

"Wait… what's going on?" I asked. For a split second, I was envisioning some sort of petty betrayal, like the kind that led to the awkward love triangle of my high school years. Fortunately for me, Steve was decidedly *not* Mel's type.

His breathing seemed heavy and labored. "It's… it's my daughter, Brick," he told me between burdened breaths. "I'm here with her at urgent care in Malibu."

"Is she okay?" I asked him, panic seeping into my chest.

"We don't know what's going on with her," he admitted, his own voice echoing my rising panic. "She's got a 104-degree temperature and her lips are blue and she's lost her sense of smell and she can't taste anything and I can't get ahold of Gwen and I don't know what to do…" A sob clotted his voice. It sounded like he was crying on the other end of the line.

"Oh, my God," I breathed into the phone. "What are you going to do? We've got the show in just a few hours…"

Steve stuttered momentarily. "I… I… I can't leave her."

"So, you're…" The realization dawned on me suddenly, sharply, like a knife to the sternum. "You're going to miss the show, aren't you?"

"I am *so sorry*, Brick," he told me with an earnest sigh. "I was going to bring her with me tonight, you know? I thought maybe she and your daughter could hang out. But she's in no shape to come with me."

I could feel my breath getting more and more ragged. "I get it. I understand," I told him. And I did. Intellectually, I *completely* understood the need to put family first. Physiologically, however, I was veering from steady waters towards jagged rocks.

"I know this show means a lot to you," he said. "And I'm sorry that I let you down… again." Once more, it sounded like he might be crying – but all I could think about was my own swelling panic. "I just can't figure out any other solution."

I took a deep breath.

Coping mechanisms, I reminded myself. *Coping mechanisms*.

"It's okay," I reassured him. "We'll make it work. Just worry about your daughter, and I'll take care of the rest." I was about to hang up, but I added one last addendum before I ended the call: "Some things are more important than rock and roll, right?"

Once again, I found myself at a musical crossroads.

For a split second, I envisioned some grand, triumphant repeat of the Gilman Street show, with me standing front and center at the microphone while our sidelined lead singer sent his condolences and disappeared beyond the horizon – never to be seen again.

But only for a split second.

And then that feeling was gone.

For the briefest of moments, before the overwhelming anxiety started to kick in, I had delusions of grandeur, imagining myself as the victorious protagonist in some picture-perfect movie-script ending. But, just as quickly, I realized that Call Field's return to the stage was a simple house of cards – and the King of Hearts had just removed himself from the foundation. The entire flimsy structure was about to collapse.

For this reunion concert, I had expected to hide behind the impenetrable armor of my keyboard fortress, to use my 88-key instrument as a shield from the invisible forces of anxiety and fear. Apart from that one show at Gilman Street, I hadn't ever handled lead vocals for Call Field onstage. Sure, I wrote most of our songs with my thin voice accompanying the acoustic guitar in my trembling hands… but there's a huge difference between strumming in the solitude of your dorm room and thrashing around onstage in front of real, live human beings. As it was, I already had enough anxiety welling in my body to drown an army of depressed poets. Now, suddenly, I needed to relearn an entire setlist's worth of songs in the final hours leading up to the show.

After ending the phone call with Steve, I immediately started hyperventilating. My lungs started throbbing in quick, uneven bursts, that familiar balloon of panic inflating inside my chest. I closed my eyes, trying to will away the anxiety that threatened to constrict my wind pipe and suffocate me. Even with so many years staring down the demons in my prefrontal cortex and battling the dark shadows of depression that hovered over my heart, I was still just a scared little boy fighting against overwhelming forces.

What am I going to do? I asked myself.

With my brain and my gut engaged in dubious battle, I started stomping upstairs to my office.

Right foot. Left foot.
Right foot. Left foot.
Repeat.

Right foot. Left foot.
Right foot. Left foot.
Repeat.

I forced myself to move up the staircase, step by step. Trying my best to quiet my brain, I focused on the ricocheting echoes of my footfalls.

Right foot. Left foot.
Right foot. Left foot.
Repeat.

Right foot. Left foot.
Right foot. Left foot.
Repeat.

When I reached the landing at the top of the stairs, I turned to the right and crossed the threshold into my office. Try as I might, I couldn't suppress the nervous pressure that kept expanding and swelling up from my heart. I was hyperventilating and sobbing.

I collapsed on the hardwood floor.

It was happening again.

I was starting to fall apart.

I was having a panic attack.

It turns out that the antagonist, the villain of this tale, hasn't been Steve Öken or Call Field or the cruel hand of God…
It's been mental illness.
It's been me.
This isn't a story of "man vs. man," but "man vs. self."
The conflict has *always* been inside of me.
And it might remain there forever.

I can't do this, I thought.

I can't do this.

Like so many fragments of shattered vinyl,
scattered across a hardwood flood…

I was broken beyond repair.

I was a ship unanchored,
unmoored from the shoreline.

I could feel myself slipping away.

Getting smaller.

Disappearing.

I was almost gone.

I was almost gone.

And then I saw it.

Just when I felt like my old nemesis, Anxiety, might choke the life out of me, I was jolted back by a flicker of sunshine that glinted off the floor of my office. A sliver of hope broke through the darkness – like a pinprick of illumination in the curtains of night.

It was my father's guitar.

A slant of sunlight refracted off the lacquered surface of the instrument's upper body, beckoning me towards it.

I sat up.

With my hands on the ground, I crawled forward like a corpse exhumed from its grave. In that moment, I was a shattered vinyl record drawing the pieces of myself back together, every groove etched into me like a sympathetic scar.

Slowly, deliberately, I crossed the room and wrapped my hands around my dad's acoustic guitar. Pulling it off its stand, I caressed the tuning pegs on the headstock and ran my fingers along the embossed frets that stood up from the plateau of the fretboard. I stroked the cool surface of the rosewood under my fingertips.

And I took a breath.

I tilted the guitar back and forth in my hands to examine the mystifying refractions of light. As I angled the wooden rosewood of the body in front of me, I saw my own reflection peering back in a sepia-toned mirage. Maybe it was a trick of the light, but the visage that stared back at me with its thinning hair and horn-rimmed glasses and crooked smile –

Was my father.

I'm sure you can attribute this to genetics and family resemblance and poor eyesight and a host of other rational explanations. But, in that moment, I saw a whisper of the man who raised me, who taught me almost everything I know. And with that dim reflection, that surreal slant of light, a sense of peace washed over me – not like a bucket of ice water, mind you, but a calming mist.

My father was there.

When I needed him the most, my father was there.

As he had revealed to me the summer that I turned fifteen, my father had struggled with anxiety and depression throughout his life.

While he was able to wear a deceptive mask of cheery normalcy, he suffered quietly inside for years on end. Yet, despite that beastly intrusion into his heart, he never let the darkness defeat him.

And neither would I.

I slipped my father's acoustic guitar onto my lap and started to play those familiar songs of my youth, the ones that had allowed me to share the most tender, honest pieces of myself with the world – my frustrations, my fears, my insecurities, and my triumphs. It was only a few hours until showtime, but as I strummed, I channeled the incalculable resilience I envisioned my father possessing as a wizened old man. In my moment of clarity, I let that imperceptible strength flow through my veins and arteries, from my heart to the farthest reaches of my fingertips and onto the strings of my father's guitar.

For the record, I'm a skeptic.

I don't believe in ghosts.

But that doesn't mean they don't exist.

That moment felt like a divine, angelic possession, a benign bolstering of my soul. My father's spirit coursed through me and gave me the strength to face my own demons. As absurd and ridiculous as it sounds, I felt like my father was with me in my time of need.

Everything was going to be okay.

In my core, I knew that to be true.

In the end, it didn't matter if it was an optical illusion or an incorporeal visitation from the dead. To be honest, I really don't care.

When I needed him the most, my father was there.

CHAPTER FORTY-NINE
"We're Together Again"

A few hours later, I found myself waiting in the wings of Oxnard Shores High School with my old butterscotch Fender Telecaster strapped across my shoulder. After Steve's frantic phone call, I spent an hour and a half relearning all of the songs that I'd written for Call Field, as well as the handful of covers we'd chosen to play that evening. As much as I thought that it would be a devastating task to adopt the frontman role at the last minute, I quickly fell into a natural rhythm – as if my heart was willing my body to maintain momentum on the treadmill of my life, despite the interminable anxiety that I had been unable to shake. Though my obsessive-compulsive tendencies still ached for more practice and preparation, I knew that I would be ready. Not like I had a choice, mind you, but the longing was there, nonetheless.

A quick shower and a short drive later, I was once again stepping foot on the grounds of my home-away-from-home, Oxnard Shores High School. The mood backstage was pretty jovial, though I found myself answering an endless array of questions.

When the boys in the band finally arrived and asked about Steve's whereabouts, I reached back into the dusty vaults of memory to explain. "Remember that Gilman Street gig?" I asked. "Well, this show is going to be the sequel…"

Still, though, *"Where's Steve?"* became the question of the evening. Repeated over and over. And repeated again. *Ad nauseam.*

Each time, I calmly explained that Steve's daughter had fallen sick with some bizarre, mysterious illness, and he had made the executive decision to put his family first. I can't blame the guy. And I found myself once again repeating my father's age-old mantra: "Some things are more important than rock and roll."

The warmup act for the evening was none other than the Oxnard Shores High School Jazz Band. Jacob, the soft-spoken blonde student in my AP English class who had thoughtfully contributed to the class discussion about "Incomplete," was actually one of the featured performers: little did I know, this quiet, unassuming kid was a pyrotechnic guitar prodigy. As the band swayed to some old Duke Ellington tune, Jacob's fingers flew around the frets in an insanely prodigious solo. It was almost like watching a teenage Ethan while he was in the zone, with extravagant guitar acrobatics and death-defying improvisations woven throughout the performance. It really was something to behold. And though I had never seen Jacob outside the confines of the classroom, I felt an immense pride swelling within me as I watched this bright young man – one of *my* students – shine in such a familiar forum.

As their half-hour opening set started to wind down, I felt a tug on my shirt sleeve. Turning around, I saw Veronica standing several inches taller than usual; decked out in a long, elegant evening dress and ridiculously high heels, she once again looked older than her seventeen or eighteen years. For a brief second, I imagined her as an adult: a sophisticated dentist with a family of her own and a topnotch wardrobe to match. Though it would be many years – maybe even a decade – until she finished dental school, I had no doubt that she would eventually actualize her dreams.

Heck, she managed to get Call Field back together, which is nothing short of a miracle. If the girl can pull *that* off, then grad school should be a breeze.

"Are you ready, Mr. Smith?" she asked.

"As ready as I'll ever be," I told her.

"It's not too late to back out, you know," she said, contorting her mouth into an apologetic grimace. "Especially with the Steve situation. No one would blame you for canceling."

I laughed. "I'm pretty sure that if I tried to back out, you'd beat me to death with your dad's x-ray machine."

"Mr. Smith!" she called out, melodramatically holding her right hand over her heart. "I would never do such a thing!" She lowered her fingers and gently smoothed out the folds of her dress. "Besides, an x-ray machine would be too heavy. I'd just use a bonding agent to glue you to the stage." She chuckled at her own cheesy joke and slapped me on the bicep.

That Veronica. What a kidder.

"In any case," she continued on, "you're out of time. This is the jazz band's last song, and then you guys are up." Once again, she looked at me strangely, with an awkward mixture of concern and comprehension. "Are you sure that you'll be okay?"

I glanced up at the stage, watching the members of the jazz band take their final bow amid roaring applause. "You know, Veronica, I think I am. For the first time in a long time, I think I'm going to be okay."

She patted me on the back like an encouraging teammate in the baseball dugout. "You've got this, Mr. Smith. You're going to be great."

As the students in the jazz band packed up their gear and lugged it out to the wings, Veronica sternly straightened her posture and approached the stage manager about some last-minute changes to the overhead lighting. The fragile floorboards moaned under the weight of the jazz band's multitudinous members and musical instruments. This theater *definitely* needed some restoration.

With only moments until showtime, I looked back at Chunk and Ethan and Victor, half-expecting them to turn tail and run to the parking lot. But the boys simply beamed with eager excitement.

"Are we really doing this?" I asked, my eyebrows bunched up in worried lines.

Chunk nodded his head up and down in pure, unadulterated delight. "I think we are, Brian," he said, unable to repress the smile that was forming across his face.

"Call me *Brick*," I told him. "I am only one solid piece in the architecture of this band. And I couldn't have done anything without you guys."

Ethan placed his hand in the center of our huddle, and the rest of us followed suit. "*To the past...?*" he suggested.

"To the *future*," Victor corrected him. Then he tentatively looked over at me. "Unless you have another idea, Brick."

Suddenly, a grizzled voice chimed in from behind us. "What about *Cooper...?*" the voice suggested.

We all whipped around to see Steve Öken jogging towards us from the hallway. It was like *deus ex machina...* or, in our case, *deus **ex-lead singer***. Or something like that.

A monumental wave of relief flooded throughout every limb of my body. I *might* have finally been ready to share my timid voice with the world, to stand up in the center spotlight... but I also knew that Steve was a far more formidable singer than I will ever be.

It's always the song *that's most important*, I reminded myself, *not the singer*.

"You made it!" I yelped out. "What about your daughter? Is she okay?"

"She's going to be fine," Steve told us, as we parted to make room in the circle for our indomitable lead singer. "I finally got ahold of Gwen, and she volunteered to take our kids for the night." He looked directly at me then. "Sometimes," he said, "even the ones who wound us the most can end up saving the day."

I gave him a solemn nod, and my lips curled into an earnest smile. "I think there might be a song in there," I said.

"Oh, yeah?" Steve asked, an irrepressible grin growing across his own face. "Maybe for the next album?"

"Maybe," I echoed back.

"I'm not going to let you down again, Brick," Steve told me as he threw his arm around my shoulder. "I promise you."

There was a sweet, silent moment of kinship. No matter what had transpired before, we would have each other's backs when it mattered most.

"Soooo… *Cooper*…?" Ethan asked, his wide eyebrows and stubbly chin nudging us forward through the pause.

I smirked back at him – and the rest of my brothers in the band. "*Cooper*," I agreed, grinning wildly.

Ethan, Chunk, Victor, and I gave each other a knowing smile before quickly laying our hands on top of Steve's.

"1… 2… 3…" Steve counted off for us.

"*COOPER!*" we all shouted in unison.

And then it was showtime.

Call Field was back.

At long last, the hour had arrived. Veronica went bounding onto the stage in her chic gown, exuding that improbable, paradoxical mixture of youthful giddiness and premature confidence. She was like a car with one set of tires raised up on the curb and the other set dipping down onto the street. And yet, for all that nearly imperceptible adolescent awkwardness and clumsiness, the crowd whooped for her as if she was a movie star descending to the unwashed masses.

"And now, ladies and gentlemen," she announced into the microphone positioned centerstage, "the moment that you've all been waiting for! Together again for the first time in two decades… the original members of Call Field!"

The crowd erupted in hoots and hollers and cheers and applause. Although our school's auditorium can't seat more than a thousand or so, it sounded like ten times that number of people in the audience.

As we jogged onstage with our instruments in hand, the crowd went *nuts*. Of all the concerts that we had played over the years – from our high school talent shows to the Warped Tour to the Fillmore – we had never, ever received a blissfully enraptured greeting of that magnitude.

That night, the audience at Oxnard Shores High School gave us a chance to begin again.

We had played countless times in bars and coffee shops and concert halls, but I had never actually felt like a real rock star until we walked onto the stage that night. Ironically, it wasn't until my worlds collided and the band of my youth crossed over into the realm of my professional present that I finally experienced the undiluted ecstasy of honest adoration. It was simply intoxicating – more potent than any drug or drink or pharmaceutical remedy.

"Good evening, Oxnard Shores High School!" Steve chimed into the microphone.

The crowd roared back their unrestrained response.

"Thank you for coming out tonight! We are the Call Field band from Ojai, California, and we're honored to play for you this evening!"

Right on cue, Chunk tapped out the four-count for our first song.

We were off to the races.

On the fifth beat, I hit that oh-so-familiar opening *A* chord that signaled the start of almost every show we ever played. This time, though, it wasn't the bass I was thumping: it was my butterscotch Fender Telecaster electric guitar, that life-changing Christmas gift I'd received from my parents when I was thirteen years old. Our opening song was bringing everything full circle, taking us back to the very beginning of the band.

"I wanna' be your time bomb!" Steve wailed into the mic as I strummed the electric guitar behind him. The unassailable grit in his voice announced to the world that Call Field had returned.

After that first line, the guys pummeled their instruments, playing with a sense of urgency that felt more like the kinetic energy of teenagers than the tired thrumming of forty-year-olds. Every thump of Chunk's kick drum, every screech of Ethan's guitar, and every boom of Victor's bass seemed to conjure up the spirits of our youth. As Steve cupped his brazen hands around the microphone and howled, his voice was imbued more with a vivacious gratitude for life than an angry resentment for how the years had tormented and traumatized us. It was a moment of musical majesty.

As for yours truly… I was enjoying every second of it.

All the anxious trepidation that had been welling up inside of me for two decades – all of my fears about returning to music and performing onstage and reuniting with the band – simply flooded forth from my body in beads of baptismal sweat and cleansing breath. I felt like my soul was molting, expelling the dead layers of skin that had accumulated over the years. Even with my last-minute panic attack earlier in the day, a sense of calm serenity washed over me as the band thundered through its setlist. It felt a little like finding peace in the eye of a storm – albeit a storm that had raged violently inside of me for twenty years. Though I would inevitably have to confront the other side of the cyclone – and, in the evening's aftermath, I would have to take a cold, hard look at my own wrinkled reflection in the mirror – I felt weightless and free as I feverishly strummed my guitar onstage.

While Steve hollered his way through the song, I thought back to the fifteen-year-old kid who had written "Time Bomb" – that eager, excited young man who was so smitten with his Chemistry classmate that he composed his first real song about the aching and longing he felt for her. I couldn't help but think about Serena, that confident but impetuous girl whose buoyant presence on the soccer field belied the yearning that she felt for some explosive, all-consuming romance. Though I was the one initially left disconsolate, discarded like superfluous seaweed from the hull of a boat, I wasn't the only teenager nursing a broken heart: within a few short years, my first crush would end up crushed herself. While I found myself sidelined by Serena's attraction to the handsome new kid in town, Steve Öken, their teenage conflagration was only the prologue to years of doomed devotion. As it turns out, that kind of explosive, all-consuming romance tends to leave a swath of destruction in its wake.

As Steve growled his way through the last chorus, the lyrics proved to be especially prescient for the fifteen-year-old writer of the song. *"This blaze, high above the sea, will consume you and me,"* he sang. And it was true: Serena, that brilliant shining light of our graduating class, found herself captivated and consumed by the Adonis-like lead singer of my band. Did she ever recover from that blistering relationship? It had been so many years since I'd last seen her, I had no way of knowing.

When the final, ringing notes for the song echoed through the theater, I held my breath.

Will this work? I wondered. *Will they love us? Will they hate us? Or, worst of all, will they simply feel indifferent about us?*

As it turned out, my fears were unfounded. Again. While the last power chord fizzled out into the subtle, static hum of my amplifier, the audience members sprang to their feet and responded with rapturous applause. The sound felt deafening, like thousands of ice pellets hailing from the sky onto a tin roof. Steve turned back to face the rest of us, his eyebrows curled up in confident satisfaction. And, as I looked over at Ethan and Victor, they seemed giddy with excitement. Even Chunk, usually so irrepressibly stoic, beamed with pride.

With this embellished energy guiding us, Steve twisted back to face the audience. "This next song is an anthem that we played at our high school graduation," he announced. "It seemed like an appropriate choice for a show in a high school auditorium."

Our leader singer's soliloquy elicited giggles and grins from the darkened theater. Steve was a musical snake charmer, staring down the cobra of coolness and skepticism that inhabits every crowd, and somehow managing to mesmerize them, nonetheless. Despite the audience's potential rock and roll rowdiness, Steve would tame them. He continued vamping through his introduction, and the crowd lapped up every last crumb of his monologue. Meanwhile, the band members onstage simply soaked up the unbridled buzz of the theater's energy.

As I stood there beside Steve, Fender Telecaster draped over my shoulder, I scanned the aisles for familiar faces. Even with the floodlights blurring out most of my vision, I recognized a handful of students and families behind the auditorium's orchestra pit.

Right there, front and center in the first row, I spotted the familiar silhouettes of my immediate family. Mom, Uncle Jeff, and Aunt Alyssa – the benevolent baby boomers who had essentially given birth to this band

(and, in fact, had literally birthed two of its members) – were beaming proudly at us. To Mom's right, I saw another trio of familiar faces: my sister, Marina; her husband, Reggie; and their teenage daughter, Jayden. My niece looked like a mirror image of her father, with the same athletic build, mahogany skin, and thick coils of black hair that framed her face. Marina, Reggie, and Jayden had made the trip down to SoCal from their home in San Rafael just to see the reunion concert – though they also planned on catching a Lakers game and touring some SoCal universities (including my *alma mater*, UCLA). I was a lucky man to have such dedicated and devoted family in my corner.

Just a few seats down on the stage-left side were Mr. and Mrs. Jones. Undoubtedly, they were there to support their daughter – the mastermind of this whole event. Both of them seemed utterly entertained as Steve casually chatted with the 1,000 human beings seated below him. Adjacent to the Joneses in the front row sat Brenna and the Silverman family. I recognized Mr. Silverman from our supermarket run-in earlier in the week, but I counted three children of various ages seated immediately to his right. Of course, I identified Brenna immediately, but flanking her on either side were slightly younger doppelgängers: a middle-school-aged brother and a petite sister who didn't look much older than Sam. Like the Joneses, Brenna and her siblings sat bright-eyed and spellbound by the proceedings.

In the second row, behind the Joneses, I recognized Veronica's best friends, Rita and Charlie. A little further back, I spotted half a dozen of this year's AP English students: Alexandria and John and Riya and Lekendra and Bryce and Jason were all grouped together in one long centipede of a row. I could also make out a few other kids from last year's Advanced Placement classes: Charlie and David and Randall and Susan and Julie sat in two rows on the stage-right side of the auditorium.

My daydreaming was interrupted, though, as Chunk counted us off and I started strumming the four-chord introduction to "Different Seasons." Ethan's slippery lead lines slithered in and around the chords while Victor's bass boomed below us.

"Days have passed and so have dreams..." Steve howled into the microphone. *"We are children grooooooown..."*

I had felt so old, so prematurely weathered, when I wrote those words on the precipice of my eighteenth birthday. Little did I know just how dramatically my world would twist and turn in the years ahead, how much fate would leave me staggering in the wake of unexpected pain and suffering. I envisioned myself on the day of my high school graduation, cloaked head-to-toe in a black robe, feeling so paradoxically loved and lost and lonely. Looking over at Chunk and Ethan, I remembered us sitting off in the corner of a bustling classroom before we marched down to the field – feeling like icons and outcasts, all at the same time. I've seen countless students like that over the years: kids who build a sense of celebrity in their high school microcosm, but still inhabit worlds of loneliness and isolation. It was bittersweet to think back to that time, remembering the aching sensation that I could never quite extinguish – even in celebratory moments of victory, like that long-ago commencement ceremony.

"When the time comes for different seasons," Steve sang on the chorus, *"a change of weather for the heart... We'll stand tall knowing that we've come this far..."*

It was true: the group of us on that dilapidated stage had come so far since our days as Sespe Creek High School's resident punk band. In the two decades that had passed since graduation, we had lost parents, friends, even spouses; but we'd also gained confidence and careers and children. And, somehow, like the grains of sand that accrue at the bottom of your shoes after a trip to the beach, we'd also amassed the knowledge and wisdom that accompany experience. We had gone from naïve, arrogant kids to wiser, humbler adults.

A change of weather, indeed.

When we finished "Different Seasons," we immediately launched into a punk-rock version of Johnny Cash's "Ring of Fire" – a simultaneous nod to ol' Johnny and his musical descendants, Social Distortion. We cranked the amps "to eleven" (as Spinal Tap would say) and pounded away at the song that June Carter wrote about her future husband, finding comfort in the unrequited love that lay at the heart of the lyrics. The song felt like a sweet reminder of our early days as a band, emulating the punk rock heroes that we idolized so earnestly. And now, here we were: aging punk rockers entertaining the next generation of would-be singers and screamers and strummers and drummers.

In thematically appropriate fashion, we followed up "Ring of Fire" with my paean to the Cash & Carter love story, "(Won't You Be My) June" – which also served as a thinly veiled expression of my *own* tortured romance with a certain Hawai'Irish girl in the UCLA dorms. Suddenly, I saw myself in Westwood on that sweltering September move-in day, carrying boxes up to my dorm room. I spun around to look over at Victor, my "gaysian" roommate from that first year of college, and I gave him a grateful smile. As different as we might have been, Victor had always offered an open ear for my adolescent angst, and he'd supported me in one of the most trying seasons of my life. As I longed for that beautiful girl across the hall – maddeningly close, yet so far away – Victor and I had spent hours talking about life and love and all the mixed-up emotions of young adulthood. I didn't appreciate him enough at the time, but Victor had been a great friend and collaborator, someone who was willing to drop his sketching or his organic chemistry homework to pick up his bass guitar and jam along to my newest musical composition.

"*My heart is swinging like the Tennessee Two,*" Steve sang into the microphone, "*every time I get close to you…*"

I plucked the strings on my Telecaster, trying to emulate the *boom-chicka-boom* sound that Johnny Cash developed with Luther Perkins and Marshall Grant way back in the 1950s. God, how many hours did Victor and I spend strumming guitars underneath that poster of Cash that I had hanging on our dorm room wall? Victor was an integral piece of my life, if only for a few fundamentally formative years, and I was grateful for the chance to see him once again. If nothing else, Call Field's reunion would have been worth it to reconnect with my erstwhile college roommate and long-lost friend.

After "June," the band made its way through all of the "greatest hits" in the Call Field catalogue, bringing a new sense of urgency to the songs of our youth. As we careened through "Sherilyn" and "Barbed-Wire Skies," it felt at times like Casey Jones barreling down the railroad ties – exhilarating and powerful, but almost at the precipice of flying off the tracks. Invariably, there were a few flubs – I missed a chord change in "Stop & Talk" and Chunk couldn't quite get in the pocket on "Canaan Road" – but our sheer desire to succeed kept us between the rails as we raced to the finish line.

By the time that we got to "Beautiful Girl from Heaven," our captive audience was unequivocally captivated. They clapped and cheered and applauded in all the right spots, offering us the support we craved – and, perhaps, desperately *needed* – to make it through the evening. It was hypnotic, trancelike, a shared mesmerism between the players onstage and the crowd seated below. Strumming along to "Beautiful Girl," I thought back to my prolonged courtship with Lani – our shared classes, the scratch marks and ink stains of her purple pen, the scent of hyacinth and tangerines that permeated her dorm room across the hall. I remembered the aching, the longing, the second-guessing of every nuanced movement and uttered sentence.

With a tenderness heretofore underutilized, Steve crooned out the chorus of the song as the rest of us harmonized with him. *"All I can do… is wait for you… So, I fall and I fall again for the beautiful girl from heaven…"*

When Lani came to see Call Field play at the Ventura Theater during that sweltering summer night in 1998, it was a turning point in our relationship. During our freshman year at UCLA, we had grown closer and closer – best friends who impatiently pined for each other. It wasn't until that late-July evening that things shifted between us: she had recently broken up with her boyfriend and I jumped at the opportunity to swoop in while she was single. It was a risky move – composing a song for a girl who may or may not reciprocate your feelings – but it might have been the best decision I've ever made. Writing "Beautiful Girl from Heaven" felt therapeutic and liberating, as if I was finally naming something ethereal and weightless that had haunted me for a long, trying year of heartache.

Although I had been diligently searching for them most of the evening, it wasn't until the final chorus of the song that I spotted Mel and Sam in the audience. Just like that night opening for blink-182, Mel watched me with awe and admiration – virtually ignoring the far-better-looking lead singer who captured everyone else's attention. This time, though, Mel wasn't accompanying my parents; instead, she sat by the side of our daughter. The *Beautiful Girl from Heaven* had given birth to another beautiful, heavenly girl: Samantha.

A lot can change in twenty years. The scene before me was incontrovertible proof of that.

When the last Weezer-esque notes of the song subsided, the audience once again clapped and chanted their approval. Without hesitation, we quickly plunged into the next tune, a rapid-fire version of "Wurlitzers & Women" that owed more to the Ramones than to Willie Nelson. When we finished up with that song, we plowed through a rollicking rendition of "Don't Want to See You Tonight" that brought out a bit more of the song's rockabilly swing than our recorded version on *A Different Slant of Light*. After that, we blasted off through "Sam Cooke's Soul" and "Photocopy" and our fan-favorite cover of the Ramones' "I Wanna' Be Sedated."

At the end of "I Wanna' Be Sedated," Steve drew his left arm up to his head, wiping his sweaty brow with a half-closed fist.

"Thank you, Oxnard Shores High School, for inviting us here tonight!" Steve rasped into the microphone. "It's been a few years since we've played together," he said as he whipped around towards the rest of the band scattered around the stage, "but I think we've got most of the kinks figured out."

Steve chuckled and the crowd laughed along with him. As usual, the audience was in the palm of his hand. Whereas, once, I might have felt jealous, this time I actually felt relieved; whatever anxiety I harbored about performing in front of hundreds and hundreds of people was quelled, thanks to Steve. For now, at least.

"In all seriousness, though," Steve continued, "this is a pretty remarkable experience. The last time the five of us were onstage together, we were still in college. Heck, we were barely out of high school. And now look at us… we're back in high school again." Once more, the crowd genuinely grinned along with Steve's banter.

You had to hand it to him: even after all those years offstage, he was still a natural-born entertainer. Once upon a time, I would have envied him – would have jealously scowled from the sidelines as he held court. But now, after so many years of teaching and parenting and simply growing up, I felt comfortable with my vantage point from the side of the stage. Was it humility? Maturity? Anxiety? I don't know. But, regardless of the explanation, I felt at peace with my role.

For once, I didn't long for a spot in the spires astride the apex of the building. I was comfortable being a simple brick in the foundation.

We ripped through a few more songs, from a truncated "Patterns in Snow" to a ramshackle, rocked-out version of the Beach Boys' "Surfer Girl." Yup, even twenty years down the road, Call Field still recognized our debt to Brian Wilson and company. And while *Pet Sounds* might not have been a household name for my AP English students, I definitely saw some folks in the audience singing along to every word of the song.

Including Sam.

That alone made the entire night worthwhile for me.

After we wrapped up the final notes of our Beach Boys cover, Steve once again turned to the audience and began his proselytizing. In my stubborn skepticism, I still half-expected more self-aggrandizing words and bold boasting. Needless to say, I was unprepared for what came next.

"We have one more song for you tonight," Steve panted into the microphone. "And I have a feeling you've probably heard this one before…"

Although he was in great shape for a forty-one-year-old ex-athlete, he was dripping with sweat by this point in the show. And yet, despite the greasy glint of his hair and the wet spots seeping through his tight black t-shirt, he still looked like a movie star. The bastard.

"But before we play our one big hit song," Steve continued on, over the rising volume emanating from the audience. "I want to introduce the members of our band."

It seemed like such a simple gesture, something that should be expected of every lead singer at every concert. But, considering how things ended that night at the Fillmore, the unpretentious introduction of the band came across as an earnest endeavor for forgiveness – like waving a white flag in the bloodied remains of a burned-out battlefield.

Apparently, I wasn't the only one with regrets saddling my shoulders for two decades. Despite seeming like the vile villain of my life story, Steve – yes, the antagonistic *Steve Öken* – had done some soul-searching in the intervening years. If his behavior onstage was any indication, it's a distinct possibility that Steve had been bearing his own burden of guilt for quite some time.

"Behind me, on the drums," Steve announced, "is the coolest comic-collecting cat I know. Originally from Ojai and now a resident of Marina Del Rey, we have *Charles 'Chunk' Smith!*"

As Chunk beat out a familiar surf-rock shuffle, the audience applauded wildly. I imagine that somewhere in the darkened theater, Uncle Jeff and Aunt Alyssa were beaming with pride over their comic-book-loving drummer son.

"And over here to my left," Steve continued, "we have our extraordinary lead guitarist, the coolest agricultural scientist to ever strap on a Gibson SG. Ladies and gentlemen, please give a round of applause for *Ethan 'Golf Course Guy' Hidalgo!*"

Almost immune to the roar of the crowd, Ethan started riffing on a scale in the key of D, his flashing fingers flowing fluidly over his fretboard. He made a slight bow with his torso, never missing a note of his arpeggiated sweep picking.

"Next up, all the way from Santa Maria, California," Steve shouted feverishly, "is the creator of the webcomic *The Didactic Dinosaur*, an alumnus of UCLA *and* USC, and an all-around remarkable guy. Let's give a round of applause for our bass player, *Victor 'Dino Dude' Wu!*"

Sheepishly, Victor grinned, his face flushing crimson as the audience applauded and screamed for him. He thrummed along on the bass, following Chunk's shuffle and Ethan's languid lead lines. As he palm-muted an open D-string, he raised his left hand to wave to the auditorium. As shy and reserved as Victor might have been, he seemed genuinely thrilled to be up onstage with us.

After the applause for Victor had swelled and quelled, Steve swerved around to face me. "Now, Oxnard Shores, it's time for your hometown hero…" He whipped the microphone cable around and reached out his left hand for my shoulder. "A long time ago, back when *we* were in high school, I met *this guy* on the football field. It wasn't exactly camaraderie at first sight –" He shot me a knowing grin that was equal parts humble acknowledgment and apology. "But we had a chance encounter in the locker room that changed everything. I was sitting there, wiping the sweat and grime off my uniform and I was belting out some old song…"

"It was Social Distortion's 'Ball and Chain,'" I interjected, leaning into the microphone.

"That's right," Steve said, rubbing his chin with his left hand. "Man, this guy has an incredible memory! No wonder he became a teacher…"

The crowd chuckled along with Steve's commentary. Though I felt uneasy being the subject of such a prolonged soliloquy (strangely enough, it reminded me of listening to the best man's speech at a wedding), I could tell that this was Steve's way of issuing a public apology. And *that* was definitely worth any discomfort I might have felt.

"Anyway, after he heard me singing in the locker room, he asked me to come jam with his band," Steve continued. "And when we all got together, it just *clicked*. It was like I finally knew where I was meant to be. Not only that, but all of us in the group complemented each other. While I ended up being the lead singer, I couldn't write a song to save my life."

Once again, the audience chuckled along with Steve, their eager faces illustrating just how mesmerized they were by his speech.

"And that's why *this guy* became the heart and soul of our band," Steve said, taking a step back to look at me and gesture outwards to the audience. "This next song… heck, *all* of these Call Field songs you're hearing tonight – all these melodies and lyrics – they're all written by *this guy* right here."

Steve patted me on the back and then gripped my shoulder. And that deferential act, that simple physical contact, meant more than he could possibly know.

"Ladies and gentlemen," Steve continued, "I am proud to present to you the hero of this story… The multitalented knight in shining armor and horn-rimmed glasses that you know and love… The English teacher extraordinaire who was the spiritual leader and brains behind our band… And one of the best friends I've ever had… *Brian Richard 'Brick' Smith!*"

The sound that erupted from the audience was unlike anything I've ever heard or felt in my entire life. It's human nature to crave validation, to yearn for acceptance, to long for love; and yet, so often in our day-to-day existence, we feel like our work goes unnoticed, that our worth is undervalued, that our labor is unrewarded. As a teacher, I have far too many days when I wonder if what I'm doing with my life has any impact on my students. I question if I made the right choice to cage myself in a classroom five days a week with a captive audience of teenagers. But, when the spectators in that high school auditorium jumped to their feet, hooting and hollering and screaming and clapping, it felt like everything that I'd done with my life – everything that had led me to this moment – had been worth it.

In that moment, I felt complete.

As much as I like to hide from the spotlight, shirking away the blinding illumination, it felt *really* good to soak up that long-overdue applause. Of course, being the softie that I am, I found myself choked up and a little overwhelmed. It reminded me of that famous Sally Field Oscar acceptance speech: *"You like me, you really like me!"*

Twenty years ago, Steve would have swooped in and stolen the attention for himself. This time, though, he let that applause linger and loiter. I think, deep-down inside, Steve felt guilty for the callous cruelty of his youth; this small moment of sharing the spotlight – *literally* – was his way of trying to rectify his past mistakes. And though it's impossible to ever truly repair the wreckage of the past, this felt like a small step forward.

Steve gently gestured me towards the microphone on its petrified stand, extending his muscular arms like semaphore flags. For a split second, I thought about stepping up to that glistening mic and launching into a heartfelt monologue; I contemplated using the opportunity to set the record straight and tell the crowd just how much this moment meant.

But that's not who I am. I'm not the spire at the top of the tower. I'm not the needle with an aching arm extended to the heavens.

I'm the concrete at the base of the building.

I'm the brick foundation.

And I'm okay with that.

Slowly, deliberately, I shook my head. "I don't need to speak," I told Steve in a hoarse half-shout away from the mic. "You've been singing my words all night long."

Without hesitation, Steve just nodded and acquiesced. He understood. As he walked back to the microphone stand, he raised his arms above his head and started clapping quarter-notes along with Chunk's rhythm.

"Ladies and gentlemen," Steve called out to the crowd, "We didn't think we'd ever get the chance to do this again… but here we are." He glanced behind him, surveying the four of us scattered across the stage, before turning back to face the audience. A big smile swept across his face as he pointed at me. *"Hit it, Brick!"*

On his command, I started strumming the song that changed my life – all of our lives. Ethan swooped in and slid through the octave chords that comprised the intro riff. Victor bashed the D-string on his bass. Chunk pounded the drums like a tank slamming into roughhewn soil. Steve lurched into the microphone like a man reborn.

"California can be cruel in the summer…" he roared.

And the crowd erupted.

When you're young, life is full of infinite possibilities. Your hopes stretch higher than the heavens and reach farther than any ocean could ever take you. As you get older, however, those dreams diminish. The wear and tear of age and responsibility dim the horizons.

If you're lucky, though, those hopes can be resurrected for fleeting moments. Dwindling ashes can give birth to fiery hours. Maybe it's just hearing your favorite song in concert or feeling the gentle brush of the autumn wind against your bare skin – but those moments are priceless, valuable beyond words.

For the briefest of moments, you can be infinite once again.

Miraculously, we were just as good as we had been twenty years ago – if not better. We thrashed our way through "Incomplete" as if it was the last time that any of us would ever appear onstage, strumming and singing and screaming and sweating like a unified force of nature – like an omnipotent tidal wave, completely unstoppable and unbreakable.

On our own, each one of us was a single, solitary stream.

Together, we were a riveting, righteous river.

Nothing could stop us. Nothing could tame us. We were brothers-in-arms, unified by music and bound to one another with the anchors of the past, the tethers of the present, and the threads of the future.

And when our voices joined together in harmony, when the waters met the sand, the world was ours.

CHAPTER FIFTY
"Keepin' the Summer Alive"

Against all odds, Call Field's reunion was a smashing success. In addition to the psychological and spiritual rewards of playing the show, we raised something like $30,000 for the school. We also received some good press and renewed interest in the band: Mel told me later that *#CallField* was trending on social media, with photos and videos of the band flooding Twitter and Instagram and TikTok and Facebook and Snapchat and whatever other platforms everyone is using these days.

Plus, I was able to put my ghosts to rest.

When the concert ended and guests had been greeted and hands had been shaken and equipment had been loaded, we gave each other hugs and promised that it wouldn't be another twenty years before we played another show. It felt like being a kid again – minus the insecurity and jealousy and petty infighting, of course. I never thought that my life could've taken such a dramatic set of twists and turns.

And maybe it wouldn't have without Veronica Jones.

After almost everyone had gone home and the custodial staff was wheeling in oversized plastic trash bins, Veronica caught up with me. She had changed out of her fancy-schmancy evening attire and put on her usual garb: jeans and a t-shirt. Instead of her ubiquitous BYU sweatshirt, though, she was wearing an unzipped black hoodie.

"What do you think of the t-shirt?" she asked. She stretched out her top from the bottom-fold stitching so that I could see the screen-printed graphic more clearly.

For a split-second, I thought it was a Ramones shirt: it had the familiar star-laden black-and-white circle with a set of names ringing around the middle image. But instead of *Johnny, Joey, Dee Dee,* and *Tommy*, it listed a different set of characters: *Brick, Chunk, Ethan, Steve,* and *Victor*. And while the Ramones logo featured a presidential bald eagle at the center, emblazoned on Veronica's shirt was the image of a phoenix rising from a blazing pyre. In weathered font above the graphic was a familiar set of two words: *Call Field*.

Yup. Veronica Jones was wearing a Call Field t-shirt.

I stifled a surprised chuckle. "Where did you get that?" I asked her. "I've never seen that design before…"

"We had these printed *especially* for this show," she explained in her typically bouncy manner. "And did you see the writing inside the banner?" she asked, pointing to the base of the graphic.

I squinted my eyes to examine the image on her shirt. At first glance, I had overlooked some subtle, nearly microscopic text: it was a brief sentence, a concise clause stringing together three simple words.

Hindsight is 2020, it read.

"Rita came up with the design," she clarified. "I know how much you love the Ramones, and we thought t-shirt sales would be an easy way to raise some additional money for the theater."

I couldn't help but grin. *This kid thinks of everything*, I mused to myself.

"Plus," she added, "we thought it would be a great way to immortalize our *Captain, My Captain*." She paused, suddenly unsure of herself. "Do you like it…?"

"How could I not?" I chuckled back.

A brief silence started to settle on us like a fine film of stardust. As much I hate baring my soul to anyone – let alone a *teenager* – I knew that I needed to thank this remarkable kid in front of me.

"You know, Veronica," I began sheepishly, "I really didn't want to do this."

"Do what?" she asked.

"You know…" I said, gesturing around us at the stage and the theater. "*This*… Playing music again. I thought that I had left that piece of my life behind me, buried in ashes and debris. I used to get panic attacks just *thinking* about Call Field…" I stopped talking and took a deep breath.

"But now…?" she asked, urging me on.

"But now I know how much I missed having this in my life… and how much I'm going to need it in the future, too. So, thank you."

"You're welcome, Mr. Smith," she said. And then she punched me in the arm. "I knew that you had it in you the whole time."

It was hard to believe that my worlds had converged at such an unlikely juncture. I stared up at the rafters, envisioning the multitude of outcomes that could have lain in store for me, if only one or two things had gone differently in my life. In some ways, it was an accumulation of an infinite number of small choices and results, all of which guided me to this exact moment in time. I looked back at Veronica, that precocious twelfth-grade student, and sighed.

"You know, Veronica, my life could have gone in so many different directions. I could have tried to stay in the music business. I could have tried my hand at journalism. Heck, I could have gone to law school. But, instead, I chose to become a high school English teacher."

"Do you think you made the right decision?" she asked me.

I turned back to face Veronica, paused, and looked her in the eyes. "Absolutely," I told her. "Maybe I could have gone back to the band, gone back to a career in the music industry. But if I had done that, I would never have met so many amazing kids – so many remarkable *human beings* – at this important intersection in their lives." I gave her a knowing grin. "And I never would have met you."

"Aw, shucks," she smirked.

"That's the thing about teaching. You might not have the superficial rewards of fame and fortune, and you *definitely* get humbled along the way, but you also have the chance to make real human connections. And I wouldn't trade my time with you and the thousands of other students I've taught. Not for anything."

Veronica looked away from me, her eyes traveling up to the dulled lights that hung half-illuminated from the metallic rafters above us. "It looks like you've done it all, Mr. Smith. You went to college, got married, had a kid. You did the rock star thing. And now you've done it again." Her gaze, steadily focused on the horizon, never wavered as she spoke. "So, what do you do after your dreams come true?"

"You become a high school English teacher," I told her. "And help young men and women achieve *their* dreams. And maybe, just *maybe*, one of those students will go off to college, sing in a couple of coffeehouses, and then return home to take over her dad's dental practice. And one day, that favorite student of yours – no matter how big of a pain she might have been during her senior year of high school – will end up becoming your favorite dentist."

Veronica turned to me and blushed. "Thank you, Mr. Smith," she said.

"Thank *you*, Veronica," I echoed back. "It turns out you were right. I *did* need that root canal, after all."

Veronica snorted an honest laugh. "Well, now that you have your root canal, and the band is back together, anything can happen. You have an infinite number of paths in front of you. The world is yours for the taking, Mr. Smith. Expect the unexpected!"

After so many years of anxiety and depression and frustration and bitterness, it felt like the interminable darkness of night had faded into the promising hues of a new sunrise.

It seemed like the bright crest of the horizon was hovering just within our grasp, ready for a new chapter of limitless potential. For a few brief moments, it felt like everything was golden and magical and laced with endless possibilities.

And then, a few weeks later, the world shut down.

A lot can happen in a year and a half.

Eighteen months is enough time for a global pandemic to sweep across every continent and every country, leaving billions of souls frantic and afraid. It's enough time for a novel virus to infect over two hundred million people, with a trail of over four million dead in its wake. That's *four million* families who have lost a daughter or a son, a mother or a father. And I know exactly how devastating that can feel.

The Portuguese have a word, *saudade*, which describes the deep, melancholy longing that we feel for someone who is absent from our lives. The collective trauma of the last year has left us all grieving. It's not an exaggeration to say that this simmering sentiment of *saudade* has become a permanent companion, an unwelcome passenger wherever we travel. All it takes is one hundred and eighty days to twist us around 180°. And we've lapped that ring three times since the world shut down.

A year and a half is enough time for the improbable to become possible, for modern sentences to etch themselves into history books. It's enough time for a volatile presidential election, a terrorist takeover of the United States Capitol, and the proliferation of countless condemnable conspiracy theories. But it's also enough time for a new presidential term, with the country's first female vice-president, as well as a slew of other brand-new elected officials. It's enough time for a new day in America – and the rest of the modern world.

Eighteen months is also enough time for brilliant scientists, working at a blistering pace, to utilize cutting-edge mRNA technology to manufacture a vaccine administered to billions of individuals, leading to the greatest number of lifesaving inoculations in almost a century. It's enough time for these real-life heroes to save the world.

And it's also enough time for a mild-mannered almost-rock-star turned English teacher to finish writing his entire life story.

Veronica was right, but not in the way that she anticipated. The unexpected *did* happen: COVID-19 swept across the world, causing unprecedented disruptions to our lives. For the remainder of that spring, we faced lockdowns and quarantines and face masks and a frenzy of other frustrations. Seemingly overnight, the world as we knew it changed in a multitude of unforeseen ways.

Just as everything in my life seemed to be a dream come true, as I was once again sailing high in the heavens with wings made of wax, the blistering heat of reality sent us all spiraling towards the unpredictable waters below us. As we crashed into those cold, unforgiving waves, we were forced to reevaluate what we hold dear.

All of the simple things that we took for granted, with expectations of permanence and predictability, retreated from view. And, while it was hard for *all* of us, it was uniquely challenging for high school kids.

No prom. No senior ball. No baseball or swimming or track & field. No jam-packed graduation parties. No celebratory summer trips overseas. No warm embraces from dear friends or acquaintances.

California *was* cruel last summer – but not because of cold fronts or gray skies or sunburn-giving girls. It wasn't the weather that weighed down our souls and anchored our lives. It was something bigger, something vaster than all of us combined.

Speaking of sunburns…

A few days after the Call Field reunion show, just before the world went into lockdown, I received a beige envelope in the mail from an unfamiliar address – but with vaguely familiar handwriting. The swooping, curling cursive was like a match in the dim, dusky darkness of my brain, reminding me of a towering presence from the caverns of my past. When I opened up the fresh, tender envelope, I realized what it was.

A letter from Serena Rios.

It's been years since I've seen her or spoken with her or even written to her. Though I had once spent every waking hour thinking of Serena, hanging on her every word, I was no longer the love-struck teenage boy that had been so smitten with her. I'm not sure why I was so nervous, why I trembled when I tore open the beige envelope, but I guess there was still some small, imperceptible piece of me that felt throttled when that looming shadow of my past darkened my present. With trembling hands, I held the letter in front of me and read.

> *Dear Brick,*
>
> *I hope that this letter finds you well. Imagine my surprise when I flipped open my Facebook feed a few days ago and saw all*

the headlines and photographs from your recent reunion show! My husband and my kids didn't understand how big of a deal that was, how reading something about a silly high school band could have such a profound effect on me. I guess that's because they don't know the whole story.

I'm still "friends" with Steve, despite everything that transpired between us (he's the one who forwarded your mailing address to me), and he simply flooded social media with snapshots from your benefit concert. Reading through it all, I felt myself involuntarily choking up and thinking about the good old days. Never underestimate the power of nostalgia, right?

I've thought about you quite a bit these last few years. I've wondered how you've been, how your life has developed, where fate has taken you. Are you settled? Are you happy? Do you wish you could have done things differently?

I still listen to your old albums. Before, it used to be about Steve: his voice, his face at the front and center. But now I look past his shadow. I listen to the words and the melodies and I realize... It's you.

It was always you.

I get a little teary-eyed sometimes, and I realize that things could have happened very differently. In those days, I was blinded by youth and by Steve's good looks. I didn't see what was right in front of me the entire time. I understand that now.

I can't help but wonder: how differently would our lives have turned out if I had made different choices? What if I had chosen the writer instead of the messenger?

I guess we'll never know.

Take care of yourself, Brick.

Love,
Serena

I stood there at the kitchen counter for a few minutes, reading and rereading her letter. It was strange to hear from another ghost of my youth – but, I suppose, no stranger than any of the other events that had transpired over the months leading up to the concert. As my eyes scanned over the words captured in the girlish calligraphy of her handwriting, I felt a slight shiver up my spine. Those swooping, curling characters reminded me of old sunburns, those aching feelings of yesteryear that had been buried deep in the trenches of my heart. It was a little like running fingers over an old wound that has healed and left behind a barely visible blemish – scarred, but no longer sensitive to the touch.

Serena was right: we'll never know. But I'm okay with that.

There is something I believe firmly in my heart: my life turned out better with Mel than it ever could have with Serena. While the young Miss Rios might have been my first fleeting love, she wasn't my last. The final, forever romance that I couldn't have foreseen when I was fifteen years old is still playing out its lifelong trajectory.

And that forever romance was standing only a few feet away from me.

"What's that?" Mel asked.

"It's nothing," I answered with a smile. "Just another ghost from high school."

I crumpled the letter, opened the creaking metallic lid of the trashcan, and threw away this relic from my past.

But I digress.

In the weeks that followed Call Field's resurrection, teachers everywhere (including yours truly) were forced to reinvent themselves: Zooming replaced Xeroxing, FaceTime calls replaced face-to-face conversations. Somehow, though, we completely revitalized an age-old profession for these unprecedented times.

After my students completed an online administration of the AP English test (fun fact: Brenna told me that she quoted "Incomplete" in one of her essays), it was a short – but seemingly endless – sprint from final exams to graduation. And, when the Oxnard Shores High School class of

2020 held their drive-through commencement ceremony at the Channel Islands Harbor (live-streamed, of course, for those at home), I was waiting for them on the stage…

Guitar in hand.

Two years ago, it would have been unfathomable for me to consider playing music in front of my students – virtually *or* in-person – as part of a graduation ceremony. But, two years ago, it would have been impossible to predict that an international pandemic would completely reshape our lives.

Expect the unexpected, indeed.

When it came time for Oxnard Shores High School to plan that year's ceremony, Veronica Jones had one last favor to ask of me. My star student, Sam's favorite babysitter, wanted to sing at graduation. But, as with the Winter Spectacular talent show, she needed a guitarist.

"You won't even need to learn a new song," she reassured me via a Zoom meeting. "It's one that you're very, very familiar with."

"What did you have in mind?" I asked.

"Well, Mr. Smith, you've inspired me this year," she began to say, before rushing through a caveat. "And I'm not talking about the Call Field thing or the UCLA thing or even anything related to school at all."

I laughed to myself. "If it's not school and it's not Call Field, what else is left?"

"You'll be happy to hear that I've been listening to the Beach Boys pretty much nonstop for the last few months," she said. "In-between my daily doses of Call Field, of course."

"*Of course*," I murmured back to her in the ironic, self-deprecating tone that's become my trademark.

"Anyway, I'm finally starting to understand why you and your dad were so obsessed with the band. There's some really good stuff in their catalogue… like *really* good."

"You don't have to tell *me* that," I reminded her with a grin.

"So, there's one song in particular that I think would be perfect for me to sing… I mean, for *us* to play. And it's one that you'll really appreciate, I think."

"And what song is that, Veronica?"

She hesitated for a split second, her eyes diverting away from the camera, and then quickly looked back at me. "I want to sing 'Love and Mercy' at graduation," she said.

"*'Love and Mercy,'*" I echoed aloud. After all that I'd been through with Veronica, she was bringing things back to very personal territory. And now that she'd heard my complete, unvarnished story, she knew exactly how much that song meant to me.

"I mean, I know it's *technically* not a Beach Boys song," she sputtered, "but it's still Brian Wilson. And I know how you feel about him."

There was something truly uncanny about the wheel of my life coming full-circle like this. Again. The last time that I had played "Love and Mercy" in public, it was on a high school stage at my father's funeral. And now, twenty years later, the young lady whom I had come to consider an adopted second daughter was asking me to play the song at a high school commencement ceremony.

For my father, it had been an ending.

But for Veronica, this would be a new beginning.

And while a fortune teller would have come in handy during the chaotic mess that was 2020, you don't need a crystal ball or perfect vision to forecast what happened next.

When Veronica and I sauntered up to the makeshift stage by the Channel Islands docks on the day of her high school graduation, it was a breezy, lazy almost-summer evening. The sun was slowly cresting towards the horizon, scattering gold and auburn hues across the heavens. As the crowd of a few dozen masked onlookers (Veronica's family and the school district's camera crew among them) watched us with rapt attention, my fingers started to move in their mechanical rhythm, picking out the chords for Brian Wilson's undisputed masterpiece.

"This song is a prayer for peace in all the seasons of our lives," Veronica said into the analog hum of the microphone, as I made my way through the instrumental opening bars of the song. "And even with everything that's going on in the world right now, I'm grateful that I get to sing this song for you tonight with our very own Mr. Smith…"

The small crowd of staff members, district personnel, and family members cheered and clapped. And I couldn't suppress the smile that was slowly, earnestly forming around my lips.

Veronica began to sing the first verse of the song as a heavier breeze drifted towards us from the nearby water. Despite the less-than-ideal conditions, her voice reverberated gorgeously across the dock, captivating everyone within earshot. When it came time for the chorus, I stepped up to my microphone and harmonized with Veronica's shimmering voice.

"Love and mercy…" we sang together as I strummed that simple, repeating chord progression. *"Love and mercy…"*

We made our way through the song, our voices melding together more confidently with each successive line. When it came time for the big choral moment, when an army of vocals usually bombards the listener, I stopped plucking the guitar strings and let our unaccompanied voices soar together in the evening air. For the final chorus, Veronica looked over at me, glowing in the glory of her big moment. *"Love and mercy…"* we sang together.

Love and mercy. That's what the world needed when Brian Wilson wrote his signature song in the late 1980s. And Lord knows we need that now, more than ever.

When it was all over, Veronica rushed over in her flowing black robe and sandal wedges. With tears brimming in her eyes, she folded her hands in front of her in gratitude. "Thank you!" she shouted to me over the deafening din of the wind-whipped docks. "Thank you for everything."

Even with the mandated six-foot physical distance between us, I had never felt closer to my star student than at that moment in time.

As she turned away, I surveyed the dozens of folks on the ground before us. I sheepishly waved at the crowd before slipping offstage.

It was my first time performing at a high school graduation as a staff member. But I have a feeling that it won't be my last.

CODA

I got lost sometimes in the melodies of my mind,
where I tried to find what I need.
And the crashing tide swept me off my feet,
But you've made me feel complete now for a while...
And it's just like your smile.

EPILOGUE
"The Last Song"

It's just one step at a time.
Right foot. Left foot.
Right foot. Left foot.
Repeat until the end of the story.

Though it's summer and I have no reason to wake up early, I couldn't sleep. When I glanced over at the red numbers on the face of the digital clock this morning, the digits beamed at me brilliantly across the room with a bright *5:19 AM* registered on the screen. Despite the unholy hour, I knew it was time to get up.

After quietly creeping out of bed, I stealthily changed into my running gear, laced up my shoes, left a note for Mel, grabbed my keys, and headed out the front door before my girls could wake up. As I stepped outside, the morning air was crisp in its misty August chill. Without much forethought, I cued up my iPhone and pressed play. The Beach Boys came streaming through my earbuds, the swirling opening strains of "Sail On, Sailor" chiming along as my feet cycled through step after step.

Right foot. Left foot.
Right foot. Left foot.
Repeat until the end of the story.

As I continued jogging down Harbor Boulevard – that gray, rootless boundary that separates Oxnard Shores from the neighboring city of Ventura – the shimmering sounds of the Beach Boys filled my ears. Over the course of my run, "Sail On, Sailor" made its way into "Wouldn't

It Be Nice" and segued to "Good Vibrations," my heavy footfalls muted by the music blaring through my noise-cancelling AirPods. By the time that I got to "Heroes and Villains" and "God Only Knows," I was already a few miles deep into my run, the Ventura pier and fairgrounds somewhere just beyond the horizon.

It was an interesting convergence, the music in my ears and the scenery around me swirling in my mind with images of years gone by, and I thought about my first concert after the COVID lockdown. It was a "concert in your car" show at the Ventura Fairgrounds – kind of like those old drive-in movie theaters, but with a massive scaffolded stage instead of a static supersized screen.

You can probably take a wild guess which band we went to see.
The Beach Boys.

It was the first night of Oxnard Shores High School's October break, almost one year (to the day!) after Veronica Jones initially interviewed me about my time with Call Field. Though it was truly bizarre to watch a live concert from the vaguely comfortable cushions of my car, the stars seemed to have aligned for me: The Beach Boys. Here. Just a few miles from where I live in Oxnard. During a pandemic that prevented the performance of any and all live music. Needless to say, I was in heaven.

As the Beach Boys have done many times over the years, the Mike Love incarnation of the band (minus Brian Wilson and Al Jardine, unfortunately) played the aforementioned Ventura Fairgrounds in our fair sister city to the northwest. The throngs of people who attended the show were probably ignorant to the fact that two of the band's most important (not to mention *founding*) members were absent from the show. In fact, I would assume that most of the attendees were probably just excited to hear key hits from the *Endless Summer* or *Sounds of Summer* compilations.

Heck, after half a year in lockdown, they were probably just excited to get out of their houses and see some live music.

Of course, the Beach Heads in the crowd (like yours truly) went in with a much more discerning eye. We recognized that what we would see onstage was not a perfect facsimile of our beloved band in its 1960s heyday; rather, it was a resurrected reincarnation of that mythic group from Hawthorne, CA. But, as someone whose band has only recently risen from the ashes, I can't speak ill of any other musical phoenixes out there.

I won't badmouth Mike Love or Bruce Johnston – or even John Stamos, for that matter. I respect all of them for preserving the Beach Boys' legacy in the face of such overwhelming odds. I mean, how many other bands of their caliber can still respectably tour after fifty long, tumultuous years together? Call Field couldn't even make it through one complete decade, so I have no right to disrespect a band that's been around (in one incarnation or another) for half a century.

The whole is greater than the sum of its parts. Brian Wilson wasn't the Beach Boys. Brian, Carl, Dennis, Mike, Al, David, *and* Bruce were the Beach Boys – and, if you're going to get super-technical, so were Ricky Fataar and Blondie Chaplin and Glen Campbell. The Wilson brothers and all their compatriots (familial and platonic) were a heavenly choir harmonizing over raucous rock 'n' roll, finding common ground in the shared music where they defined themselves and their places in the world.

Call Field was no different.

It's been arrogant of me all these years to believe that I was the only "true" member of the band. For too long, I thought Call Field was nothing without me – and they thought I was nothing without them.

The truth, however, was somewhere in the middle.

We were nothing without each other.

Our reunion concert showed us that we still have an audience. There are folks out there whose lives we touched with our melodies and lyrics and concerts and albums. And they like us enough to come out and watch us play on a ramshackle high school stage. Not bad for a bunch of punk rock songs from our youth.

Recently, Steve has been in contact with a few record labels – some big and some not-so-big. They've expressed interest in bringing us out of retirement, planning a tour, and perhaps even arranging for some studio time to record new material. Steve has been advocating for us to follow that path, to join hands and saunter up that Yellow Brick Road towards the improbably attractive Emerald City of fame and fortune.

It could be a rock and roll renaissance for Call Field… or it could become an unmitigated disaster of feuding egos and financial catastrophe. Would our reunion be an exercise in nostalgia or a victory lap? Could it be both?

If we look to the Beach Boys for guidance, it's easy to believe that we could make *something* work – put some incarnation of Call Field out on the road and relive our glory days from the turn of the century. Maybe we'd even beat the odds and churn out some inspired new material that resonates with our old fans, while culling new audience members from the throngs of music-obsessed teenagers who weren't even born when *A Different Slant of Light* was released.

But, as with The Beach Boys, it's impossible to guarantee that our semi-permanent reunion would lead to longterm prosperity. After Brian Wilson and company reached brilliant heights in the 1960's, they struggled to define themselves in the aftermath of that stratospheric success. Sure, they had some remarkable albums scattered throughout the early 1970s, but they floundered for a long time until their unlikely renaissance with "Kokomo." It took The Beach Boys a while to understand their impact, but their music is like an iridescent gem that shines brightly in the face of ever-present darkness. You just need to brush off the accumulated dust and sand that sometimes obscure their legacy.

Can Call Field come back from the dead and create a worthy successor to *A Different Slant of Light*? Can the band resurrect itself from the dusty graveyard of one-hit-wonders and find sustainable success?

Honestly, I don't know. But I'm at peace with that uncertainty.

To circle back to the concert: that evening's Beach Boys show was a bittersweet one. It was a serendipitous opportunity to see our family's all-time-favorite musical group, but Samantha didn't get to experience the concert with the band's biggest fan: her grandfather.

I'm sure Mel will say that my Beach Boys obsession is a desperate attempt to cling to the fading vestiges of my father's life. She's probably right. But it's more than that. We inhabit these songs and these albums because they are passports to different places, different lives. We all need some fun, fun, fun to make it through the day. Because in a world of shattered vinyl, every scratched trace of the past matters. Every record counts.

I have no doubt that my dad, the man Samantha's heard countless stories about (but whom she never met), would have *loved* to sit next to his luminescent granddaughter, swaying in time with all of those old hits from his youth. No matter how polished, professional, and charming the assembly of musicians onstage might have been, something pivotal was missing for me.

My father – Samantha's grandfather – wasn't there.

Maybe because of that overwhelming absence, the most wonderful moments of the show (for me, at least) happened offstage: it was the way Samantha's eyes lit up when she recognized the opening, cooing vocals of "Surfer Girl" and the way that Mel slipped her fingers into mine when the band struck up the chiming guitar arpeggios of "Wouldn't It Be Nice." Despite what the young Brian Richard Smith, Jr. thought twenty years ago, music itself should not provide the defining moments of a person's life; rather, music is merely the vehicle for awakening emotions in its listeners. The best music reminds us that we live blessed lives, and it enhances the enlightening emotions that we feel. For years, the Beach Boys have done that for me – and I would like to think that Call Field's music might have done that for someone else.

Alas, there were no fireworks at the fairgrounds that time.

When Lani and I came to the fair on our first date, we were just wide-eyed kids with an irrepressible sense of wonder. We were barely out of high school, and the whole world seemed full of limitless possibilities. We didn't know the heartbreak that we'd endure, the magnificent heights we'd climb, or the subtle joy that aging would bring to us in our autumn years.

Young love starts with the explosions of fireworks, but eventually settles into a comfortable candlelight. It's been twenty-three years since the night that Lani and I shared our first kiss. Since then, we've weathered our fair share of peaks and valleys; yet, no matter how dark the veil, we've refused fate's attempts to extinguish our flame. Sometimes, in the turbulent winds, our candle might flicker and tremble. But we never let our shared light go out.

Returning to the fairgrounds with Samantha that day, it felt like everything was coming full circle. When I was young, I went to the county fair to shuffle through the rows of neon lights with my parents; years later, underneath a fireworks-laden sky, Lani and I shared our first date there; and that night seeing the Beach Boys, I set out to share the illumination with my beautiful wife and daughter. What more could an almost-rock-star turned English teacher possibly hope for?

Right foot. Left foot.
Right foot. Left foot.
Repeat until the end of the story.

Last week, Sam came and sat next to me at the dining room table while I diligently typed away on the keyboard of my laptop. I've been working on this autobiography for months now – from October break of 2019 through the pandemic shutdown of 2020 and into the summer of 2021. To borrow a phrase from the Grateful Dead, it's been a *long, strange trip*. Seriously.

I've kept myself busy this summer, with every spare moment spent in a mad-dash sprint through the chapters of my life. Needless to say, all those weeks off from Oxnard Shores High School have definitely been put to good use. Now that the days are drawing to an end, however, I'm once again racing against the clock to finish before I run out of time.

I've been lucky, though. While Mel has been at her *Oxnard Breeze* office (undoubtedly banging her head in frustration as she edits innumerable not-ready-for-print articles), Sam has been at "Mermaid Summer Camp" all day, swimming mile after mile at the pool and in the ocean. My daughter is clearly living her best life.

I, on the other hand, find myself glued to a hazy computer screen, recounting all my explosive exploits, errors, and extrications. From what I've read about writing books, I assumed that it would take a lot longer than it has. Of course, when you're working uninterrupted for more than eight hours a day and averaging two-to-three pages an hour, you can get a lot more accomplished than you might anticipate.

Anyway, as I was saying, I was writing yet another chapter in this rigorous retelling of my life's story, when Sam situated herself next to me at the table, her bony frame hunched near the laptop screen.

"How's your book coming along, Daddy?" she asked.

I yawned and stretched out my arms, feeling the invisible weight of seven hours worth of typing flow through my aching fingers. "It's going really well, actually," I told her. "I mean, I *think* it's going well. It's my first time writing a book, so I can't really say if I'm doing a good job or not. I just don't know what I don't know, you know?"

Sam gave me a quizzical expression. "I have no idea what you're saying, Dad." She rolled her eyes at me, before looking over at the computer screen.

Samantha is starting to get kind of sassy for a soon-to-be fifth-grader. But, as long as she doesn't break any more of my priceless vinyl artifacts, I'll cut her some slack.

Samantha squinted and studied the header in the upper right-hand corner of my Microsoft Word document before turning back to face me. "Daddy, why is your book called *Incomplete…*?"

"Well, Sam," I explained, "that was the title of the most popular song that I wrote. It makes sense to use the most famous thing that I've done as the title for my life story, right?"

"Okay…" she said, not entirely satisfied with my explanation. "But what does it *mean*…?"

"It means that everything in life is a work-in-progress," I told her. "As long as I'm alive, my story will continue to be written, even when I'm done with the last page of this book. And that's one of the big, essential questions that I'm trying to address: is life ever *really* complete?"

"Only when you're dead," she answered. She curled up her lips in distaste, as if death was a bite of bitter broccoli. "So… as long as you're still living, your life is incomplete?"

"That's right, Sam," I agreed, tucking a rogue strand of hair behind her right ear.

"Then I hope that your story stays incomplete forever," she told me, her smile brightening as she grabbed my hand. "And I hope that you'll be with me for as long as I live."

"I can't be with you *forever*, Sam," I whispered softly into the afternoon air. "But I'm going to stick around for as long as I can."

She leaned into me and squeezed me tightly. "You promise?"

"I promise you, Samantha." I sighed and kissed the top of her frizzy head. "Because there is nothing in this world more important to me than you."

Right foot. Left foot.
Right foot. Left foot.
Repeat until the end of the story.

I'm thinking about last night's show. Unlike the big hoopla surrounding Call Field's reunion last year, the coffee shop gig less than twelve hours ago was a simple, understated affair – just a guy and his guitar in front of a small crowd, no different than any other other obscure small-time performance in an indistinct small-town American suburb. However, despite all its commonplace qualities, it was a momentous occasion for me: it was my very first solo show.

It also would have been my father's seventy-fifth birthday.

To commemorate the event, to celebrate three quarters of a century since Dad was born, I figured I would honor my father's memory by doing something I had never done before. So, on August 14th, 2021, I played my first concert. Kind of.

More importantly, I took my dad's sage advice to heart: *I sang the hell out of it.*

When Steve told me twenty-five years ago that I would never make it as a singer, it crushed me, silencing my still-developing voice. I was content playing the director for a long time, letting others take center stage while I patiently stood in the wings, watching from a distance; now, though, I understand how important it is to let the spotlight shine in your face and let the songs pour forth from your lungs.

The opening act was (who else?) *Veronica Jones*, in her very first coffee shop performance. That same precocious kid, the star student who once shared with me that she had a lifelong dream of playing her own café gig, finally got to live out one of her folk-rock fantasies. As she weaved her way through the eclectic mix of songs in her set, covering Fleetwood Mac and the Civil Wars and Death Cab for Cutie, she was backed by the strumming of my now-former student, Jacob – the blonde kid whose jazz-band chops so impressed me the night of Call Field's reunion show. Throughout their set, Jacob confidently strummed as Veronica stood front and center, captivating the small crowd with her crystalline voice. It was a sweet, endearing, imperfect set of folk songs from two of my favorite students.

Mel and I have put Veronica to good use a handful of times since that graduation performance, allowing our spunky daughter a few more opportunities to visit with her favorite babysitter. Each time, Sam lights up the second that she sees Veronica cross the threshold into our humble home. Despite the near-decade age difference between the two girls, it's like they're long-lost friends who have finally been reunited after years apart. Of course, I know that they'll eventually outgrow each other as they move on to the different seasons of their lives. But I have a feeling that one day, when Veronica Jones opens her very own dental practice, she'll have one very excited young patient ready to share smiles with her favorite former-babysitter once again.

When it was my turn to take the stage, I was surprisingly nervous. Though I've played countless shows with Call Field over the years, I've never been alone on stage before (notwithstanding my graduation audition and my father's memorial service, of course). Just like I've been doing all year, though, I took a succession of deep breaths, calmed myself, and forced myself to step out onto the makeshift stage.

I played some of my favorite Call Field songs – albeit in a stripped-down manner, reminiscent of the late evenings in which I wrote most of the melodies in a lonely bedroom or garage or dorm room. Of course, I sang "Sherilyn" and "June" and "Different Seasons." And I even played a countrified arrangement of "Time Bomb." Though the tunes sounded drastically different than the punk-rock versions Call Field recorded in the late 1990s, the "unplugged" environment better mirrored the solo settings in which I wrote these songs. Even without all the dramatic fuzz and flourish of the boys in the band, my lyrics and melodies still managed to keep the crowd entertained throughout the set.

"That's how you know if a song's worth its salt," my dad once told me. *"If you can play it on an acoustic guitar and it still stands up."*

By my dad's standards, I would say that my songs stood up pretty well last night.

In between my original compositions, I interspersed some well-chosen covers, including (of course) some Brian Wilson tunes: "Surfer Girl," "Sail On, Sailor," and "Love and Mercy." Everyone instantly recognized "Surfer Girl" – it *is* a fan-favorite Beach Boys song, obviously – but "Sail On, Sailor" drew some quizzical looks from the crowd. Not everyone is a card-carrying Beach Head, I guess. Whatever. It's still one of the best things the Beach Boys have ever done.

When it came time for "Love & Mercy," I invited Veronica up onstage to sing with me. This time, however, we traded off verses in a duet – like the musical partners that we've become over the past year and a half. Even if the kid has some growing left to do, the girl can *sing*.

Throughout the whole set, Samantha stared at me, wide-eyed and broadly smiling. Leaning back in her seat, Sam curled up against Mel, whose bronze arms wrapped around our daughter's diminutive frame. The expression that Samantha wore seemed eerily familiar: it was the same look of pride and amazement that I had shown my dad when I saw him play guitar and sing with the Stuttering Surfers at his fortieth birthday party. If nothing else, the night was worth it to see Sam beaming with pride. In that moment, I felt loved and supported and whole.

In that sweet, sweet moment, I finally felt complete.

It wasn't an epic performance. In fact, I only played for about 45 minutes before I introduced the final song for the evening.

"This next one might sound familiar to some of you," I told the small audience of family and friends and students. "I wrote it about this really cute girl who used to live across the hall from me in the dorms at UCLA." I smiled over at Mel, my precious wife, who (I think) was blushing. It was hard to tell from my seated position on the stage, semi-blinded by the lights overhead. I'd like to *think* she was blushing, at least.

"Anyway," I continued, "when I wrote the song, we had just seen Brian Wilson play a concert in Northern California... You see, Brian Wilson was my dad's favorite musician, and I kind of inherited that from him." I wistfully looked away from the crowd below me. Even today, years and years after my father's death, I still miss him. And it's hard to let go of that aching, that longing for the life we once had.

When I looked over at Sam, though, I saw something in her crooked smile, a yearning expression that reminded me of years long forgotten – a brief refraction of myself, a blessed reflection of my father. It was a reminder that even though the man I once knew is gone, a little piece of him lives on in me. And in his granddaughter.

That thought bolstered my spirits enough for me to soldier on and suppress the lump that was growing in the alcove of my throat.

"For the *kids* in the audience who don't know," I explained, "Brian Wilson was the mastermind behind the Beach Boys. He is, without a doubt, one of the best songwriters in the history of music, responsible for some of the greatest melodies ever written. But he wasn't the only member of the band." I paused, deliberating about how much I should share with this cloistered coffeeshop crowd. "You see, it takes a village to write, record, and perform music. I learned that the hard way with Call Field, thinking that I was the chieftain of our little group. But what's a chieftain without anyone to lead?"

The room grew a little quiet – awkwardly so. Had I overshared? Did I reveal too much? Was this revelation a little too personal?

Right about then, a gruff voice called out to me from the back corner of the room. "Brian Wilson's got nothing on you, Brick!"

As I squinted, I could just barely discern the Adonis-like features of a very familiar lead singer. Steve stood there, smiling brightly, his arms wrapped around his two daughters as the trio of Ökens swayed back and forth in place.

"You want to come up here and sing with me, Steve?" I shouted out across the room.

For a split second, I thought I saw his frame start to lurch forward, his arms beginning to lift off the shoulders of his daughters. But then, he suddenly stopped cold. "Nah!" he called out. "I want to hear *you* sing it tonight!"

From somewhere in front of me, someone (Veronica? Jacob? Rita?) started to clap. The sound of applause crept across the room like the beginning of rainfall on a summer night. Mel and Sam beamed proudly, and I felt like I'd fallen onto the surface of a trampoline, suddenly propelled heavenward by the smiling faces around me.

"Okay," I conceded, "I guess the matter is settled." I took another deep breath, ready to start my final song of the evening. "So, this is how I wrote it, late one chilly October night in my sister's living room in San Rafael. And this is the first time that an audience will hear it the way that it was born into the world half a lifetime ago."

A compact curtain of applause swept across the room.

With that, I launched into the song.

"California can be cruel in the summer..." I sang into the microphone, shaky and nervous at first, but steadily growing more confident with each word.

It might not have been the greatest-ever rendition of the song, but it was honest and heartfelt – qualities which, at this point in my life, matter more to me than pristine perfection. As I strummed and sang, the audience grinned and nodded along. When I got to the first chorus, a number of the parents – and even a few of the kids – sang along.

"I get lost sometimes in the melodies of my mind… where I've tried to find what I need…" I belted into the mic, my voice bolstered and elevated by the quiet chorus of audience members who (in various degrees of pitch) accompanied my own humble voice. *"But the crashing tide has swept me off my feet… and left me incomplete for a while…"*

Though no arms encircled me, no bodies pressed against mine, I felt like an entire room – of family, friends, and fans – was lifting me up in a moment of victory.

"…And it's just like your smile…"

After twenty years full of twists and turns and unexpected diversions, I had finally taken the reins and given myself a chance to sing from my heart.

I had finally found my voice.

And I sang the hell out of it.

After the show, Samantha walked up to me sheepishly, her big eyes bright and shimmering. She was sporting a custom-made Stuttering Surfers t-shirt in a children's size, the band's stick figure logo of Sammy the Surfer featured prominently atop his ubiquitous surfboard. Samantha hugged her petite arms across her chest, obscuring the shirt's graphic design. Behind Sam stood Mel, her arms ushering our nervous daughter forward to the stage.

Before Samantha could say anything, though, we were approached by a trio of family members: Mom, Marina, and Chunk. The three of them bounded up and enveloped me in a big bear hug, squeezing tightly as if I might disappear from their embrace. As Sam folded herself under my arm, Chunk placed his thick hands on my shoulders.

My cousin, my childhood doppelgänger, was grinning from ear to ear. "That was a great show, Brick!" he bellowed as he pulled away from me. "It really brought me back to all those early days in the garage."

"You mean when I couldn't sing to save my life?" I asked. I was only half-joking.

Mom clucked loudly and slapped my bicep. "Not at all! You've come a *long* way, Brian. You should be really proud of yourself. You're not just a second-rate stand-in. You're the real deal."

I patted Mom appreciatively on the shoulder. "Thanks again for coming, guys. It really means a lot to have you here tonight."

"Wild horses couldn't drag us away, Brian," Marina said. My sister's eyes traveled down to the diminutive figure hiding beneath my armpit. "Is that Baby Samantha down there?" she asked.

"I'm not a *baby* anymore, Aunt Marina," she protested. "I'm going into *fifth grade* next year. I'm practically a teenager."

Marina kneeled down so that she was eye-level with my daughter. "You'll always be Baby Samantha to me, sweetie. Even when you're taller than I am." She patted Sam's cheek gently and gave her a wicked grin.

And then, as if he had just noticed what she was wearing, Chunk poked her in the belly. "I love your t-shirt, kiddo! My dad would be proud that little Baby Sam is sporting a *Sammy the Surfer* t-shirt!"

Samantha blushed crimson and stretched out her shirt, proudly displaying it for us all to see. Even though Sam's recent discovery of Call Field was a revelation for her, she's seen the Stuttering Surfers dozens of times over the years. Still, though, Uncle Jeff's band held some rock star mystique for my daughter.

"I know that they're not as famous as The Beach Boys," she told us. "But I love them. The Stuttering Surfers are kind of like the next-best-thing."

Chunk reached his right hand deep within a hidden compartment of his jacket. "And that reminds me," he said, extracting a small metallic shape from his pocket. He shared a conspiratorial glance with Marina and Mom before turning his attention back to me.

"We've actually got a little surprise for you, Brian," Marina said.

"A congratulatory gift," Mom added, "if you will."

With that, Chunk grabbed my hand and placed the object in my callused palm.

It was a flash drive.

"What's this?" I asked.

Chunk wore a look of smug self-satisfaction on his face. "Rumor has it that a certain vinyl record might have met an untimely fate," he explained. He winked down at my daughter and gave her a little pat on the cheek.

Sam looked down at the ground, embarrassment and guilt creeping into her expression like storm clouds in a crystal-blue sky.

Without missing a beat, Chunk placed a reassuring hand on Samantha's shoulder. "Luckily for *you*," he said, "Uncle Charles is here to save the day." He looked back up at me and his eyes softened. "I pulled a few strings and worked some tech magic. It's the Stuttering Surfers single that your dad sang on."

I could feel the blood rushing from my head, and I must have blanched ghostly white. "But… how?" I asked him. "I thought my dad had the only copy."

"Remember Mountain Dog Musicworks? Where we recorded the *Bookhouse EP* back in the day?"

"Of course," I said, glancing down at the compact capsule in my open palm. I still felt lightheaded as I waited for him to explain.

"Well, I told my dad what happened with Sam's little accident, and he dug through the garage until he found the original acetate disc from the recording session. I borrowed it and passed it off to the owner of Mountain

Dog, Tim Frantz. Tim took my dad's acetate, hooked it up to some fancy equipment, and ripped a WAV file from the original vinyl. He also included MP3 and AAC files, just in case you wanted those, too."

My eyes drifted back and forth from the metallic minor miracle in my hand to my cousin and my sister and my mother.

All three of them stood tall and proud.

"I know it's not a replacement for…" Mom left her sentence unfinished for a moment, letting me fill in the blanks myself. "You know. It's not the same as the real thing. But it's a pretty great substitute." Mom adjusted her watch strap and caressed her wrist while she waited for my reaction.

My eyes brimmed with tears, and my hands started trembling. "This is amazing, guys," I told them. I reached forward and pulled all three of them into an embrace.

My mother, my sister, and my cousin are the best kind of kin – the type of family that love and support unconditionally. And they gave me back something I thought had been lost forever: a piece of my father's past, an artifact of a life that I thought had been irreparably broken. It wasn't gone, though. The ghost had simply been released from its shell. I realized in that moment that the legacies we leave behind outlast our fragile frames.

Our bodies might be analog, but our souls are digital.

"Hey, watch out for me!" Sam yelped as she was caught between the four towering figures above her.

My three full-grown family members and I pulled apart, leaving space for the mischievous munchkin between us. Even with the gap of aging wedging us apart, we were fastened together by something infinitely stronger than any adhesive: the bond of family.

As our drummer, Chunk had kept the band's rhythm steady for all those years. But, more importantly, my family had kept my life anchored with their affection. And that's worth more than a million snare drums.

"I've gotta' split," Chunk told me, chuffing deeply with the warm, recycled air of the coffee shop. "The wife and kids are waiting up for me back home."

"I think that's my cue to exit, too," Mom said, throwing her arm around Marina. "It's past my bedtime."

I gave them a grateful glance. "Thank you, guys. Seriously."

"It was nothing, Brick." Chunk patted me on the shoulder one last time, pinched Sam's cheek, and then sauntered off into the cool, black night.

As I watched Chunk, Marina, and Mom leave, my fingers threaded through Sam's. She leaned her small frame against my waist, tapping out a messy morse code rhythm on my palm. Instinctively, I leaned down and gave her a kiss on the top of her head.

Yes, this little *pitseleh* has given me more than a few gray hairs over the years, but she's still the most important thing in my life… even if she did shatter my irreplaceable prized possession. I have a feeling that my dad would understand, though.

From the side of the stage, Mel hesitantly approached us. She gave me a curious look and raised a speculative eyebrow. "Did she ask you yet?" Mel bit her lower lip, just as she's always done when faced with an unforeseen challenge.

"Did *who* ask me *what*…?" I inquired.

Samantha pulled herself away from my arms and turned to face me. Her muddled expression was hard to read, and I wasn't sure what might be hiding behind those twinkling eyes.

Mel casually approached us, like a zookeeper trying not to scare a skittish lion cub. She looked down at our daughter, glanced up at me, and then looked back to Sam. "Your daughter has something to ask you," she prompted.

I leaned down so that I was eye-level with Sam. Although she's been growing like a weed this last year, sprouting inches taller every few months, I still see the sweet, sensitive, mermaid-loving child whose arms wrap tightly around Cinnabunny each night when she drifts off to sleep. She may not be a "daddy's girl" forever, but I'll appreciate the time that we have left before she turns into a fiery teenager. Lord knows, I already spend enough time with high schoolers.

"Daddy…" Samantha began, her eyes averted to her shuffling feet.

"Yes, Sam?" I asked, kneeling down in front of her and gently placing my left hand against her blushing cheek.

My daughter's eyes trailed from her scuffed sneakers up to the blue tartan plaid of my shirt, before settling on my face. She muddled up her mouth and opened her lips to speak. "Can you teach me how to play guitar?" she asked.

As could be expected, I choked up. You know me: I'm a big old softie when it comes to this kind of stuff.

I wrapped my arms around my daughter and hugged her tightly, tears fomenting from the corners of my eyes. "Nothing would make me happier, sweetie," I whispered to her, smiling as I pulled her into my shoulder. "And nothing would have made your grandfather prouder."

When I glanced over Sam's shoulder at the stage, I saw my father's guitar sitting prostrate on its stand. It might have been another trick of the light or the kaleidoscope vision of tears clouding my eyes, but I saw a familiar reflection shining back at me: a balding, bespectacled man with an earnest expression peeking through a litany of tears.

And I swear that I saw my father in that instant. As I grinned, so did he. And when I kissed my daughter on the top of her head, his eyes were my eyes and his smile became my own.

Right foot. Left foot.
Right foot. Left foot.
Repeat until the end of the story.

So, dear reader, you've made it through the many chapters of my life, the "pocket symphonies" of my personal and professional journeys. At this juncture, some of the more discerning, critical readers of my story might be thinking something along the following lines:

Brian, why is this autobiography so long? Can't it be pared down and distilled to a more concise narrative? And why did you have to include all those tangential side-notes about The Beach Boys and Twin Peaks and Emily Dickinson and neckties and treadmills? Doesn't that just muddy up the story at hand?

In many ways, all of those complaints are perfectly valid.

But here's the thing about life: it's messy and convoluted and contradictory and disjointed. Unlike literature, life doesn't come wrapped in a tidy bow with concise plot threads and perfectly sewn narratives. I'm living proof of that.

Does that make my story any less real, any less credible? Does that make my grief or my anxiety or my depression any less truthful? Does that make my late-in-life resurrection any less victorious? I can't say. You'll have to make that call. Or *Call Field*, as it were.

If I've done my story justice, it might resonate deeply with you, might serve as an analog to your own journey. Although the word *analog* is often used as the antonym for *digital* – the world of cassette tapes and tube amps and rotating clocks – it also refers to similarities and comparisons, much like the word *analogy*. Perhaps this story is an analog to your own, full of the hiss and hum and creaks and cracks that parallel your own life. In such circumstances, I hope you recognize that this is not just a tale about a would-be rock star who became a quirky high school teacher – this is really a story about clemency and complexity and completion and closure.

And, yes, it's about rock and roll.

Though I've made a ridiculous number of pit-stops along the way, I hope that you've been able to find some small semblance of truth buried in these pages, tiny tidbits of wisdom or insight that can help you through your own messy, complicated life.

That's what the best literature does: it forces us to reflect upon our own lives, reminds us to treasure the people who surround us, and provides us with a chance to appreciate the subtleties and nuances of our worlds. Art and music and film are best understood when aligned with a personal context. If I've moved you in any small way with my words or my songs, then I've done my job.

You are alive. Treasure that.

And make the most of it.

Right foot. Left foot.
Right foot. Left foot.

Repeat until the end of the story.

These are the memories that keep me moving while my feet pound the pavement, one step at a time.

For the first time in a long time, I'm off the treadmill and I'm venturing into the streets. No longer am I on the same course, day after day, confined to the repetition that I've come to embrace as my inevitable (albeit comfortable) fate. Suddenly, the rotating motor of the treadmill is not my guiding engine. I can move at my own speed and work through the rhythms of my heartbeat to find my own pace.

Don't get me wrong: while it can be liberating to step off the treadmill, it's also intimidating to see city streets stretch out before you with countless paths, endless possibilities.

These last few months have been stranger and more invigorating than I could have ever imagined. Not so long ago, I was comfortably confined by my routine – content with my static, suburban, middle-class existence – marking mile after mile on the treadmill safely secured in my garage at home. And though I'm not quite like Huck Finn "lighting out for the territory ahead of the rest," I can't deny the fact that things are different now.

I don't know what's going to happen next – the next sentence, the next paragraph, the next page, the next chapter, the next book.

None of us do.

Nothing is promised. Nothing is guaranteed.

But there is an honor in not knowing.

There is a peace in the unseen.

I don't know where these roads might take me or how long my heart will hold out or how much time I have left on this earth.

But I'm going to make every mile count.

A NOTE ON THE TYPE

Once again, the principal text of the novel was composed in Times New Roman, 12-point font. As I said before, you can take the boy out of the English classroom, but you can't take the English classroom out of the boy. I promise that I'll try a different font next time.

ACKNOWLEDGMENTS

This is a book about fathers and mothers and sons and daughters. Though parenthood is like wearing ill-fitting clothes in a never-ending fashion show, I'm incredibly grateful that my own mother, Marion Levin-Welch, has been such a powerful role model in my life. She taught me early on that the answer to almost any question is simple: *love*. I only hope that I can provide my own children with the kind of inspiring, encouraging environment that she gave me and my siblings. Her decades of dedication have shaped me into the person that I am today, and I'm only one little bough among the many branches that she's nurtured with her selfless sacrifices. She isn't just a Master Gardener among the foliage – she's a Master Gardener of the heart for everyone she meets.

While fatherhood can be a tricky river to navigate, I've been blessed with a few influential father-figures over the last four decades: Richard Feldan, George Stassi, James Welch, John Young, and (of course) Mark Levin. These men have provided me with a rich foundation from which I can build my own life, reminding me that dads can be gracious, giving, and goofy in equal measure. With my own children, I have done my best to live up to the extraordinary examples that they set.

I wasn't always the best role-model for this piece of sage advice, but I've learned over the last eleven years that *family comes first*. Thank you to my siblings, Richelle Feldan and Matt Levin, as well as their respective branches of our family tree (Max, Ashley, Dillon, and Casey), for keeping me tethered to *terra firma* when I'm dreamily drifting towards the atmosphere. I also have immense love and appreciation for my extended family: my aunt and uncle, Murray and Julie Levin; Paris, Alan, and Hazel Levinovitz; my mother-in-law, Edie Stassi; my wife's grandfather, Sal Stassi; Aunt Susan, Uncle Galen, and Julie Onizuka (along with Nathan and Maia, obviously); Johnny, Trevor, and Nicole Wu; and Karen, John, Madden, and Jackson Blomquist. I love you all.

I realize that *Incomplete* had the longest acknowledgments section ever printed, so I'll keep the list more concise this time. I'll start with my insightful and encouraging beta readers: Christine Young, Alissa

Charvonia, and Theresa Olivier. These three brilliant young women provided insightful and illuminating feedback during the revision process of *Incomplete* and *A Different Slant of Light*, guaranteeing that the final draft you hold in your hands is exponentially more polished and pristine than the rough woodwork of words that they initially encountered.

In the world of teaching, it's nearly impossible to separate the personal from the professional. Fortunately for me, I work with some of the most wonderful colleagues in the realm of public education: Annie McGavren (who is still the best human being I know) has been an absolute godsend, a font of encouragement in the drought of the last few years; Kelly Herrera bolsters my spirits and restores my confidence when self-doubt threatens to derail me; Kevin Downey is my longterm partner-in-crime, an indefatigable presence who inspires everyone he meets; Heather Arrambide is my confidante and catalyst for spiritual growth; C.J. Foster brightens my days when we geek out over *Star Wars*, Funko, indie rock, science fiction, and Stephen King; Emmet Cullen not only provided the headshots for my two novels, but he also inspires me with his acts of heroism – inside *and* outside the classroom; Frank Davis provides the camaraderie and comedy that make this job so fulfilling; Tina Perez brings humor, wisdom, and compassion to our shared workspace; and last (but *definitely* not least), Kathleen Olivier is the best coworker *ever*, full of grace and kindness and wit, and I couldn't survive my daily library workload without her. *Go, Bulldogs!*

Although Veronica Jones is obviously a fictional character, she has inherited a variety of admirable traits from my former AP English students, including (but not limited to): Aricka Wilde, Nick Jones, Megan Mueller, Danielle Pelkola, Allison Knight, Shannon Householder, Jeff Dunne, Alexandria Jason, Jenny Allen, Sarah Shaffer, Hanna Colman, Brenna Neri, and Sophia Morales. These remarkable young men and women made my time in the classroom a rewarding experience, and they've all pursued their own praiseworthy passions. I'm grateful that our paths crossed during those brief windows of time, and I hope that I inspired them as much as they inspired me.

In addition to being my dentist, Dr. Stephanie Hwang Kroll is one of the most brilliant students I've ever encountered – and is also one of my favorite human beings. Her encouragement and support during the writing, editing, and revision of the *Incomplete* saga has been absolutely priceless, and her dental expertise helped add authenticity to the "root canal" chapters of *ADSOL*. Stephanie and her husband, Bryan Hwang, are truly wonderful people, and I'm grateful that I've watched their relationship develop from its earliest stages into the lifelong romance that they share.

Much gratitude goes to my graphic design team: Lucas Schultz, Madison "Maz Spaz" Lonis, Lux Reid Dumas, and Claire Laminen. The preternaturally gifted Mr. Schultz designed Call Field's phoenix logo and the Stuttering Surfers' Sammy the Surfer, and I'm blown away by the pieces that he created for this book. Madison painted the beautiful "surfer girl" image that became the foundation of Call Field's Fillmore poster, and I'm thrilled that I was able to commission this gorgeous piece of artwork for my novel. Lux was my Photoshop savior, designing the logo for Call Field's name, creating the shattered vinyl image for the front cover, and basically working digital magic on an assortment of design elements. Without Lux, the dust jacket of the novel would have looked much less eye-catching and professional. Claire Laminen graciously gave me permission to use an inspiring sunset-washed photograph of her husband, Marshall, for Call Field's *A Different Slant of Light* album cover. Marshall is a *much* better human being than Steve, though, so don't let their uncanny resemblance spoil your perception of the lovely Laminen family.

Many thanks to the litany of talented musicians I've worked with over the years. For almost two decades, I've been galvanized and challenged by my bandmates in Far From Kansas and the Briar Rose Ramblers (Matt Levin, Danny McDermott, Dr. Frank Cruz, Diana Essex-Lettieri, Mark Pohl, Chris Dixon, Natalie Leichtfuß, Willie Makiling, Jon Crocker, Devon Hammond, Jeff Dunne, Josh Brock, Jason Dinkler, Mike Cromie, Jordan McWethy, Samantha Perkins, Jamie Allen, Emily Bradvica, and Brittany Oliver). I've also been incredibly blessed to collaborate with Nani Edgar and Danny Carvalho (a.k.a. Kailua Moon), two remarkable musicians who continue to inspire me with our musical partnership. *Mahalo!*

Although nostalgia *is* a beautiful liar, I'm thankful for all of the close friends who helped guide and shape my life over the last few decades: Keith Flores, Chris Land, Jeffrey Jacob Mendel, John Cabral, Dr. Ruben J. Valencia, Rich Letus, Sara Brucker, Lindsie Brennan, Kerry Haggerty, Denise Duran Maloney, Chris Perez, Josh Burnell, Tom Kranzler, Josh Collins, Jim Hill, Jon Paillette, Shane Beck, Erin Young, Zachary Levi Pugh, Lizzy Martin, Adam Politis, Andy Davies, Ray Nagatani, Brendan Barrett, Meghan Clarke, Melissa Binder, Jaime Jones, Anna Levy, and the Vogelbaum family.

While the term "book club" might conjure insulting images of tedious teatime and lackluster literature, I can safely say that *my* book group is more of a family than a futile snooze-fest. Many thanks to Marilyn Beal, Brooke Gant, Dawn Maloney, Cheryl Wheeler, and Amie Lyans for sharing a robust love of reading and engaging in passionate literary discussions. I am so lucky to have them on my team.

Special thanks to Chris Jay and the Army of Freshmen, who graciously allowed me to include them in this novel. I've been fans of theirs since 1997, and I'm thrilled that I was able to sneak them into the final draft of *ADSOL*. Chris was also an early champion of *Incomplete*, spreading the literary rock and roll gospel in true Springsteen-ian fashion.

I'm massively indebted to the real-world local businesses that gave me permission to reference their institutions in this novel. Thanks again to Tim Frantz at Mountain Dog Musicworks Recording Studio for letting me include his name and business as pivotal plot points in *Incomplete* and *ADSOL*. Likewise, much appreciation goes to Todd Winokur, who allowed me to use his historic coffee shop, Café Voltaire, in the *Incomplete* saga. I'm grateful that Brandon Salzer gave me his blessing to use Salzer's Records as the setting for one particularly important scene in *ADSOL*. Fun fact: I wrote the very first pages for *Incomplete* while standing in line outside Salzer's on Record Store Day 2014 (April 19th, to be exact). With the line wrapped around the building, I started typing out the diner date scene on my iPhone, scripting dialogue and character descriptions as I inched closer to the store's entrance. It's an honor to include Salzer's in *ADSOL*, and I feel like it brings the writing of this story full circle.

Much gratitude goes to the proselytizers of my prose, most notably Bobbi Powers, Nicki Mitchell, Bryan Freeberg, Kate Bello, Lindsie Brennan, Bethany Marrie-Wood, Maynard Raguine, Lauren Rad, Andrew Coates, Jamie Allen, Jennifer Kaplan, Susan Barber, and Sara Small. These generous folks shared their praise on social media, providing me with a larger soapbox to preach about my rock and roll literature.

Thanks to my fitness gurus at Cal Coast Strength & Conditioning, Eddie Raburn and Martha Benavides, for helping me stay on the right path with my health. I want to see my daughters grow up and blossom, and I couldn't do that without the significant health and lifestyle changes that the Cal Coast crew has fostered and supported.

Brian Wilson and The Beach Boys obviously play a large role in *Incomplete* and *ADSOL*. Though I've never met the gentlemen in the band (apart from a brief autograph signing with Mr. Wilson), I'm forever indebted to them for crafting some of the most important music of the last century. I hope that the *Incomplete* saga inspires new listeners to delve into the wealth of beautiful recordings that this band has created.

Endless thanks to Nicole, Shamus, and Gabriel Auth – the unofficial "bonus" members of the Levin family. Whether we're wildly waving Hogwarts wands or wistfully watching Marvel movies or vigorously venting about teaching, they're always the most supportive, sympathetic friends we have.

My wife, Kathleen, is my pillar of strength, the beaming lighthouse helping me reach the shoreline when I'm tempest-tossed in the overwhelming ocean. If our little household was a band, she would be the drummer – the member who guides the entire group through the various rhythms of life's music. There isn't enough sauvignon blanc in the world to thank her for all that she's done for me.

To my daughters, Alexandra and Charlotte: music might just be "one monotone color in the broader palette of life," but you fill up my horizons with vibrant, endless shades of love. Nothing in this world means more to me than you. Thank you for making my life complete.

READER'S GUIDE

READING GROUP DISCUSSION QUESTIONS

1.) Throughout *Incomplete* and *A Different Slant of Light*, Brian foreshadows the darkest days of his life. Did the band's self-destruction, the death of Brian's father, and/or Brian's breakdown surprise you? How has Brian's adulthood been affected by these traumas and tragedies? In what ways has he been humbled or emboldened by his life experiences?

2.) Call Field's 2020 logo, printed on the shirts that Veronica orders for the reunion concert, features the image of a phoenix rising from the ashes. How does Brian's narrative – and the story of Call Field – parallel this mythical creature's story?

3.) How does Brian's life mirror that of his namesake, Brian Wilson? What similarities do Call Field and The Beach Boys share in their cycles of self-destruction and rebirth? Will Call Field's reunion last? Do you think the last living members of The Beach Boys will ever reunite?

4.) What significance is embedded in the names of the novel's characters and settings? Take another look at the names of supporting cast members and locations (perhaps with the help of Google Translate). How do the names of these characters/locales reflect their roles in the story and their relationship to Brian?

5.) Once again, the motifs of water and dry land are threaded throughout the novel. What does water symbolize for Brian and the other characters in *A Different Slant of Light*? In what ways has Brian's life been a "journey from the mountains to the sea, from sandy suffocation to the untamed liberation of the ocean?" Will Brian ever make peace with life's unpredictable waves?

6.) Were you surprised by the backstage brawl at the Fillmore? Did you anticipate the fistfight that splits the band in half? Who did you think would be the instigator for this showdown? Who did you think would throw the first punch?

7.) Veronica spends a great deal of time planning out Call Field's reunion with the help of Mel (and Brian's old bandmates, of course). Does Mel have the right to make those decisions for her husband? How would you have approached the situation, if you were in Mel's place?

8.) How do you imagine Samantha's relationship with her parents will develop in the years ahead? Will she become a bold mini-Veronica, as Brian predicts? Or will she inherit her father's sensitivity and anxiety? Will she pursue music with the same passion and intensity as Brian?

9.) The last few chapters of the novel include an *American Graffiti*-style coda that sheds light on the fates of the book's supporting characters. Were you surprised at all by how these characters' lives unfolded? Whose lives seem to have turned out the happiest and/or the rockiest?

10.) The author writes that "People don't change… Except when they do." In what ways has Brian grown from the insecure, anxious little boy introduced in *Incomplete*? In what ways do you think Brian will continue to change? Have you had any similar transformations (health, romance, confidence, etc.) in your own life?

11.) In the novel's final chapters, the story's trajectory is derailed by the COVID pandemic/shutdown. How does the pandemic interrupt Brian's moment of glory after Call Field's reunion? How did Brian's prior experiences with mental health and grief prepare him for the collective trauma of the global coronavirus pandemic? Was your experience with the pandemic similar to Brian's? In what ways was it different?

12.) *A Different Slant of Light* ends with a "Lady or the Tiger" moment, as Brian contemplates the various potential paths that lie before him. What do you think Brian will do after the credits roll? Will he resume his normal life and continue teaching, or will he quit the classroom and pursue music full-time? Will he join Call Field out on the road, or will he emulate Brian Wilson – his namesake and hero – and let the band tour without him? Which path would *you* choose?

BIBLIOGRAPHY

Anderson, John, and Joe Thomas, directors. *The Beach Boys: Doin' It Again*. Brother Records, 2012.

Boyd, Alan, director. *Endless Harmony: The Beach Boys Story*. Brother Records, 2000.

Carlin, Peter Ames. *Catch a Wave: The Rise, Fall & Redemption of the Beach Boys' Brian Wilson*. Emmaus, PA: Rodale, 2006.

Dillon, Mark. *Fifty Sides of the Beach Boys / The Songs That Tell Their Story*. Toronto, Canada: ECW, 2012.

Fusilli, Jim. *Pet Sounds*. New York: Continuum, 2005.

Gaines, Steven. *Heroes and Villains: The True Story of the Beach Boys*. Da Capo Press, 2002.

Hilburn, Robert. *Johnny Cash: The Life*. First Edition ed. New York: Little, Brown, 2013.

Leaf, David. *The Beach Boys and the California Myth*. Grosset & Dunlap, 1978.

Love, Mike, and James S. Hirsch. *Good Vibrations: My Life as a Beach Boy*. Blue Rider Press, 2016.

Morgan, Johnny. *The Beach Boys: America's Band*. Sterling Publishing, 2015.

Sánchez, Luis. *Smile*. Bloomsbury, 2014.

Stebbins, Jon. *The Beach Boys FAQ: All That's Left to Know about America's Band*. Milwaukee, WI: Backbeat, 2011.

Was, Don, director. *Brian Wilson: I Just Wasn't Made for These Times*. Lionsgate, 1995.

White, Timothy. *The Nearest Faraway Place: Brian Wilson, the Beach Boys, and the Southern California Experience*. Henry Holt and Company, 1994.

Wilson, Brian, and Ben Greenman. *I Am Brian Wilson: a Memoir*. Perseus Books, 2016.

Wilson, Brian, and Todd Gold. *Wouldn't It Be Nice: My Own Story*. Harper Collins, 1991.

SOUNDTRACK PLAYLIST

A Different Slant of Light draws from a deep well of popular music, with a hefty selection of Brian Wilson and the Beach Boys (for obvious reasons). Please enjoy this suggested soundtrack of songs to accompany your reading of the novel.

"Think About the Days" (Brian Wilson & Joseph Thomas) — The Beach Boys, *That's Why God Made the Radio*, 2012.

"(What's So Funny 'Bout) Peace, Love, and Understanding" (Nick Lowe) — Elvis Costello and the Attractions, *Armed Forces*, 1979.

"Sail Away" (Brian Wilson, Joseph Thomas, Jim Peterik, & Larry Millas) — Brian Wilson feat. Blondie Chaplin, *No Pier Pressure*, 2015.

"Rock 'N' Roll High School" (Joey Ramone & Dee Dee Ramone) — The Ramones, *Rock 'N' Roll High School*, 1979.

"Absolutely (Story of a Girl)" (John Hampson & Brian Desveaux) — Nine Days, *The Madding Crowd*, 2000.

"Santa Baby" (Joan Javits, Philip Springer, & Tony Springer) — Eartha Kitt, *Santa Baby*, 1953.

"She" (Billie Joe Armstrong, Mike Dirnt, & Tre Cool) — Green Day, *Dookie*, 1994.

"Ruby Soho" (Lars Frederiksen, Roger M. Freeman, & Tim Armstrong) — Rancid, *...And Out Come the Wolves*, 1995.

"Bad Reputation" (Joan Jett, Kenny Laguna, Ritchie Cordell, Marty Joe Kupersmith) — Joan Jett, *Bad Reputation*, 1980.

"Left of the Dial" (Paul Westerberg) — The Replacements, *Tim*, 1985.

"Bulletproof in Baggy Jeans" (Chris Jay, Owen Bucey, & Aaron Goldberg) — The Army of Freshmen, *The Army of Freshmen*, 2001.

"I Wanna' Be Sedated" (Joey Ramone, Dee Dee Ramone, & Johnny Ramone) — The Ramones, *Road to Ruin*, 1978.

"Our Prayer" (Brian Wilson) — The Beach Boys, *20/20*, 1969.

"Surf's Up" (Brian Wilson & Van Dyke Parks) — The Beach Boys, *Surf's Up*, 1971.

"Black Muddy River" (Jerry Garcia & Robert Hunter) — Bruce Hornsby & DeYarmond Edison, *Day of the Dead*, 2016.

"No Hard Feelings" (Timothy Seth Avett, Scott Yancey Avett, & Robert William Crawford) — The Avett Brothers, *True Sadness*, 2016.

"Healer in the Sky" (Laura Elizabeth Rogers & Lydia Lane Rogers) — The Secret Sisters, *Saturn Return*, 2020.

"Summer's Gone" (Brian Wilson, Joseph Thomas, & Jon Bon Jovi) — The Beach Boys, *That's Why God Made the Radio*, 2012.

"Time" (Tom Waits) — Tori Amos, *Strange Little Girls*, 2001.

"Fade Into You" (Hope Sandoval & David Roback) — Mazzy Star, *So Tonight That I Might See*, 1993.

"This Beautiful Day" (Brian Wilson & Joseph Thomas) — Brian Wilson, *No Pier Pressure*, 2015.

"Bored to Death" (Mark Hoppus, Travis Barker, Matt Skiba, & John Feldmann) — blink-182, *California*, 2016.

"Beyond the Veil" (K. Nick Jones) — Tiger Army, *Retrofuture*, 2019.

"Ring of Fire" (June Carter Cash & Merle Kilgore) — Social Distortion, *Social Distortion*, 1990.

"Truckin'" (Jerry Garcia, Bob Weir, Phil Lesh, & Robert Hunter) — Grateful Dead, *American Beauty*, 1970.

"Love and Mercy" [Live] (Brian Wilson) — Brian Wilson, *Love & Mercy: The Life, Love, and Genius of Brian Wilson*, 2015.

"Landslide" [Live] (Stevie Nicks) — Fleetwood Mac, *The Dance*, 1997.

"I Will Follow You Into the Dark" (Benjamin Gibbard) — Death Cab for Cutie, *Plans*, 2005.

"From This Valley" (Joy Williams, John Paul White, and Phil Madeira) — The Civil Wars, *The Civil Wars*, 2013.

"The Long Way Home" (John Paul White) — John Paul White, *The Hurting Kind*, 2019.

"Last Ride" (K. Nick Jones) — Tiger Army, *Retrofuture*, 2019.

"Sail On, Sailor" [Live in Las Vegas, 2014] (Brian Wilson, Tandyn Almer, Van Dyke Parks, Jack Rieley, & Raymond Kennedy) — Brian Wilson feat. Blondie Chaplin & Al Jardine, *Brian Wilson and Friends*, 2015.

ABOUT THE AUTHOR

J.D. Levin is a mild-mannered librarian by day… and a mild-mannered rock & roller by night. He has worked as a public school educator for almost two decades – first as an English teacher, then as a Teacher Librarian. Outside of the classroom, he's written songs for Far From Kansas, The Briar Rose Ramblers, Kailua Moon, and Grammy-nominated slack-key guitarist Danny Carvalho. Levin is a graduate of UC Berkeley (BA '01), Stanford University (MA '02), CSUN (MA '09), and CSULB (TLSC '15). He lives on the central coast of California with his wife, two daughters, and cluttered collection of musical instruments. *A Different Slant of Light,* the sequel to *Incomplete*, is his second novel.